*To
Dottie,*

His Fair Lady

Kathleen Kirkwood

Warmest wishes,

Kathleen Kirkwood

Cover Artist: Delle Jacobs
Cover Flat: Bydand Publishing
Anna Tyukhmeneva at **www.depositphotos.com**

ISBN-13: 978-1-62454-001-1

DEDICATION

For my beloved grandparents,

George & Marie
and
Guy & Charlotte

You are never far from memory and always in my heart.

SPECIAL APPRECIATION

My heartfelt thanks and deep appreciation to

Linda Abel, Publisher, *The Medieval Chronicle*, for her thoughtful review and insightful feedback for this newly revised edition of *LADY*; and to

Anne-Caroline for her generous guidance on all things French, especially for helping to resolve a number of finer details and points of minutia that kept niggling at me.

PART I

The Squire

"Dieu li volt!"
"God wills it!"

—Motto of the Crusaders

Burgundy, June A.D. 1190

"The Lionheart awaits! We press on to Vézelay!" Sir Hugh FitzAlan bellowed his command and galloped back along the column of men, beasts, and wagons traveling the age-worn road.

Royce promptly followed on his sturdy roncin, shadowing the great knight as a squire's duty demanded. Watchful, Royce held his steed at a precise distance behind the charger, determined to prove his worth for the honor so recently bestowed upon him.

Again came Sir Hugh's full-throated cry as he heartened his troops and inspired them onward.

The Lionheart. Vézelay. The words burned in Royce's chest and his pulse thumped in his veins.

Surely Heaven's grace shined upon him. When Sir Hugh's squire broke his leg a fortnight past during practice in the lists, 'twas he—Royce de Warrene—whom the great knight singled out to replace the other noble. Soon after, Sir Hugh secured the funds he'd so fervently sought, enabling him to leave England apace with his retainers and join the king's army amassing across the Channel in Burgundy, poised to embark on Crusade.

Beyond all hopes and imaginings, Royce now traveled in a train of gallant knights and stout men-at-arms, a red cross emblazoned upon his shoulder. Each amongst them was sworn to war against the infidel and to win back the Kingdom of Jerusalem for Christendom.

Failure was not possible, Royce deemed as he trailed closely behind Sr. Hugh. Did not the three most revered monarchs alive join forces and lead their armies east? Who could withstand them—England's King Richard, *Coeur de Lion*, the very flower of chivalry itself; France's illustrious Philip Augustus; and the renowned Holy Roman Emperor, Frederick Barbarossa?

Soon the devil, Saladin, and his Saracens would taste Crusader steel ten thousand times over. Justice would be exacted for their black deeds—the bloody seizure of Jerusalem and its Frankish king, the butchery of the captured Templars and Hospitallers, beheaded by the hundreds, and the enslavement of thousands of Christians.

Even now, the emperor, Frederick, and his host proceeded to the Holy Land whilst the armies of Richard and Philip gathered at Vézelay, their departure imminent.

Royce drew an invigorating breath, his heart drumming solidly against his chest. Surely Heaven's grace did smile on him that he—a newly made squire of scarce ten-and five years—should accompany the valorous knight, Sir Hugh FitzAlan, on Holy Crusade to campaign beneath the banner of the Lionheart. One day, Royce vowed, he, too, would attain the spurs of knighthood and wield his sword and fight for right. Upon his honor, 'twould be so.

The blustery shout of a roughened voice broke Royce's ruminations, drawing his attention to a flush-faced man on a small bay mare. Royce recognized him as Beuvan de Luce, the oldest of the bachelor knights in Sir Hugh's employ. At the knight's boisterous call, Sir Hugh reined his charger to a halt, Royce doing likewise behind him.

"Do we march the night through?" Sir Beuvan asked, shoving back the coif of mail from his head, revealing grayed, sweat-dampened hair plastered to his skull like a cleric's cap. "Vézelay yet lies three days hence."

"Aye, Beuvan. We need close the time to two or we risk missing the king's departure." Sir Hugh lifted his bearded face to the dulling sky then returned his gaze to the knight.

"The moon shall be high and full this night and shall well light our way. We press on hard for now but take heart, friend. I have word, by Richard's arrangement, a fleet awaits the troops at Marseilles to bear us across the sea to Acre. We shall take our rest once aboard ship and strengthen ourselves for the test to come."

With that, Sir Hugh turned his charger toward the head of the column and rode swiftly forward. Royce kept pace on his roncin though his body ached with fresh complaints for the endless hours spent in the saddle these past days.

He ignored the shafts of pain splintering down his spine and through his legs, refusing them the least concern. Instead, his mind remained fixed on the knight's words and the very core of his concerns.

'Twas urgent they hasten, lest the Lionheart depart without them.

The dusky veils of eve descended as the soldiery passed through the lush, rolling lands of Burgundy, their cloak of summer green darkening to black as the light faded completely. Hour upon hour, the retinue persevered along the ancient pilgrim road, the moon's glow alone now silvering their path and brightening their way.

Royce welcomed the cool of night and gave himself to thoughts of the days to come—of sailing with the king and of what a Saracen might look like.

Beneath the solid tread of his roncin, the road dipped and rose and dipped again, following the countryside's gentle contours. Lost to his thoughts, Royce scarce took note of those undulating rhythms until the road turned sharply upward, the climb steeper than any before. Glancing ahead, his gaze drew to the horizon as the entourage trod on and approached the crest of the road.

Royce blinked when a stain of color appeared beyond the top of the rise—an eerie ruddy gold, illumining the underbelly of the pitch-dark sky.

At the sight, Sir Hugh spurred his horse forward to gain a better view. Royce scarce won to his side, along with several retainers, when Sir Hugh threw up his gloved hand and signaled the troops to a halt. In unison, their gazes riveted on the scene below.

Royce's stomach fisted tight as he spied a sizable village beyond, its patchwork of fields and crowd of thatched houses set ablaze, firing the midnight heavens. Faint cries drifted to their ears—piteous cries filled with horror, hysteria, and abject misery.

Sir Hugh vented a curse, his mien hardening as he turned in his saddle and addressed his companion knights and men-at-arms. "A foul deed hath been wrought this night," he roared. "God's test is upon us! Ready your blades and keep vigilant, men. We know not what cur we meet."

With that he unsheathed his sword and commanded his men forward, leading them down into the vail. Instinctively, Royce set his heels to his roncin, keeping pace with the knightly host, unquestioning of whether he should do so or not. A squire did not join his lord in combat, true, but he need keep near to hand all the same.

Heart racing, he leaned into his mount. When the ground leveled out, he reached back for his spear, lashed on the roncin's rump along with Sir Hugh's spare weapons.

Royce's blood ran hot in his veins. How often had he craved to rise to such a moment? Like all knightly candidates, he longed to hone his skills, gain the experience of battle, uphold the chivalric code. Freeing his spear—the only weapon allowed him as a squire—he gripped it tight, prepared to aid his lordly knight and do whatever the Almighty required of him.

Turning off the main road, the retinue hastened toward the village on a broad lane. Within minutes they galloped between burning fields where flames leapt high, devouring crops and vineyards and casting the soldiers in a molten glow of crimson and gold.

As the troops emerged from the fiery stretches, they reached the first sheds and houses on the outskirts of the village proper, aflame as was all else. Keen to danger, the knights sought signs of those responsible for the foul handiwork they now came upon—oxen split open from gullet to tail, the entrails spilt out, pigs and goats dissevered, their parts strewn across the ground.

Royce glanced at a lumpish mass nearby then realized 'twas a man lying face down in a pool of blood, his head smashed open. Several feet away lay a second man, his eyes staring vacantly to the heavens, his throat sliced wide, his arm cleaved from its joint.

Royce swallowed the bile that scaled his throat and fought down his revulsion. Looking to the seasoned soldiers surrounding him, he found them stone faced, their expressions shuttered as they continued to seek the perpetrators.

If the gruesome sight moved these warriors, they concealed their emotions entirely, so single-minded were they to their task. Embracing their example, Royce steeled himself and proceeded on.

At Sir Hugh's gesture, the troops slowed, moving more cautiously now along the principal lane, flanked by a blazing forest of peasant houses. Each dwelling stood apart on a small parcel, a network of paths running between them, the fires feeding upon their flimsy wattle-and-daub constructions. Fences lay shattered all about, the yards overrun and the livestock butchered, feathers everywhere.

Death met Royce at every glance—scores of villagers slain, lying in twisted heaps, male and female, young and old alike. 'Twas as though he'd entered Hell itself.

His stomach again threatening, Royce clamped down on his emotions, determined to not embarrass himself or his station. Diverting his gaze from the carnage, he scanned for the enemy host but found none. 'Twould seem they'd long departed, their devastation complete.

Moments later the lane ended, opening onto the heart of the village—the central green. To one end stood a substantial stone church and to the other, the manor house of the resident lord, it too of stone, encompassed by a wall and situated back toward the river. No doubt 'twas the Yonne that flowed there—the same river that accompanied the pilgrim road to Vézelay, coursing ever near.

Royce hardened his jaw as he surveyed the village green and the wreckage there. Bodies scattered its length, the peasants cut down as they'd fled for the protection of the sanctuary.

Of those who'd survived the attack, many now moved amongst the dead, wailing in utter despair. Others attempted to fight past the smoldering buildings lining the green, striving to reach neighbors who'd fallen beyond. Still more cowered in the doorway of the church, shock carved in their features and rooting them there.

Royce kept his roncin to a steady trot behind Sir Hugh as the troops filed onto the green. At the sight of the armed soldiery, the villagers began to shriek and disperse in every direction. But a handful halted, spying the red crosses that adorned the warriors' garments, and called the others back.

Recognizing the Crusader emblem, the villagers stayed their retreat. Relief shone on their stricken faces. With hands outstretched, tears of desperation spilling over their cheeks, they rushed to embrace their deliverers. Royce found himself quickly enveloped, as did the others in the retinue, as the peasants pleaded for help and sobbed out their doleful tale.

Sir Hugh sought to calm the crowd but to little effect. Just then a snowy-haired man, bent with age, grasped Sir Hugh's booted foot, thanking God for sending His chosen defenders, however late.

"Who hath plagued you this night, old father?" Sir Hugh demanded as the man continued to cling to his boot. "What foe besieged this place and wreaked such havoc?"

The old man looked up with haunted eyes and shook his head. "Could not tell, could not tell," he jabbered. "'Twas a surprise raid, a large company of soldiers. They wore no livery to identify them, only garments of black to shroud them in the night."

Sir Hugh's brow deepened. "Did you see who commanded them? Did you recognize any amongst them?"

"No, no. But the main force rode for the manor house." The man released his hold on the knight's boot and lifted a bony finger toward the structure. "'Twas as if they knew Lord Hamelin was in residence, returned these two days past to accept the rents."

Worry slashed the man's weathered features afresh, his voice quavering. "I fear what has befallen our lord and his family. The raiders purposed death to all here in Vaux. Of that I am certain."

Sir Hugh swore sharply then barked orders directing a portion of the troops to attend to the survivors and learn what they could of the attack. Motioning for the others to follow, he rode toward the manor house. Without hesitation, Royce followed and within minutes passed through the manor's stone enclosure wall and into the courtyard.

Royce sucked his breath at the sight of the ground, thick

with slaughter. What killing fury had visited this place? he wondered as he drank in the horror spread there. What dark enemy had this Lord of Vaux?

His gut twisting, Royce guided his mount behind Sir Hugh as they picked a path through the bloody tangle of corpses, everywhere spines broken, limbs severed, heads gashed and lolling. Again his stomach lurched, on the brink of revolt, but he clenched his jaw tight and pressed on.

Arriving before the steps of the manor, Royce dismounted on uneasy legs, his knees gone soft as curd. Grim reality awaited once more—a half-dozen guards sprawled lifeless upon the stairs, having made their final defense here. Their obvious failure did not bode well for those within.

Working his way around the fallen men, Royce climbed the steps behind Sir Hugh, dreading that the manor now served as a tomb. At the top, the massive entrance door stood ajar, all dark within.

First to gain the landing, Sir Hugh seized a torch from one of the iron brackets that flanked the entry. His sword in hand, flashing with firelight, he bid his men forward and entered. Instantly, the soldiers surged after him, jarring Royce aside where he'd hesitated before the portal. Swallowing deeply, Royce tightened his hold on his spear and forced himself across the threshold.

Smoke stung his eyes and a stench assaulted his nostrils as he stepped into the hall. Covering his lower face with his hand, Royce squinted through the haze and sought Sir Hugh and the other knights. As before, no foe met their steel. Only the dead remained.

Glancing to the hearth, he located the source of the smoke and loathsome odor. There, several of the lord's great hounds had been cut open and tossed upon the fire.

Revolted, Royce backed away, his steps faltering as he moved toward Sir Hugh. Turning his attention to the heart of the hall, he guessed the nobles had been enjoying late-evening entertainments when the attack occurred. Tables, which had yet to be dismantled for the night, now lay overturned, a gaming board and playing pieces scattered in the rushes.

On the floor nearby stretched the body of a woman, gowned in ivory silk, a ruined lute beside her. Her filmy veil twisted about her, torn and disheveled, exposing gold-spun hair, matted with blood at her temple. Surrounding her lay four—nay, five—men in blue-and-silver livery. A personal guard perhaps?

Royce compressed his lips, finding it odd that their attire differed so markedly from those of the defenders who lay without. Mayhap she was the lord's wife, he reasoned, though among the slain he spied another woman crumpled in the rushes across the room, her garments no less fine.

Royce continued toward Sir Hugh then halted as his foot connected with something substantial, immovable. Dropping his gaze, he discovered a large bulk of a man in velvet robes edged with fur. Royce gaped at the hole in the man's chest, a bloody pulp. 'Twas the lord of Vaux, stabbed countless times, his eyes put out.

Royce staggered back a pace, a cold sweat breaking across his forehead and coating the palms of his hands. Spots sprang to life, mottling his vision, while the room began to move beneath his booted feet. Dimly, he heard one of the soldiers call to Sir Hugh from across the room.

"They are all dead above stairs, sire—the children, servants, everyone."

"Craven whoresons be they who did this!" Sir Hugh swore in a burst of temper. "God's teeth! Would that we had time to give pursuit."

Swearing fiercely once more, he pivoted in place and started forward. Abruptly, he halted in his footsteps as his gaze alighted on Royce.

Surprise fired the knight's eyes. Or was it confusion? Royce could not read his shifting expression. Perhaps he'd mistakenly expected to find his former squire and didn't readily identify him. But as Sir Hugh's brows collided over his nose, his eyes darkening with displeasure, panic unfurled through Royce, head to toe.

Should he not have accompanied the knights after all? Skimming a glance about the chamber, Royce realized with a start that no other squires stood present within save himself alone. Heat swarmed into his cheeks. Though he stood to the height of most knights' shoulders, Royce felt he'd just shrunk to the size of a gnat.

His heart thudded heavily as Sir Hugh turned brusquely aside and signaled to the man nearest him. In an instant, Beuvan appeared in the corner of Royce's spotty vision.

"Take de Warrene and search outside," Sir Hugh growled in a voice not to be challenged.

Royce opened his mouth to speak, shaken that the knight he served should order him from his side. Had he erred so greatly? Did Sir Hugh think to dismiss him altogether for this lapse?

"Now!" the knight snapped, then gave Royce his back and moved off.

Beuvan moved to stand before Royce, studying him closely. A moment later he expelled a breath and turned on his heel. "This way, lad. Have a care where you step."

Stinging with embarrassment, his stomach yet roiling beneath his belt, Royce followed Beuvan to the back of the hall where the service rooms lay. They passed along a narrow passage between the buttery and pantry and came to a short flight of steps leading down to a small chamber.

Here an oaken tub stood, half-filled with water, much of its contents sloshed over the stone floor. Woodenly, Royce observed that someone had recently bathed here. A slab of soap melted in one of the many puddles pooling the floor. Like life itself in this place, the water had gone cold.

Proceeding outside and into the yard, Royce drew deep of the fresh air, clearing his lungs. Unfortunately, it did naught to soothe his touchy stomach.

"By the saints!" Beuvan spat suddenly.

Royce traced his gaze to the sheep fold where the animals had met the same fate as all the other livestock in Vaux, here the entire flock destroyed.

"'Twould seem someone wished to annihilate the very village itself, eh, lad?" Not waiting for a response, Beuvan looked toward the river and gestured to the mill complex situated beyond a stand of trees. "Come, lad. Best we inspect that too. No telling what it might yield. Keep alert. I doubt the raiders left it untouched."

With his spear firmly in hand, Royce followed Beuvan, challenged to keep pace with him. Though he felt drained and unsteady, he was thankful to distance himself from the manor and the devastation that surrounded it.

Passing the stand of trees, they continued toward the complex that appeared to be two separate mills of differing sizes with an adjoining house, all backed to the river. As they approached the buildings, they spied several lumpish forms in the grass, illuminated by the moon's glow.

Beuvan sprinted forward and closed on the shapes. Royce joined him moments later, panting for breath. Instantly, he froze as his gaze lodged on what remained of the miller, his wife, and two daughters, all mercilessly cut down, the man's brains spilled out.

Royce's fragile hold over himself broke completely and his stomach convulsed. Dashing for the river's edge, he scarce gained the bank when he dropped to his knees and began to heave. A blackness swept through him and again he retched. At last his stomach emptied and his sight began to clear.

Shame flooded him. He was a weakling, an *enfant*, not fit to serve as squire to any knight. He wanted to crawl into the nearest hole.

"First time is it, lad?" Beuvan moved to stand behind him. "You've yet to see battle, have you? This is your first taste of such bloodletting, then?"

Royce nodded, humiliated.

"You'll toughen up," the older man assured with gruff confidence. "There will be far worse to see in Jerusalem."

Royce hung his head. How would he endure it? How could he serve Sir Hugh? All his high dreams and aspirations for himself and the future crumbled in his mind's eye. What a worthless candidate he was for knighthood. How could he hope to uphold the Code of Chivalry if he be ever on his knees, unable to cope with the sight of death?

"Will you tell Sir Hugh?" Royce rasped out.

"Tell him what?" Surprise tinged Beuvan's voice.

Miserable, Royce swiped a hand across his mouth and looked up to the knight. "That he's made a sorry choice for a squire. I've shamed myself, and therefore shamed him. How can I attend Sir Hugh at the field of battle if I cannot control my stomach here?" He dropped his head again, wholly dispirited. "Surely he'll wish to leave me behind and choose another."

For a moment Beuvan did not speak. Then he squatted beside Royce and cocked his head to one side. "Here now, lad. Do you not know why Sir Hugh sent you from the hall just now? 'Twas apurpose."

Royce lifted his eyes to Beuvan. "Apurpose?"

"Aye, to save face—*your* face before the other knights. I've no need to tell him what he already knows. He could read the sum of it in your ashen face."

Royce looked away, his disgrace biting deep to his soul.

"Ah, lad, all the brotherhood have stood—or knelt—where you do now, spewing out their insides. Knights are not born, young Royce, they are made. None ever becomes fully immune to the grim realities of our profession. But they do harden. So shall you. No one goes to war but he does not come back changed. No lad can go on Crusade and not help but come back a man."

Beuvan gave a reassuring clout to Royce's back and rose. "For now, wash your face and take a moment to steady yourself. I'll search further along the bank."

Beuvan started off then turned back to Royce. "Sir Hugh has no intention of dismissing you, rest assured. I will tell you this—you are skilled, lad. You have passion and heart, though not in greater measure than a dozen others."

"Then why did he choose me for his squire?" Royce asked, perplexed.

"Because he saw something in you—a bit of himself I believe. You're sharp and clear minded, to be sure, but also self-reliant, independent in your thinking. Those qualities will serve you well, lad, though they may also lead you into a few mishaps, as they did this night." Beuvan's lips spread in a smile. "Now see to yourself. I'll look about."

Royce moved to the river's edge and splashed his face with water then sleeved himself dry. Catching up his spear from where he'd dropped it, he stood to his feet.

As he cast a glance down the river, he saw Beuvan bending over another form in the grass. Royce looked away, unable to bear more. Not this night. Spying two small boats overturned on the bank nearby, he strode tiredly toward them, thinking to sit awhile.

Was Beuvan right? Would he harden with time? What if he handled himself no better in time to come—in view of the Crusader knights, or, worse, the Lionheart himself?

His spirits plummeted once more, failure looming as a very clear possibility. If he could not stomach the discoveries of this night, how could he withstand the bloodshed to come, warring against the infidels?

Downcast, Royce halted before the boats. Despite his years of training, he'd failed before he'd begun. Be he a squire or knight, it mattered not if he couldn't rise to the demands of his calling. What good was he to anyone? He castigated himself, plopping down heavily on the craft nearest him.

Instantly, a squeal issued from beneath the boat, followed by a thud. Royce sprang to his feet, his senses sharpening. He held his spear aimed at the boat. When all remained silent, he gave a solid kick to the craft's side.

Again came a high-pitched squeal, followed by several knocks and thuds against the underside of the boat, something shifting about there. By the high pitch of the squeal he held certain 'twas no man hidden beneath. Some animal then? Surely not a dog. The cry did not suit that of a cat either. A kitten, perchance? Or piglet?

Cautiously, Royce set his spear aside, then moving swiftly, he gripped the side of the boat by its edge and hoisted it up, flipping it back and over. Another squeal filled the air as Royce's gaze locked with two huge eyes set in an elfin face.

'Twas a child, a young girl of no more than seven or eight years. She was hunched in a ball, wrapped in homespun toweling. A halo of silvery hair spilled about her, pale as the moon.

"By all the saints—" Royce muttered his astonishment.

In the darkness and death that gripped this place, she shined like the brightest little star plucked from heaven, an angelic waif, who'd somehow survived the night.

The child continued to stare at him, trembling fiercely as she clutched the thin toweling about her. Taking in her bare shoulders and limbs, Royce realized she was naked beneath the cloth. Had she been snatched from her pallet whilst she slept and deposited here, he wondered?

Unfastening his cloak, he draped it about her, then lifted her from the ground, up into his arms. At once, she began to squeal and wriggle, panicked as though she feared he'd harm her. With little effort, Royce held her against his chest. She weighed no more than a feather.

"Shhh, now, little one. I'll not hurt you," he soothed.

She continued to writhe and nearly slipped from his arms, but suddenly she went still, her gaze fastening on his shoulder. Her little fingers lifted to the red cross, caressing it as if she recognized its significance. In the next breath, she wrapped her arms about his torso and clung to him with surprising strength.

Royce fell back a pace, his breath leaving him. "Ho there, sweeting! Ah, could you . . . ease your hold, just a little? . . . No, I guess not. Er, let's sit over here." Royce moved toward the second of the overturned boats. "That's right, easy. Nothing to fear, I'll protect you."

Circling his arms about the child, he lowered them both to the boat, shifting her onto his lap. As he did, she looked over to where the miller's family lay in the grass. Shuddering against Royce, she buried her face in his chest.

"Are they your people, little one?"

She said nothing but burrowed deeper into him, continuing to grip him tightly.

Royce let the moment pass, content to provide her the haven of his arms. Poor girl. What horrors she must have witnessed from her place beneath the boat, her family slain before her eyes. Minutes more passed then, finally, he leaned back and gazed on her features, so delicately modeled. A small, captivating mole marked the corner of her upper left lip.

"Do you have a name, little one?" he coaxed softly. When she didn't respond, he pressed again for a name to put to her. Still she would not speak. He smiled gently. "What shall I call you then? Mary? Margaret? Joan?"

The girl lifted her face to his, her brows crimping together as though she searched her mind and could not quite find the answer she sought. At last, her little lips parted. "Ana," she whispered petal soft.

Royce's smile widened. "Ana, is it? 'Tis a lovely name and suits you well, child."

He continued to smile but was unable to win the same from her. Instead, she lay her head against his heart and rested there as if listening to its calming beat. Moments later she sighed, her little slip of a body conforming to his, the tension passing out of her. Royce stroked her bright hair, finding himself touched by her trust and innocence, savoring his sudden role as protector.

"What have you there?" Beuvan's rough voice broke the spell of the moment as he returned. "Why, she's a little mite is she not?"

Ana's hold tightened on Royce as the knight reached out to touch her.

Beuvan chuckled. "A bit shy, is she?"

"I believe she's the miller's daughter—an orphan now." Royce continued to stroke Ana's hair, calming her. "Did you find anything along the river?"

"A woman, looked to be a servant of some manner." Beuvan scratched his whiskery cheek then vented a wearied breath. "Best bring the girl along. We need get back. Surely someone will take her off your hands."

Royce rose and trod behind Beuvan, feeling suddenly reluctant to relinquish the child. No matter. Ana remained twined fast about him.

In minutes they rejoined the others, finding they'd quit

the manor and moved to the village green.

"This has all the markings of a *chevauchee*," Sir Hugh was saying to a handful of his closest knights. "With France's king departing on Crusade, no doubt there will be many more such raids amongst the local lords. Rivalries run bitter and deep in these parts I am told."

Seeing Beuvan's approach, Sir Hugh acknowledged him with a nod, then swept a glance to Royce and the child. He returned his attention to the circle of knights.

"Spread word we are moving out. We will escort the survivors to the next village, a place called Vincelles. Some of Vaux's men have agreed to stay behind to bury the dead. The people of Vincelles can send others back to aid them. We can do no more. Precious time is lost to us already."

As the troops and villagers prepared to depart, Royce moved among them, seeking to find someone who might know the miller's child and agree to take her. But the people gave him little heed, seeing only to themselves and their own, their emotions and senses still ravaged by the terrors of this night.

Unable to tarry longer, Royce moved to his roncin. "You'll ride with me, sprite," he informed Ana, trying to pry her arms from beneath his arms and about his middle. She clung all the tighter. "Come now, up you go. I'll mount right behind you, I promise." She continued to squeeze him, unwilling to separate from him one inch.

Chuckles sounded around him, the knights finding amusement in his plight. Royce made a swift decision, placed his foot in the stirrup, and, with Ana firmly attached, pulled himself upward and into the saddle with all the grace of a pregnant cow. As he settled them together in the saddle, Ana melted into him, a contented smile tilting the corners of her little mouth.

Laughter broke out among the knights.

"'Twould seem Royce has won a heart this night," Renaus FitzOsbern declared in a booming voice for all to hear.

"Such devotion, gained in so little time. What's the lad's secret?" Roger de Bray's tone glowed with admiration.

"Fathers best lock away their wives and daughters when young Royce grows into his manhood," Henry le Toit warned, then burst with laughter, the others joining him.

Royce leveled them a cross look, then clicking his tongue, guided his roncin to his accustomed position behind Sir Hugh.

At that, Sir Hugh ordered the men and villagers to move out. Leaving behind the smoldering village, they rejoined the pilgrim road.

Dawn split the skies as the train of soldiers and peasants arrived in Vincelles.

Ana awoke from her slumber, snuggled against Royce's chest and warmed by his cloak. As she shifted against him, he dropped his gaze to her. His breath caught his eyes met hers—two glorious emeralds shining up at him. In the dark, he'd been unable to discern their color. Now, with the morning's light, he found himself entranced by their exquisite shade of green.

The blare of a horn snapped his attention to the front of the line where Sir Hugh's herald sounded their presence to the inhabitants, signaling their peaceful intentions.

In short time, the village elders met with them at the edge of their boundary and Sir Hugh advised them of the attack on Vaux. Generously, the people of Vincelles welcomed those of their sister village, agreeing to give them shelter.

"Lad, come quick," Beuvan called from where he'd been mingling among the peasantry.

Royce dismounted, and with Ana still securely attached

in his arms, he strode to Beuvan's side. The knight grinned wide and turned to a couple who appeared to be of middling years.

"Lad, this is Georges, the village brewer, and his wife, Marie. They wish to see the girl."

The woman came forward, clasping her hands before her as she consumed Ana with her gaze. "Oh, Georges, the Lord has heard our prayers," she exclaimed softly.

The brewer blinked back the wetness that appeared in his eyes. "*Vraiment*, and He has answered them as well." He pulled his eyes from the child and looked to Royce and Beuvan. "Marie and I, we have no *enfants* to fill our home. We will take the girl and raise her as our own."

The couple moved to relieve Royce of Ana, but she clung to him as ever she had throughout the night.

"Sweeting, you cannot come with me where I am going," he explained.

It took the four of them to disentangle the girl from Royce and give her over to Marie's arms.

"Her name is Ana," Royce explained to the couple, avoiding the heart-wringing look in the girl's emerald eyes. "Her parents and sisters were murdered before her eyes. She isn't inclined to speak much."

Tears now streamed over Ana's pale cheeks. Why did he feel like such a blackguard for leaving her here? He fumbled for the leather coin bag tucked inside his belt and gave it over to Georges.

"Here, use this to feed and clothe her. She has nothing in this world, not even a simple gown." By the shabbiness of their garments, Royce noted the brewer and his wife obviously had little of their own as well. Still, compassionately, they would take in this child.

"*Merci*, young man." Marie smiled, her face full of gratitude. "Your kindness will not be forgotten."

As the couple turned to leave with Ana, she screamed for Royce, thrashing in Marie's hold and reaching out her arms to him. Her anguish tore at his heart. Something broke deep inside him at that moment—broke for this child, for all she'd endured, for all she yet faced in time to come among strangers, having lost everything.

Royce balled his hands at his sides. By all that was holy, if there be a reason to master himself and embrace his calling, then here it be before him. Upon his honor, he would earn his spurs and uphold the knightly code, protecting the weak and the powerless. For all the little Anas in the world, he would fulfill his destiny and become the man he must.

Remembering the cross about his neck, he drew its chain from beneath his tunic and over his head. Quickly, he moved to Ana.

"Shhh sweeting," he soothed. Gifting her with his cross, he placed it around her neck, then thumbed the tears from her cheeks. "God will protect you, little one, and keep you safe. Remember me in your prayers, sweet Ana, that I can be strong and do all required of me."

Impulsively, Royce pressed a kiss to Ana's forehead. Turning on his heel, he strode quickly away and mounted his roncin behind Sir Hugh.

With a final glance back to Ana's angelic face, he rode out with Sir Hugh and the other soldiers and pressed on for Vézelay.

PART II

The Knight and the Maiden

"Now is the time at hand,
Love come to blossom,
Ripens the little maid,
Swells now the tender breast,
Vainly hath all been done
If all is ended."

—Late twelfth—early thirteenth
century, Anonymous

2

The Palace of Westminster, England Autumn A.D. 1200

"Look there, cousin. 'Tis the great Crusader knight, Sir Royce de Warrene," a feminine voice murmured, awe drenching her voice.

"Are you sure 'tis he, the hero of Acre and Ascalon?" a second female's voice asked, her interest obvious by her tone.

"I had it from Lady Margaret, who had it from Lord Bromley, that Sir Royce landed at Dover this week past, returned from the Holy Lands. He sent word ahead of his coming and was to arrive here at court any day," the first confided, breathless with excitement. "Besides, the knight is the only man in the chamber I cannot put a name to. And mind you his tanned features and the sun-brightened streaks in his hair and beard. Surely 'tis he."

"Mmmm, I'm inclined to agree," the second voice purred, as if relishing some treat. "By his size and bearing alone, 'tis evident he is a warrior of some import. *Certes*, he towers above all the other nobles present here. I venture he possesses more brawn than ten of them together. One would need such strength to slay the infidels by the hundreds, single-handed."

"Hundreds? Oh nay, cousin, by the *thousands*, 'tis told." A sigh issued from the first female. "He's very handsome, is he not? And look at the length of his sword and scabbard.

You know what 'tis said about a knight's sword?" Her voice dropped a fraction, conspiratorially. "The armorer makes each sword specifically in proportion to its owner's size."

"How deliciously intriguing," the second voice purred once more. "I would very much enjoy examining the size of yon knight's *blade* for myself—fully unsheathed, of course."

A tinkle of mischievous feminine laughter sprinkled the air.

"Has he a wife?" the second pressed.

"Shhh! He'll hear."

Royce turned at the approach of the Yeoman of the Chamber, a wiry man with hawklike features carrying an ornate staff.

"His Majesty will see you now." The man gave a shallow dip of his shoulders in semblance of a bow and bid the knight follow.

Casting a swift glance toward the two ladies who'd been so avidly discussing him, Royce acknowledged them with a nod and appreciative smile. Their cheeks flamed instantly.

Royce's smile widened as he turned, taking in their shocked realization that he'd overheard all they'd spoken. In truth, their comments were heady wine for a man just returned to his homeland after baking these ten years past in the desert. Then, too, the court ladies in their bright gowns and finery were as sweet as honey to his eyes.

Royce continued behind the official, making his way through the forechamber and crush of lords, ladies, and clerics, proceeding toward an immense oaken door at the far end of the chamber.

The official halted there to exchange brief words with the guards. Eying the knight, they required he divest himself of his weapons before proceeding further. Royce complied, though he felt naked without his sword and the small dagger he kept sheathed on the back of his belt. Satisfied, the guards moved aside, allowing the two forward. With decided ceremony, the yeoman struck the door thrice with his staff. Moments later, the door drew open from within and Royce found himself face to face with a moon-faced clerk.

"De Warrene? Enter, enter." The clerk waved him in with a rapid flapping of his hand.

Royce crossed the portal as the clerk scurried off across the chamber, stopping where a flock of nobles and ministers attended a richly garbed man of abbreviated height. The clerk wormed his way through the congestion then dropped to his knee and waited to be recognized.

Royce fixed his gaze on the man at the center of everyone's interest. He stood at a thick-planked table, silhouetted against a glazed window that soared upward into a graceful arch. Methodically, the man affixed his signet ring to wax and parchment, approving document after document proffered by the royal administrators. He completed the task, then waved them away and stepped apart of the table, extending his arms. Instantly, a servant bustled forward and aided him into a luxurious fur-lined robe. The servant, presumably his tailor, quickly sank to the floor and began fussing with a noticeable sag in the hem.

Royce absorbed the sight of John Plantagenet, consecrated King of England since May of the year past. He was sturdily built though surprisingly short for a Plantagenet, having none of King Richard's height. He did possess the reddish Angevin hair of his father and brothers, however, and if rumor had it right, their quick temper. Even as he waited for his tailor to right the wayward hem, John paced this way and that, displaying a hot, restless energy so characteristic of the Angevins and their diabolical energy.

Royce continued to wait, regretting he'd not returned from the Holy Lands sooner to aid the Lionheart. Perhaps, had he been at the siege of Châlus to serve the king, he might have prevented . . .

Royce shut off the thought, knowing his presence would have made not one dram of difference. Richard had been impulsive, foolhardy, riding up to the castle wall to inspect the progress of his siege machines, courting danger, not even taking the precaution of donning his armor. A cross-bowman upon the upper ramparts handily discharged a bolt into his shoulder. Richard died ten days later, his wound turned gangrenous.

Royce refocused on the new sovereign. John now wore the crown, having wrested it from his young nephew, sired by old Henry's third son, Geoffrey—now also deceased. England's greatest barons, including William Marshal himself, refused to support the boy, who was much spoiled and dominated by unprincipled counselors. They feared his yoke would prove far worse than John's.

Were they right to support John, the youngest and only surviving eaglet of Henry II? Royce had questioned their wisdom all the way from the shores of Jaffa to those of Dover. He did not trust John. Few did.

As Royce beheld the restless man before him, he wondered what to think of the new king. Old Henry and his brood were not called "the demoniac Angevins" for naught.

After pressing his ring to yet another glob of wax and parchment, the king snatched up his goblet and turned, nearly trampling the moon-face clerk who still waited on bended knee. After taking notice of the clerk and then heed of his words, John jerked round, swinging his gaze across the chamber to Royce. His face brightened.

"Ah, Sir Royce de Warrene!" he exclaimed buoyantly. "I've looked forward to your arrival since news of your landing at Dover."

"Majesty." Royce bowed deeply, touching a knee to the floor at the king's approach, noting how the tailor scrambled after him, still connected by needle and thread to the royal hem.

Oblivious, the king came to a halt before him, continuing to smile. Meanwhile, the tailor knelt at his side, his needle flying.

"Rise, Sir Royce," John bid heartily. "I am anxious to hear of your adventures. No doubt word of your return has spread throughout all of England by now. The clerics at Dover are like gabbling old women, scratching down every morsel of news that comes to their ears and relaying the latest buzz to Canterbury and beyond."

"The temptation is understandable, Majesty, what with the traffic of pilgrims and travelers that pass through Dover's port." Royce pressed to his feet.

Truth be told, he'd indulged in several hours' gossip himself over cups of ale with the chroniclers, gleaning what he could of the status of the realm since Richard's death,

"Yes, yes, understandable, but while the scribes report of your return, 'tis the court that shall be the first to hear of the latest deeds of chivalry wrought by her knights for all of Christendom."

John paused of a sudden, studying Royce closely as if seeking to take his measure. One side of his lips lurched upward into a crooked smile. Just as quickly, he whirled round and gestured to the moon-faced clerk.

"Wine! Wine for Sir Royce!" Impatiently, John crossed the space to meet the clerk halfway. The tailor gasped and scuttled after the sovereign once more, snatching at the needle dangling from the royal hem.

Seizing the goblet from the clerk's pudgy hands, the king turned on his heels and strode back to Royce, thrusting the vessel into the knight's hands. In the same moment, the tailor shrieked, having stabbed himself with the needle. He shoved his finger into his mouth and caught up his needle with his other hand, then bent to the hem once more.

"What's this?" The king glanced down and pinned the tailor with an irritable look. "Ralph, are you yet to be done?"

"I will be if your Majesty will do me the kindness of standing still," he replied waspishly.

John grinned like a mischievous child who'd vexed the man apurpose and now gained precisely what he desired. "So be it, so be it," he allowed and strove to stand motionless while Ralph took his stitches, though the king's efforts proved less than successful.

John angled a glance to Royce. "Stories of your prowess burgeon your name, Sir Royce. I vow they rival the deeds of my late brother."

Again, Royce sensed John searched him out. Certainly, Royce had distinguished himself in the East, but he stood nowhere near the stature of Richard, only in his shadow, as did most men.

"Sire, you know how the people love to exaggerate." The image of the women in the forechamber sprang to mind.

"You fought with Richard at the Battle of Acre, did you not? Knighted on the field of battle, I am told."

Royce caught a combative note in John's voice, containing a sudden sharpness and swift change of mood. Had he misspoken somehow, Royce wondered?

"Aye, sire. The stories are true."

John downed a mouthful of wine then touched his forefinger to his lips. "Let me see if I have the right of it. Sir Hugh FitzAlan's destrier was killed beneath him, the beast falling atop the knight and trapping his legs."

"Aye, Majesty."

"But then you, his high-hearted squire, ran onto the field of battle, snatched up his sword, and wielded it with all the ferocity of a Norse berserker, slaying three hundred infidels on the spot and sparing your knight."

Royce's lips twitched upward. "The number has a tendency to grow in people's telling, Majesty, but essentially the tale is true. I fought on till the Saracens either lay dead about us or withdrew at the sound of retreat. By God's grace, Sir Hugh lived to fight other battles." Seven more before he fell a final time.

"And my brother knighted you on the field of battle, did he?"

"'Twas Sir Hugh who gave me the *colée*, once we'd freed him from beneath his horse. 'Twas his privilege, though the king looked on."

Royce remembered the proud moment, the knights Beuvan and Renaus supporting Sir Hugh while he delivered the ceremonial blow to his cheek, Roger de Bray and Henry le Toit looking on. Now they all lay in the dust of Jerusalem, save Beuvan who yet lived and chose to remain in Haifa.

The tailor completed his task and bit off the thread with his teeth. Full of thought, the king strode back to the table, flipped open the lid of a jeweled casket, then began slipping costly rings onto his fingers and settling a great chain and medallion of gold about his neck.

He turned back, his expression shuttered. "Such gallantry and skill as yours are invaluable to the realm. I understand you even campaigned with the Templars."

"For a time, Majesty."

"Yet you chose not to join their order? Curious." John's eyes lodged on him, narrowed, crafty.

Royce cast about in his mind for a tactful response. While he'd once considered joining the order, he'd decided against it due to a taint of fanaticism that infected those hardened warriors. He did embrace much of their strict discipline, however.

"For most of my stay in the kingdom of Jerusalem, I employed my sword securing the road between Acre and Ascalon and defending Jaffa. But 'twas always my intent to return to England's shores."

Reaching beneath his tunic, Royce produced a small scroll, feeling now to be the best time to broach the reason for his requested audience.

"Before your brother, King Richard, departed the Holy Lands—for services I rendered beneath his banner, particularly those during the bitter retaking of Ascalon—he granted me a portion of land to claim at the time of my return. Knowing I desired to remain a while longer in the East, he assured a seneschal would be appointed to oversee the estate in my absence. Now, at long last, I am returned to assert my claim in person."

Royce gave over the scroll to the king then released a long breath, feeling a mixture of joy and edgy uncertainty collide in his chest as he embraced his future, no longer a landless knight.

Richard had assured the land boasted a fine castle and prosperous village. In addition, Royce had accrued a modest fortune while in the East. The years ahead boded well. Once he'd secured his new land, seen to the castle and its defenses, he would consider establishing his own house, his own bloodline. For that he need seek a good marriage, preferably one with an important heiress who could increase his station, bringing him more titles and more lands. Royce was determined to secure a place of import and influence for himself in England now that he'd returned.

The king's brows drew upward, surprise lighting his eyes as he scanned the parchment bearing his brother's seal. "In truth, I was unaware of this particular grant, Sir Royce, or of this estate being named among the royal holdings."

Royce's breath stilled in his lungs. He felt as though a

great fist had just reached out and squeezed his heart. What intent lay behind the king's words? Did he think to deny him the Lionheart's behest and keep the estate for himself? Royce's doubts about John reared their scaly heads.

The king continued to peruse the document then, with head bent, he cut his eyes up at Royce.

"I confess, I am surprised Richard had royal lands left to give, or that he would grant them without a price. He would have sold London itself had he been able, so that he might finance his wars. The kingdom never finds rest," he murmured, returning his gaze to the parchment. "Always a wolf at the door."

John straightened abruptly, rolling the document with quick fingers. "Of course, I shall support Richard's wishes. Like my brother, I recognize you to be a worthy and *loyal* subject of the realm?" His words held a question in their tone.

"That I am, sire," Royce returned, meeting the king's penetrating gaze.

"Then certainly you are deserving of such reward," John said simply. He became all movement again. Returning to the table, he motioned his counselors and attendants to leave him and seized upon an iron-bound casket.

"I shall have my counselors examine the grant and determine precisely where the property lies." He fitted a key to the casket's domed lid and opened it. "There is still much to learn of my domains. 'Tis my intention to rule personally, but thus far I've completed a tour only of my Continental holdings. In the weeks to come, I shall begin a circuit throughout England. Who knows? Perhaps, I shall chance across your new lands."

John tossed Royce a smile, then dropped the scroll in the casket and secured its lid with a click of the key. "Rest assured, I shall have the matter examined forthwith as you'll wish to settle and make preparations before winter."

"My gratitude, Majesty." Royce bowed deeply once more, discomforted that the king retained his only proof of Richard's grant, a document he'd painstakingly guarded through the years. Before he could rise, the blare of trumpets sounded loudly from without.

"Ah, the feasting is to begin anew." The king smiled wide. "We are yet celebrating my new bride's coronation, Sir Royce. You will join us, of course, as our honored guest. Isabella will delight in your tales of gallantry and valor, as will all the court."

Royce pulled his gaze from the casket, feeling a twinge of distrust in his gut. There was naught he could do at the moment about the scroll.

"You are most gracious, Majesty."

Again the trumpets sounded.

"The queen awaits!" John snatched up his crown from where it rested haphazardly on a nearby chair and lodged it onto his head.

Bidding Royce follow, he hastened from the chamber, taking long strides on short legs, his robes flowing and jewels sparkling, a smile splitting his bearded face. Obviously, this youngest of the Plantagenet brood enjoyed all the advantages and attentions of kingship, a station that for many years must have seemed beyond his reach.

Royce trailed after the king, matching his brisk pace. Surprisingly, the courtiers and attendants who'd held audience with the sovereign stepped aside for Royce before they themselves joined the royal progression. He could only wonder at their seeming deference. Presumably, many a man enjoyed stations far greater than he. Perhaps 'twas the favor the king afforded him that now governed their actions, Royce reasoned.

Much bowing and scraping accompanied the king's passage through the antechamber as the lords and ladies opened a path for the sovereign and his train to proceed toward the White Hall. Whispers followed them and it bemused Royce to hear his own name repeated upon those noble lips as a "great Crusader knight" and "hero."

Queen Isabella waited before the doors of the feasting hall, surrounded by her elegant ladies-in-waiting and flanked by the most powerful barons and clergy in attendance. At her husband's approach, she sank into a deep curtsy, a vision of exquisite beauty and grace. Though Royce had heard glowing descriptions of her comeliness, 'twas still jolting to behold the new queen in person—for reasons beyond her loveliness.

As Royce understood it, after John's coronation, he immediately set out on a tour of Normandy and the Acquitaine. There, he encountered the beautiful heiress of Angoulême, Isabella, and became wildly enamored of her. Inconveniently, she was already engaged.

When John made his intentions clear, Isabella's parents were all too happy that their daughter attain a queenship. They moved to break the engagement and arrange her hasty marriage to the English monarch. But scandal swirled darkly about the newly wedded couple. Whilst John was a man of prime years being two-and-thirty, Isabella was a child of barely twelve.

Royce pushed aside his thoughts as John took his young queen by the hand. Raising her to her feet, he pressed a lingering kiss to her fingers. By his look alone, 'twas plain the man was utterly besotted with his bride.

The king placed Isabella's small hand on his forearm, his larger one lingering to cover hers, then turned to Royce. "My lady-wife, this is Sir Royce de Warrene, the heroic knight of whom I spoke, just arrived from the Holy Lands. He warred with Richard there. I'm sure he will be agreeable to entertain us tonight with gallant tales of the Crusades and of the years since my late brother's departure from *Outremer*, the lands beyond the sea."

Royce bowed low and, at once, the diminutive queen lifted her free hand to him to be kissed.

"Rise, Sir Royce. I shall take pleasure in your stories of chivalry and am pleased that you are returned safe to England's shores."

Royce dropped a light kiss to the queen's ring then rose. He paused for a moment as he gazed upon her enchanting face. His brows began to draw together, then realizing the gesture, he willed them smooth lest others think he found displeasure with the queen.

In truth, Isabella reminded him of someone, but he could not quite puzzle out whom. She was a delicate creature with lively eyes. Her bright, flaxen hair draped over her shoulders in two long plaits, each wound with satin ribbons and ending in jeweled clasps. A veil of net spilled from her fair head, held in place by her queenly crown. Gemstones glittered on her mantle and gown, the latter a shimmering creation of gold sendal over an ivory undergown, all lavishly embroidered.

Royce regarded the queen for only a brief moment before she turned to gaze admiringly into her husband's eyes. Next, he found himself presented to the dignitaries surrounding the royal couple, among them Hubert Walter, the Archbishop of Canterbury; Geoffrey FitzPeter, the king's justicar; and most notable and impressive of all, the very paragon of knighthood itself, William Marshal, Earl of Pembroke and Lord of Leinster.

The earl took a keen interest in Royce and was just expressing his interest in hearing of the latest developments in the East when a fanfare of trumpets, drums, and pipes signaled the ceremonials for dinner to commence.

The king and queen led the procession into the hall, followed by the dignitaries and nobles in descending order of rank. Royce held back, waiting for the others to pass before he himself joined. But the king halted and gestured him forward, indicating he should remain near.

The White Hall proved to be a great aisled chamber, high-ceilinged and of significant expanse. Tapestries and painted screens enlivened the cold stone walls, warming them by color, if not in fact.

Tables, draped with snowy linens, lined the length of both sides of the hall. At the far end, the king's high table held place of precedence, situated upon a raised dais beneath a crimson canopy. Left of the dais stood the *aumbry*, a sideboard crowded with gold vessels, exhibiting the king's wealth. To the dais's right stood a separate table intended for the honored guests who, like the sovereigns, would be clearly visible to all in the hall.

As the king and queen assumed their places upon the dais in the sole company of the Earl of Pembroke and the Archbishop of Canterbury, Royce again found himself at a loss, wondering where exactly he should assume a place. Just then, the Marshal of the Hall appeared with his white wand and led him forward to the table of honor. Royce seated himself, amazed to find himself in company with such important personages of the realm.

A fresh flourish of trumpets announced the beginning of the rituals. Issuing from the kitchen passage at the opposite end of the hall emerged a procession of noble servitors and squires of gentle birth. First came the ewerer and his assistants, white cloths over their arms, bearing lavers and pitchers for the washing of hands. The king and queen were first attended then the other lords and ladies, their hands cleansed with fragrant herbal water.

Next in the cadre came the carver and cupbearer, the

pantler and butler, and the almoner, who led the chamber in prayer. More servers followed bearing great platters of food and tureens of soups, comprising the first course—offerings of flesh, fish, and fowl. While the meats were sauced and broken, two noble youths paraded a subtlety around the room then set it upon a stand for viewing. Robert de Beaumont, Earl of Leicester, who sat beside Royce, informed him that the marzipan sculpture was of the queen's dower castle, gifted her upon her recent marriage to the king.

The bustle continued in the hall with a constant traffic of servers coming and going. The mingling of harp, dulcimer, and lutes played in the background while guests partook of the feast and chattered with their table mates. Minstrels, jugglers, and dancers entertained between courses while servers paraded the subtlety round the hall again. Trumpets heralded each new course, the multiplicity of dishes continuing—lampreys and eel dishes, venison pastries, stuffed pig, puddings, capons, woodcock, jellies and tarts, quince in comfit, almond cream, fried minnows, and more, all washed down with spiced wine and ale.

Royce restricted himself to a light sampling of a few dishes for the variety was staggering and more than he cared to manage. Throughout the meal he gave himself to answering his companions' questions. As he was discussing recent events in Jaffa, he caught sight of the two women who'd taken a sharp interest in him earlier in the antechamber. They sat with a third woman, a matron, perhaps in her early thirties. She stared at him with dark, compelling eyes, then tipped her head toward the other two, asking some question, her gaze never leaving him.

"Beware, Sir Royce," Lord Robert advised goodnaturedly. "That is Lady Sibylla, Countess Linford, a fine catch for her wealth and estates, though she's buried three husbands to manage it. She's known to be looking for fresh prey and has a particular liking for men younger than she." His smile disappeared behind his goblet as he downed its contents.

Again the trumpets blared, declaring the final course. But before the procession of food began, a single youth—one of the ushers of the hall—appeared. He ran toward the dais and dropped to one knee, flustered.

"Your Highness forgive me. I tried to stop him but—"

An aged noble entered the hall, his hair like snow and his robes a rich brocade edged with marten. He made his way slowly, painfully, down the length of the hall with the aid of two canes and servants supporting him on either side. With dragging steps he came to stand before the main dais.

"Majesty, a thousand pardons," the man said in a deep booming voice, bowing as low as he could manage. His servants aided him upright once more.

"I am Lord Gilbert Osborne of Penhurst and I seek the knight, Royce de Warrene. On good word, I am told he landed at Dover two days before last and departed there for Westminster Palace. Happily, I was at Canterbury when news of his return reached my ears."

The king exchanged a swift glance with Royce. "Dover's scribes are far busier than I imagined," he uttered in obvious amazement, his brows arching high.

The old lord shifted his weight, leaning heavily on his canes. "Sire, I have urgent business with the knight. 'Tis a matter of honor and of dire urgency. If he be present, pray direct me to him."

Royce rose slowly, purposefully to his feet. "I am he whom you seek," he said, his rich voice carrying through the hall. "I am Royce de Warrene."

Lord Gilbert turned and fastened his eyes on him. For a moment he held silent. Then his features twisted, a mixture of anger and torment flooding his features. He shuffled his stance and turned back toward the dais.

"Majesty, I demand justice!" he bellowed, striking the floor with his cane.

Murmurs rippled along the high table and throughout the hall.

"Justice?" the king blustered, his expression confounded. "Sir Royce has just this hour arrived, returned after a decade in the Holy Lands. What possible justice could you seek?"

"Justice for a grave wrong he has committed regarding my granddaughter!"

Gasps echoed all around and many a lady's eyes leapt to Royce, stabbing him with knifelike looks as though he'd wronged all womankind.

"I know not of what you speak," Royce stated flatly, maddened to be falsely accused and denounced before all. "Ever have I acted honorably toward those of the gentle sex. Never have I brought ill on the least of them. Who is your granddaughter, sir?"

"The lady Juliana Mandeville, child of my daughter, Alyce, and of the great Marcher lord, Robert Mandeville, God rest their souls. Surely, you know of Sir Robert. He served King Richard on Crusade. 'Twas at Acre he fell."

A face and blue banner flashed in Royce's mind. "I recall the knight, but I know nothing of his daughter."

"Ah but you do!" The old man jabbed at the air with one of his canes. "And because of you, she has been lost to me these many long years. I demand you restore her to me!"

Again the hall erupted in murmurings and babble. Royce steeled himself, a knot forming in his chest.

"Upon my honor, I know naught of what you speak. But if I have unknowingly wronged the lady, I shall right it."

"Aye, upon your honor, right it you will!" the old man snapped. "Hear me out then."

Gathering his composure, Lord Gilbert bid his servant bring his folding stool. This done, he lowered himself onto the piece with considerable effort and continued to grip his canes before him. Silence fell over the hall, its occupants' attention fixed upon the old lord as he began to address them.

Glancing to the royal minstrel who stood right of the dais with his lute in hand, Lord Gilbert gave him a nod. "Take heed of my words if it pleases you, for 'tis a doleful tale, worthy to be remembered in verse, though at present it owns no end."

Pausing, the old lord drew his gaze over those in the hall, lingering momentarily on Royce, then bringing it finally to settle on the king and his young queen, who appeared particularly enrapt by his presence. Lord Gilbert drew a deep breath.

"Ten years past, when the Lionheart put forth the call to arms for the Third Crusade, my son-in-law, Sir Robert Mandeville, crossed the Channel with his soldiers to meet the king at Vézelay. His wife—my daughter, Alyce—and their only child Juliana, accompanied him as far as Rouen. My own wife, Thérèse, God rest her soul, was of French birth. Alyce, our daughter, desired to visit her mother's relatives, something she was accustomed to do every several years.

"From Rouen Sir Robert sent Alyce and the child on with a small host of men-at-arms to Senlis, where they visited a widowed aunt. From there, they journeyed southward, destined for Châlon, where a second aunt lived in cloister. Their travels brought them to the village of Vaux, where they stopped to seek lodging for the night with the local lord."

Royce kept his gaze fixed rigidly on the old lord, masking all emotion from his features as the memories of that long-ago night swarmed back in all its harsh detail.

Lord Gilbert shifted on the stool. "Tragically, that very night the village and manor were attacked and laid waste." Tears collected in his pale eyes. "The source of the attack remains in question even after these many years, though 'tis suspected a feud amongst the French nobles lay at its cause. The lord of Vaux was not without enemies. To point, the attackers specifically sought out all those of noble blood and put them to the sword. Evidently, 'twas their intent to exterminate the lord and all his kindred."

Lord Gilbert bowed his snowy head, his voice quavering. "My daughter, Alyce, was among those slain. But the child, Juliana, was never found."

The hall remained hushed as a tomb. Royce closed his lids, remembering the death and wreckage in the manor house, envisaging the noblewoman laying dead in the rushes, blood saturating her golden hair. Fallen about were her personal guards. He'd wondered at the time about their blue-and-silver livery, which differed so markedly from that of the other guards. Now he understood. The lady was of another, much nobler house. She was Alyce Mandeville.

Royce took a deep swallow and opened his eyes. Directly across from him, Lord Gilbert drew a handkerchief from his sleeve and mopped his face and wiped at his eyes. He then struggled to his feet, his eyes and features enlivening as a fresh fury stole into his face. He turned and cast Royce a searing look.

"These long years have I searched for my granddaughter. This much have I learned—Sir Hugh FitzAlan and his men came upon Vaux that murderous night and aided the survivors to a neighboring village. A child fitting little Juliana's description was seen directly after the attack, in the care of Sir Hugh's own squire. Apparently, she held a particular liking for the lad and rode clinging to him all the way to Vincelles, where he gave her to a peasant family—the village brewer and his wife."

Royce wavered at the revelation then clenched his hands to fists as Lord Gilbert continued his tale.

"For these many long years, I have searched tirelessly for my granddaughter but, alas, to no avail. The brewer soon left Vincelles with his little family to seek better fortune elsewhere, using the coin the squire reportedly gave him."

He stabbed Royce with another accusing look then turned toward the dais once more.

"There is no way to know if Juliana yet lives, but her looks are as exceptional as they are distinctive—silvery blonde hair, eyes like emeralds, and a distinctive mole marking the corner of her upper left lip."

Ana. With crystalline clarity, Royce recalled the angelic creature who'd wrapped herself around his person and around his heart. He stole a swift glance at the queen then dropped his gaze away. 'Twas Ana of whom the child queen reminded him, not in age but in her glowing beauty, pale as the moon. Royce's pulse drubbed heavily in his veins. How was he to have known the child was of noble blood?

Lord Gilbert's thundering voice jerked Royce's attention back to the hall.

"Sir Hugh and his retainers were in such haste to join the Lionheart that they took no time to inquire about those in their care," he railed, his features collecting into a choleric mien.

Turning, he raised his cane and shook it accusingly at Royce.

"'Twas *you* who served as squire to Sir Hugh. You, Royce de Warrene, are the one who gave my highborn granddaughter into the charge of peasants, robbing her of her birthright, her station, and what is left of her family—

me, her grandfather!"

Royce started to speak, to tell Lord Gilbert how, at the time, he'd sought to find the child's relatives among the survivors of Vaux, to tell him how she'd called herself only "Ana," obviously not remembering the full of her name. But the girl had been severely distraught by the butchery she'd witnessed. As Royce opened his mouth to say as much, the old lord cut short his words.

"Juliana is my only surviving blood relative and I, hers. My days grow short. I am unwell and nearly crippled, as you can well see, and I am unable to continue my search."

A fit of coughing overtook Lord Gilbert. Somewhat defeated, he lowered himself onto the stool, his servants bracing him. His throat settled, and he lifted his gaze toward the dais, a great sadness in his eyes.

"If there be one thing I wish above all in this life, 'tis to behold my little Juliana with these old eyes before I close them forever. God willing I shall."

He struggled once more to his feet, seemingly gathering the last of his strength about him.

"Majesty, when I heard of Royce de Warrene's return, I recognized his name and came at once to find him. Now I demand justice—that Sir Royce take up my quest and find Juliana and restore her to me and to her rightful place as a highborn lady and heiress. Sir Royce, I demand you right the wrong you wrought so many years ago."

Royce stood stunned, unable to find his voice. Clearly he was at fault and Lord Gilbert's outrage justified. His unwitting mistake tore at the fabric of his honor and stained his very name as a worthy knight of the realm.

The queen moved first. Visibly touched, she laid her hand on the king's arm and leaned toward him to whisper in his ear.

John's lips parted in a wide smile. "Yes, my dear, a

quest. How splendid! Just as in days of old, and here we have a knight of renown to see the quest through," he blurted triumphantly, like a delighted child.

The queen smiled, clapping her hands together as rumbles of approval reverberated throughout the hall. The king rose from his place, assuming a more sober aspect.

"Upon my oath, no domain under my crown shall lose even one of its fair damsels," he proclaimed magnanimously. "Sir Royce, as a knight of the realm, you are bound to defend—and rescue —maidens in distress. Considering your role in the matter, I charge you with this quest. Find the heiress Juliana Mandeville by whatever means you must and restore her to her grandfather, Lord Gilbert Osborne."

The king stepped from the dais, approached Lord Gilbert, and proffered him his royal hand and ring, which the old lord kissed. John then crossed to where Royce stood at his place.

"We will talk anon of your lands, Sir Royce. My counselors will have the details sorted out by the time you return and your quest is complete. There will be a boon for you when you do," he added cheerfully. "The court looks forward to your swift return. After all, how many places can an heiress hide?"

"Indeed, Majesty." Royce forced the words past his lips, still reeling from the swift turn of events and subsequent royal command.

The king started toward the dais then halted and turned back. "Report to my scribe. He shall draw up letters of introduction and authority in the matter. Perhaps Lord Gilbert will wish to add his own letters to these."

Royce reined his emotions, his years of training and discipline taking over as he embraced his knightly duty. Wrong must be set to right, especially since he was the cause of that disservice. 'Twas long ago at Vincelles that he committed himself to succoring the weak and the powerless—for "all the little Anas of the world," he'd avowed. Now, duty and destiny called that he, once more, aid Ana herself.

Royce bowed deeply to the king and queen.

"Majesties, by your leave, I shall hasten to Dover and set sail on the first ship for Boulogne. By God's grace when you next see me 'twill be with the heiress, Juliana Mandeville, at my side."

3

Chinon, in the region of Touraine, France—
one of the Plantagenet domains of King John

Ana silently slipped her cloak from the peg by the door and stepped out of the house into the predawn quiet. The chilled fresh air of early morn nipped at her cheeks and nose while somewhere in the dark a lone dog barked. Obviously, like herself, the animal could not sleep.

Traveling to the end of the narrow street, Ana headed for the main square, anxious to reach it before the first rays of light fell over Chinon and turned its walled castle and the cliff it sat upon all to gold. 'Twas a spectacle she loved to behold. This would be her last time to steal out so freely and do so—leastwise, as a maiden. Today was her wedding day.

Ana turned onto a crooked lane, hastening her steps past half-timbered houses, squeezed side to side. Again a dog barked while the tantalizing aromas of hot bread and meat broth teased at her nostrils, masking the foul odors that ever pervaded the streets. Ana continued on, her heart beating light and quick. In minutes, she emerged onto the square.

Already there was some movement there. A pair of veiled-and-wimpled matrons ambled toward the well at the square's center, their buckets looped over their arms, their heads together as they shared some tattle. Several merchants opened the horizontal shutters on their store fronts, propping the topmost plank upward to create a canopy and dropping the lower one onto legs to serve as a counter to display goods and conduct business.

Directly across from Ana rose the substantial church of St. Maurice, dominating all else on the square. Her lips parted in a smile. In the coming hours, she would stand upon the church's hallowed steps for all to see and exchange marriage vows with Gervase.

She drew her cloak snugly about her, thoroughly content. Was she not the most fortunate maid of Chinon, to have won the cooper's heart? Gervase was a good, God-fearing man, dependable, pleasant to look upon, and the owner of a profitable and stable business—making wooden casks. He would be amply able to provide a secure life for a wife and family.

She was indeed lucky to be marrying such a man. Life would be good with Gervase, well worth her wait to marry. And she'd waited longer than most maids. Some, including her foster mother, Marie, feared she might never agree to wed. But, then, they didn't understand her reasons—deep, heart-held reasons—for waiting.

Out of habit, Ana lifted her hand to the silver cross suspended on a chain about her neck and closed her fingers around it. She doubted anyone could understand her feelings even if she attempted to explain them. Why even begin?

Her thoughts went back to her bridegroom, a warm joy spreading through her.

Gervase had struck a friendship with her foster father more than a year ago. On the occasion of her eighteenth Name Day—a day chosen randomly since she knew not her true one—she relented and decided to accept Gervase's suit, which he'd been pressing for nearly six months. Since their betrothal, four weeks past, she and her foster mother had prepared for the happy event, baking endlessly and making great quantities of fresh ale and beer, which now filled Gervase's new casks.

Ana blew at a wisp of hair that had fallen across her forehead and eyes, then released a breezy sigh. 'Twas a fine match and she cared deeply for Gervase. She'd been fortunate to be able to choose a spouse for love. And it was that—love. After all, true love involved deep respect and fond regard for one another, beyond simple attraction or momentary desire.

Yes, she loved Gervase and he loved her. 'Twas evident by the sparkle of longing ever present in his eyes when they were near. Admittedly, much of that "sparkle" had to do with Gervase's anticipation of their wedding night. He did naught to conceal it. Still, she knew he loved her.

A fluttery sensation, akin to a host of butterflies, rose from her stomach and flittered upward, inside her chest. A few days past, her foster mother had explained the physical aspects of marriage and what she might expect. When Ana had expressed shock, Marie quickly assured she need not worry. Gervase was a mild-mannered man and would likely be a considerate lover, especially during their first couplings.

Ripples of unease traveled through Ana. She could not think on these things or the night to come. Her foster parents' own relationship seemed happy in all regards. She would draw encouragement from that. Surely she would survive Gervase's passion and possession of her. In time, perhaps, she'd come to even welcome it.

Bird chatter began to fill the air as the first rays of dawn spilled over the city and into the square. Ana raised her eyes toward the sprawling fortress on the cliff as both began to glow. She inhaled a deep, renewing breath and smiled. 'Twas going to be a splendid day.

Just as the castle and cliff magically paled to gold, the

clatter of a horse's hooves sounded on the cobblestones, drawing her gaze. Ana retreated into the shadows of the nearest building to watch as a single rider appeared on the square astride a large black stallion. He rode apace, heading directly toward the lord mayor's dwelling, which stood adjacent to the church.

As Ana continued to observe him, the women at the well scuttled off. She sharpened her gaze over the stranger. He was impressive in size and bearing, attired in knightly garb—a long, sleeveless surcoat worn over a hauberk and leggings of mail. A close-fitting hood of additional mail covered his head, while a bright scarlet mantle flowed from his shoulders. Facially, she could discern little of his features owing to his mustache and beard, though both were neatly trimmed. Drinking in the sight of him, her gaze drifted slowly downward then stopped at the great sword he wore at his hip.

A sudden sense of foreboding washed through her. Ana clutched the cross in her hand once more as she watched the knight dismount and approach the entrance to the lord mayor's residence. As he disappeared inside, she shook off the prickly feelings, aware that the fine hairs on the back of her neck and arms had lifted on end.

Ana clamped down on her emotions. Strangers in the city were not uncommon. Obviously, with day breaking, the night guard had opened the city gates and permitted entry to those who waited without. The knight's business lay with the lord mayor and had nothing to do with her. She'd not dwell on him one moment longer.

But the fluttery feeling she'd felt in her stomach and chest moments before had turned to lead. Ana set her jaw. She refused to believe in omens. 'Twas the sight of the knight's sword that unsettled her so, that and no more. Such weapons ever conjured dark memories from her past.

Ana turned on her heel and quit the square. Retracing her steps back along the crooked street, she quickened toward her foster parents' house, forcing her thoughts to the hours ahead and the coming celebration.

'Twas her wedding day, and she'd allow nothing to spoil it.

Hours later, the wedding party swept Ana and Gervase along the streets of Chinon amidst great noise and merriment. Musicians led the procession, skipping about as they played bright tunes on their flutes and tamped out rhythms on beribboned tambours.

Well-wishers and onlookers joined the festivities along the way, many offering jovial advice to the bridegroom for the wedding night. Gervase laughed good-naturedly and replied with his own cheerful banter. When his twinkling gaze fell upon Ana, consuming her whole, heat shot to her cheeks and she felt herself blush completely.

In truth, Ana found his attentions most flattering. She smiled up at him, feeling radiant and pretty in her new dress, a light green wool, embroidered about the neck and sleeves. A circlet of flowers crowned her wealth of pale hair, flowing freely past her waist. Completing her bridal dress, soft leather slippers adorned her feet. Beside her, Gervase looked wonderfully handsome, clean and smooth shaven and dressed in his best clothes.

Happiness filled Ana's heart. After the nuptials and mass, the wedding party would return to her foster parents' home to feast and dance and sing till dark. A bubbling pork stew awaited them, plus rounds of barley bread, fish pasties, and eggs by the dozens. To wash it all down, there was a plentitude of ale and beer and even a barrel of watered wine—gift of a local vintner and patron of Gervase's fine casks.

As the party progressed through the winding streets, their numbers rapidly multiplied, swelling to a sizable crowd as they entered the main square and advanced toward St. Maurice. Ana looked expectantly to the great arched doors where the priest would emerge momentarily, carrying an open Bible and the wedding rings.

Gervase gave an affectionate squeeze to her hand as they began to mount the church steps. She smiled into his brown eyes. In scant moments they would speak their vows and be joined for the rest of their mortal lives. Today would be one of the most important and memorable occasions they would ever experience.

Transferring her gaze to the church's central door, she saw it slowly draw open and the priest's figure appear. As he stepped from the church's dim interior into the light, she noted that Pere Armand did not appear his normal, robust self. Rather, he looked ill, his face pinched and his complexion waxen. Ana's gaze fell to his hands and found they were empty.

Before she could think on it, a movement just behind the priest drew her eyes. In the next instant, the blur sharpened into the figure of a man. As he came to stand beside the priest, she recognized him at once as the stranger she'd observed at dawn.

The knight was impressive in stature and commanding in presence, much taller than she'd expected and exceedingly broad-shouldered. She saw now that the surcoat he wore over his mail was deep blue, enhancing the color of his eyes. Those eyes sought hers at once, their expression containing a vibrant intensity that sent bolts of apprehension flashing through her.

The priest suddenly cleared his throat and turned to the knight. "This is Ana of whom I spoke, the daughter of Georges, the brewer, and his wife, Marie. Does she favor the maid you seek?"

The knight swept a long gaze over her, from the top of her flowered head down to her slippered toes and back, skimming everything between, then lingering a moment at the mole on her upper lip. A muscle moved in his cheek as he locked his eyes with hers.

"'Tis she," he declared in a rich, full voice, his words filled with certainty.

Ana's eyes widened at the exchange, heat shimmering through her at the knight's intimate perusal.

Maid you seek?

She looked to Pere Armand, then Gervase. Her bridegroom made not the slightest move to intervene on her behalf, but stood gaping at the knight. In truth, no one in the crowd so much as twitched, their gazes riveted on the stranger. Glancing to her foster parents, she saw alarm piercing their eyes, their hands gripped together as they took measure of the man.

Ana returned her gaze to the imposing knight. For what possible reason did he meddle here, spoiling her wedding day? Seeing that he continued to scrutinize her, she jutted her chin upward, a spark of defiance emboldening her.

"Pere Armand, am I to be examined like goods at market on the church steps when I have come to wed? Pray tell this knight to seek elsewhere for a maid if he be in need of one. I am bespoken for. Pray, let us begin the ceremony that Gervase and I might speak our vows and marry."

"That will not be allowed!" the knight declared, his tone sharp, commanding, possessive.

Ana went to stone as gasps broke among the crowd. Whether 'twas due to her boldness or the knight's swift temper she could not say, their words had flown so fast.

His gray-blue eyes continued to bore into her. They held a vague familiarity. Ana shook away the notion. Impossible, she told herself, a flood of indignation welling inside her. What right had this stranger to interfere here, particularly in her choice of a husband? Plucking up her courage, she faced him squarely.

"I assure you I will marry whomever I please, Sir Knight." She managed to hold his gaze without flinching, though inside she quivered like a mass of half-baked pudding.

"Child, mind your tongue!" Pere Armand admonished. "This is Sir Royce de Warrene. He comes at the behest of King John of England, our own liege lord, and also at the urging of a certain Lord Gilbert Osborne."

Smarting at his rebuke, Ana directed her gaze to the priest. At the same time she wondered why Gervase still stood beside her like a log and said naught.

She afforded the churchman her sweetest smile, hoping her effort didn't appear forced. "How agreeable that the knight is acquainted with such imminent personages, but what has that to do with me?"

"Lord Gilbert seeks his lost granddaughter, Juliana Mandeville," the priest offered.

Ana flicked a glance to the knight and back. "Then I wish Lord Gilbert good fortune in finding her, but this knight is mistook if he believes me to be able to help. I know nothing of this Juliana Mandeville."

Nervously, Pere Armand rubbed his hands together, one within the other. "The girl disappeared ten years ago, from the village of Vaux on the night of its burning."

Ana's heart jolted in its place at the implication of his words. Still, she refused to grant them any significance in regard to herself.

The knight stepped forward, claiming her attention. Again he studied her with intense, probing eyes. His gaze swept to Georges and Marie then back again.

"Is it not true that the brewer and his wife are not your natural parents, but rather, your foster parents? In fact, you were brought from Vaux on the night it was savagely attacked and given to their care in the neighboring village of Vincelles, ten years ago."

Ana felt the blood drain from her face that this stranger should have such knowledge of her past. "That night is most painful to me. Why do you resurrect it on my wedding day? If you must know, I was orphaned that night. I am the only surviving daughter of the miller of Vaux."

"Of the *miller*? Do you not know—?" The knight halted his words, surprise touching his eyes. He began to speak again but stayed what he would say once more. "Have you no memories of that night, or of your people?" he asked at last.

Ana shifted her weight from one foot to the other. "A few memories of the attack. Nothing before it. Nothing of my kindred either," she admitted, feeling a familiar pang in her heart.

The images of fire and bloodied swords flashed before her mind's eye. She pressed her lashes shut, thrusting back the disturbing pictures and casting them into the recesses of her mind.

"I am Ana, the miller's daughter, none other," she stated flatly, her breathing suddenly shallow and quick, her patience short. "The one who found me claimed it to be so for he'd also discovered my family laying slain in the grass nearby. Now, if you please—"

"The lad was mistaken, fair maid," the knight spoke softly, a note of sadness—or was it regret?—in his voice.

"'Twas not your family who lay there, though indeed 'twas the miller's. In truth, you are the daughter of Sir Robert Mandeville and his wife, Lady Alyce."

Ana's eyes snapped to the knight's. Again it perturbed

her that he should possess such details of her life. How could he possibly know of her squire?

"Tragically, Lady Alyce died that night during the attack on Vaux and your father later, whilst on Crusade," he continued. "Your grandfather has searched for you these many years, but now he is too enfeebled to continue and the quest has been given to me."

"Quest?"

"Aye. I am charged with the task of finding you and returning you to your grandfather in England, where you will take your rightful place as a highborn lady and Lord Gilbert's sole heir."

"Nay, that cannot be so!" Ana reeled round to Gervase and gripped his forearms, her eyes pleading for help. But she found only confusion in his face. Shaken, she darted a glance to her foster parents, then to the priest.

"Someone tell him, I am not this Juliana. My place is here in Chinon at my husband's side." Even as the words left her lips, a crushing feeling overtook her. Would no one help her?

Gervase finally moved. He took her hands in his and fumbled with her fingers, seemingly unable to find his tongue. He searched her face with a questioning, confounded look. Meanwhile, the murmurings among the crowd increased in her ears. A surprising number seemed pleased with this turn of fate.

"This man is not your husband," the knight spoke again, his voice weighted with galling authority. "Be warned, any marriage made without Lord Gilbert's permission will be promptly annulled."

Anger boiled up in Ana's soul. Quest or not, the man had no right to appear on the church steps on her wedding day to seize control of her life in the name of another.

Frantically, she searched her memories, reaching back to

that night long ago, striving to press past it to find the name Alyce or anything that might reveal the truth of her parentage and station. But she could find naught but darkness there. Darkness, except for her squire.

Ana could still remember first seeing his handsome face as he lifted the boat and discovered her crouched beneath. Remembered traveling the road to Vincelles, snuggled against him on his fine mount. 'Twas the only memory that lingered bright and undiminished in her mind—that and being given over to the care of Georges and Marie and then the misery of her squire's departure.

Ana looked to the knight. Why did he come this day to ruin the life she'd come to know and love? The entirety of her life's memory was confined to a few slender years, most spent happily here, in Chinon. Now when she would marry a man she loved, one well regarded by her foster family and who could provide her with a secure future, the knight sought to alter her life's course, snatch her from her home, and place her under the mastery of strangers.

Though her memory may be faulty, Ana knew one thing with certainty. The world was an unpredictable and frighteningly dangerous place. Happiness, and all that was known and dependable, could be lost in the blink of an eye. Georges and Marie had restored the gift of joy to her heart. Still, she craved the familiar—nay, she clung to it. And even more important, she coveted security. Now, callously, this man would rip her away from all she held dear.

Just then the knight moved forward and lifted his gloved hand to take her arm. Ana bristled.

"I assure you, I am not the maid you seek. I am but a commoner, 'tis plain to see."

The knight's eyes widened a fraction, then narrowed. "Your manners may be that of a commoner, but your blood is most noble. The mistake made long ago must be righted.

You will be restored to your grandfather who waits for you across the Channel at the court of King John."

"A second mistake will not right the first." She glared at him. "I possess no drop of noble blood, and I'll not leave my home and family for an alien shore and nameless faces. Pray, leave me in peace to wed my copper. What possible difference could it make to you?"

"Difference?" he barked, his color rising, challenge in his tone.

Ana drew back toward Gervase, panic churning in her breast as anger flashed across the knight's features. She'd stung his pride. Or was it his honor? Knights were so full of the one and zealously protective of the other. 'Twas unwise to inflict a dent in either.

"What difference amending the past—*your* past—makes to me is not at issue," he ground out. "By orders of King John—Chinon's liege lord as Duke of Normandy and the Acquitaine—you are required to accompany me to the royal court in England."

"I will not!" Ana gasped out, then realized no one moved to help her. She cast her gaze over the stunned crowd. "This knight plays me a sorry jest and on my wedding day. Will no one stop him? Gervase? Pere Armand? How can you allow him to take me?"

Ana heard the desperation in her voice and despised her sense of powerlessness. In the next moment, Georges and Marie hurried to her side, wholly distressed, her foster mother enveloping her in her arms. Ana gathered her strength, hardening her resolve.

"I'll go nowhere!" She hurled the words with defiance then turned to those gathered before the church. "This knight has yet to present one scrap of proof to support his claims. He has no authority over my person. Perhaps he means harm to me, sent for some vile purpose."

"Enough! Bind your tongue, maid," the knight bellowed. "If 'tis proof you desire, you shall have it."

He reached beneath his surcoat and withdrew a packet. As he opened it out, it proved to be two leaves of parchments folded together, one bearing a large red seal.

"Any schooled in letters may inspect these documents for themselves," the knight called loudly, holding up the pages. "One contains the king's commission, granting me authority in the matter of the heiress, Juliana Mandeville. The other is a missive rendered in Lord Gilbert's own hand. "In it, Lord Gilbert outlines the dates and circumstances that brought Lady Alyce and her child to Vaux on the night of its destruction. He also gives a detailed description of his granddaughter." His eyes fixed on Ana. "Lord Gilbert writes that she possess hair of a rare, silvery blonde color and eyes like emeralds. He adds that she can be identified by a distinguishing mark—a mole upon the upper left corner of her lip."

The knight's gaze shifted to the mole Ana bore upon her lip, just so, then to her fall of silvery hair. He then stared straight into her eyes—eyes Ana had ever been told shone like emeralds.

"All these traits you possess, fair maid." The knight continued to hold her gaze.

She gave a laugh, half choking. "'Tis hardly proof at all! Maids other than myself own such features."

Ana felt herself flush as the knight's eyes drew to the chain she wore about her neck, tracing it to where it disappeared into the top of her gown.

"There is one thing more," he said, his tone weighted. "On the night of the attack on Vaux, when Sir Hugh FitzAlan and his soldiers escorted the survivors to Vincelles, you rode with his squire. Is that so?"

"*Oui*, 'tis so." Her heart picked up its beat. She distrusted the path of his questions.

"Before he departed, the squire gifted you with something personal, something that belonged to him alone—a silver cross."

"You can't possibly know that." Shaken, she stepped free of Marie's arms, back and down one step, then another.

The knight tracked her steps as he came forward and began to descend. "The cross once belonged to the squire's own father. On the back side it bears an inscription—the knights' ancient and hallowed oath, *Par bouche et des mains, je suis votre homme.*' 'By mouth and by hand, I am your man.'"

"Nay!" The denial burst from her lips, her heart plummeting.

Halting on the step above her, scarcely a breath apart, the knight removed his gloves and reached forth. His fingertips grazed the swell of her breasts as he drew the chain forth from her gown, exposing a silver cross. Turning it to its back side, he held up the piece and displayed the engraving there.

"Let this cross stand as proof for any who require it," he proclaimed for all to hear.

Ana bent her head, feeling as if her heart had been torn from her chest. Somehow she found her voice and offered a final protest.

"The cross proves only that I am the girl the squire found in Vaux. There could still be a mistake."

"Patience, my child," Pere Armand soothed, coming forth to stand beside the knight. "Perhaps, on meeting with Lord Gilbert, he will confirm you are not his granddaughter after all, and you will be allowed to return to us." His gaze swiveled toward the knight. "She will be free to do so in that event, will she not?"

"I will escort her myself," the knight vowed.

Ana knew she should take solace in that, but she could

read in the knight's eyes he held no doubt as to her identity. He'd not the slightest expectation of returning with her to Chinon.

"So shall it be then. We must abide by the king's command." Pere Armand looked to Ana. "There is no other choice."

Ana steeled herself at the truthfulness of those words. "'Twould seem not," she said through stiff lips. "Certainly not for a simple maid, even on her wedding day."

She glowered at the knight—a man who so willingly would ruin her life at the behest of his king. His heart must be of stone.

"I shall hold you to your word, Sir Knight. Upon this cross, I shall." She snatched back the holy object from his fingers and enclosed it protectively in her hand.

The maid's eyes continued to slash at Royce, two green shards, stabbing him with her anger. She looked to detest him wholly—loathe him, even. Royce expelled a long breath. This encounter had not proceeded at all well, certainly not as he'd hoped.

Royce had been elated this morn when his latest lead proved fruitful and the lord mayor confirmed a maid fitting Juliana's description lived in Chinon. By God's grace, he'd arrived barely in time to prevent the disaster of the noble heiress marrying a commoner.

Admittedly, Royce had been astounded by the maid's transformation from a mere twig of a girl into a ravishing young woman. Still, there could be no mistake as to her identity. Aside from her distinctive features, he recognized the brewer and his wife. Though much older now, he'd placed them at once as the couple to whom he gave the child "Ana" that fateful night in Vaux. Like the maid, however, neither appeared to recognize him.

The thought nettled, particularly that Juliana showed no sign of knowing who he was. 'Twas understandable. Last she'd seen him, he was a bony, bare-faced lad, yet to sprout into his height. Then too, his coif of mail concealed most of his head and all of his hair. His mustache and beard masked everything beneath his nose and cheekbones. What could she see of his face but his brows, eyes, and nose?

In truth, Royce had intended to reveal himself as the squire who'd found her beneath the boat—not that he was eager to make known his role in losing the little heiress and displacing her amongst the peasantry. But the maid's stubborn defiance and sharp tongue allowed him no opportunity to do so at first. When she disclosed that she held no memories of her past, not even of her true parents, the revelation gave him pause. He'd expected her to recall something of her family and be agreeable, if not pleased, to accompany him to her homeland and to her grandfather.

The maid continued to blister him with her look. He need tell her he was the one responsible for leaving her at Vincelles. But not now, not here. She'd challenged every word to cross his lips thus far. Coupled with the fact that she didn't recognize him, 'twas unlikely she'd believe what he had to say. That would leave them arguing further still on the church steps before all. Best to tell her later, without a crowd surrounding them. As for her foster parents, he deemed 'twould make little difference whether he revealed his past identity or not. More importantly, he was the one who prepared to take Juliana from them now.

Royce glanced to the brewer and his wife, saw the heartbreak in their eyes that he should deprive them of the child they'd raised. He felt like the lowest of wretches to cause them this misery.

"Do not be distressed," he heartened. "Your foster daughter—once acknowledged as Juliana Mandeville—will assume her rightful place and live with great advantages as a noble lady and heiress. What more could be desired?" The words rang hollowly in his own ears.

He cleared his throat. "I have been authorized to generously compensate you for your privation."

Actually he had not, but witnessing these people's anguish, he felt moved to do so. Pulling a pouch of coins from his belt, he looked between the maid's foster parents and her bridegroom. In fairness, he need compensate the cooper as well. After all, he was depriving the man of a wife.

Royce emptied half the coins into his palm and gave them to the brewer. He then handed the remainder to the cooper, who seemed quite astonished by the sum.

The maid crossed her arms, fury firing her features. "I am not a parcel of goods to be bartered or sold!"

Royce turned his attention to her, a weariness setting into his bones. "For both our sakes, I advise that you hold rein on your tongue. By order of the king, you *will* come with me and do as you are required."

Her look darkened. "Be assured, I have no desire to come with you. If you dare to take me from Chinon, I promise, you will be most sorry!"

"I already am," Royce replied tiredly, a pain piercing his temples.

"I shall go neither willingly nor quietly, and I vow to resist you at every turn."

"Be that as it may, still you will go. Now, have you belongings you wish to collect from your home?"

She raised her chin. "What possessions I have shall remain here, awaiting my return."

"So be it. Let us not tarry then. Make your farewells and we shall depart."

Royce waited as the maid hugged her foster parents fiercely, then bestowed a kiss on the cooper's cheek. "Wait for me," she said through her tears.

Royce signaled to the lad whom he'd employed to tend his horse and bid him to lead the stallion forward. With his quest complete, he chafed to be away with the maid.

Seeing now how she stood motionless and wide-eyed before the monstrous-size horse, Royce afforded her a smile.

"Until I can secure a gentle palfrey for you, we'll ride together."

"We will not!" she cried, appearing scandalized to the marrow.

By all that was holy, would the maid give him no respite? Undeterred, Royce swung the maid up in his arms and tossed her onto the stallion's back. He then climbed up behind her. She gasped as he wrapped his arm around her waist and drew her back firmly against his torso.

As he turned his mount, she twisted in his arms to glimpse the faces of her foster parents and cooper a final time.

"I'll soon return," she called out, determination and hope mingling with her promise.

Urging the stallion forward, Royce rode from the church square, the beautiful, yet mettlesome maiden captive in his arms as he departed Chinon.

4

The city of Tours, a day later

"I'll *not* ride. I choose to walk." Ana crossed her arms over her chest, her brows knocked together as she scowled her best at the overbearing knight.

"'Twill be no kindness to your feet. 'Tis a long walk to Boulogne," he replied as he fed an apple to his horse.

By the crispness of his tone and the narrowing of his eyes, Ana knew she tested the limits of the man's patience. Well, he'd brought it upon himself and she'd warned him full well. He'd find her to be neither docile nor compliant if he purposed to see through his "quest." 'Twas no less than an abduction, royally sanctioned or otherwise. And he deserved no less than her contempt.

"There is nothing the matter with my feet." She notched her chin, and thus her nose, into the air, aware how the other travelers in their company slid glances their way.

"There may be naught the matter with your feet, but the same cannot be said of your slippers. They are not intended for trekking long distances over rugged roads and will soon be in shreds, and your feet bleeding."

"I am not so fragile as you assume, Sir Knight. I am accustomed to walking and will do so, as will most of our companions." She nodded to the sundry band of pilgrims, tinkers, tradesmen, scholars, religious, and more as they assembled at St. Martin's tomb, on the city's west side, preparing to depart on the main road north.

Pivoting on her heel, Ana mentally closed the matter and stalked gracelessly away to join the others. Against her better judgment, she cast a glance back over her shoulder only to find fire kindling in the knight's eyes. She smiled inwardly, taking a perverse pleasure in the knowledge she'd aroused his ire, which, as a noble knight, he was bound to hold in check. 'Twould be unchivalrous to reproach a "lady" publicly, she mused.

Moving toward the back of what might loosely be called the retinue's line—a jumble of people, donkeys, packhorses, carts, dogs, and crates of chickens—she released a long sigh. The knight was entitled to be angry, she supposed. When he failed to find a suitable horse for her to ride, he sold his fine saddle for one of different design, fitted with a small cushion at the back. It would allow her to ride behind him "pillion," as he called it. She was unsure how, exactly, one rode pillion but she was certain she'd not like it.

"Hannibal will not harm you, if that is your concern," the knight called, breaking into her thoughts as he led the beast forward by the reins and rejoined her. "You need not fear his size. He favors you."

Ana cast a skeptical glance over the brutish stallion, then cocked her head to one side. "He *favors* me? How can you be sure? Did he tell you as much?" she taunted.

The knight locked his gaze with hers. "I warrant, you'd know if he did not." He let the implication of his statement hang between them, weighting the air.

Ana grew uncomfortable under his continued stare and shifted her eyes toward the monstrous horse once more. Hannibal looked like he would simply gobble up anything, or anyone, he disliked. In truth, the beast did unnerve her, but that wasn't the reason she refused to ride. She'd ridden the full distance from Chinon to Tours pressed against the knight's chest, his arm fastened securely around her. She could still feel the memory of his steely hold on her—about her waist and beneath her breasts.

She eyed the small cushion where she would be expected to ride pillion. Presumably, in order to remain seated, she would need to wrap her arms securely around the knight's middle. That would result in her breasts being pressed into his back for the entirety of the journey. She had no desire to endure such nearness, or intimacy, with the knight.

Then, too, there was the matter of the mail hauberk he wore beneath his surcoat. Her back still prickled from where she'd leaned against it during her journey here, the ringlets of iron overlaying the knight's hardened frame. Her backside had also suffered, and not a little, from the long hours spent in the saddle.

Instinctively, her hand sought the abused area and she rubbed at the soreness there. "'Tis not your horse that concerns me. I've had enough of riding for a time and much prefer to walk."

The movement of her hand drew the knight's gaze. Comprehension lit his eyes. Ana dropped her hand away instantly and shifted her stance. 'Twas a mistake, she realized at once, for now, his eyes fixed on the curve of her backside then slowly trailed upward. A tingling warmth passed through her.

"Very well, my lady." The knight cleared a roughness from his voice, one not present the moment before. "I shall walk with you and give Hannibal his leisure for now."

He raised steel-blue eyes to hers, sending waves of unease cresting through her. Was she ever to be affected so by the man's slightest attention toward her? He merited her scorn, not a blushing response.

"I am not your *lady*. And you needn't trouble yourself on my account. Ride if you wish."

"I find I, too, prefer to walk," he returned genially—too genially—one side of his lip tilting upward in a half smile.

Irritating man, she fumed silently. He knew full well she had no choice but to endure his presence.

Within the hour the travelers set forth from the city, heading north toward the duchy of Normandy. Tours had reminded Ana greatly of Chinon, with its narrow streets and half-timbered facades. Now, as with Chinon, the landscape outside the city walls quickly gave way to forests thick with oak and beech, opening from time to time onto luxuriant fields and vineyards.

As the road wound once more through the woodland, tiny, plump goldcrests swept overhead, twittering their high-pitched "zee-zee-zee" as they disappeared into the forest's canopy, ablaze with the reds and golds of autumn.

Ana stole a glance at the knight as he walked beside her, matching his pace to hers. He positively towered over her. She took in his mail hauberk and the unsightly, head-conforming hood that encased his hair. His trim beard and mustache were golden brown in color, and the bare portions of his face—what little showed of it—were tanned as though he'd labored long in the sun.

The knight's eyes suddenly shifted to hers and she quickly dropped her gaze away. Directing her attention frontward over their assorted companions, she shored up her nerve then blurted the question at the fore of her mind.

"How do you bear walking so long in your armor? It looks to be heavy and uncomfortable. Must you always wear it?"

"'Tis of little consequence and the day is most pleasant." He shrugged. "One must be ever prepared for the dangers of the road."

"Dangers?" Ana darted a glance along the fringes of the forest. Finding nothing of concern, she settled her eyes once more on the knight. "I know little of such things, though I've heard tales of travelers' plights. Since arriving in Chinon many years ago, I've left its safety but once. My family traveled to Samur on a matter concerning my foster father's business."

"Then consider your journey to England a great adventure," he said lightly, almost cheerfully.

Ana stiffened. Was the man callous? He'd wreaked havoc on her life, preventing her marriage and stealing her from those she loved and from all she knew.

"What holds the prospect of adventure to you, Sir Knight, holds naught but heartbreak for me."

He blinked over eyes lit with surprise.

She ignored the look and drew her mantle close about her—a thin, unsubstantial shield between the knight and her frayed emotions.

"This morning you said we will travel first to Le Mans," she remarked, changing the subject.

"Aye. First to Le Mans, then on to Rouen and the coast at Boulogne. From there, we'll cross the Channel and land at Dover."

Ana pressed her lips together. She'd never sailed upon the water, nor seen *La Manche*—the Channel—or any great body of water for that matter.

"And what then will happen, once we land at Dover?"

"Then we'll seek the royal court, and I shall deliver you into the keeping of Lord Gilbert, your grandfather."

"He is *not* my grandfather," she said flatly.

"I have no doubt that he is."

"Your lack of doubt matters not one whit, Sir Knight. You shall be proven wrong and, by your own oath, you shall be required to return me to Chinon. 'Tis forgone."

He looked down his perfectly straight nose at her, at the same time hiking one brow high.

"You've a saucy tongue, one most unbecoming a lady. 'Twould be in your interest to harness that member before you assume your place as a highborn maiden and heiress. A sharp tongue could gain you unwelcome results."

He pulled his gaze from hers to stare straight ahead. "And my name is not Sir Knight. 'Tis Sir Royce de Warrene. You may address me as Sir Royce."

Ana lifted her chin. "As you wish, Sir Knight, but I am no lady and intend to prove it so."

A small muscle twitched at the corner of his eye as he glanced down at her. He regarded her with a narrow look. "By your mouth and manners you have already succeeded, but by blood you have not, as I've said before. Let us leave it at that."

Ana flinched at his censure, his opinion abundantly clear. Well, she'd wanted him to agree with her, had she not? And he did. In his eyes, owing to her behavior, she was no lady.

The thought rankled.

She cared not at all what he thought of her, she told herself. Not one speck, crumb, or jot. Not at all. She wished only to return to Chinon, to her foster parents and to Gervase, the man who loved her. Still, her curiosity needled.

Seeing the knight had lengthened his stride and pulled ahead of her with his massive horse, she quickened her steps to catch up with him, falling in by his side.

"Tell me, Sir Knight, should Lord Gilbert believe I am his lost granddaughter—not that I am, understand—but should he believe so, what will befall me then?"

He skipped a glance to her then returned his gaze ahead. "Why the very best things imaginable. He will recognize you as his heiress and install you at Penhurst, his estate. No doubt he'll engage tutors to instruct you in the skills you lack and will need as a lady of import, and then he will seek a match for you."

"A match?" she frowned.

"A husband. I know naught of Lord Gilbert's standing or the extent of his holdings or titles, but I am certain he'll seek a fine match to improve your station and his whilst he lives. 'Tis the way of things."

Ana deepened her frown.

Seeing this, his own brows dipped. "Does that trouble you?"

"What say shall I have in this match?" Ana asked, fresh apprehensions clawing through her.

"What say need you have? Your grandfather shall choose best for you. He has your interests at heart."

"But he knows not my heart. I alone do. I would have a say in the choice."

The knight leveled her a patient, forbearing look. "You may express your feelings toward a prospective bridegroom, but your grandfather, being your guardian, will have the sole and final word in the matter. You must trust in his judgment."

Ana rooted to the ground, her fists flying to her hips, her arms bent akimbo.

"You mean, I am to have no voice in this? I am expected to wait, utterly mute, as a complete stranger to me makes a decision that will affect the rest of my life? That is monstrous! 'Tis known the way of nobility is different, but in this, this . . ."

She tossed her hands skyward, anger and indignation colliding in her, clogging her throat.

"I'll be no one's pawn, or puppet, or cat's-paw," she spat out at last. "You castlefolk scorn those of common stock, 'tis well known. But be assured, we enjoy freedoms far greater than your own. At least in this. I may have been raised as no more than the daughter of a townsman, but as such I have enjoyed a direct say in whom I would accept in marriage and who would have rights to my person, to my-my body," she blurted, shaking now.

Ana wrapped her arms protectively around her middle, having said far more than she'd intended, far more than what was wise.

The knight studied her, his expression perplexed. "I am sure your grandfather will consider your feelings in the matter. I did not mean to indicate otherwise. But, he does have the final decision."

"And I must obey, even if I do not agree with his choice?"

"Aye."

She clenched her teeth, her temper mounting. "And so a stranger, not even of this land—one claiming to be my grandfather—will have the right to give me over to yet another stranger as a bridal prize. And that stranger, in turn, will carry me off to another, more distant place, filled with even more strangers. Is that the way of it?"

"Lady Juliana," he soothed in his rich voice. "You will have a fine castle to oversee and servants—"

"I am not Juliana!" she flared, drawing the attention of the others. She lowered her voice, though only slightly. "I don't want castles, or servants, or strange men to take their pleasure upon my person or to tell me what I may and may not do. I want my cooper, Gervase. He will love me and care for me, even if humbly so." She dashed away a traitorous tear, searing the corner of her eye. "I'll speak no more on it."

Ana forced down the emotions that threatened to overtake her. Struggling to compose herself, she inhaled deep of the woodland's cool, earthy scents and drew into herself, shattered that—should she prove to be the lost heiress—she was destined to be gifted to some faceless man, a prize trophy for his carnal appetites, one to beget his heirs upon. His own requirements, of course, would be based solely on his rank, power, and wealth. 'Twas what mattered most to nobles, all they truly understood.

Her foster mother's description of the sexual act seized Ana's thoughts, preyed upon her fears. She dreaded the prospect of such personal, physical invasion, of such total possession of her body. And what if the man selected for her was cruel? What if he abused her, beat her?

She'd chosen well in Gervase. He was a gentle man with a pleasant humor, one who would treat her kindly in all ways. He was also reliable and steadfast, a man she could depend upon and work beside in life, aiding him in his cooping business, loving him as his wife—partners, really. For all the castles and finery and luxuries in the word, she'd not trade the freedom she'd known these years—or Gervase—for any one of them.

Ana drank in another deep breath of the crisp autumn air. Its cool tendrils spiraled downward, filling her chest and wreathing her heart, chilling her there. She felt so vulnerable, so powerless. Yet, she wasn't truly so, her instincts told her. She was only as helpless as she allowed herself to be.

With each step, Ana collected her strength about her, her thoughts darting, swift as the goldcrests in the branches overhead.

She must escape. 'Twas the only way. Somehow, she must get back to Chinon and find Gervase. Then, they would both need flee and hide for a time—in a large city, one under the protection of the king of France, not John of England. *Paris!* Yes, that was the answer. She and Gervase could begin their life anew in Paris. Perhaps, her foster parents would join them there too.

Ana's spirits rose. When several of their companions started to sing a *rondeau* to pass the time, she even joined in the parts, which gained another surprised look from the knight. She granted him a smile, plotting her escape as she did. 'Twas urgent she learn all she could about their surroundings, direction, and other possible paths. When the right moment presented itself, she would elude Sir Royce de Warrene and slip away.

Royce gaped when the maid smiled at him—a flash of white teeth, her emerald eyes shining. He noted how she picked up her pace, her step livelier. The limp she'd tried to conceal the last hour disappeared altogether.

Inexplicably, her whole mood had altered, significantly so. Royce pondered that. What could account for her sudden change of temperament, one minute snarling at him, the next minute gracing him with a bewitching smile?

And it was bewitching. She was beautiful when she smiled. God's toes, she was beautiful when she did not, and equally so even when she railed at him, anger firing her eyes, rendering them a deeper green.

The delicate waif he'd left in Vincelles a decade ago had certainly changed. No longer the timid little girl he'd found shrinking beneath the boat, she'd grown into an entrancing creature—spirited and strong willed and with the keenest of tongues.

He released a breath. Transforming the brewer's daughter, Ana, into the heiress Juliana Mandeville would be a challenge for her tutors. 'Twould require much work and patience to remold her manners and polish her common edges. Yet, he was reminded of a gemstone found in the rough and of the exquisite result it yielded once refined. 'Twould be someone else's task to transform this jewel, God give him or her strength. Surely 'twas worth the effort. Yet, would she ever accept her new place, even given time?

Royce watched Juliana sing, stepping forward as she

joined in a repetition of the verses. His eyes skimmed over her bright, silvery hair and fine features, then slipped downward, tracing her high, full breasts, trim waist, and the swell of her hips. Even should the tutors fail and her manners remain lacking, he imagined it would forestall few suitors who would willingly take her to wife and climb into her bed.

Strange that she should be so averse to taking a husband of noble breeding. But then her objection lay not in the rank, but in being bedded by a stranger. Royce scratched his jaw through his beard. She wouldn't be the first maiden to be nervous about the intimacies of mating. Still, had he not discovered her on the church steps, about to wed? She must have come to terms with the realities of marriage in some measure. Or was it that the maid desired only the cooper?

Royce mentally chewed on that. Admittedly, he'd wondered whether Juliana was yet a virgin. 'Twould be no surprise if she weren't, given the practices of commoners. Upon being betrothed, 'twas said many couples of that class sought their fleshly pleasures before taking their wedding vows, not waiting for the sanction of the Church.

The image of Juliana coupling with the oafish cooper soured Royce's thoughts, and he blotted it from his mind. Perhaps the maid had had a bad experience with the physical aspects of lovemaking. Again his thoughts leaped back to the cooper, his mood darkening once more. Had the man been rough with Juliana in some way? Had anyone ever sought to harm her, sexually, over the years? Royce hardened his jaw, the question burning in his chest.

A loud thwack, followed by a crash and the splintering of wood seized his attention. Ahead, the dogs began to bark as the air filled with feathers and clucking chickens. Escaping the dog-drawn carts and their demolished cages, the birds flopped and flapped and scuttled into the woods. The company of travelers ceased their song, many rushing into the underbrush to recover the birds. At their lead was Mother Agnes and her four nuns. She urgently appealed to the others for help as the fowls were meant for their poor convent in Rouen.

The subsequent hours were spent collecting the chickens and recaging them in hastily repaired coops, putting the group sorely behind schedule. They'd anticipated reaching a Benedictine hostel outside Le Mans and stopping there overnight. Now, they were forced to camp along the roadside. Fortunately, they located a small clearing just off the main path, one backing to a stream.

Juliana's improved humor continued and no sharp words passed between them. They shared a meal in companionable silence, a simple affair of hard biscuits, dried meat, and cheese, plus a bladder of wine, which she instantly pronounced unfit for even Hannibal. Her foster father's beer and ale, she declared, were far superior.

As she nibbled a strip of venison, she glanced his way from time to time. Still, not even a hint of recognition appeared in her eyes. It pricked his pride. Why, exactly, he was unsure. 'Twas reasonable she wouldn't associate the scrawny lad he'd been with the man he'd grown to be, a decade older at that.

He studied her profile as she turned to gaze toward the neighboring campfire. There, Piperel, the juggler who traveled in their company, entertained the others, deftly tossing apples and pears in the air, keeping them in constant motion.

Royce tugged his beard. Perhaps now was an agreeable time to reveal his identity to Juliana. She deserved to know he was the squire who'd found her in Vaux long ago. 'Twould further lay to rest questions of her identity.

He set aside the chunk of cheese he'd been slicing and

started to speak. But when he looked up again, he found she'd risen and now strode toward the others, fascinated as the juggler exchanged knives for the fruit, manipulating them with great dexterity. Ending with a flourish, Piperel bowed deeply and held out his ragged hat. Juliana smiled then stepped off to join Mother Agnes's little troop. Together the women headed into the woods, presumably to see to their personal needs.

Royce vented a breath. Another time would serve as well to speak with Juliana on his role in Vaux. Many days of travel still lay ahead of them.

He rose and gathered the remnants of his meal and returned them to the leather pouch that rested on the ground beside his new saddle. He next set aside his sword and scabbard, then stripped away his surcoat, hauberk, and undertunic, baring his arms and upper torso.

Royce caught up the skin of water he'd filled earlier from the stream and doused his hair and chest, rinsing away the sweat and dust gained in the day's travels. As he toweled himself dry, he moved toward Hannibal to groom him as he did each night. At his approach, the stallion nickered a greeting. Royce grinned.

"Here we are again at eventide, old friend. Tell me, have you any advice for dealing with mettlesome maidens?"

Hannibal bobbed his head then nuzzled Royce's hand, then his pantleg, seeking a treat.

"An apple? 'Twill take more than that to win Juliana's cooperation."

Royce took up a cloth and began rubbing down Hannibal with long, rhythmic strokes. When the women did not soon reappear, he glanced toward the point where they'd entered the forest. Diverting his gaze to the men in their small encampment, he studied them closely, counting their number, but noted none to be missing.

Royce turned back to the stallion. Perhaps the women lingered by the stream to refresh themselves or rinse their clothes.

One thing for certain. They wouldn't have ventured far. The sun descended quickly now, dipping behind the trees. 'Twould soon be dark.

Ana quickened her pace, anxious to place more distance between herself and the nuns. Thankfully, she'd been able to slip away unnoticed when the sisters settled themselves beside the stream to say their evening Office.

Pressing through the underbrush, Ana hastened deeper into the forest. When she came upon a narrow trail, she immediately followed it, believing it to be a heavenly sign. Surely, God guided her steps. She'd prayed for His help and He'd answered, swiftly so, providing her this opportunity to escape. Now, she must seize the moment and make good her flight.

Yet, fear gnawed at her nerves. She'd had little time to think through a plan, scarcely any. She must reach Tours, then Chinon, that much she knew. She owed the earlier ordeal with the chickens to Divine intervention. The delay had prevented the group from reaching the Benedictine hostel where she would have been closely watched and where 'twould have been nearly impossible to escape.

Her earlier conversation with the knight still galled her. The ways of the nobility regarding unwed maidens were loathsome. She'd not be herded to England like a prize cow, to be tethered by some ancient lord in his castle till he saw fit to give her to another of his choosing. She'd have none of it.

Though it frightened her to the bone to place herself in possible danger, circumstances demanded she be both brave and bold. She'd take this one risk in order to return to

Gervase and seek a new life with him. It stood to reason, if the Almighty provided her the opportunity to escape, He would also protect her.

Ana hurried on, brambles and branches clutching at her mantle and gown, tearing at her hair. She thought only of fleeing the knight and finding a place to hide. If she could successfully elude him this night, then with the first rays of dawn, she could follow the road back to Tours, keeping to the edges of the forest. Once there, with luck, she could join another group of travelers heading south. For now, she'd not think on the possibility of vagabonds or thieves who might plague the highway. She'd encountered none on her journey thus far, and with luck, she'd reach the city before sunset tomorrow.

"Faith, Ana," she mumbled to herself, gripping hold of the silver cross about her neck as she rushed on.

Pain twinged her feet, sore and blistered from the day's walk. Now acorns, sticks, and other debris on the forest floor bit through her thin slippers and into the soles. She tightened her jaw tight against the pain, knowing she'd no choice but to suffer it.

The sun blazed through the leafage of trees like a great orange ball, sinking lower with each passing minute. As Ana continued along the winding trail, she realized with a start 'twas likely a path used by the forest animals. The thought offered little comfort for her nerves, but there was no help for it.

Minutes later a distinct rustling noise sounded in the undergrowth off to her left. Ana halted, her pulse leaping. She quickly scanned the area, her gaze drawing to a feathery, knee-high bush that shivered and shook. In the next moment, a large hare sprang out of the foliage and scampered away, disappearing down the trail.

Ana gasped, then expelled her breath, her heart beating

madly in her chest. Collecting herself, she forced herself on. From some unseen perch, an owl called, a haunting sound that sent chills along her spine. Other woodland dwellers added their own whistlings and chitterings as the forest came alive with dusk.

As Ana won further into the wood, she again heard rustlings in the underbrush ahead, as though something rummaged there. The vegetation quivered and trembled, much like before. Ana smiled, thinking the hare to be there, perhaps tussling with a furry cousin.

"Ah, 'tis you again. Did you find a friend?"

The words barely left her lips when her gaze touched upon the ground in front of the bush. Acorns lay scattered over the soil beneath an aged oak. Sections of earth lay turned and bare where, presumably, some of the delicacies had been devoured. A set of hoofed tracks imprinted the dirt, leading into the underbrush.

Ana swallowed, her breath sealing in her throat, as the rustlings there turned to agitated thrashings. Something skulked beneath the forest cover. Something of significant size.

Her blood went to ice as a wild boar emerged from the leafy growth—a *sanglier*. 'Twas a hideous creature, massive and humpbacked, teeth bristling from its mouth. Her eyes widened at the size of the beast's fierce, curving tusks. They could rip her to shreds in an instant.

A strangled cry rent the air. A woman's cry. *Juliana!*

Royce dropped the cloth, spun from the stallion to snatch up his sword, then bolted headlong into the forest.

Coming upon the nuns where they huddled round-eyed by the stream, he scarce spared them a glance but splashed through the water and sprinted on in the direction of the maid's screams. Quickly, he came to a path and followed it.

Within moments, he closed on an ancient, spreading oak. To his surprise, Juliana clung to its lowermost branch. Below, a large black boar slashed at the tree's trunk with its tusks, squealing and grunting as it did.

"Sohow! Sohow!" Royce shouted, drawing the beast's attention to himself, casting off the scabbard from his sword as he did.

The boar turned, snorting fiercely, fury burning in its savage little eyes. Again Royce clamored at the animal, waving his arms and blade, striving to lure the animal away from the tree, away from Juliana.

Royce steeled himself, knowing the perils of challenging a boar on foot. Better to face such a creature mounted, with a long spear and a dozen hounds to aid him. But he did not have that advantage. He'd only his sword and one chance to slay the beast. Should he miss his mark, the boar would dispatch him with a single swipe of its tusks, splitting him from groin to chest.

Royce gripped the pommel of his sword with both hands, holding the blade before him. He studied the animal for the telling signs that would signal the onset of its attack.

The beast watched him as well, with eyes full of malice. Clashing its tusks over its teeth, sharpening them, it took several steps forward, then backed once more beneath the branch where the maid yet clung. Should she lose her grip, she'd land atop the animal and meet a swift and grisly end.

Royce shouted again, anxious to draw the boar off. "Here, you snout-faced monstrosity. Over here!" He waved his blade, baiting the creature.

The boar snorted, the bristles raising on its black hump, its ears flattened against its head.

"What are you waiting for?" Royce harried. "Come, taste my steel."

At that, the beast rolled its eyes, pricking its ears and

lowering its head as it drove toward Royce, enraged.

Royce braced his stance, tightening his grip on the pommel as he targeted the beast. His heart thundered in his chest as he watched the boar close the distance. At the last possible moment, Royce sidestepped the creature, inverted his sword, and plunged its point into the swine's neck. His muscles shuddered as he drove the blade full to the hilt and sundered the beast's heart. Squealing and thrashing, the boar stumbled, dragging Royce with it to the ground as it brawled with the steel and finally convulsed. At last it grunted and slackened upon his sword.

For a moment, Royce lay heaving where he lay, eye to eye with the beast, its tusks having laid open several inches of his forearm. His hands gripped the pommel so tightly, at first, he was unable to pry his fingers loose.

Voices sounded around him—the tinker, mason, several of the pilgrims, and others—awed that he'd killed the beast single-handedly. Royce pushed to his feet, then made his way toward the oak on unsteady feet. Glancing up to the maiden, he noticed for the first time how her gown bunched upward, revealing long legs, bared and scratched. He noticed, too, the panicked expression that remained on her face.

Exhausted and with little strength left to climb trees, he held up his arms to her. "Can you manage to swing down? I shall catch you."

Shakily, she unwound herself from the branch. Freeing her legs, then releasing her hold, she dropped into his arms. Royce staggered back as he caught her, his hands tangled in the skirt of her gown and her hair tumbled across his face. As he secured her against him, he felt the warmth of her palms on his shoulder and that of her body pressed against his.

Lowering her to the ground, she slid down his length.

But when the maid's feet touched the earth, she suddenly flung her arms about his middle and squeezed him tight. Suddenly, the long years that had separated them since Vaux shrank to naught. Once more, she seemed the terrified waif he'd discovered beneath the boat. Instinctively, his arms enveloped her.

Several minutes passed before he came back to himself. 'Twas no child he held, but a young woman. A young woman who'd purposely taken to the forest this night and nearly cost him his life.

Ana shook against the knight's chest, her arms entwined about him. But as the horror of the moment passed, she realized her cheek lay against the bare, sculpted muscles of his torso.

Ana jerked back, releasing her hold on him. She shoved her hair from her eyes and looked up at him through the fading light. The knight's virile good looks stole her breath. 'Twas the first time she'd seen him without his hood of mail. Seen him half-naked, with a thick mane of hair flowing to broad, well-defined shoulders.

She dropped away her gaze, then saw the injury to his arm, suffered because of her.

"You're hurt." She voiced the obvious, at a loss for words.

"Aye, that I am," he stated in a tone unexpectedly stern. "Why did you come so far into the forest?"

The question surprised her, as did his look, which held something in it more akin to anger than to relief or thankfulness that the ordeal with the boar was past.

"I-I became lost," she replied defensively. "I wandered away from the sisters and must have gone in the wrong direction."

"A lie." His eyes narrowed. "The camp is visible enough

from the stream. You did not stray from the sisters. You were seeking to escape."

"No, truly I—"

"Have you no sense? The forest is filled with wild creatures, any number of which would happily dispatch you and make a fine meal of you."

Heat rose to Ana's cheeks. "I knew God would protect me and He did!"

"So, you did seek to escape."

Not waiting on an answer, he seized her by the arm and moved toward the beast. He drew his sword from its carcass, then turned to Juliana and directed her back along the path. The others could do what they wished with the swine.

"You're right," he growled at Ana. "God did protect you. He sent me after you—to save you from yourself. Remember that, should you think to run off again. I've no intention of letting you slip away. Upon my oath, you are in my keeping, and so shall you remain."

5

Outside the city of Le Mans, the following day

She'd have to steal Hannibal. There was no other way.

Not steal him, exactly, Ana corrected. She'd only borrow him until she reached Chinon. Then, she'd leave him in the keeping of Pere Armand until the knight arrived. No doubt he'd follow her and swiftly so, given that she'd possess his prize stallion and would have foiled his quest. By the time the knight gained Chinon though, she and Gervase would be well on their way to Paris.

Ana looked to where Mother Agnes tended Sir Royce's forearm, unwrapping the bandage that showed a fresh seepage of blood. Carefully, the nun began cleansing the wound. The knight minded her ministrations as he stood patiently, his upper armor and garments removed, down to the linen shirt he wore next to his skin.

The shirt was of obvious quality, Ana deemed. 'Twas short-sleeved, low and open at the front, revealing a sprinkling of hair upon his chest. She noted the tan he bore there, matching that on his neck, face, and what was visible of his arms. Her gaze trailed over his thick fall of hair. In the day's light, she realized its color was darker overall than that of his beard. Yet, 'twas brightened throughout with golden streaks as though gilded by the sun.

Ana pondered that. 'Twas odd for anyone to bear so deep a tan this late in the season, or for his hair to be blanched by the sun's rays. She'd understood the climate of

England to be similar to that of France. What could account for the knight being as brown as a field laborer at the height of summer?

Her eyes drew to the gash he bore on his arm, a nasty piece of work wrought by the swine's tusks. Mother Agnes had cleaned and stitched it last night. Now, having washed it anew, she layered it with a poultice and began binding it with clean strips of cloth once more.

Ana felt a stab of guilt that Sir Royce should have been wounded on her account. For a fleeting moment, the entire episode flooded back and she tasted fear once more. The knight could have been killed confronting the boar, and she would have been to blame, little better than a murderess. Yet, he had proven himself to be a warrior of exceptional skill. Perhaps he'd not been at such great risk after all in dispatching the boar. Perhaps.

Ana shifted, uncomfortable with the shallowness of that thought. Still, she refused to accept all the blame, all the guilt, should real harm have befallen Sir Royce. He needn't have placed himself in danger's way to begin with, she reasoned. She'd not asked for his help. In truth, she'd been doing quite well by herself. She'd had a firm grip on the oak's limb and the boar would have tired of attacking its trunk after a while. Even boars must tire. Eventually.

Ana shut off the troublesome thoughts and transferred her gaze to where Hannibal nibbled the grass. She smiled inwardly. Her new plan was sound, far more so than her one of last night. The stallion could carry her southward, swiftly and safely, back to Chinon, without need of keeping to the forest.

If only she'd managed to slip away with him earlier, before the group had reached the outskirts of Le Mans. Then, the knight would have been at a loss to acquire a second mount to pursue her. The only animals in their company able to carry a man were donkeys, and they could offer little speed.

Ana shielded her eyes against the sun. They were in sight of the city. She could make out its walls from where she sat on a stump, looking across open fields. For now, she'd need to bide her time and wait until their little group of travelers was well beyond Le Mans and on their way to Rouen—far enough so the knight would be unable to reach another city easily to buy a fresh horse.

Perhaps the delay was for the best, she thought as she studied the stallion. She needed time to befriend Hannibal and win his trust before she stole him. If the knight had the right of it, Hannibal liked her. She hoped 'twas true. When the moment seemed right—when the group stopped for one of its customary rests, as now, and while Hannibal was still saddled—she'd mount him and ride off. How difficult could it be?

Sir Royce's masculine voice drew Ana's attention as he thanked Mother Agnes. Looking up, she saw that he'd left the nun's side and now walked directly toward her. A minute later he halted a step away then bent to retrieve his garments, which lay next to the stump. After drawing on his tunic, he reached for the heavy hauberk. Ana quickly rose to assist him, taking hold of the hem of his mail shirt.

"Here, let me help or you'll have yourself bleeding again."

He paused, seemingly surprised by her offer, his steel-blue eyes boring into hers. Without a word, he allowed her to aid him into the hauberk, flinching once as they eased the metal sleeve over his injured arm. Still, he uttered not a sound, but Ana could see by the look in his eyes and the muscle that leapt in his cheek that it pained him greatly.

With the hauberk in place, he drew up the concealing hood, leaving naught but the oval of his face visible. Slipping on his blue surcoat, he next belted his sword in place then turned to Ana.

"You've been limping all morning, my lady, and your shoes, as predicted, are in ruins. I'll brook no argument. You'll ride Hannibal until I can purchase you suitable boots."

Ana opened her mouth to object, both to his suggestion and to his address of her as "my lady." Reconsidering, she pressed her lips back together, then moistened them with her tongue. She sorely needed the practice of riding and for the stallion to become accustomed to her.

"As you wish, Sir Knight. Indeed, I find the opportunity to ride Hannibal most welcome just now." She smiled graciously, bringing another look of surprise, but then of suspicion to his eyes. She'd have to remember in the future to not agree with him so readily.

At that, the knight turned toward the stallion and whistled a command. Hannibal lifted his head, his ears swiveling. The beast then gave an answering neigh and shake of his neck and mane, then abandoned the patch of grass and ambled toward his master.

Ana's spirits sank. If the knight could summon the horse with naught but a whistle, she'd need choose the moment to escape with the animal with great care.

"Stand upon the stump," Sir Royce directed Ana as he left her side and strode forward to meet his steed.

"The stump?" She scrunched her face, puzzled as she came back to the moment.

"Aye," he called as he mounted Hannibal in one graceful movement, using the strength of his legs alone to climb into the saddle, sparing his wounded arm. He turned the stallion toward the stump and guided him toward it.

Realizing Sir Royce's intent, Ana stepped onto the stump as he'd instructed. Seconds later, he reined Hannibal beside her and extended his sound arm.

"Grasp hold of my arm with both your hands," he bid, leaning out from the saddle and catching her by the elbow and upper arm.

Barely had Ana clasped hold of him when he swept her off the stump and up onto the padded cushion behind him, as though she were no more than a feather sack.

Ana grabbed for the back of the saddle to steady herself, her legs dangling together over the left side of the stallion's hindquarters. Instead, she caught hold of Sir Royce, low on his hip and to the front, touching his thigh and abdomen. She jerked her hand away, abashed, then clutched for the saddle once more, nearly toppling off her seat in the process.

Unlike Sir Royce's first saddle, which possessed a high back, this one owned no more than a small lip, with the leather cushion extending behind it, intended for a second rider. Ana seized onto what she could of the saddle's sorry back and held herself perfectly still, perfectly straight. She'd no wish to share any unnecessary closeness with the knight. Yet, how was she supposed to stay atop the horse?

Ana felt the knight shift in front of her. Glancing up, she found that he'd twisted in the saddle to look back at her.

"You'd best put your arm around my waist."

"You're w-waist?" she stammered, transferring her gaze there and remembering suddenly how he'd looked last night, naked to the top of his braies. Even viewing him upside down in the poor light, she'd been able to make out the well-defined muscles of his upper torso. She could envision them even now, beneath his chainmail and surcoat.

"Aye, around my waist—lest you fall, my lady. Hannibal is a monstrous-sized beast and 'tis a long way to the ground."

Ana wrenched her gaze from Sir Royce's back and glanced downward. Why did the distance to the ground seem so much farther than before, when she'd ridden in front of him?

Raising her eyes, she saw how the other travelers in their company were assembled and beginning to set forth. Not a few watched her and the knight openly, curiosity and smiles lighting their faces. 'Twas as though she and Sir Royce provided some entertainment and they now waited to see what would pass next. Did they expect her to fall off the stallion's hind end, or was it her contending with Sir Royce that amused them so?

Ana drew herself up, arrow-straight. "I can see for myself how far it is to the ground, Sir Knight," she said brittlely continuing to sit rigid, motionless, clutching at the back of the saddle.

"Come now, take hold of my middle," he urged her. "I won't bite."

"I'm not so certain of that," Ana muttered.

Wary, she looped one arm lightly about his waist. The gesture forced her to lean forward, but she managed to keep her body from touching his. To her surprise, she thought she heard him chuckle.

"Is there something that amuses—" she began, irked, but just then the stallion moved beneath her, the muscles of its flanks bunching and stretching.

Feeling herself slip upon the seat, Ana seized the knight about the waist with both arms and held tight. This time Sir Royce's amusement was distinct—a full, rich laugh escaping him as they rode forward.

As the band of travelers passed through the thick towered walls of Le Mans, Ana was struck by the rubble and charred remains of buildings that greeted them. Proceeding along the cobbled streets, they encountered whole sections of the city under construction and other portions so new that the structures displayed little weathering.

Ana's thoughts leapt to King John. She cast about through her memories of the year just past and the tales she'd heard of him.

John—then a princeling—had been present in the fortress of Chinon when news of the Lionheart's death arrived. She'd seen his troops depart the city as he raced to seize his brother's crown and to oppose those who supported his nephew's claim.

What happened afterward, she'd heard recounted many times since, mainly by her foster father, Georges, who lost no opportunity to bandy the details over cups of ale with his customers and friends.

Traitorously, the citizens of Le Mans championed John's nephew, closing the city gates and refusing the prince entrance when he arrived. Pressing on to Normandy, John remained in Rouen long enough to accept the ducal coronet and be confirmed in his office. Then, before sailing for England, he returned to Le Mans at the head of a Norman army and took his revenge.

'Twas devastating, by the tales Ana had heard. John destroyed the city. What he and his men did not burn, they leveled to the ground, and on parting took with them many of Le Mans' leading citizens as prisoners.

Evidence as to the truth of those accounts lay all about, Ana observed as Hannibal continued to pick his way along the twisting street. She withdrew her gaze from the sight and brought it to the knight's back. Had Sir Royce served John at the time? Had he lent his own sword arm to carry out John's wretched act of vengeance?

The thought set ill in the pit of her stomach for as she looked on the ruin of Le Mans, memories surged to mind of Vaux—slender memories, but dark ones all the same.

The travelers arrived on the main square and halted by the well, agreeing to meet and continue on in an hour's time, after they'd replenished their supplies.

Spying a cobbler's stall, Royce directed the stallion toward it, then dismounted. As he lifted his gaze to the maid, he found her eyes fixed upon him, her brows pulled together, her look sharp, assessing. He started to speak, to offer her an arm down, but the cobbler bustled forth.

"Ah, gallant sir, have you need of a pair of sturdy new boots? Or comfortable shoes, perchance? You will find mine to be of the finest grade of leather and the best construction in all the city."

Royce saw how the man's eyes skipped from his mailcoat to his sword, symbols of his knightly status and the promise of silver weighting his purse.

"I have need of neither, but my lady does of both."

"I'm not your—" Juliana began to protest, but the man moved quickly to where she perched upon Hannibal and frowned at her ragged slippers.

"What have we here? The lady's shoes are—"

"Worthless. Fit her with your most durable leather boots. Ones that will bear up walking a distance. A pair of kid slippers too, if you have them."

The man shot Royce an odd, frowning look, then taking measure of the maiden's feet with his experienced eye, he scuttled off, disappearing into the back of his stall. Moments later he returned with a pair of low-topped boots.

"Your accent—'tis Norman is it not?" The cobbler kept hold of the boots, his eyes stabbing Royce, keen and bright.

Royce inclined his head, wondering what the man truly sought. Given what Royce had learned since his return from the East—mostly from the monks at Dover—he could guess the bitterness the citizens of Le Mans must hold to-

89

ward the Normans, as well as toward their overlord, King John.

It did surprise him, however, that this commoner could not distinguish between a Norman or English knight. Admittedly, there was nothing about his armor, bearing, or language that would mark him as one or the other. Equally true was the fact that England's Angevin kings—dukes of Normandy and the Acquitaine—spent more time on this side of the Channel than on the other, as did their barons and men-at-arms. Forsooth, in all of the Lionheart's ten-year reign, his feet walked upon English soil little more than the span of five months.

"If 'tis an accent you think to detect in my speech, good cobbler, 'tis that of the English court. Norman-French is the language spoken there amongst the royals and nobles—but that is well known."

"You are John's man then." The man spewed a stream of spittle on the ground, his words more statement than question. He held forth the boots. "These will fit your lady. Three silver deniers for the pair. I have no slippers."

"Three?" Royce choked. 'Twas thievery, pure and simple.

Seeing how he'd begun to draw glowering stares from the neighboring merchants, he reached for his pouch, not wishing to provoke the moment. Obviously, like the cobbler, these simple people suspected any knight who served King John to have been party to the attack on their city.

Royce held out the coins, believing the man to have doubled his price specifically for him. After snatching the silver pieces from Royce's fingers, the cobbler bit each one with his back teeth. Satisfied as to their quality, he gave Royce his back and retreated toward his stall.

Royce heaved a sigh, then turned to the maid. He halted his footstep, finding that she too, glared at him from her place atop Hannibal. But this time a condemning light burned in her emerald eyes, as though she'd made some decision concerning him.

What next, he wondered tiredly, as he proffered her the boots. Why did he have a sinking feeling that it was going to be a very long day?

"Best try these on before we depart. I've no wish to be cheated twice in one day."

Ana had listened closely to the exchange. The knight served King John, certainly in regard to herself. Sir Royce carried out his quest at the king's behest. Being that he was a skilled knight—as demonstrated by his slaying of the wild boar—it stood to reason he'd honed those skills in the service of another lord. Likely, he'd served the king for some time and had used his skills in the destruction of Le Mans.

Her heart sank at that thought. What sort of man was Royce de Warrene? Certainly one willing to deprive her of her family and bridegroom and deliver her to the royal court and an unclear future. One who would never allow her to return to Chinon.

Ana's gaze fell to the boots he held out to her. Better that she walked barefooted than accept charity from his hands.

"I want nothing from you, king's man," she clipped out, her voice tinged with indignation.

Some emotion flickered in the knight's eyes, one she could not put a name to.

"Consider these gifts from your grandfather then," he replied evenly.

Ana's temper multiplied. "How many times must I say it? I have no grandfather. I never had, not even a foster-grandfather."

"Are you so sure, Lady Juliana? Do you not wish to

know for certain?"

His words stopped her cold. All her angry judgments of the knight fell away, supplanted by his question. She crossed her arms over her middle, confusion and doubt bubbling to the surface of her heart.

"Don't call me by that name," she said at last, unable to think of anything else to say.

She told herself not to listen to his words, but to concentrate instead on what she must do this day to gain her freedom and flee the knight.

But some place deep inside her refused to ignore his challenge. She'd long assumed she had no living relatives. Not only was she an orphan, but Georges and Marie had learned from the survivors of Vaux that neither the miller nor his wife possessed relatives that lived, at least none known to them.

But what if somewhere, there was someone who shared the same blood as she? The same forebearers? Who knew something of her earliest years? The very thought was seducing.

Ana shook away her musings. There was no one, she told herself. Not here in France, and certainly not across the waters in the person of an old man. If anyone was to carry her blood it would be her children, and she'd have a say as to who their sire would be.

Ana fell to silence, remaining so as she and Sir Royce rejoined their companions and departed the city, heading for Rouen.

Ana winced. The boots hurt her feet. 'Twasn't that they were not of the proper size but, rather, her blisters pained her. Added to that, the boots were stiff, unbroken, having yet to become supple enough to conform to her feet. Thankfully, she would be riding, not walking, when she made her escape southward.

And that time drew near.

Ana drew off the boots once more and set them aside. She glanced to where Mother Agnes inspected Sir Royce's arm, then to the others who milled about the clearing alongside the road, seeing to their various needs. Fortunate for her, she seemed to be forgotten for the moment. Most gave their attentions to a man named Guy of Lisors, a minstrel who'd joined their company in Le Mans. At the moment, he captivated their interest with a *lai* he chanted, having promised such entertainment for the duration of the trip in exchange for food and drink.

Ana inhaled a breath of the cool autumn air and looked away. As predicted, their band had journeyed several hours north of Le Mans before halting for this brief respite. They would begin again, proceeding several more hours before they stopped for the night at the small Cistercian hospital of St. Giles—or so the knight informed her.

Ana recognized that the present moment offered her best opportunity to slip away with Hannibal. If she waited longer, till they neared the hospital, there stood the chance the monks might have something faster than a donkey or mule to offer the knight to pursue her. No telling whether the abbot there enjoyed worldly ways. But if she successfully escaped now, Sir Royce would be forced to return to Le Mans on foot before he could secure a horse. That would give her all the advantage she needed to make good her flight. A movement caught her eye. Looking up she saw that a couple of tradesmen approached Sir Royce, admiration beaming from their faces. 'Twas a scene she'd seen repeated many times throughout the day. As before, the men appeared to be congratulating the knight on his kill of last night. Using wide gestures, they simulated Sir Royce's movements and how he'd spitted the boar on his sword blade. The minstrel, having finished his *lai*, joined the spirit-ed men who launched into a fresh demonstration of the feat for his benefit. It appeared Guy of Lisors wished to set verses to the tale and asked for them to repeat it as he picked out a tune on his lute. Ana rolled her eyes. They would swell the knight's head if they didn't desist. He was insufferable enough as it was.

She gave her attention to a more important matter—Hannibal. Best that she move closer to the stallion and position herself for what she must do. Ana knew little of horses, but enough to realize 'twould be unwise to startle the animal. She would soothe Hannibal with a calming voice and offer him an apple. If all went well, she'd win his confidence enough to remain near as she waited for the right moment to present itself to make her escape.

She could do naught till the knight stepped out of sight. Surely he would do that, she thought. Surely, before the group resumed their travels, the knight would seek to refresh himself in the woods. He hadn't done so thus far, she'd been careful to note. But once he was out of sight, Ana knew she must mount the horse at once and ride fast along the road—fast out of whistling range.

Ana rose, her heart quickening as she gathered her boots and walked toward the stallion with the most casual gait she could affect. Freedom waited just minutes away. Soon now she would be on her way, back to her family and Gervase. The realization fortified her, causing her blood to thrum through her veins.

As Ana approached the stallion, she was careful to stay in his line of sight and not surprise him with a sudden gesture. He appeared larger with each step she took toward him. Indeed, as the knight oft said, Hannibal was a monstrous-sized creature.

Ana swallowed down her fear, noting, for all his size,

how he picked through grass and leaves selectively, almost daintily. He wasn't the devil he appeared to be. Besides, Sir Royce had remarked himself, Hannibal favored her. There was nothing to fear, Ana told herself.

"Hello, boy. Hello, Hannibal," she called softly.

The stallion lifted his head and regarded her with his huge eyes. Seemingly satisfied that he knew her, he gave a swish of his tail and went back to his grazing.

Ana saw how his reins were looped on the branches of the nearest bush and decided they'd present no problem when the time came to release them. She noted, too, the height of the stirrups. She'd need to lift her foot rather high to reach it. That would be her first challenge. Her boots would help somewhat as they would provide a solid sole to protect the bottom of her feet against the stirrup's iron bar, especially as she mounted.

She set the boots down, then drew out an apple from the folds of her gown, one she'd been saving since earlier when she'd slipped it from the knight's saddle pouch. Cupping her hand about the fruit, Ana held it out to the stallion, her arm wobbly.

"Here you are, boy. You'll enjoy this better than what you're finding on the ground. We're going to be great friends, aren't we?"

Suddenly, Ana sensed a presence looming behind her.

"Best hold your hand out flat." Sir Royce's voice sounded in her ear. "Hannibal might mistake it for a delectable treat and try to sample it."

He reached around her and straightened her fingers with his own, his arm alongside hers, only longer and half enveloping her.

As Hannibal took the apple in his teeth, Ana snatched her hand away and in doing so, fell back a pace. Instantly, she came up against the wall of Sir Royce's hard frame. Discomposed by the knight's abrupt appearance and his disturbing nearness, Ana stepped clumsily to one side, putting space between them.

"I didn't know. I haven't been around horses much. I've seen them pass in the streets, of course, but my family has never owned or cared for one." She knitted her brows. "Would Hannibal really eat my hand?"

"Not apurpose, fair maiden."

He smiled then, a flash of white teeth through his beard. If her pulse hadn't already been leaping madly before he'd appeared, she would owe it to the knight's closeness. It disconcerted her as much as his smile.

Sir Royce stepped toward the stallion and patted his shoulder, then glanced back at her.

"We shall feast tonight at St. Giles. Our companions believe our monkish hosts will not object to roast boar. They do not eat meat themselves, but there are many travelers needing to be fed as well as the sick in their hospital."

"I thought 'twas agreed to send the boar with the sisters to their convent along with their chickens."

"Thoughts of a rare and succulent feast got the better of the men, though their argument was that the swine's flesh would not keep long enough to reach the nun's convent." He smiled again.

"I see." She rotated her ankle, working the soreness from her feet, then sat down to draw on the low-topped boots. She grit her teeth as she slipped her foot into the first. Ana felt the knight's eyes upon her and inexplicably went warm.

"Those appear to fit well enough." He commented, breaking the silence that had fallen awkwardly between them.

"Well enough," she mumbled, her nerves a tangle. The knight wished to make small talk. She wished for him to leave and do what he would do in the woods, so she could take his horse and be on her way.

Ana said nothing more, busying herself with the second boot, hoping he'd take the hint that she did not want his company. Instead, Sir Royce squatted down beside her and pushed back his coif, revealing his sun-kissed hair. He hesitated a moment, his eyes clouding with some thought.

"Lady Juli . . Ana, there is something I must—."

Relievedly, Piperel took that moment to appear with Guy of Lisors, bearing a score of questions. Sir Royce stood and began to send the two away when several more men joined them, commending his skills and urging him to come away.

Sending an apologetic look to Ana, he excused himself and withdrew with them. The sincerity of his look and his courtesy surprised Ana, but she had no time to think on it. Surely Piperel's and the other men's appearance was a sign of Divine intention. For as she glanced in their direction, she saw that they not only occupied Sir Royce most thoroughly, but the lot of them were making their way into the forest.

She touched her cross through the cloth of her gown and sent up a hasty prayer. The moment for which she'd waited was upon her. May God guide her path. And Hannibal's too, she added swiftly.

Ana moved as swiftly as she dared toward the stallion, grimacing as fresh pain lanced her blisters. She hobbled forward, stopping when the stallion lifted his dark head and gave a shake of his powerful neck. For a moment, she was unsure whether he was warning her to come no closer or simply taking her measure once more. But in the next breath, he stretched his neck and nose forward and sniffed at her gown.

"There's nothing hidden there, boy, but you can have all

the apples you want if you'll just take me to Chinon."

She reached forth a tentative hand and stroked his long nose. Then, hands shaking, she moved toward the bush and reached for the reins. They came free with a tug and blessedly the horse did not bolt or pull away.

Ana stepped to the stallion's side and took a long swallow. "All right, Hannibal, I'm going to mount you now. Be a good boy and hold still."

Reaching upward, she grasped for the saddle's horn and at the same time, lifted her foot to the stirrup. She could reach neither easily. Not to be thwarted, she raised up on her toes and hopped—once, twice—then seizing hold of the outer edges of the saddle, hauled herself upward and shoved her left foot into the stirrup. An agitated sound—somewhere between a whinny and a squeal—erupted from Hannibal and he took several steps backward.

"Easy, boy. It's just me, Ana," she puffed as she clung to the saddle, struggling to drag herself upward into the seat.

But Hannibal would have none it. He stamped his foot and flicked his tail, barely missing her. Ana tightened her grip on the saddle as, suddenly, the stallion began to turn in a circle, his ears laid back, white showing in his eyes.

Round and round he circled, snorting and stamping, his pace increasing. Panic seized Ana and she forced herself upward, grabbing for the saddle horn and managing to throw her waist partially across the seat. But Hannibal liked that movement even less and squealed loudly, his front legs coming off the ground, then dropping back down.

Voices sounded all about and Ana next made out a blur of people gathering around her and the twirling horse. One rushed forward, a man.

Her heart plummeted. This couldn't be happening. She couldn't fail, not now. Somehow, she must gain control of the stallion and be away.

Frantic, she shifted her weight to stand in the stirrup and, at the same time, tossed her free leg high, attempting to swing it over the saddle, so she might ride as she'd seen the knight do. Disastrously, she succeeded only in kicking Hannibal in his flank with her booted toe.

The stallion squealed in earnest, rearing upward and pawing the air as he sent Ana hurtling from his side. One moment she felt herself flying weightless through the air. In the next, her back and head collided with something solid, then together with it, she crashed to the ground.

Ana lay unmoving, dazed as she blinked up at the cloudless stretch of sky overhead. The object that had broken her fall lay beneath her, an uncomfortable lump of no discernible shape. The lump shifted of a sudden and began to mutter. 'Twas a man's voice—Sir Royce's.

Ana gasped and scrambled off the knight, but as she started to her feet, he trapped her wrist. Looking down at him, she saw a large red mark marring his cheek where the back of her head had obviously connected with the bone.

Sir Royce continued to keep hold of her wrist as he pressed slowly to his feet, drawing her with him, fury in his face.

"You would steal Hannibal?" he roared.

"Steal? N-Nay, borrow 'tis all, and only for as far as Chinon."

"Do you know the punishment for stealing a knight's horse?" he bit out, his anger not abating one jot.

"Well, I, no . . . but I wasn't steal—"

"Hanging, and directly so."

"You wouldn't!" she gasped aloud, then glanced frantically to those who gathered about them.

"And why wouldn't I?" he snarled, bringing her eyes back to his.

"Because . . . because, you must deliver me to Lord Gilbert unharmed. 'Tis your quest."

He bent down to her, eye to eye, nose to nose. "My quest was to find you and return you to your grandfather. Nothing was said about the condition in which I need deliver you."

"*Condition?*" she sputtered, her thoughts sprinting wildly. "Well, Sir Knight, I'd think you'd be better tending to your own condition. 'Tisn't so very agreeable at the moment!" She nodded at the bruise forming on his cheek.

He seized her by the shoulders, at that, fire blazing in his eyes. She thought he'd throttle her right then and there. But just when she braced herself, expecting the worst, he went still as stone. The corner of his mouth twitched upward.

"At least there is truth in that statement, lady." His grip slackened and he straightened. "I've fared none too well in your company. But heed me well. I've suffered far worse and will not be deterred from my purpose or from fulfilling my quest. Now, unless you wish to be shackled for the rest of our travels, you'll cease these foolhardy efforts to escape back to Chinon. Is that understood?"

Ana dropped her gaze, giving a brief nod of her head.

"Pledge it, upon the bones of the saints."

"Bones?" Her eyes flew to his.

"In my sword's pommel." He released her shoulders and, taking her hand, placed it over the large, disc-shaped end of his sword's hilt, protruding from his scabbard. "Swear it," he growled.

"I-I swear."

"Swear you'll not seek to escape to Chinon or steal horses to do so," he pressed her to repeat the words exactly.

"*Oui.* I mean, *non*, I'll not seek to escape to Chinon or steal your horse . "

"Any horse."

"*Any* horse," she parroted, glaring at him.

He freed his hold on her hand, then stepped away to see to Hannibal.

Hearing the unexpected sound of a musical note, then a second, Ana turned to discover the minstrel nearby, plucking at the strings of his instrument. He looked to be composing new verses. Ana glowered at him, at the same time ignoring the snickers that drifted amongst the crowd.

Drawing herself up, Ana straightened her garments, brushed the dirt and leaves from their folds, then fingered the debris from her hair.

She'd *not* give up, she promised herself. She'd just have to think of another way to escape the knight, one that would not violate her oath. She needed God on her side, after all. Though at the moment, she wondered if He was truly listening.

6

Beyond Rouen, on the way to Boulogne

Sanctuary. Yes, that was the answer. She'd flee to the protection of Mother Church. No one, not even the king, could force her from those hallowed confines.

Ana smiled as she rode pillion behind the knight. When he turned his head to glance over his shoulder at her, she realized, in her momentary joy of determining a new way to escape, she'd tightened her grasp on Sir Royce's middle. As embarrassment unfurled warmly through her, she relaxed her hold, then gave her thoughts back to her plan and what she need do.

There'd been numerous churches and shrines along the road ever since leaving Chinon. Ana understood from the pilgrims who traveled amongst them that such was common. There was never a want of a church or monastery-operated hostel to ease one's plight, ever offering Mass and a bit of broth and bread. Leastwise, there was never a lack of any along the main highways used by the pilgrims to journey from one venerable place to another.

Ana took heart. The pilgrims followed official guide books and the maps they contained. Since many of the pilgrims had continued beyond Rouen with their small band—destined for England and the shrines at Walsh-ingham and Canterbury, they said—then it stood to reason there would be many more churches lining the road they now traveled, all the way to Boulogne. She'd have ample opportunity to escape into sanctuary.

Pleased, Ana smiled again, wondering why she'd not thought of the plan before now. 'Twas far less dangerous than taking to the forests or purloining horses. Best of all, as regarded her sacred oath, she'd not be breaking it. She'd be merely stepping off the roadway to enter a church.

Her mind decided, Ana knew what she must do. When the group came upon the next church, she need only reach the church doors in order to claim sanctuary. No longer did one need to actually enter the church and gain the altar itself, as in times past. They need only reach the outer doors of the church. Some buildings even possessed an iron ring, affixed in the stone of the church's facade. One need only grip hold of the ring and proclaim sanctuary in order to gain the church's protection.

Hope, mingling with anticipation, swelled in her breast. Her plan would work. It must. However, she'd a far better chance of success if she could garner someone's help—someone who could slow the knight. 'Twas forgone that he'd give pursuit, and he could easily outrun her. Given Sir Royce's size and strength, perhaps she should enlist the aid of several "someones."

Pensively, Ana drew her gaze over the other travelers. Many of the faces had changed. The good sisters had left their company in Rouen, as had the master mason and stone cutters who'd journeyed there to work on the cathedral of St. Ouen. Piperel, too, remained in the city, though Guy of Lisors traveled on, ever entertaining them with his lute and verse.

On reflection, Ana realized that most of those who'd set forth from Le Mans—those who'd been with them at the time Sir Royce slayed the boar and had been impressed with his courage and skill—would be averse to challenging him in any way. On the other hand, there were newcomers amongst them who'd not witnessed the feat, having only just joined their party. Even when they heard the tale, they'd likely think it much embellished. There was not even the swine itself to give proof to the story, having been eaten many leagues back.

Ana's gaze paused over two of the newest members of their troop—a pair of wild-looking Scotsmen in their strange, voluminous wrappings. They wore their hair and beards long and shaggy and wound great lengths of plaid cloth about their persons, these over saffron-colored shirts with baggy sleeves. Their legs they left bare, and they wore rawhide shoes, ankle high. Both men were of a good size, she observed, not so large as the knight, but they appeared to be hardy and strong enough to hinder Sir Royce for a space of time. Despite all, she hoped they wouldn't hurt the knight too badly.

Ana suddenly realized the Scotsmen were snatching looks her way, one then the other, interest etching their eyes. 'Twas not uncommon for her to draw the interest of strangers, owing to her hair. Many found its moon-pale color a great curiosity. Perhaps she could use that attraction to her advantage, she considered. If she could play upon whatever protective instincts these Scotsmen might harbor toward the gentler sex, convince them that the knight did ill by her, then mayhap they would be of a mind to help her.

Ana studied the men more closely, assured they'd be able to delay Sir Royce long enough for her to gain the church doors and claim sanctuary. She could picture the scene in her mind's eye. Oh, but the knight would be furious when she outwitted him. Her lips curved upward at the thought.

"Does something amuse you?" Sir Royce asked, glancing back at her once more.

Ana straightened her posture, easing her hold on his

middle, which, perturbingly, she'd tightened again.

"I'd a pleasant thought, 'tis all," she tossed back, feeling lighthearted and well amused. "I do prefer to walk for a time and join in the song. The others are beginning a *rondeau*, I see."

Sir Royce sent her a suspicious glance, then gave a shrug. "I suppose it could do no harm. We'll both walk."

Reining Hannibal to a halt, the knight dismounted, then aided her down.

Ana quickly removed her boots before taking a further step, for her feet still pained her. Wiggling her toes, she gave forth a contented sigh. "Ah, freedom," she uttered, drawing a sharp look from the knight.

Ana caught up her boots and started forward, not caring what he might think. Instead, she bent her attention to where the Scotsmen took part in the *rondeau*, singing loudly and off-key in their odd, warbly voices. The sounds grated on her ears, but when they stole a glance her way, she only smiled. In the next instant, their eyes shifted to the knight's and they turned frontward again, continuing in their song without a further glance toward her.

Glancing to Sir Royce, Ana saw the menacing look he'd just sent them still darkening his face. Impossible, arrogant man, she simmered, pelting dark thoughts his way. Well, a little look would not daunt these rough-hewn Scotsmen, she was sure. Nor would it her.

Ana fixed her smile in place, demonstrating to the knight that his intimidations and overbearing manners did not faze her. Inside, however, her thoughts grew more anxious. With each passing hour, her plight became more desperate. Once she and the knight reached the coast and boarded a ship for England, 'twould be impossible to make her way back on her own. All hope would be lost.

Ana's chance to speak with the Scotsmen came when the band paused on the outskirts of a small village to water their animals and refresh themselves.

While Sir Royce saw to some pebbles that had collected in Hannibal's hooves, she made her way toward the bright little stream that flowed just beyond a stand of beech trees. She strove to make her movements appear natural and unsuspicious. Trailing behind a small number of their companion travelers, she kept somewhat apart of them, making sure the Scotsmen saw that she was approachable.

The two stood a little downstream, downing some form of drink she'd heard them call *uisge beatha*. Ana bent to the stream, sending them a glance they could not miss, then splashed her face with water and sleeved away the droplets. Rising, she sent them what she hoped was an utterly forlorn look, then went to sit by the trunk of one of the towering beech trees. Mindful, she settled on the stream side of the tree, out of the knight's view.

Scarcely a minute passed, but the woolly-looking Scotsmen stared boldly her way, exchanging several words between them. Wiping their mouths, they started toward her, disregarding the knight's earlier warnings, as she predicted they would. At their approach, Ana caught up the hem of her skirt and dabbed at the side of one eye, as though to catch a tear.

"Does somethin' distress ye, m'lady?" the older of the two, possessing a mass of fiery red hair, inquired as they came to a stop by the tree.

Ana kept her lashes demurely lowered. "I am not a lady, not a real lady, but only a humble maid of Chinon and a most anguished one at that." She wiped at her eyes again.

"How so, lass? Who causes ye sooch distress?" he pressed.

"Yon knight does." She sniffled and gestured past the

trunk, back in the direction of Sir Royce. "He took me from my home, my family, the very steps of the church."

"The kirk steps?" The second man, dark and thick-chested, squinched his eyes and brows, his tone appalled.

Ana nodded, miserable. "*Oui*, on my wedding day."

"Och, what gall and a cursed thing tae do," declared the first man.

"My betrothed is heartbroken, as am I. He waits for me even now." Ana slipped a peek at the men, finding disappointment in their eyes at the mention of a wedding and a bridegroom. She sniffled all the more loudly. "He waits for me upon the church steps, day and night, unwilling to leave them. But alas, 'tis all in vain."

"'Tis a bluidy outrage," clamored the dark-haired man.

"But that is the least of it." She raised doleful eyes to theirs.

"There be more, lass?" The two exchanged glances.

Ana slipped a glance around the tree trunk, toward where Sir Royce attended Hannibal. He appeared engrossed with some matter concerning the stallion's hoof and unconcerned with her at the moment. Ana returned her gaze to the Scotsmen, then nodded meekly.

"The knight takes me to England as a bridal prize to present to an ancient lord across the water. I—" She allowed her voice to catch. "I am to be no more than a slave to a man's, er, earthly needs."

"*Earthly* needs?" The red-haired man canted his head.

"I mean earthy, his earthy cravings." She looked from one to another, finding their looks nothing short of dense. "Uh, base desires. His passions."

The younger man's face brightened. "Och, ye mean the man wishes tae—"

"Och, she knows wha' she means." The older man jabbed him with his elbow, then turned back to Ana. "Dinna fash yersel', lass. Ian and I will put an end tae the knight's foul schemes." He started to move off.

"Nay, not here or now, good sirs. Sir Royce de Warrene is a man of great skill and will lop off your heads in an instant if he reaches his sword. Even if he doesn't, no one will aid you. The knight takes me with the express approval of King John. He carries papers bearing the king's seal."

"John Softsword? Och, there be the devil's spawn." The older man spat in the dirt, the other after him.

Ana nodded gravely. "The same. But there is a way to foil their plans—the king's, the knight's, and the ancient lord's."

"Ye may count on us, lass. We're listenin'."

Ana stood to her feet and gazed back at the knight. He appeared to be done with Hannibal and wiped his hands on a cloth. At the same time, he cast his glance about, undoubtedly seeking her. Ana turned back to her companions, knowing she must speak quickly.

"Such brave men you are. Very well then, this is what I have in mind . . ."

Juliana was up to something. Royce could smell it in the air. See it in the glow of her face. If that was not enough, he'd been garnering dark looks for the past hour. Curiously, they were leveled at him from those newest to their company, particularly the two barbarous-looking Scotsmen.

Royce pondered that, scanning the horizon and the rolling landscape, awash with burgundies and golds. High overhead, a hawk circled with easy, gliding grace.

He drew his thought back. Perhaps 'twas the ugly bruise spreading over the left half of his face that drew the frown—the bruise *and* the speculations amongst their new companions as to how he'd gained it. Yet, that wouldn't explain the looks of disapproval—censure, really—that he thought to read in their eyes.

The Scotsmen—Ian and Malcolm MacGregor by name, he'd learned—had exchanged words with Juliana by the stream. They'd moved off once Royce had finished with Hannibal and started toward the maid. What might they have discussed, he wondered. Despite Juliana's recent oath, he far from trusted her. On the other hand, the maid could be amazingly naïve at times. Was she unaware of the Scotsmen's keen interest in her? Had she not seen the wolfish looks in their eyes?

Royce sharpened his gaze over the men, taking their measure, then decided he best keep a close eye on them. At least Juliana's mood had improved for the moment, and for that he was grateful. Yet, 'twas not necessarily a good sign, he conceded. In recent days, her apparent happiness was naught but a prelude to new mischief. Best he redouble his vigilance concerning the maid. She was far too clever for her own good.

Just then the tinsmith who'd recently joined them sent Royce the blackest of looks. He blinked at that, wondering what he'd done to bring such disfavor. In recent days, he'd been hailed as a hero for saving the maid and slaying the vicious boar single-handedly. Now, 'twould seem, he was regarded as something akin to a species that fed at the bottom of a lake.

The woodlands progressively diminished as the travelers entered the Bray region with its flat, open stretches, broken periodically by valleys and streams. It was only after crossing the Somme River that they came upon another forested area. According to Sir Royce, 'twas the *Forêt de Crécy*.

The trees soon disappeared once more, but in time the group came to a small wooded valley. As the road dipped downward, Ana caught sight of a building of pale limestone set against a backdrop of golden foliage. By its lofty belfry, pricking at the sky, she knew it at once to be a church.

Ana's excitement rose and doubled. 'Twas the first church they'd come across since she'd laid her plans. On the other hand, she knew her companions had no intentions of halting here, for there remained ten miles yet to travel before reaching their destination of Nouvion.

It mattered not, Ana decided. She must seize the opportunity waiting for her here in the valley. There might not be another such occasion this day.

As the group trod on, following the road into the valley, drawing ever nearer to the church, Ana studied it intently. It sat back from the road further than she might have hoped to find, but 'twas not at an impossible distance. The architecture itself delighted the eye with elaborate carved moldings upon its facade and a great semicircular tympanum, sculpted with figures, crowning the entrance. What interested Ana most, however, were the two great double doors, which she could see clearly now.

Ana steadied her nerves and prepared herself for her flight into sanctuary. Her thoughts suddenly dropped to her boots, and she chided herself for having put them on again. There would be no opportunity to remove them. But her feet had become unexpectedly chilled without them while she rode motionless behind the knight. Though the weather had been unseasonably warm for the past week, the day had turned suddenly nippy as they neared the coast, a heavy moistness hanging in the air. Ana assured herself 'twould be more comfortable inside the church, something she'd soon enjoy.

When at last the group came even with the church, Ana brought her gaze from the sacred building and caught the Scotsmen's gazes. The flame-haired one gave her a subtle, knowing nod as if to say "Be on your way," he and his friend, Ian, would see to the rest.

With that encouragement, Ana willed herself to action. Loosing her hold on Sir Royce, she pushed herself from her seat and leaped to the ground. Pain splintered through her ankles as she landed with a solid thud and pitched forward onto her knees. Catching herself with her hands, Ana lost no time but shoved to her feet and launched herself in the direction of the church. A shout sounded behind her, but she hastened on, fast as she could in the blasted boots, which smarted with each step. She expected to hear Hannibal's hooves at any moment, eating up the ground behind her. Instead, 'twas not his hooves she heard, but the stallion's agitated squeal, followed by the brawl of male voices.

Ana snatched a glance over her shoulder, catching a blur of the Scotsmen's plaid as they converged on the knight and rider. The man, Ian, trammeled the stallion's reins, while the other dragged Sir Royce from his saddle. Together the Scotsmen fell atop the knight, the three of them dissolving into a wild broil of feet, elbows, and fists.

Ana swallowed back her horror and restrained an overwhelming impulse to hasten back to aid the knight. Instead, she forced herself to turn from the sight and press on toward the church steps. But Ana had covered little distance when, from behind, came a mighty roar. Unable to ignore the clamor that ensued, she glanced back once more in time to see the mound of plaid cloth and limbs leave the ground as the knight threw off his attackers and sent the Scotsmen flying through the air. Sir Royce regained his feet, looking much like an enraged bear.

Ana's bones went to liquid as the knight turned his fury on her and drove after her. For a moment she faltered, frozen in her steps. Then sheer panic took hold of her and she compelled her feet toward the church steps. She *must* gain sanctuary. 'Twas the only thing that would save her now, save her from the knight.

Her heart high in her throat, Ana rushed for the church porch, her legs burning, her boots tearing at her blisters. As she spied an iron ring to one side of the entrance portal, her hopes revived. Frantic to reach it, she stretched out her hands before her, that her fingers might seize upon the ring even before her feet arrived on the spot.

Just as she closed on the church steps, she heard the knight bellow, his voice startlingly near. She shot a glance past her shoulder and found him bearing down on her. As their eyes met, he hurled himself at her, his feet leaving the ground. Ana screamed, turning forward once more, but just then, his hands clamped down heavily upon her shoulders and he dragged her to the ground along with him.

Ana slammed against the earth's hardness, her breath vaulting from her lungs, the knight's weight dropping atop her. She writhed and scrabbled to get out from underneath him and claw her way to the steps, just yards away. But he grabbed hold of her and rolled her onto her back, pinning her to the ground, his chest pressing solidly against hers. Together they heaved for air, their breaths mingling, their faces an inch apart, their lengths mashed together.

Besides the purply bruise that covered his cheek, Ana saw that Sir Royce now wore a cut above his opposite brow. She'd not be surprised if the gash on his arm had broken open in the struggle as well—all due to her. Saints preserve her, she thought shakily as he speared her with his gaze.

Abruptly, the knight pushed his weight off her, then seized Ana by her arms and yanked her to her feet. He spoke not a word, but dragged her along with him to where the others waited by the road, watching the scene play out. The minstrel, she noted, held Hannibal's reins, while the Scotsmen tended their battered faces.

Sir Royce muttered something unintelligible beneath his

breath as he continued to pull her along with him, leading her toward Hannibal. Coming to a halt beside the animal, the knight swung her up onto the saddle, then proceeded to tie her hands to the horn with a leather lace. He then turned to Guy of Lisors.

"Guard her well till I return, minstrel. There is silver in it for you." He looked sternly at Ana. "If you value all that is most dear to you in life, lady, you will neither speak, nor move a muscle, nor do anything other than breathe. Is that understood?"

Ana gazed at him wide-eyed, fearful to return even an answering nod. But she'd not the chance for scarcely did the words leave Sir Royce's lips than he pivoted on his heel and strode toward the Scotsmen.

Ana's heart slipped to her toes. She had failed. Deep inside she knew the knight would allow her no future chance to escape.

Having reached Nouvion, the travelers took lodging at the hostel there. It wasn't the cleanest they'd encountered, but as it had begun to drizzle, Ana welcomed the roof over her head. At least there was that for which to be thankful.

She and the knight shared a large single room with the others, stretching out on pallets on the rushes before a central fire. Shockingly, Sir Royce drew his pallet against hers, then proceeded to take out a length of leather rope. Her ire began to climb as he tied one end of the leather to her left wrist, then the other to his, leaving a short span of rope between them. He obviously trusted her not at all, Ana stewed, not that she could fault him.

As Sir Royce reclined on the pallet, Ana remained sitting and scanned the crowded room. It hadn't escaped her notice how, since the church incident, she'd been gaining dark looks of her own from their companions, much like those leveled at the knight earlier. Guy of Lisors was the only one who seemed amused by the day's events. He presently kept to himself in a corner, plucking at his strings, fitting verses to the notes. Ana held no wish to know what tales he wove.

As Ana netted another reproachful look, this time from the tinker among them, her temper bubbled up. "Why do the others look at me that way? Did you tell them some lie?" She twisted in place to level Sir Royce her most accusing glare.

He stared back at her, dispassionate. "I am a knight of the Realm, sworn to a sacred brotherhood. I do not lie. Nor do I steal horses, nor tell untruths of others."

Ana ignored the implication his words contained and looked once more to the others. "You told them something. You must have."

"That I did. I don't deny it."

"Just what did you say to them?" she demanded, indignant, ignoring the fact that she herself had spread falsehoods of him. Of course, that had been for an honorable cause, nothing short of her freedom. Likely the knight had spread stories of her out of less noble motives.

Sir Royce held her eyes with his for a prolonged moment then rose to a sitting position beside her. He then transferred his gaze to their companions. "At my request, these good people repeated what you yourself told them. I simply clarified the details for them."

"Which were?" she said hotly, then jumped when his eyes sought hers, entrapping her gaze once more.

"I told them that your aged grandfather lies dying across the Channel, his only wish in life being to see his granddaughter a final time and give her his blessing. But that you callously care naught for his pitiable plight, but only for yourself and your own desires. That you'd willingly leave him to die with a broken heart, so you might return to Chinon to marry your cooper."

Ana's voice deserted her, so stung was she by his bald observation. His words rang disconcertingly true. At least they would for anyone who believed Lord Gilbert was her grandfather. But he was not.

Ana gave herself a mental shake. The knight was wrong in his beliefs, as well as in his assumptions. She had reasons other than her cooper to draw her back to Chinon. Personal reasons she'd shared with no one, not even dear Georges and Marie. Ana lifted her free hand to where the silver cross lay, concealed beneath her gown, and fingered its shape.

"How long do you intend to keep me tied to you?" she asked at last.

"As long as I must."

Sir Royce lowered himself to the pallet once more and stretched his legs out.

"I told you, I've no intention of letting you slip away. And if you've thought of enlisting the aid of the Mac-Gregors again, don't bother. I've paid them handsomely to guard us, both this night and all the way to Boulogne. You will find beneath their untamed looks and manners, they are men of honor. They've a keen sense of familial duty, especially where it concerns aging patriarchs. Now lay down and let us to sleep. I feel greatly in need of rest this eve, thanks to you."

Ana glanced to the space beside him then back to Sir Royce. "But, we cannot share a pallet together. 'Twould be scandalous!"

"'Tis two pallets, and we're sharing neither. There's nothing scandalous about it. By order of the king, I am charged to do what I must to deliver you to England. Now, to sleep, lady."

With a tug of his wrist, he drew her down beside him. Ana turned to face away from him at once, but she next felt him move closer, his position conforming to hers as he draped his left arm over her waist. 'Twas a courtesy she knew, for otherwise she'd be forced to sleep with her arm bent backward.

Still Ana grumbled to herself for the inconvenience, keenly aware of the weight of his arm, of his nearness, of how his body had begun to warm hers. . . .

A lethargy soon overtook her. Drowsily, she sank into the knight's warmth and drifted into a deep sleep.

7

Boulogne-sur-la-mer, France

From atop the walls of Boulogne's aged fortress, Ana gazed numbly out over the waters of *La Manche*, the Channel, toward an unseeable shore and an unseeable future.

A stiff breeze buffeted her, whipping her pale hair about while overhead fork-tailed terns filled the sky, whirling and crying out their harsh "kee-urr." She watched as they dove dramatically downward to skim the waters, then winged upward again with beaks full of fish.

This place possessed a wild beauty with its white chalk cliffs and sandy shores, with its dune flats sewn with buckthorn and creeping willow. Leastwise, those were the grasses pointed out to her. She'd never stood in such a place before. The seaward views were a feast to her eyes, and the expansive sights inland she found to be astonishing. Below the fortress figures bustled about the crowded port and its lively fishing village. Everywhere there were birds of vast varieties, her favorites the comical gulls and the chunky little sandpipers that zigzagged hurriedly over the shore.

Were circumstances different, Ana knew she'd find the experience exhilarating. But circumstances were not about to change. All hope of escape was truly lost to her. In roughly a half day's time—thirteen hours, the knight had apprised—she'd be setting foot on English soil. Would she ever see her foster parents or Gervase again? Her throat caught with an unvoiced sob, the thought squeezing her heart.

Taking up the silver cross in her palm, Ana stroked her thumb lightly over its length and texture. She ignored the long strands of her hair dancing about her face and the damp cold that shivered along her spine. Keeping a firm hold on her emotions, she glanced toward the two guards who stood on the rampart about a hundred paces away. 'Twas Sir Royce's doing. He'd posted the men to keep watch of her while he went down to the village to attend to matters concerning their departure.

Ana turned back to the battlement wall, casting her gaze out over the waters of "the Sleeve," *La Manche*, once more.

She and Sir Royce had passed the night comfortably installed in the fortress, which perched high on a cliff overlooking the port. To her surprise, they'd been instantly welcomed past the gates. No doubt, 'twas due to Sir Royce's knightly rank and noble blood. However, she'd observed how a number of officials at the fortress seemed to recognize Sir Royce without introduction. Possibly they remembered him from a previous visit, she guessed when he'd passed through Boulogne's port with the king, perchance? After despoiling Le Mans?

Ana shut her mind to those thoughts and gave herself to the vista before her. 'Twas truly magnificent, unlike anything she'd seen before. Suddenly a cacophony of birds sounded directly above her. Ana sucked in her breath to see a legion of the feathered creatures blackening the sky as they winged their way southward.

Her heart settling back in place, she lowered her gaze only to discover Sir Royce approaching on the ramparts. He wore his armor, as ever he did, with the unflattering coif drawn up. At the moment, his long scarlet mantle billowed about him, filled with the persistent breeze. A second mantle draped his left arm, she now saw, feeling a mixture of suspicion and curiosity.

With the signal of his gloved hand, Sir Royce relieved the guards, then continued toward her with brisk, purposeful strides. Time itself seemed to press upon him. Unhappily, Ana realized her days in France were at an end.

"Hannibal is safely boarded. 'Tis time we do the same," Sir Royce informed, halting before her. "Here, you will have need of this for our crossing. 'Tis made of double-thick wool, fur-lined, and will keep you warm."

Without pause, Sir Royce caught the mantle off his arm and, in one fluid movement, enveloped Ana in its folds. The gesture startled Ana, jolting her back in time, back to that long ago night in Vaux.

The knight's movements struck her as identical to those her squire had employed on discovering her beneath the boat. At the time, seeing she wore no more than simple toweling, the squire had swiftly removed his mantle and enwrapped her with it, as the knight had done just now. But 'twas more than the act of drawing the mantle around her, but the motions themselves, that she found so similar—the way both the knight and the squire had achieved the task. They'd leaned forward, just so, their heads slightly tilted, as they brought the mantle about her with a distinctive flick of the wrists.

Apprehension purled through Ana, her feelings jumbled, anxious, conflicted. 'Twas but an illusion, she chided herself. There were no similarities between the two. How dare the knight remind her of her squire—one so noble, so caring, so wholly unlike this despoiler of cities.

Ana drew back a pace from Sir Royce. "I've told you before, I want none of your gifts."

Surprise appeared in the knight's eyes, then turned to a look of annoyance. "Nonetheless, you may find yourself in sharp need of the mantle once we are upon the open water and grateful to have it. The cold is far more bitter and more penetrating upon the sea than on land."

Ana resisted his argument, not wishing to agree with him on any matter. Yet a small voice of reason prodded, reminding if she hoped ever to see her loved ones again, she'd need to survive the crossing. 'Twould be foolish to freeze to death out of stubbornness and 'twould serve no purpose. Then too, the mantle was exceedingly warm, she quickly discovered. 'Twas weighty, yet soft, and possessed a deep hood that would further shield her from the elements.

"Very well, Sir Knight." She drew herself up, staring at him squarely. "I will accept the mantle and make use of it for now. But only for now."

Royce watched as Juliana turned to look out over the Channel, catching up the silver cross from where it hung suspended over her heart. Just then, the air filled with the shrill calls of a great host of lapwings. Together, he and the maid witnessed the spectacular passage of the birds overhead. *Certes*, they must number in the thousands, he thought amazed. 'Twas the time of the annual migrations, ever a stunning sight along this portion of the coast, as it was across the Channel at Dover.

Disappointingly, Juliana displayed no reaction to the spectacle, but appeared immune to the sight. So many wonders surrounded her, yet she refused to enjoy a single one. She continued to cling to all she'd left behind, her heart sternly closed, open to nothing. Yet, he couldn't fault her. 'Twas a hard thing to lose one's family. That, he knew first hand. But Juliana had lost her loved ones twice. There was also the matter of the hulking cooper, for whom she obviously cared.

Royce shoved aside his last thought, finding it unpalatable, and cleared his throat. "We need be away, my lady."

Juliana gave a small nod of understanding, fingering the silver cross as she did. But just as she began to take a step she halted, going suddenly stiff. Her brows drew together as her gaze dropped to the holy object in her hand. Slowly, she lifted her eyes to his.

"How did you know I possessed this cross?"

The question took Royce aback. He reached through his memories of the past week, striving to recall the words they'd exchanged upon the steps of St. Maurice, and how he'd cited the cross as proof of the maid's identity. 'Twas time he disclosed all to Juliana, of how their paths had touched years past, of his full identity. On the other hand, he was unable to read her current mood. They had a long journey before them aboard ship, and he had no wish to spawn new troubles with the maid.

"As I believe I explained, Lord Gilbert searched long for his granddaughter and was able to learn much of Vaux, the squire, the cross—"

"But how did *you* know of the engraving on the back of the cross? Lord Gilbert couldn't have learned of it. Not even my foster parents noticed the inscription till after we'd moved from Vincelles. They cannot read, but long assumed it to be a prayer. Yet, you claim it to be the knight's oath? How did you know?" She narrowed her eyes. "Or did you simply make that up?"

The accusation irked Royce, but he refused to let the maid draw him out. "'Tis not unusual for a knight to inscribe his sacred oath upon the cross he wears."

"Then you didn't know for sure," she charged, cutting short his next words. "You only guessed it bore the oath, and no one challenged you or thought to read it for themselves."

"Few could, I imagine."

"Pere Armand could, yet he did not. Why, the inscription might be a prayer after all, or something different entirely than the knight's oath. You said the cross belonged to the squire's father. Was that a guess, too?"

Royce started to respond, but Juliana slashed her hand angrily through the air. "You deceived me! You deceived everyone at the church. You don't know if I'm this heiress or not. And yet you forced me to go with you. You abducted me—on my wedding day—just so you could be done with your quest."

Royce's temper spiked. The maid had assaulted his honor. "The cross *does* bear the oath, exactly as I gave it," he said between his teeth. "There are at least two scholars traveling in our company. Either one of them can read the inscription for you, if you care to consult them."

The maid looked poised to further argue the point. His forbearance at an end, Royce decided to clear his conscience and disclose all. "Lady Juliana, there is something about the night in Vaux I must—"

"I am not Juliana!" she screamed, her emerald eyes blazing. "And there is nothing, *nothing*, you have to say that I wish to hear. Not today, not tomorrow, not ever! You have ruined my life!"

The maid spun in place, gripping the battlement to steady herself.

Her words struck Royce at his core. Twice now he'd altered the course of Juliana's life—first, by mistakenly placing her in the care of commoners, denying her her rightful place amongst the nobility and robbing her of precious years with her sole living relative, her grandfather, Lord Gilbert. Now, he deprived her of the only family she'd known during the last decade, the only one she could remember.

He *had* ruined Juliana's life. For that, he felt himself a miserable wretch and equally torn. The angelic child, Ana, had inspired him to prevail over his own weaknesses and to become the man, the knight, he had become. He'd won his spurs and committed himself not only to the service of God, but to the weak and powerless, pursuing worthy and valorous deeds. He'd spent additional years in the East, believing himself useful to those in need of him there. Indeed, he'd become that noble defender for all the little Anas who had no one to protect them. But now, the source of his inspiration, Ana herself, despised him fully as he sought only to right things in her behalf.

Royce clamped his jaw tight. Very well, then. He deserved her wrath. 'Twas just recompense, he deemed, for he'd caused the maid untold distress. He would honor her wish and not attempt to explain aught or to speak of the past. 'Twould make no difference anyway. Juliana was who she was, an heiress of noble blood. No doubt, she'd loathe him forever for taking her away from her sainted cooper. Yet, such a marriage would never be allowed by her guardian.

He would do his duty by the maid, Royce told himself. He would see her to court and to Lord Gilbert's keeping. Then he would give himself to matters concerning his own future. He would take possession of the lands and castle granted him by the Lionheart and set about establishing the House of Warrene.

Ana wished to cry, but she refused to shed a single tear in the knight's presence. She had no wish to be perceived as weak or defeated, or that her spirit had been in any way conquered, for it had not.

Ana closed her fingers around the cross, its silver metal cool to her touch. A thought suddenly unfolded in her mind and she dropped her gaze to the piece. Perhaps her valiant squire yet lived, returned from the Crusade. She'd long hoped he would find his way to Chinon, but he had not.

Still, if he'd survived the infidels, she might find him in England. And if she did, then mayhap he would take pity on her and come gallantly to her aid once more and save her from her awful plight. Truly, there was no one else to help her.

If only she knew the squire's name. But that lack would not deter her. She would seek him, or news of him, among those at Court. Perhaps someone knew of the company of knights that had stopped at Vaux and aided its people.

Ana tried to conjure the squire's image. She'd seen him in naught but moonlight and torchfire and at the breaking of dawn. She remembered his hair as being similar in color to the knight's, only darker and without his sun-washed streaks. The squire's eye color was perhaps more blue, but she couldn't be certain.

What might he look like now as a grown man? She recalled him as standing to the other knights' shoulders and, therefore, not overly tall. He'd been slender in build, though when she'd clung to him, she'd discovered him to be rock hard beneath his garments and his arms like bands of iron as they offered her solid, comforting shelter.

Ana glanced out a final time over the water, feeling life itself closing in upon her. She drew into the warmth of the mantle, knowing she had no choice but to brace herself and meet her fate straight on.

"'Tis time," the knight said simply, bidding her to come away.

Ana turned and, head held high, accompanied Sir Royce from the fortress.

PART III

Times Present, Times Past

"In this world of change
naught which comes stays,
and naught which goes is lost."
—Madame Swetchine

8

Dover Castle, England

The sound of soft, feminine humming stirred Ana slowly from the depths of sleep.

As she dragged herself toward consciousness, she felt a delicious warmth surrounding her. Ana sank into that warmth, her last memories being of the bone-chilling cold of the sea and huddling in vain over a small brazier. Wherever she was now, she didn't care. She was warm and comfortable and she could feel her toes once more.

Again the humming played at her ears. Ana levered open an eyelid and saw that she was in a small chamber. Its rough stone walls and high-planked ceiling reminded her much of her lodgings in the fortress of Boulogne.

Ana blinked open both eyes and glanced toward the source of the sound, only to discover a round, wimpled woman bustling back and forth before the hearth. She wore garments of good-quality cloth. Still, she appeared to be a servant for she was preparing a bath for someone.

Ana watched as the woman emptied a bucket of steaming water into a wooden tub positioned before the fire. This done, she next set about strewing dried petals and herbs over the water's surface.

With a start, Ana realized the bath must be intended for her for no one else was present in the room. Smiling at that, she started to lift herself to a sitting position, but at once, her stomach lurched and the room began to shift. Groaning, Ana dropped back onto her pillow, drawing the woman's attention.

"Ah, my lady, good morrow. I was about to awaken you. Your bath water is . . . My lady? Are you not feeling well?" she chattered in thickly accented French.

Ana took a long, dry swallow. "I can still feel the rhythm of the waves beneath me. 'Tis as though I never left the ship."

The woman wagged her head sympathetically. "Poor dear, you suffer the sea-complaints, do you? Get that way myself, every time I put a foot in a boat. Needn't even leave shore. You just rest there, and I'll finish readying your bath."

She started to step away then stopped and turned back, crossing her hands over her generous, aproned middle. "Almost forgot. My name is Mildred, and your gentleman has engaged my services to see to your needs whilst you're here."

Ana strained to follow the maid's words, for in addition to her heavy accent, she spoke swiftly. Meanwhile, Mildred crossed to the tub, tested the water with an elbow, then set out snowy towels and a bar of soap. Ana wasn't sure she felt up to the woman's unbounded energy and buoyant good cheer. For the moment, she lay perfectly still, gazing up at the ceiling beams and trying not to move. But questions crowded in. Ana glanced slowly about the chamber, trying to remember how she got here.

"Where is this exactly? Did we land in Dover?"

"Aye, my lady. And this is Dover Castle." Mildred smiled. "You were sleeping like a babe when your ship docked. Your fine knight arrived with you in his arms at the castle gate. Fast asleep you were. He didn't walk all the way from the shore, of course. Rode that black beast of his."

"Hannibal?"

Mildred gave a small lift of one shoulder. "Don't know the animal's name, but your gentleman, Sir Royce, would allow none but himself to see to you. Once in the keep, he carried you up the many flights to this room, saying you'd taken ghastly ill on the crossing."

The last part Ana remembered clearly. She'd huddled against Sir Royce on the ship, his arm steadfast around her. That was after some rather unpleasant bouts of sickness. She hadn't taken well to the choppy waters, and she didn't wish to think on it overlong now, lest she make herself ill all over again.

Ana drew her hand idly across her waist and let it rest there. Startlingly, she felt her bare flesh. Peering beneath the coverings, she realized someone had undressed her. She lay naked beneath the sheets.

"Who . . . ?"

"Now, don't you worry yourself, my lady." Mildred smiled, jabbering on. "Once your knight laid you abed, I saw to your needs myself. Shooed him out, I did, and stayed with you through the night. But oh, what a handsome one your knight is, my lady." She sighed. "He obviously cares for you very much."

"*My* knight? No, you don't und—"

"Would you like a little wine, mayhap? Or a bit of cheese and bread? That might settle your stomach. Or if you'd like to try something more substantial—"

Ana held up a hand to stop Mildred's flow of words. "A sip of wine, thank you, but nothing more. I doubt my stomach will tolerate anything solid at the moment."

"Yes, my lady." The maid scuttled over to a corner table laid with a small repast. "'Twill take time to readjust. But you'll be fit and hale again before the day's half spent, mark my words. Here you are now," she said, returning. "Sip the wine slowly."

Ana accepted the goblet and took a small taste of the cloudy liquid. Fortunately, Mildred had turned away again and didn't see her grimace. The drink was intolerable. Ana vowed, should she ever be given the opportunity, she'd brew her own ales and beers and ciders and never touch what these English called wine.

Mildred crossed to the bedside once more, smiling. "Shall I see you into your bath now, my lady, before it goes cold? You'll feel much improved after a good soaking."

Ana found it embarrassing to have a total stranger help her naked from her bed. Still, she required a steady arm on which to lean. She felt weak and uncommonly stiff.

With Mildred's aid, Ana stepped into the tub of hot, fragrant water. The scents of lavender and rosemary drifted pleasantly to her nostrils as she rested back, her bones melting into the heat. It felt glorious.

Accepting a block of soap from the maid, Ana found it perfumed with the same floral-and-herb blend. She set to work on herself, relishing the silken feel of the soap as it slid over her skin. 'Twas utter luxury, an apt reward after the wicked Channel crossing. She could linger here all day, she believed.

But the exuberant Mildred had other ideas and took a second bar of soap to her hair, lathering and washing it thoroughly. After numerous rinsings, Mildred pronounced Ana clean from head to toe and held out a large towel for her to step into. After wrapping Ana snugly in its folds, the maid left her sitting by the fire drying her hair while she bustled back to the bed and began laying out a host of new garments.

"Your knight favors you greatly, my lady," Mildred said past her shoulder. "He's spared no expense on your behalf."

Ana's eyes widened at the assortment of clothes covering the bed. She could no longer see its surface.

"Sir Royce had them delivered early this morn," the maid continued. "There are several changes of gowns, traveling robes, undergarments, and slippers. . . ." Her voice trailed off.

Stunned, Ana rose from the stool and joined the maid, surveying the spread of clothing as she did. There was a change of chemises, several gowns and overgowns, veils, gloves, girdles, slippers, and more.

A small storm began to gather deep inside Ana. She wanted no gifts from the man and didn't intend to accept them. But when she searched for her own gown among the others, she realized 'twas not in sight.

"Mildred, where is my gown? The one I was wearing when I arrived, what has become of it?"

"I sent it to the laundress to be cleaned, my lady. And, if you will pardon my saying so, 'twas in sore need of it."

Ana stayed the words poised on her lips, remembering how deathly ill she'd been on the ship and how Sir Royce had seen her through that time—holding her in his arms, helping her the many times she heaved over the side—a very unladylike experience, to be sure. No doubt her dress needed cleaning, from the crossing as well as the long days spent traveling on the roads.

"I do expect my gown to be returned." She spoke a bit sharply, then softened her voice, seeing the maid's look. "You see, 'tis my wedding dress and, therefore, very special to me'"Twas the truth. Ana intended to wear the dress still, when she married Gervase.

"Of course, my lady," Mildred smiled. "And you needn't concern yourself. Our laundress, Marguerite, is excellent with cloth of every kind. She'll make the gown like new, you'll see." She winked, her smile widening. "I do love weddings. And I always trust my senses about such matters. My senses tell me you've chosen well in Sir Royce."

"Sir Royce?" Ana sputtered.

"Aye. You've a great defender in the knight, by the looks of him. And so considerate and handsome he is too. Considerate I say because he took a different bed for himself last night and let you be, knowing how sick you were and all. But don't you fret. Plenty of time for cozying up. He'll get you with many a beautiful babe, and you'll have no complaints about how he accomplishes that, I vow."

"Sir Royce and me?" Ana choked out, feeling herself flush to her toes. But the cheeky maid had already spun away before Ana could correct her misconceptions.

"He waits below for you now with Brother Giraldus," Mildred gabbled on as she held up one of the chemises. "Best we see you dressed and down to him."

Ana started to press the issue and explain that Sir Royce and she were not wed. But instead, she found herself tongue-tied as she fought down images of herself and Sir Royce intimately involved. Such a preposterous notion. Outrageous, really.

Were she a true lady of noble blood, Ana knew she should redress the maid for her boldness. As it was, judging by the quality of Mildred's garments and the fact that she was in service to nobles, Ana questioned whether Mildred's station might actually be higher than her own, for she herself was merely a brewer's daughter. Regardless, Ana decided to let the matter lie and gave herself over to the maid's ministrations.

With Mildred's aid, Ana first slipped into a long linen chemise. The garment's cloth was light and finely woven, infinitely more comfortable against her skin than the wool she normally wore. Next, she drew on colorfully patterned hose, which the maid gartered for her at each knee.

Relying on Mildred's judgment, Ana chose a creamy gown, embroidered with gold thread about the neck and hem and possessing close-fitting sleeves. 'Twas made of the most wondrous fabric, something Mildred called *chansil*, a silk blend, she explained. Ana ran her fingers over it, delighting in the smoothness of its texture. But Mildred interrupted, assisting her into an overgown that she called by its English name, a kirtle. This was of a sunny-gold wool, its skirt falling only to the knees and its wide, turned-back sleeves to the elbows.

Mildred turned Ana around and laced the gown up the back, and when done, Ana found that the gown hugged her shape to the top of her hips most revealingly. To finish the attire, the maid fastened a girdle low about her hips, suspending from it a small mirror and purse. The latter, Ana discovered, held a single denier. Evidently, Sir Royce did not wish her to be without coin, but was not about to allow her enough to buy passage back to France. Last came slippers, the leather soft as butter.

"Now, my lady, let us see to your hair." Mildred led her back to the stool by the fire and began combing out her long tresses. But as she drew her hair back and began to work it into a braid, Ana stopped her.

"But, my lady, a married woman always binds her hair," the maid objected.

"Sir Royce prefers it loose and flowing," Ana returned, unsure he cared one way or the other, but nevertheless not wishing her hair bound.

"Very well, my lady."

Mildred crowned her hair with a light flowing veil, transparent and shimmery, spilling down Ana's back to her hips. This the maid secured with a twisted silken cord, repeating the colors of her gowns.

"You look ravishing, my lady," Mildred praised. "Here, see for yourself." She handed Ana a disc-shaped mirror of polished metal.

The reflection that gazed back from the mirror startled Ana, and she found herself astonished by her own transformation. Quickly, she set the mirror aside. She mustn't allow herself to become seduced by such luxuries and temptations, she told herself. 'Twas an illusion she saw in the mirror, created with elegant clothes and costly novelties. Gervase waited for her. She must keep her thoughts on him. She intended to regain her freedom and return to Chinon to become a cooper's wife, that and no more.

"Sir Royce awaits, my lady." Mildred spoke at her elbow. "Are you ready to go down?"

"As ready as ever I shall be."

Quitting the room, Ana followed the maid through a long vaulted corridor, then down a flight of spiraling stairs. As they turned into another passage, Ana saw a large glazed window at its end. She found it curiously appealing, with its regular gridwork of panes. Glancing ahead to the maid, Ana continued to follow her, but then an odd, prickling sensation crept over her. Hesitantly, she returned her gaze to the window. 'Twas somehow familiar.

Without warning, an image gripped hold of Ana. In her mind's eye she saw a young girl, no more than eight, with flowing hair, silvery like her own. The girl laughed and giggled as she ran along the corridor toward that same window. A nursemaid chased behind her, both playing a game of some sort. Their laughter echoed in the passageway, resounding in Ana's ears as though having just been uttered.

The child glanced back over her shoulder, and when she turned forward again, she discovered a tall man at the end of the corridor, outlined before the window. He caught her up, joining in the laughter as he twirled her around, holding her high above his head. As he lowered the girl and held her against his chest, she spied something upon his shoulder, something that attracted her. The child reached out to touch it, but before she did, the image vanished.

Ana stumbled sideways toward the wall, throwing her hands out to catch herself as she fell against it. Mildred moved instantly to her side, bracing her up by the waist and elbow.

"My lady, are you all right? My lady?"

Ana gulped for breath, the space around her swirling slowly to a halt, the corridor empty save for herself and the maid.

"Y-Yes, I'm fine." She massaged her forehead. "'Tis only the effects of the crossing that I still suffer. I'll be all right."

But would she? Ana wondered, unable to account for the strange incident.

"Come, my lady," Mildred urged. "'Tis just a little further now and you can rest."

Brother Giraldus cocked his tonsured head to one side, eyeing Royce's injuries. Then a deep rumbling laughter rolled upward from his belly and out of his throat.

"Do you mean to tell me . . ." He paused to swipe the tears of mirth from his eyes, chuckling through each word. ". . . to tell me that you battled Saracens for a full decade and returned without a scratch, only to suffer all manner of cuts, stitches, and contusions when you fetched a simple maid from the country?" He erupted with laughter once more.

"I never said I hadn't been wounded by the Saracens, and I assure you, there is nothing simple about the maid. Not this one." Royce lifted a forebearing brow at the jolly cleric. Annoyingly, at the mention of his stitches, they began to itch along his arm where the flesh healed. 'Twas a bothersome reminder of his Ordeal-by-Juliana.

A solid rapping sounded at the door, drawing both

men's attention. As Brother Giraldus pulled the door open, Royce turned to discover the source of his injuries framed in the portal. He sucked a breath.

Juliana was stunning. She illuminated the very space in which she stood, like the sun and stars rolled into one.

Royce struggled to find his voice as his eyes roamed downward from her silvery blonde hair to her golden gown, and slippered feet. Her veil added to the effect, a shimmering mist of fabric cascading to her hips. Juliana appeared every inch the finest of court ladies—certainly the lady she was ever meant to be. Would that this vision could persist.

"Come in, child. Come in." Brother Giraldus broke the spell as he ushered Juliana into the chamber and waved away the servant woman who stood without. "Bless me! Are you the maid who bested the great hero of Acre and Ascalon? And such a little thing you are." His eyes danced merrily as he glanced to Royce.

Confusion crossed Juliana's face, but still her gaze remained fixed on Royce, consuming him as it had from the moment the chamber door first opened.

"Hero?" she asked, the words whispering from her lips.

"Why, yes, my child." Brother Giraldus's eyes shifted between the two. "Did you not know? Sir Royce is a famed Crusader knight."

"*Crusader?*" She blinked at that, her brows knitting as she came out of her reverie and turned to the monk.

"Yes, child. Sir Royce departed with the Lionheart years past and has only returned this last month. My child? Are you all right? You look pale."

She did look pale, Royce realized with a start. He moved instantly to her side and supported her arm, his free hand moving to the curve of her waist.

"Lady Juliana is still recovering from the Channel crossing," Royce explained. "She did not take well to the experience, I fear."

Juliana turned huge eyes to his and said nothing as he led her to a chair. She only stared up at him, appearing as wordless as he had been moments before, when his gaze first alighted on her.

"Would you care for something to drink, my lady?" he asked gently. "Brother Giraldus has some ale that I think you might find passable." He gave a small smile, knowing how particular she was in matters of drink.

"I thought you served King John." Juliana's words came softly, her brows pinching together once more.

"In truth, the only service I've given him thus far is in finding you."

Her gaze fell away at that, and she rubbed her temple as though a pain stabbed her there. "I think I will have some ale, if you please," she said a moment later.

Brother Giraldus promptly filled a cup for the maid and brought it to her. "Here you are, my dear. We haven't been introduced, but I am Brother Giraldus. I'm one of three chroniclers who maintain a cell here at Dover. Sir Royce was just about to tell me more of his experiences whilst on Crusade. 'Tis a special undertaking of mine to set the tales down with ink and vellum, so they might be preserved for generations yet to come."

Distracted by some sudden thought, the monk put a forefinger to his chin and turned to Royce.

"Ah, but first, Sir Royce, you wished to know of the king. Latest word has it that he has been touring the countryside and that the queen is at Wallingford, awaiting his arrival. From what you've told me, 'tis likely you'll find Lord Gilbert there, comfortably established and cared for by the royal physick."

Royce pondered that a moment. "Wallingford Castle shouldn't take overly long to reach, given that 'tis in nearby

Oxfordshire and on the Thames."

"No time to reach at all," Brother Giraldus agreed. "If you and Lady Juliana delay your departure till the morrow, your arrival will likely coincide with that of the king's. Better still, 'twould allow the lady more time to recover and you time to share more stories of *Outremer.*"

"*Outremer?*" Juliana tilted her head, her gaze lifting to Royce then moving back to the monk.

"Yes, child—the 'lands beyond the sea.'" Brother Giraldus smiled as he took a chair opposite her, drawing it up to a scarred oaken table where his writing supplies lay. "The tales Sir Royce told me upon his return were most astounding," he said, taking up his quill. "There is nothing like a personal account, I can assure you."

Ana strove to collect her wits. She'd hardly begun to recover from her bizarre experience in the corridor when the striking sight of Sir Royce—no longer in his dust-laden armor but bathed and garbed in rich robes—stole her breath and the rest of her senses clear away. Then, before she could even begin to compose herself, she discovered he was not the contemptible despoiler of cities she'd assumed him to be, but a gallant Crusader—a hero, no less—who'd fought with the Lionheart.

Ana downed a mouthful of ale, ignoring its taste, then drew on the cup again. How she wished to curl into a tight ball and hide away in some lone corner while she sorted everything through. But she could not. And Sir Royce's gray-blue eyes remained upon her even now, sending unaccountable feelings sliding through her.

Perhaps 'twas only the awe she felt, learning he was a knight of the Holy Crusade. Or could her feelings be ones of relief, that he'd not aided King John in his loathsome revenge on Le Mans? Ana reminded herself that even though all that may be true, it changed nothing between them. Sir Royce had turned her life upside down and brought her to the English shores against her will, no more than a prisoner.

Her gaze drifted to the knight once more. He stood speaking with Brother Giraldus at the moment, concerning some entry on the monk's parchment. Taking another small sip of ale, Ana continued to gaze discreetly over the rim of the cup, her eyes lingering on Sir Royce's tall frame.

Gone were the layers of padding and mail with the un-flattering coif concealing most of his head. He now wore a rich crimson tunic over black chasusses and boots, all show-ing his masculine form to advantage. He'd obviously bathed. Even his tanned skin appeared lighter, as did his hair, which had seen a trimming, along with his mustache and beard.

As he spoke with the monk, his bruised side turned away, Ana realized the truth of Mildred's words. Sir Royce was indeed a handsome man. Not that such an admittance in any way diminished her feelings for Gervase, or the fu-ture she wished to share with him. Still, she found herself scarce able to keep her eyes from Sir Royce, as she had since first entering the chamber.

Ana thought back on all she'd been told. The knight was a hero of places called Acre and Ascalon and had spent years in the East. 'Twould explain his unseasonal tan and sun-streaked hair. She'd been wrong, sorely wrong about him. But what else did she not know?

As Ana shook away her musings, she realized Brother Giraldus was pressing the knight for a new story.

Sir Royce glanced thoughtfully out the chamber's nar-row window, then turned back. Leaning his hip against the wall, he crossed his arms over his chest.

"I know you wish to hear of battles and victories, Giraldus, but perhaps 'tis best to begin at the beginning, when the armies of Richard and Philip met at Vézelay. That too is important for your records, and I believe you will find the events intriguing on their own merits."

Brother Giraldus's head bobbed in agreement as he laid out a fresh parchment and prepared to write. In the same moment, Ana's gaze leaped to Sir Royce at the mention of Vézelay.

He'd been there, of course, as had her squire. Ana's heart quickened. Perhaps the two might have met. Perhaps, Sir Royce knew something of her squire's fate.

"'Twas estimated eight thousand soldiers gathered at Vézelay," the knight began. "Our own forces arrived belatedly, but I can attest to the number for troops thickened the ground like locust for miles around."

Eight thousand soldiers. Ana's hopes sank. 'Twould be a miracle for Sir Royce to have encountered her squire, even briefly, in so vast a company.

The sound of the monk's quill scratching across the dry parchment drew her thoughts back. Ana returned her attention to the knight, listening intently for whatever he might reveal of Vézelay and the time that followed, imagining what her squire must have endured after he'd left her at Vincelles.

"Upon our arrival at Vézelay, we learned of the death of the emperor, Frederick Barbarossa, and that his army had turned back to their homeland. Naturally, it cast a pall over our high spirits," Sir Royce was saying. "Quarrels erupted between Richard and Philip, as they ever did throughout the campaign. But then, omens plagued us too. When the armies started forth and the kings picked up their pilgrim's script and staff, Richard's staff broke. He ignored it, of course, not believing in portents but only in himself, and led the troops forward."

Ana propped her chin on her hand as she continued to listen, gazing on Sir Royce's features. His eyes had lost their blue, turning steely, and his gaze was now distant, his expression intent, as he relived those days.

"The two armies marched south together, English and French. 'Twas an impressive sight. But at Lyons came our first mishap. The bridge collapsed under the weight of our army as we crossed the Rhône. I nearly drowned myself. King Richard ordered boats lashed together, thus we eventually gained the other side."

Sir Royce began to pace. "Next, at Marseilles, where the Lionheart expected a fleet of a hundred ships to meet his army, and for which he'd paid most handsomely, none awaited. Furious, he hired the first three ships he could find, but most of us were forced to march overland, as did King Philip, who distrusted travel by water."

A chill spiraled through Ana as she thought on what the soldiers must have endured as they crossed one inhospitable land after another, making their way to the desert lands. Her own few days and minor discomforts traveling through France's countryside could not compare to the hardships borne by the Crusaders, borne by her dear squire.

"Further delays followed, not the least of which came when Richard's irrepressible mother, Queen Eleanor, arrived with a Spanish bride for him, the Princess Berengaria. The two eventually wed on the island of Cyprus, but not before the bride and the king's sister, Joan, had been kidnapped. But that tale is best left for another time."

Sir Royce ceased his pacing and, lost to his thoughts, drew his hand along his bearded jaw. "In all, 'twas not until ten months after our departure from Vézelay that the armies of Richard the Lionheart and Philip Augustus arrived in the Holy Land to face Saladin."

Ana listened, enthralled, to Sir Royce's account,

thoughts of her squire slipping away. There was much more to this knight than she'd ever begun to guess. Who was this man, Sir Royce de Warrene? And after enduring years in the East, what strange twist of Fate had sent him on a quest to Chinon?

9

Wallingford, Oxfordshire

Wallingford Castle rose majestically above the Thames in white dazzling splendor. Even from the distance of the docks, the immense stronghold promised everything Royce had ever heard it to be—the "marvel of England."

Disembarking the *uissier*, a transport ship equipped for animals, Royce led Hannibal down the planking and onto the quay. Juliana followed, speaking not a word, her gaze yet raised to the great castle. 'Twas an awe-inspiring sight, even for one such as himself who'd seen many wonders of architecture in the East.

Mounting Hannibal and settling the maid pillion behind him, Royce guided the stallion along the main road, which led through the heart of the ancient town, and brought them to the north gate at its far-most end. There, they entered onto a paved causeway leading directly toward the castle and its massive fortified gate.

Wallingford, Royce knew, was among the Conqueror's earliest and most important castles constructed. Over the years, it had been converted from timber to stone and much improved upon, especially by the Plantagenet kings.

Advancing toward it, Royce again gazed in awe at the result of their passionate endeavors. Three defense walls rose in tiers, each succeeding wall higher than the one before it, protecting the massive keep within the inner ward. During a siege, the castle defenders could man all three battlements, aiming their weapons over the heads of their comrades on the lower ramparts. In addition, mural towers projected at regular intervals along the curtain walls for as far as he could see. These, Royce knew, would allow archers to take aim from any angle and to thwart enemies who might attempt to scale the walls.

Most impressive of all was the castle's gatehouse, which loomed directly ahead. 'Twas a solid structure, flanked by two huge drum towers. The whole of the castle—its walls, towers, gatehouse, keep—was limewashed so that its white surface reflected the sun and shone brilliantly over the surrounding countryside. Adding to the power of the effect, the parapets bristled with soldiers, and Royce saw now that the king's standard, bearing three gold lions on a red ground, fluttered high above the drum towers. John was in residence.

Royce felt Juliana press against him as she leaned forward and looked past his shoulder. Her hold tightened about his middle when they crossed onto the drawbridge, this of timber stretching over a deep, watered ditch. Hannibal's hooves clumped dully on the wood as they continued forward, totally dwarfed by the enormity of the structure before them.

'Tis a monstrous-sized castle, Sir Knight," Ana spoke at his ear, her tone filled with wonder. "Are all in England like this one?"

"Nay, fair maid. Wallingford is an Honor Castle, a strategic royal stronghold, impregnable. It retains over a hundred knights to secure it, never less. No one enters here without permission."

"Or leaves without it either, I imagine," Juliana added dryly.

Royce smiled grimly at her observation, which held truth to it. Once past the gates, he knew he could relax his vigil over the maid and cease worrying from one moment to the next what new scheme she might hatch in order to escape. 'Twould be a welcome relief to give that particular responsibility over to another.

Yet, 'twould be odd, after spending these many days and nights together, to be wholly free of Juliana. He would leave her with her grandfather and withdraw from her life both for now and evermore. 'Twas as it should be, of course. So why did the thought prick at him? The child Ana had been an angelic waif, he thought, envisioning her sweet face. Grown to maidenhood, though, she'd become a rose with many thorns.

Royce released a long breath, slowing Hannibal's pace as they closed on the towered gate. His quest was complete. Complete, that was, if Lord Gilbert was installed at Wallingford as Brother Giraldus believed him to be. Forsooth, he hoped the good brother was right. The old lord and his granddaughter need be reunited and proceed with their lives. He need do the same.

In truth, over the past days, he'd felt increasingly anxious to get on with his purpose for returning from the East—to claim the estate awarded him by the Lionheart. 'Twas an agreeable property in Kent, King Richard had assured, Birkwell by name, well situated and with prime potential.

As Royce understood it, Birkwell was one of the adulterine castles, slighted when Richard's father had assumed the throne and sought to break the power of England's unruly barons who'd built without license. Even when it became a royal holding, Birkwell had been, and continued to be, overseen by the neighboring bishopric, responsible for collecting the rents and taxes, contributing a portion of the profits to the church for its stewardship, and applying the remainder to the upkeep and improvement of the land and castle buildings.

Over the last years, Royce had received reports from Richard's royal accountants, confirming this to have been done in his behalf. He'd received no reports, however, since the Lionheart's death and John's ascendancy. 'Twas what had prompted his return.

Had he been wrong to remain in *Outremer*? Royce wondered. Any other knight would have ridden home apace to claim his new lands. But trusting the king's word that an able steward would oversee Birkwell, he elected to remain longer in the East. He hadn't intended to stay as long as he had, but there had been so many needs amongst the people there. So many still. . . .

Whether he'd been right or wrong in his choices, Royce knew he must ride for Birkwell as soon as possible and assess the estate's condition. Already the days pressed toward November. Winter would soon be upon them.

"Who goes there?" the watchman shouted from the gate, signaling Royce to stop.

"Sir Royce de Warrene on business of his majesty, King John," he called back, reining Hannibal to a halt. "I bring with me Lady Juliana Mandeville."

The watchman strode forward, his spear gripped firmly in hand. "Have you papers?" he asked brusquely, his gaze moving to the fading bruise on Royce's face, then to the scab above his brow.

"Aye." Royce withdrew the parchments from his surcoat and handed them over. "I seek Lady Juliana's grandfather, Lord Gilbert Osborne of Penhurst. Do you know if he is here at Wallingford?"

The guard's eyes shifted to the maid, skimming her closely—too closely for Royce's liking—before returning his gaze to him. "Nay, I know naught of your lord but the Constable will." Returning Royce's papers he waved them through. "You may pass."

Juliana remained silent, her grip tightening about Royce once more as they passed beneath the gate's archway and iron-clad portcullis. Entering a short tunnel, light spilled down on them from murder holes overhead and streamed through arrow slits piercing the walls on either side. Ahead, Royce spied another gate, positioned to slide into place, making the tunnel a death trap for any who dared to come with malice in mind or against the king's will.

Emerging from the jaws of the gatehouse, they traversed a second bridge, suspended over a second moat, this one with swans gliding over its watery surface. The sight seemed to delight Juliana, for she eased her hold on him long enough to point them out, saying something he did not quite catch. At the next gate, Royce again presented his papers and again endured the guard's scrutiny of his face before being motioned through.

Next they came upon the castle's lower ward, filled with workshops and abuzz with people. Hammers clanged on steel and on iron as armorers and smiths worked at their crafts. Carpenters axed and sawed their wood, wheelwrights pounded metal stripping onto wheels, the castle crier bellowed some message lost in the din, while a clutch of men argued loudly over a vat of crimson dye. Throughout the ward, the smells of livestock, smoke, and the caustic concoctions used by the craftsmen choked the air.

At the third and last gate, Royce identified himself and Juliana once more and asked to be led to the Constable.

"Constable Howarth is just over there, the man in the fur-collared cloak." The guard gestured with his spear to a figure in the inner ward, not two hundred paces away. His gaze returned to Royce, skimming over the side of his face and to his brow.

Royce's patience eroded. At least he didn't have to admit to these soldiers 'twas the sweet-looking maid perched behind him who'd dealt him such damage. Hopefully, he'd finish healing in the coming days, though by then, he'd be far from this place. With luck, no one would press him for explanations in the meantime.

Setting his heels to Hannibal's flanks, Royce urged his steed forward and entered the core of the castle. There the royal keep rose before them, an immense, square tower dominating the inner ward. Again they discovered a great bustle of activity, though the personages here appeared to be of a more noble stamp and the air proved sweeter.

Dismounting, Royce lifted Juliana to the ground beside him. After retrieving his saddle pouches, he gave Hannibal over to one of the young grooms, who conducted him toward the stables on the east side of the ward. Royce slipped a glance to the maid, who appeared somewhat overwhelmed by their surroundings. To her credit, she remained outwardly composed. Still he noted how she clutched her mantle close about her as though it might provide some security.

Lifting his hand lightly to the small of her back, Royce ushered Juliana toward the man who'd been identified to them as Wallingford's Constable. They stood waiting several minutes as he finished instructions to one of the squires, then, at last, took note of them.

"Good sir, good lady, forgive me. I did not see you standing there. Might I be of help?"

"Hopefully so. I am Sir Royce de Warrene and this is—"

"Sir Royce! Her majesty the queen bid me watch for your coming. Welcome to Wallingford. 'Tis an honor to meet you. I have heard of your bravery in the East—Acre and Ascalon," he enthused, reaching out a meaty hand and clasping Royce's. "I am Constable Howarth."

"Constable." Royce acknowledged the man as he freed

his fingers, aware of the maid's eyes widening over him at the man's effusive greeting. "May I present Lady Juliana Mandeville. We are in hopes of finding her grandfather, Lord Gilbert Osborne, here."

"Lord Gilbert? Aye, exactly so. He resides in the northwest tower I believe. I will find out precisely. Meanwhile, you will wish lodgings and a chance to wash and change."

Juliana, who'd remained docile for the whole of their journey from Dover, suddenly came alive and turned toward Royce, stepping before him. "Is there need, Sir Knight? Surely, once Lord Gilbert verifies my identity— leastwise, who I am not—we shall depart and be on our way back to the coast. The day is not so very late after all."

Royce steeled himself, her words like a burr beneath his skin. Had he mistaken the maid's silence for acceptance of her lot? He loathed to think what Juliana's reaction would be once she realized she was indeed the lost heiress and destined to remain on England's shores. Likely, she'd resort to her wiles and deceits again—lying, stealing, and taking every opportunity to flee. He need warn the enfeebled Lord Gilbert to be on guard. No telling what mischief she might cause, even in such a place as Wallingford.

Royce leveled her his sternest look. "You will wash and change and make yourself presentable for Lord Gilbert. Must I remind you, he has waited years for this moment—a full decade to be exact. You will not spoil it, no matter whom he decides you to be," he warned tersely.

Juliana pressed her lips together, fire flashing in her eyes as she glared back at him. "Then let us be done with it for my betrothed awaits me across *La Manche*, and my foster parents are surely sick with worry."

Royce ground his teeth. He did not wish to hear another word of her "betrothed," though he did sympathize with Georges and Marie.

"I agree, let us be done with it," he said between his teeth, the wound on his arm beginning to itch as his temper rose.

Had the maid a grain of appreciation for Lord Gilbert's plight, for his loss and for all he'd done to find her over these many long years? The maid would have to accept facts sooner or later. He only hoped she didn't break the old man's heart while stubbornly resisting what Royce already knew to be true. She was Juliana Mandeville and would not be returning to Chinon.

"Doubtless Constable Howarth will lodge you in the ladies' chambers in the keep." He slipped a glance to the man and found him nodding, his eyes rounded wide over the two. Royce returned his attention to the maid. "I will seek you there in one hour's time. Prepare yourself to be presented to Lord Gilbert. And if you have forgotten your own observations, escape is not possible from Wallingford. 'Twould be unwise even to consider it. There is an entire garrison and all the castle folk to call upon to find you if need be."

"Escape, Sir Knight?" Juliana stiffened and tipped up her chin. "Surely you jest. I have no need to attempt it when in an hour's time they will be open to me when Lord Gilbert sends me on my way."

"An hour's time then," Royce growled. "Be ready. We will see whether you leave or stay." He turned to the constable and gave over the leather pouch containing the maid's clothes. "If you will point me to where the king's ministers convene, there is a matter I must see to. I will seek you again, forthwith."

Constable Howarth appeared momentarily flustered by the couple's heated exchange. But after apprising Royce that he would find the court officials in the south tower, he bid the maid follow him.

Plucking up her skirts, Juliana tossed Royce a stinging look, then turned on her heel. With head held high and defiance starching her spine, she trailed Constable Howarth to a flight of stairs at the side of the keep.

Royce heaved a sigh. He'd been right. 'Twould be good to be done with this particular quest and attend to matters concerning his future. 'Twould also be beneficial to his temperament, which had remained ragged since first encountering the maid. He need only survive the coming hour, when he would relinquish her to her grandfather's keeping. Juliana would then be another man's concern.

After checking on Hannibal, Royce went in search of the king's ministers to request an audience concerning the Lionheart's grant and the conferment of Birkwell. That done, he verified Lord Gilbert's whereabouts, as well as Juliana's, and took up quarters for himself. An hour later, having washed and changed from his mail hauberk, he arrived at the chamber set aside for the noble maidens of Wallingford and knocked soundly on the door.

Duty had been served, honor preserved, his wrong righted, Royce told himself, straightening his tunic. After delivering Juliana, he would seek the document and license required for Birkwell, find his pallet early, and depart at first light. 'Twas a sound, orderly plan.

The door drew open revealing a needle-thin woman, one of the ladies' maids by her garments. She eyed him closely, but before he could speak, a patch of color across the room caught his eye, a beautiful rose-pink that he well remembered. As his gaze drew toward it, he found Juliana standing profiled against a window as she gazed out on the courtyard below. She wore one of the gowns he'd had specially made for her, its rose-petal color the most flattering of all the gowns to her pale beauty.

As she sensed his presence and looked toward him,

Royce's throat went dry. God help him, she looked part angel and part temptress—all sweetness and purity on the one hand, and on the other, the very embodiment of a man's most secret, passionate fantasy. At least his.

The admittance surprised Royce. He realized now he'd been holding the feeling in check, suppressing his attraction.

Royce's anticipation to be rid of the maid suddenly diminished. He should savor these last moments with Juliana, he told himself. True, she'd been a thorn in his side all the way from Chinon, but she would always hold a special place in his heart—especially the memory of the child she once had been.

Royce cleared his throat. "Are you ready, my lady?"

For a moment Juliana hesitated, lifting her hand to the silver cross that lay over her heart, as ever she was wont to do. Unknowingly, Juliana kept a part of him with her as well, Royce mused. To his surprise, he found that pleased him.

As Juliana joined him at the portal, Royce offered her his arm. When she looked uncertain of what to do, he took her hand and placed it upon his forearm, leaving his own hand covering hers as he escorted her from the room. They made their way along the corridor and down the winding stairs and passed long minutes later onto the castle grounds and proceeded wordlessly toward the northwest tower.

Royce did not miss the keen interest Juliana drew—the looks cast her way, or how the men paused in their various tasks and halted in their tracks. 'Twas to be expected. Juliana was exquisite. If only her admirers knew the full extent of the maid's capabilities, they might seek to flee rather than gawk. His injuries were proof of that.

Who was he fooling? Royce chided himself. 'Twould be no difficult matter to find the maid a husband even if she remained nettlesome and unpolished. What man would not wish to climb into her bed?

Without thought, Royce tightened his hand on Juliana's.

Feeling the strengthening pressure of the knight's fingers upon her hand, Ana lifted her eyes to his. Was he conveying reassurance or protectiveness in that touch? Or was it only a reflex, made for no reason at all? She could not tell.

Ana continued on with the knight, keeping her gaze diverted from those in the courtyard who openly stared at her. She felt painfully self-conscious and completely out of place. Except for her brief stay in the fortresses at Boulogne and Dover, she'd never been in anything remotely similar to a castle, let alone a royal stronghold such as Wallingford. The fortresses had been stark in their furnishings, intended primarily to house the garrisons, she guessed. But here, she'd found the ladies' chamber to be hung with silks, its windows glazed, and even possessing a fine fireplace, decoratively sculpted and lined with tiles. Such luxury she'd never known.

Fortunately, she'd not encountered any of the noblewomen who occupied the chamber. She'd been told they were currently in other parts of the castle, some with the queen. 'Twas just as well, Ana deemed, since she would not know how to conduct herself in the presence of ladies such as they. All in all, her brief glimpse into the lives of the nobility would be a topic for much cheerful discussion when she returned home. She now need only meet Lord Gilbert, have him see she was not his lost granddaughter, and then she would be free to return home to do just that.

Before she departed, however, there was one thing she wished to learn. If Lord Gilbert had searched for his granddaughter for as long and as extensively as Sir Royce claimed, then it stood to reason he might know something of her squire and whether or not he'd returned from the Holy

Lands. For certain, he would know the name of the knight her squire had served when the Crusaders happened upon Vaux. Lord Gilbert must have given the name to Sir Royce, for he'd spoken it on the steps of St. Maurice when he'd stopped her wedding—a Sir Hugh Fitz something. She couldn't recall the last of it, but she was loathe to ask Sir Royce to repeat it again. He was ever suspicious of her intentions, not that she hadn't given him cause to be.

Ana shivered as they entered the northwest tower and began to ascend the stairs. A wintry cold was trapped in the stones, though outside the day was most pleasant.

She slid a glance to the knight. He looked quite striking again, dressed in formal attire, his tunic a deep forest green. She'd have to endure his company for another week, of course, once Lord Gilbert pronounced her to be a stranger. Indeed, she looked forward to the shocked look on Sir Royce's face when he realized how wrong he'd been about her and that he must conduct her back to Chinon.

For a brief moment she wondered if he'd allow her to keep some of her new clothes. She'd like to keep the one she wore now, if nothing more. She'd never owned anything so beautiful as the rose-colored gown, or so soft to the touch. 'Twould be small recompense for the distress caused her.

Gaining the second floor, they arrived at an oaken door, reinforced and studded with iron. The knight gave three solid knocks upon the wood.

The scraping of a chair sounded on the other side of the door, then the quickening of footsteps as someone approached. As the door eased open, a man's narrow face appeared, a purplish blotch on the end of his nose. He pressed his fingers to his lips, shushing them.

"No visitors by order of the queen's physick."

The man started to shut the door, but the knight's arm

shot out, forcing it back open.

"I am Sir Royce de Warrene and this is Lady Juliana."

Ana's eyes leaped to his. "I am *not* Juli—"

"'Tis no matter who you are. Lord Gilbert is very ill and must not be disturbed," the odd little man grumbled. "His lordship is resting now and will need to be bled again soon."

"Bled?" Ana echoed, her revulsion for the practice ringing in her tone. "Is that necessary?"

"Young lady!" He hissed his displeasure. "You will keep your voice lowered and not, I repeat *not*, disrupt his lordship's rest."

The man put his shoulder and weight to the door as he tried to close it against Sir Royce's strength. But not to be dismissed so easily, the knight pushed against the barrier, driving the door and the little man back until the portal stood fully open.

"The lady *will* disturb his lordship and so shall I," Sir Royce avowed. "This is Lord Gilbert's granddaughter, Juliana Mandeville. And if he is as ill as you say, then all the more reason for him to see her, and at once."

"Sir Royce?" A voice rasped from the depths of the room. "Juliana? Have you brought my Juliana?"

"Now see what you've done," the little man carped as the knight swept Ana over the threshold and into the room. "You must not excite him. Sir, sir? Do you hear me?"

Ana came to a halt beside Sir Royce, midway into the chamber. 'Twas not a large room, yet 'twas warm, unlike the stairwell. A fire crackled in the fireplace, while tapestries cloaked the walls. An elaborately carved bed occupied half the room's space, its curtains drawn on three sides, the one facing the fire left open.

As Ana and Sir Royce moved deeper into the chamber, they discovered a pale figure of a man propped in a sitting position upon a wealth of pillows. His snowy hair was near indistinguishable against the equally snowy linens until he struggled to sit forward. His gaze riveted on Ana.

"Juliana? Oh . . . oh, my child, my child, you've come at last!" His voice trembled with emotion. "I knew you would. I never gave up hope. Step closer that I might better see you. These old eyes fail."

Suddenly uncertain of herself, Ana moved to the side of the bed as the old lord asked. She saw now how his eyes swam with tears and felt a hot liquid stinging the back of her own.

Lord Gilbert reached out toward her and caught her hand in his, his touch cool and dry as parchment as he drew her nearer. "Ah yes, 'tis you, my sweet Juliana. Praise God. How I've prayed to find you before I draw my last breath. And here you be." His shoulders began to shake as he further dissolved to tears. "Forgive an old man to weep so, but my heart just burst with joy."

Overcome, he could not speak for a moment. But Ana found her voice had deserted her as well, so touched was she by the man's outpouring. Tears collected in her eyes, and her throat clogged with unexpected emotion. For a moment she could almost believe she was the one for whom this man had searched so long. Wanted to believe it, if only to please him. Ana could not explain the strange feelings surging inside her.

In her mind's hearing, a small voice clamored that she shared no relation with this man. And yet, there seemed a vague familiarity about the old lord's features—his faded green eyes of a hue not unlike her own, and his brows that arched wide over his eyes reminding her of . . . someone. She could not say who. Perhaps 'twas an illusion, a trick of mind, no more than a desire to not disappoint this man, who was so obviously unwell.

Recovering himself, Lord Gilbert wiped his eyes and

gave a small squeeze to Ana's hand.

"You have grown so since last I saw you, dear Juliana. You were just a wisp of a little thing. A breeze could have carried you away. But despite the years, I would know you anywhere, could pick you out of any crowd. You are so like your mother, Alyce, and your grandmother too—my beautiful Thérèse, God rest her soul. They both had that same little mole on their upper lips, only your mother's was here, on the right side." He tapped a finger to the place above his own lip, giving a small, joyful laugh. "Come sit here on the bed. Dear child, we have years to catch up on, and I wish to hear everything about you."

"By your leave, Lord Gilbert," Sir Royce spoke from where he'd remained standing in the center of the chamber. "As Lady Juliana is obviously in good hands, I will withdraw now and leave you undisturbed."

Lord Gilbert's eyes brightened as he looked toward the knight. "But you must stay and share our joy, Sir Royce, and our thanks. You found my Juliana and so quickly. How did you manage it where I had failed after so many years of searching?"

Sir Royce smiled, giving a light shrug of his shoulder. "A piece of luck only, a lead when I stopped at Fontevrault to pay homage at the Lionheart's tomb. A man boasted of the ale of a certain brewer in nearby Chinon and of his beautiful, silver-haired daughter with bewitching green eyes."

"That they are." Lord Gilbert smiled proudly at Ana, then returned his gaze to the knight, "But Sir Royce, I see you have sustained wounds since last I saw you. Was your journey a difficult one?"

"It had its moments." The knight's lips slanted upward in a half-smile, his eyes brushing Ana's for the briefest of moments.

She dropped her gaze away, aware of a curious, fluttery

feeling in the pit of her stomach. When she lifted her eyes again, she found the old lord's inquisitive gaze moving between herself and Sir Royce. He smiled then and patted Ana's hand.

"The years have been long and many, and time doth change a man. Hopefully, you remember your old grandfather?" His words held a hopeful question as he shone a kindly, though expectant, smile on her.

Ana swallowed. She'd no wish to disappoint the old lord, but there was no way to avoid the truth, or even to bend it. Casting a glance to Sir Royce, she saw concern sharpening his features as though he feared what she might say.

His lips parted to intervene and speak on her behalf, but before he could do so she turned back to the aged man holding her hand.

"My lord, I must confess that my memory stretches back only to the night of the attack on Vaux," she said gently. "In truth, I remember nothing of the attack itself, nor of the hours, days, or years that came before it."

"Nothing at all?" Lord Gilbert asked, amazement filling his voice.

Ana shook her head, a great sadness welling up from a place deep in her soul, a dark place she knew to be there but dared not probe. Covering Lord Gilbert's hands with one of her own, she gazed into his faded eyes, unbidden tears brimming her own.

"I want to remember so very, very much," she admitted truthfully, her voice breaking. "But every time I try, I find only images of fire and blooded swords and of death all around me. For whatever reason, I am unable to push past that horrible night, or to reach any of the memories that lie beyond it."

She dropped her lashes, tears slipping over her cheeks.

She'd not expected this tide of emotion to overtake her. When she'd come to the tower, she expected only for the old lord to acknowledge she was unknown to him and to send her away. Not this. She bore a wound in her heart, one she kept her conscious thoughts ever turned from. But the wound ran deep, she knew, and had never truly healed. Confronting the past like this, she felt as though that wound had just split open.

"'Tis all right, Juliana," Lord Gilbert comforted. "Let us speak of happier times when you were small. I can tell you all about them, you know, and about your parents too. At Penhurst, I have stored many things that were your mother's and father's. Until we are able to travel there, I will fill you with stories—stories that will delight you. Perhaps something I say will stir your memories and breathe life into them once more. But I am content simply that you are here, my sweet Juliana. My heart overflows with such joy. You've come home to me at last."

Ana felt she was any place but home. Nor did she accept she was Lord Gilbert's lost granddaughter. Still, she couldn't bring herself to challenge his assumptions or blight his joy. Tomorrow, perhaps, would be soon enough to address those things. And if he had some proof to offer as to her identity, she would listen.

She glanced up to find Sir Royce's gaze lodged upon her, his look unreadable. As their eyes locked on each other's, Lord Gilbert took note of the knight.

"Sir Royce, the last time we met my words were harsh, if not scathing."

"But well deserved, my lord," Sir Royce returned. Ana's brows drew together as she puzzled their words. "Pray accept my deepest thanks and a debt of gratitude, Sir Royce. What will you do now that you've completed your quest and found our Juliana?"

Our Juliana? Ana's brows rose at that usage. She looked from one man to the other but seemed to be momentarily forgotten.

"I've an estate to claim in Kent, awarded me by the Lionheart," the knight was saying. "King John's counselors have been studying the grant. Once I collect the document, I will be away for Birkwell."

"There is nothing I can do to thank you enough for finding Juliana. But if I might give you a piece of advice, watch John," Lord Gilbert warned. "This youngest Plantagenet is a wily one. Best align yourself with one of the power barons. William Marshal would be my own choice. He is wise and much experienced in royal matters. He has had the fortune, or misfortune as it were, of dealing with the old king as well as most all of his sons. Whatever you decide though, keep a close eye on John."

A flourish of trumpets sounded from outside, drawing Ana's attention to the window.

"Ah, the call to dinner." Lord Gilbert smiled. "The king arrived this morn and Queen Isabella has ordered a splendid feast to be served. You'll not wish to miss it."

Ana blanched at the thought of supping with nobility or being in the presence of the royals. She knew nothing of how to behave in such circumstances and could only make a fool of herself.

"I would much prefer to take a meal in my chamber, if possible," Ana said.

"Nonsense, my child. You must be seen and presented to the king and queen as well. They are keenly interested in the outcome of Sir Royce's quest."

Ana groaned inwardly, wondering how she could possibly escape this.

"Sir Royce, you will do me the favor of accompanying Juliana to the hall, will you not?" Lord Gilbert entreated the knight. "These old legs will not carry me there, I fear. She'll need an escort and partner for dinner, someone to help her through the formalities. Besides, as you were charged with the task of finding her, 'tis most fitting you be the one to present her to the sovereigns."

Ana began to shake her head. "I wouldn't know how to act or what to say."

"The less said would be the better," Sir Royce suggested with a smile.

Ana narrowed her gaze at him.

"Exactly so," Lord Gilbert agreed brightly. "Allow Sir Royce to speak for you and follow his lead at dinner. 'Tis a simple matter."

"But am I properly dressed, will I look out of place?"

"You look ravishing, child. Isn't that so Sir Royce?" Lord Gilbert beamed.

To Ana's surprise, Sir Royce nodded in agreement.

"Indeed, my lord, but have no fear. I shall guard her well from all the swains in the hall."

Ana wavered when Sir Royce cast her a smile. Feeling Lord Gilbert give a squeeze to her hand, she returned her gaze to him.

"Go now and enjoy yourself, child. Come again on the morrow after chapel. We will break our fast together and you can tell me all about the royal feast."

As the old lord loosed his hold on Ana's fingers, she rose and started to step away. Turning back, unsure what prompted her, she bent and swiftly kissed Lord Gilbert's cheek.

"Until tomorrow," she said softly, watching a contented smile spread over his features as he settled back on the pillows.

She turned to Sir Royce and found a pensive look upon his face, his eyes studying her. Why she could not fathom.

Again, trumpets blared from without.

"My lady, if you will do me the honor . . ." The knight proffered his arm, waiting.

A quivery feeling traveled through her at the look he gave her now, grazing her senses. Ana drew a breath and, without a word, crossed to him. Laying her hand lightly atop his forearm, she allowed him to escort her from the chamber.

10

A brilliance of color struck Ana's eyes as she and Sir Royce entered the forechamber of the great hall. There, noble lords and ladies assembled, richly arrayed in silks and brocades—vivid reds, blues, greens, yellows, browns, and black. Jewels sparkled about their necks and across their fingers, furs in evidence everywhere.

But just as staggering as the sight of so much resplendence in one place was the veritable menagerie before her. Hooded falcons perched on the gloved hands of men and women alike, great hounds adhering close to their sides. Some nobles possessed rarer creatures—monkeys and exotic birds from the East, their breeds unknown to Ana. One lord held a raven. The lady beside him kept a weasel on a golden chain.

A fanfare of trumpets and drums announced some important arrival. Ana followed the gazes of the others and discovered the glittering personages of the king and queen as they swept briefly into view and entered the feasting hall.

"The lords and ladies will enter by rank now," Sir Royce informed quietly, bending toward her ear. "We shall wait to be announced and follow after."

"Announced?" Ana swallowed. "There is still time to withdraw to our chambers is there not? I mean, I do not mind taking a simple meal alone."

The knight smiled into her eyes, sending tiny shivers darting through her.

"Enjoy this night, Juliana. Few are privileged to feast

with royalty. 'Tis a moment in your life you'll never forget, and something to tell your grandchildren one day."

"Grandchildren? 'Tis rushing things a bit, do you not think?" Ana muttered, diverting her gaze to where nobles streamed into the hall. "I've not even a husband yet."

Sir Royce chuckled. "No doubt you will, fair maiden, and children aplenty."

Ana's gaze skipped to the knight, but he'd already turned away and was speaking to one of the court officials who next disappeared inside the chamber. Long minutes later, he returned, giving a nod to Sir Royce then signaling the herald at the door. As the horn blared, Sir Royce turned to Ana.

"Are you ready, my lady?"

Ana shook her head, shrinking back, her knees gone to water. But Sir Royce covered her hand where it yet rested upon his arm and drew her with him across the threshold and into the hall.

Ana felt swallowed by the sheer enormity of the room, the ceiling ascending to a great height. The walls stretched an inestimable length, and what portions were not covered by tapestries were paneled with screens, painted in colorful patterns. Beneath her feet, herbs sweetened the rushes, giving off the scents of costmary, pennyroyal and tansy as she and the knight passed over them, proceeding down the center of the hall toward the far end.

It seemed she traversed another world entirely, Ana reflected. 'Twas alien to all she'd ever known. As she and Sir Royce continued on, a low buzz arose in the hall. Stealing a glance to either side, Ana saw that the lords and ladies settled themselves at the linen-draped tables paralleling the walls. Their hunting birds poised on T perches behind them, the monkey as well. Unnervingly, Ana found the nobles' interest fastened upon herself and the knight as they bent their heads together, murmuring amongst themselves.

Ana felt Sir Royce squeeze her hand reassuringly and turned her eyes to his. He held her gaze with his until, at last, they arrived at the hall's far end. Looking up, Ana gasped softly. The king and queen smiled down from thronelike chairs upon the dais, positioned beneath a silken canopy of red and gold.

King John appeared much as she'd imagined him from descriptions she'd heard, these from the time he and his troops had passed through Chinon on their way to the royal fortress. Broad-shouldered and bearded, he possessed regular features plus the fiery hair of the Angevins. 'Twas the queen, however, who seized Ana's attention, her youth as startling as her beauty, her flaxen hair pale like Ana's, only hinting of gold rather than silver.

Beside Ana, Sir Royce bent in a deep bow toward the sovereigns. All nervousness, Ana started to bow as well. Catching herself, she attempted a curtsy, unsure how to accomplish it precisely. As she started to sink into a wobbly semisquat, a better idea struck her—to simply genuflect as ever she did before the church altar. 'Twas the nearest thing to a curtsy she could think of. Oh, why hadn't Sir Royce warned her of this? Dropping onto one knee, Ana bowed her head respectfully.

"Rise, child, rise. Let us have a look at you," the king's voice resounded, edged with amusement. "Sir Royce, I sent you on a quest little more than a fortnight ago. Am I to assume the maid you bring before us is Lord Gilbert Osborne's granddaughter?"

"Aye, Majesty. I present to you the Lady Juliana Mandeville."

Ana flinched at the knight's firm assertion, something not proven, leastwise to her own satisfaction.

"By the saints, but the maid could pass for my lady-wife's sister. Do you not think so, Isabella?"

Lifting her gaze, Ana found the youthful queen's smile settling upon her, her blue eyes brightening.

"Indeed, and I shall be delighted to make a new acquaintance of one just come from France. Where did Sir Royce find you, Lady Juliana?"

"Chinon, Majesty."

"A lovely city. 'Tis not so far from my family's lands of Angoulême," the queen said wistfully, then laid a hand on the king's arm. "My husband and I passed through Chinon recently, following our wedding, whilst on our way to England." She returned her smile to Ana. "Tomorrow we must speak more of these things. I will send for you to join my ladies in the garden."

"You are most gracious, Majesty."

As Ana began to straighten, the king leaned forward in his chair, his gaze searching the knight's bruised features.

"What is this, Sir Royce? 'Twould seem your quest was not without incident."

"True, Majesty, but I will heal."

Guilt stung Ana, while a new fear coiled in her stomach. Would the knight reveal her part in his injuries? What would be done to a simple maid who brought harm to a knight, especially one of his standing, a hero no less? But the knight made no elaboration, and the king spoke again.

"No doubt you will wish to see my counselor concerning your grant, Sir Royce. I shall instruct them to make time for you tomorrow. I saw Beckwell for myself in my recent travels, one of East Anglia's finer pieces of property, I vow."

The knight stiffened at Ana's side. She could not read his thoughts any more than she could the shuttered look he now wore. But, hadn't he told Lord Gilbert his estate lay in Kent, a place named "Birkwell," not "Beckwell"? Sir Royce offered no response, however. She could only guess at his reason. 'Twould be unwise to contradict the king before an entire hall of nobles. One might mistake it as a challenge, implying the sovereign was lying.

The king bid his jewel-encrusted goblet be filled with wine and brought to him. This done, he raised it before the noble gathering.

"Today, Lady Juliana Mandeville has been restored to her rightful place among her own. Let nothing more be said, no reminders given, of her regrettable absence these many years, or the misjudgments that caused it." His gaze strayed briefly to Sir Royce then returned to the hall. "Let us rejoice only that this tender maiden of the realm has been saved from her distress and restored to us."

Distress? Ana beheld the king somewhat dismayed. The only distress she felt was to be standing here before his royal personage and the queen's and a hall filled with nobles—that and the distress of being kidnapped from her groom's side on her wedding day.

Unaware of her thoughts, the king smiled widely, then downed a mouthful of wine and lifted his goblet once more. "Let the feast begin!" he proclaimed, full of good cheer.

As Sir Royce and Ana withdrew from where they stood before the dais, a finely robed man holding a long white wand approached them. He motioned for them to follow and led them to one of the tables nearby, at the upper end of the hall.

They stepped around several of the great dogs lying in the rushes and seated themselves, side by side. Within moments, liveried servants with towels on their arms and bearing pitchers and bowls moved among the lords and ladies. Ana followed Sir Royce's lead, washing her hands in the fragrant herbal water. Next, another of the many court officials—identified to her by Sir Royce as the almoner—led the room in grace.

Ana started as a fresh blaze of trumpets signaled a new procession. Instantly came a parade of squires bearing great platters of food and tureens and something the knight called a subtlety in the shape of a ship.

Sir Royce assisted Ana, choosing a variety of choice meats and placing them on the trencher they shared, a thickly sliced square of bread. Too, he saw that their single goblet brimmed with wine, and he broke open fresh rolls for them. These were made of a fine wheat flour, the texture delicate and light, the color snow white. Ana inhaled their tantalizing fragrance, then bit into the wondrous creation.

"Ah, 'tis Heaven itself, Sir Knight." She chewed on the delicious morsel, so different from the coarse barley and rye breads she was accustomed to eating. As she stuffed another piece of the bread into her mouth, she discovered several eyebrows raised in her directions. Ana looked back to the knight, who only smiled.

"You may wish to save some of your bread to use as a sop for the soups and sauces," he advised, offering her his own roll.

The next hour passed in a haze as endless offerings circulated about the hall—dishes of meat, fish, fowl, stews, puddings, pasties, and tarts of every kind. Ana believed she could feed the entire city of Chinon with this one feast alone.

She quickly discovered that the nobles possessed a penchant for sauces, these of sharp mustards, cream, wine, and fruit, served on most everything. Unaccustomed to their richness, she found more pleasure in sampling dishes made with rare spices—figs stuffed with eggs and cinnamon, gingered carp, and something called *pumpes*, small pork balls seasoned with almonds, mace, cloves, and dusted with sugar.

"How do you find the wine?" Sir Royce asked, watching as she took a sip and handed the goblet back to him.

"Tolerable. Barely." Ana coughed, trying to clear her throat of the drink's sediment, caught part way down. "I'd much prefer ale and would willingly make my own for the entire castle if 'twas allowed."

"Make ale? Like an ale-wife?" Lady Edith, who sat near, gave a shrill laugh, which ended in a snorting sound. "What a waggish sense of humor you have, Lady Juliana. Of course, we must not deprive the commoners of their livelihoods. After all, 'tis what gives purpose to their drab existence and is what they are best suited for." She popped one of the little pork balls into her mouth, then drew on her wine.

Ana's temper flared at the woman's superiority and callous regard for the very people she'd been raised among. Balling her hands, she started to rise, but felt Sir Royce's hand upon her thigh, pressing her back down onto the bench. He continued to hold her there, his hand heating her flesh through her gown. At the same time, he speared Lady Edith with an icy look.

"The humble man provides for your comfort, Lady Edith, and must not be disparaged. Besides, who is to say that one is not closer to God while brewing ale than ruling a nation? Care for another *pumpe*?"

The woman made a moue then turned her attention to her dinner companion and launched into a fresh topic, this on how extraordinarily elegant and accomplished the queen was. "That is, for one so young," Lady Edith clarified.

Sir Royce expelled a breath that spoke of impatience then gave his attention to the minstrels in the hall.

"Look there. Is that not Guy of Lisors?" He pointed to a man with a plume in his hat, plucking his lute as he roamed along the tables, entertaining with some verse.

Ana turned her eyes to the knight's, warmly aware of his hand still lingering upon her leg. "I hope he's not finished the verses he was composing on our journey."

"You mean the ones of us?" Sir Royce smiled, then a clouded look came into his eyes as though merely voicing the word "us" had triggered some thought, some emotion. He withdrew his hand from her thigh as though startled to find it there.

"Have you ever seen anything such as that, Lady Juliana?" He directed her attention to a troupe of dancers, one bending herself into a knot, others twirling about, creating undulating patterns in the air with long, colorful scarves.

As the knight fell silent, Ana gave her attention for a time to the jugglers and musicians delighting the diners while they feasted and chattered. Courses continued to arrive in dizzying variety, the traffic of servants, squires, and entertainers endless.

Ana nibbled on a sugared almond, allowing her gaze to travel slowly around the hall.

The lords and ladies supped and sopped and downed goblets of the unpalatable wine. The sophistication of the court ladies intrigued her, yet, like much of the conversation swirling about her, there was much artifice there. 'Twas obvious they added false pieces to their hair. Few could possess such abundance, Ana deemed, and the color of the extra pieces often did not match the owner's own tresses. More curious was the white powder and vermilion tints the ladies used on their faces, giving them pallid complexions and bright cheeks.

One could easily become seduced by the extravagances she found here—furs and jewels, silks and velvets, tapestries and fine furnishings at every turn. Gold plate gleamed upon the cupboard standing left of the dais, and the food was bounteous. Yet as Ana looked about, she found the dogs gnawing on bones in the rushes, one even rising long enough to relieve himself. Intermittently, the falcons would flap their wings, striving to keep their balance, and the monkey threw grapes at the diners.

Upon the dais, the queen appeared outwardly devoted to King John, yet she was a flirtatious creature, Ana noted, especially with the other great nobles who shared the royal table. Elsewhere in the hall, she saw secretive looks exchanged and private touches meant to go unnoticed.

'Twas a world apart, both wonderful and appalling, Ana thought, the experience one of extremes. Even if she were Lady Juliana Mandeville, a noble maid and heiress, she questioned whether this was truly a life to be desired. 'Twas communal, lacking of privacy, having its own strict codes and mores. Then too, women were ever used as pawns to further men's authority, given in wedlock to secure alliances to the most powerful or highest bidder. 'Twas a life of refinement, comfort, and privilege, yet one without freedom, leastwise for a woman.

Ana chewed on her lip. Perhaps that judgment was unfair. Women were granted little license anywhere, be it in a hovel or in a castle. Still, she believed she might enjoy more freedom as a townswoman than as a cosseted noble lady. Certainly, she would in the matter of love.

A pretty tune reached Ana's ears as a minstrel strolled slowly along the length of the table. Her heart picked up its beat. She recognized the tune, but could not place it. Still, she held certain she'd heard it before.

A sudden pain stabbed at Ana's temple. She recoiled, pressing her fingers there. As she did, a woman's face flashed before her mind's eyes—a woman with golden hair and wide arching brows. In the next breath, the image was gone.

"Lady Juliana, is aught the matter?"

Ana looked up and found the knight studying her.

"I'm not sure," she said in a shaky whisper, glancing about her. The lords and ladies were presently engaged with the antics of the court fool, laughing at his exaggerated lunacy.

Ana reached for the goblet and took a generous drink, then grimaced at the taste. Wiping her mouth with the back of her hand, she drew a sharp look from Lady Edith.

Trumpets sounded anew, causing Ana to wince. Yet another procession commenced at the lower end of the hall. There, four men entered carrying an enormous pie encased in a pastry *coffyn*. 'Twas so large, the men bore it on a litter, formed of two planks suspended between them and braced on their shoulders.

Conveying the pie to the center of the chamber, they lowered it onto a table with great ceremony. Again the horn sounded as one of the men, appearing to be of senior rank, drew out his knife and made a large, X-shaped incision in the crust's domed top. Within seconds, the pastry flew into bits as a host of live birds escaped the pie and flapped furiously up toward the ceiling.

Clamoring from their benches, the nobles hastened to free their falcons of their jesses and hoods and release them. To Ana's horror the hawks swept into the rafters and attacked the birds. A great screeching and crying ensued overhead, whilst bird blood rained down on those below. Ana scrambled from the bench, appalled as blood pelted her hair and gown, streaking the fabric red.

The hounds barked excitedly as the chaos continued in the rafters, pouncing on any wounded or lifeless birds that plummeted to the rushes. Inconceivably, the people laughed and cheered the spectacle, finding great amusement in the barbaric game, even as they continued to be spattered with blood. Ana fled, stumbling across the rushes and ran gracelessly on.

"Lady Juliana!" Sir Royce's voice sounded directly behind her.

Ana hastened toward the doors, slowing not a whit. But in an instant, the knight's fingers closed on her upper arm and he whirled her around against him. Without thinking, Ana pummeled his chest and struggled against his strength.

"Let me go! I don't belong here, I don't *want* to belong here. 'Tis your fault I'm here at all. Take me back to Chinon. Take me back!" she cried desperately, fighting down tears.

"And break Lord Gilbert's heart?"

When she continued to hit at his chest, he gave her a firm shake then drew her aside for a measure of privacy.

"Listen to me. Despite this night, and no matter who you believe Lord Gilbert to be—your grandfather or a deluded old man—he is failing. That much I learned from the queen's physick, before we went to his chambers. Leave and you will quicken him to his grave."

Ana wrenched free of the knight's hold and rubbed at her arms, then swiped at a wetness she felt on her face.

"You trap me with words and sentiments for someone I do not know." She hurled the accusation, trembling where she stood. "I've no wish to be a lady, especially if it means being present to such vile practices."

Sir Royce took a step toward her, and she saw now how his own clothes were spattered too.

"Juliana, I was unprepared for this, as well, though I've heard of such things."

He reached a hand toward her, but Ana shook her head and fell back a pace. She dropped her gaze to her beautiful rose-colored gown, befouled with blood.

"Look at me, my fine kirtle, 'tis ruined. Ruined, like so much else in my life." Tears spilled over her cheeks and wet the fabric, mingling with the stains. "Blood does not come out, you know. Some things in life are impossible to repair."

Ana withdrew into herself falling silent, and, at last, allowed the knight to conduct her back to her chamber.

11

The knight moves two spaces forward, then one to either side."

"Two spaces forward, but in any direction you say?" Ana concentrated on the checkered board, her brows knitted.

"That's right, like so." Lord Gilbert placed the horseman on a red square.

"'Tis very beautiful." Ana admired the small marble carving, plucking it up and turning it in her fingers.

Lord Gilbert chuckled. "In the midst of a game, dear child, I must caution you to leave the gaming pieces in position or you will gain your partner's ire."

"Oh yes, of course." Embarrassed, Ana quickly replaced the little knight on the square.

"'Tis no matter, Juliana. We play only a practice game, and I fear I've wearied you long enough with its many rules for one day." He gestured for his servant, Godric, to take the board and pieces away.

The man was not the same as the quarrelsome one with the purplish nose whom she'd encountered yesterday. Instead, Godric was large and solidly built, having sand-colored hair and a passive nature.

"I would have that item you laid out for me earlier," Lord Gilbert called after the servant, retreating across the chamber.

"Chess is a most interesting game, my lord." Ana smiled, bringing the lord's attention back to her. "Thank you for your patience with me. 'Tis very complex."

"*Very,* for everyone, child. 'Tis meant to be so. Sharpens the mind." He tapped a finger to his forehead. "Ah, here we are."

Lord Gilbert reached out to accept a small bundle wrapped in blue silk from Godric. In turn, he placed it in Ana's hands.

"Open it, child, open it," he urged, his voice bright with excitement as though he were a young boy.

His enthusiasm catching, Ana fingered the lustrous silk, her curiosity rising. Feeling something hard and flat within the folds, something having little thickness, she began to unwind the fabric. A creamy object appeared. 'Twas an elegant ivory comb, its spine carved with a profusion of flowers.

"How beautiful," Ana voiced softly as she turned it over in her hand.

Lord Gilbert's gaze remained firmly fixed on her. "Do you remember it, Juliana?"

"No, not really. Should I?"

"'Twas your mother's, the Lady Alyce. She would comb your hair with it each evening before you went to bed, and she would sing soothing songs, so you'd sleep peacefully and no nightmares would plague you."

Ana drew a finger over the comb's delicate carving. "And did little Juliana have nightmares?" she asked, curious.

"At times, but Lady Alyce and your faithful nursemaid, Aldis, were ever near and would chase them away."

Aldis? Ana sensed she knew that name.

"Of course, there are other things of your mother's at Penhurst. Your father's too. I've preserved it all. As soon as I can manage it, we will travel there. Penhurst will one day be yours. 'Tis nothing so grand as Wallingford, of course, but a fine estate all the same. You once loved your visits there as a young girl." He smiled, then gestured to the piece in her hands. "Keep the comb with you, Juliana. Perhaps 'twill awaken some memory when you least expect it."

"But I couldn't."

"Indeed, you must." He stretched to pat her hand. "Humor me, Juliana. 'Twill give me great pleasure knowing 'tis with you."

Ana held no wish to take the comb, knowing it to be so precious to the old lord, but at his continued insistence she relented.

"Thank you. I promise to take special care of it." Wrapping the blue silk about the comb, she then fitted it into her purse, suspended from her corded belt.

Strains of music drifted through the window, rising, it seemed, from directly below the tower. As a young man's voice sounded, Ana realized with a ripple of surprise that he sang words of longing and unrequited love.

"I believe you have an admirer." Lord Gilbert smiled. "The lad sounds to have been sorely wounded by Venus's arrow." He gave a small laugh. "Ah, to be young."

Her interest piqued, Ana rose and crossed to the window.

"Take care not to encourage these love-smitten swains," Lord Gilbert advised in a light but earnest tone. "Enjoy their suits and flatteries, but take care in how you respond. They have been known to go to strange and ridiculous excesses—sometimes dangerous—to win a lady's attentions. 'Tis the plague of 'courtly love' that afflicts our young men these days."

"Courtly love? I'm not sure what that is exactly."

Ana gazed down on the youth below, then smiled. Instantly, he ceased his song, sinking to the ground as his hand moved over his heart. For a moment, she feared he had collapsed of some malady, but next saw he was well and smiling, staring up at her with great calf eyes.

The clash of metal and movement on the other side of the curtain wall jerked Ana's attention away. From the tower, she could easily see over the ramparts to a space of open ground on the other side of the wall. This she understood to be the lists where the knights honed their skills. Indeed she could see a dozen men gathered there now, challenging themselves and each other at varied tasks.

Almost at once, she spied Sir Royce. He stood tall and bare chested, his muscled frame disturbingly magnificent as he wielded his sword against that of his younger opponent. Ana thought the latter to be one of the squires she'd seen in the hall last night. Surely, he was no match for Sir Royce. Presumably, the knight only tested him.

As though he could feel her gaze, Sir Royce turned his eyes briefly toward the tower, spotting Ana at the window. She smiled widely and lifted her hand in a wave, wondering if he'd purposely sought her there. But when his attention lingered a moment too long, his young partner bested him, jabbing the blunt end of his sword into the knight's stomach to claim a win.

Ana gasped, falling back a pace from the window. She continued to look out for a moment, assuring Sir Royce had sustained no injury. Satisfied, she then gazed out over Wallingford and all she could see from her vantage. 'Twas a grand place, but so foreign to her in every way.

Of a sudden, the events of last night flooded back in all their splendor and horror. Ana bowed her head, sighing as she remembered how she'd beat upon Sir Royce's chest in her frenzy to escape the hall.

"Is aught the matter, child?" Lord Gilbert called, worry creasing his voice.

Ana withdrew from the window and slowly returned to the chair beside his bed. "Last night, toward the end of the feasting, a great pie was brought into the hall. It contained live birds."

"I can guess the rest," Lord Gilbert grunted, sounding none too pleased.

"'Twas horrible. I fled the hall and disgraced myself in the eyes of the others, but I could not bear to stay."

"Poor child. I wish I could have foreseen that and spared you. I should have, I suppose. Our king is an avid hunter, and I'd not be surprised if the queen arranged the spectacle for his delight."

"Everyone seemed to enjoy it, the lords and ladies alike." She pulled at her hands, a nervous gesture.

"Not everyone I'm sure, and today the court ladies will be complaining over their ruined gowns. The laundresses will never be able to remove the stains."

"I know," Ana uttered, saddened to think of her own gown, having no hope it could be restored.

"Let us speak of happier things, shall we?" Lord Gilbert cheered, patting her hand. "I've engaged a personal maid for you, Luvena is her name. She is—or, rather, *was*—Lady Edwina Hornstead's maid, who assures the woman is of excellent character and talent."

"Am I to understand Lady Edwina discharged the maid from her own service to attend me?" Ana asked perplexed.

"Lady Edwina confided only that she desired a maid with more height." He huffed a laugh. "'Tis curious is it not, but I did not quibble. 'Tis difficult to find a maid with Luvena's recommendations. Her Majesty vouched for the woman as well. I employed the maid unseen, I fear, but if you find objection to her, you are to tell me at once and we will find another more suited."

"My lord, you are all kindness, but as I've never required a maid before, I cannot see how I shall need one now."

"I believe you will find that you will and very quickly.

Besides, 'twill be good for you to have such a companion to depend upon. Castle life, at times, can be very impersonal."

Ana could offer no argument there.

Lord Gilbert shifted against his pillows. "Now, I've engaged several tutors to instruct you in a number of areas. You will be overseeing Penhurst, and likely other estates in your lifetime. 'Twould be wise to know the basics of reading and ciphering, so no one may mislead you in important matters."

He continued on before Ana could voice a single word. "You will also need training in the running of a castle and its servants, and be given the refinements expected of a noble lady—music, painting, needlework, of course. Your diction could use a little polishing, if you will forgive me for saying so. Do you think archery would interest you? Many ladies enjoy it as a pastime."

Ana wished to object but found herself laughing instead, overwhelmed by the lord's generosity. He certainly held her interests at heart. On the other hand, the matter of her identity had yet to be resolved. She couldn't let Lord Gilbert deceive himself by continuing to think she was his granddaughter. But how could she broach the subject without breaking his heart? Sir Royce had been right in that.

Ana was still mulling her thoughts when a knock sounded at the door. When Godric opened it, a dark-haired page stepped through the portal and bowed from the waist. He appeared to be all of eight.

"Queen Isabella requests Lady Juliana to join her in the garden. I am to escort her there," he said importantly, his little chest puffed out.

Lord Gilbert gave Ana a nod and smiled. "Go along, my dear. Mustn't keep the queen waiting."

Ana reached out and squeezed his hand. "I'll return later, I promise."

"Better still, I'm feeling much invigorated since your return, Juliana. I believe I can abide being carried down to the hall for dinner. We shall dine together this night," he proclaimed happily. "I shall join you there."

"I look forward to it, my lord." Ana gave a bow of her head then followed the page from the chamber.

Lord Gilbert drummed his fingers on the bed. "Godric, go to the window to see if you can determine what interested my granddaughter so."

Following his bidding, the servant traversed the chamber and gazed out on the ward below.

"I would guess the knights working out on the lists might have drawn her interest," Godric observed.

'Twould be natural, I suppose." Lord Gilbert pulled at his chin. "She's a healthy young woman, after all. Is there anyone there you recognize?"

Godric turned back to the window, staring intently outside. "There is the knight who arrived with Lady Juliana, Sir Royce de Warrene. He has just finished with one of the squires and is gathering up his tunic to leave the lists. It appears he bears some injury."

Lord Gilbert's eyebrows rose at that. "You can see his bruises from this distance?"

"Nay, my lord, not bruises. Sir Royce's forearm is bound from wrist to elbow as though wounded there."

Lord Gilbert pondered that, thinking too of the cut over the knight's brow and what must have been a much more extensive bruise over his face.

'Twould seem Sir Royce and Juliana's journey from Chinon was more perilous than they gave me to know."

Royce toweled off his chest as he quit the lists then pulled on his tunic. As he passed through the gate into the inner ward he spied Juliana following one of the pages across the courtyard. They headed in the direction of the gardens behind the keep. 'Twould seem the queen had not forgotten the maid, he thought with some pleasure.

He'd taken no more than three strides when a young man with a cap of curly blond hair darted across the court-yard in ardent pursuit of Juliana. Skidding to a halt in front of her, he dropped on one knee and offered her a small cluster of pink campion.

God's teeth, don't take it. Royce ground his mental teeth as he watched. *The pup will think you accept his suit, and thus him-self. Don't touch it.*

Oblivious to his thoughts, Juliana smiled her angelic smile and, taking the flowers, lifted them to her nose. The swain looked stunned at first, then overjoyed. Kissing the hem of her gown, he leaped to his feet and skipped away in a fit of ecstasy.

Royce simmered. Glancing back to the maid he found her blinking after the fool, as if wondering what all the fuss was about. Then she turned, calmly no less, and continued on, trailing the page escorting her until both were out of sight.

Royce ground his teeth, his real teeth this time. He would need to have a talk with the maid—a very long talk—and inform her of the subtler customs and mannerisms of court life. As for the pasty-faced stripling who danced across the yard, Royce had a mind to escort him to the lists and take some of the curl out of that mop of his. He looked like the bookish type who could benefit from a little "knightly" instruction.

Lucklessly, he could not spare the time. He was due to speak with the king's counselor. Despite the king's words last night, Royce had been put off this morn and told to re-turn in three hours' time. Even once he settled his affairs, he had no time to search out the lad. There was another matter of import he must see to, one concerning Juliana.

Ana followed the page's lead through an iron gate and into a walled garden attached to the great keep. She recognized it at once as the same garden that was visible from her chamber window.

Fruit trees lined the inner perimeter, their leaves turned to gold and their bounty gone, excepting a few crab apples that lingered. Thrushes rummaged for berries in the low hedge that lined the path, pausing at times to drive away a pair of redwings who sought to thieve the treasures.

Arriving at the center of the garden, Ana came upon the queen and her noble companions seated before a large, ornate fountain. The women gathered around a tapestry, stretched on an oaken frame, plying their needles as they spoke of some matter amongst themselves. Nearby, a female harpist played a soft melody, her long fingers caressing the strings as if a lover.

Ana dropped into a deep curtsy before the queen, one she'd practiced after observing the ladies in the hall last night. 'Twas still imperfect, she new, but at least she managed it without falling on her backside.

Queen Isabella paused in her stitching and turned. "Welcome Lady Juliana. Rise and join us." She looked to her companions. "I'm sure you all recall our dear Juliana from her presentation at the feast last night."

The three nodded in unison. Ana could only wonder if they remembered her from the scene she made in the hall, beating upon Sir Royce's chest.

"This is Lady Blythe, Lady Arietta, and Lady Mertise," the queen introduced the others.

Lady Blythe, a round and dimpled woman, smiled with small bright eyes and scooted to one side. "There is room on the bench beside me, Lady Juliana. You can help me work the birds and vines."

No sooner did Ana seat herself than Lady Blythe handed her a needle and a measured strand of brownish-red wool. Ana placed the bouquet of campion on her lap and, with some effort, forced the bulky thread through the eye of the needle.

Ill-at-ease, Ana moistened her lips. She knew how to sew a straight line, of course, but as she surveyed the tapestry she realized these ladies were embroidering with a great variety of intricate stitches and with far more skill than she possessed. Drawing a breath, Ana applied her needle to the canvas, hoping she would not ruin the piece.

"We were just discussing Andre the Chaplain's *Treatise on Love*," the queen informed Ana, picking up the conversation. "He writes that marriage should be no barrier to love. What do you think, Lady Juliana?"

Ana blenched to be asked her opinion by the queen and to voice it before these noble ladies.

"I-I agree, totally," she forced the words past her lips. To her relief, the other ladies smiled unanimously. Emboldened, Ana pressed on.

"There is no reason not to love. My foster parents, for example, share a great love between them. There should ever be love between a husband and a wife. 'Tis the greatest happiness of all."

The women remained silent, Lady Mertise raising her brow.

"I believe Lady Juliana misunderstands," Lady Arietta submitted to the others, then turned to Ana. "The *Treatise* states, 'Marriage is no real excuse for not loving.' Chaplain Andre does not refer to love between a married couple, but states that marriage is no impediment for a husband or wife to find love with another."

"Outside the bounds of marriage?" Ana's jaw dropped open.

Queen Isabella caught the gazes of the other three and smiled gently. "Lady Juliana rightly leads us to the very proper topic of whether love can exist between a husband and wife. What say you of that, ladies?"

The three exchanged glances, avoided Ana's gaze, and looked back to the queen.

"Well, yes," Lady Mertise began. "The *Treatise* does say the only ones unable to know true love—as it ideally exists between a man and a woman—are the very young, those too old, the blind, and those possessing an excess of passion."

Ana looked at the woman, dumfounded. "I understand the first, but none of the rest."

"The old are incapable because they lose their 'natural heat,'" Lady Blythe offered.

"And the blind cannot see the lover's beauty on which their mind can then reflect," Lady Arietta said quickly, then added, "So Andre the Chaplain writes."

"And one who has an excess of passion is its slave and therefore 'cannot be held in the bonds of love,'" Lady Mertise quoted. "They are ruled only by their lowest nature and thus cannot appreciate the 'mysteries of love's realm.'"

Horse apples, Ana thought. Is there any love more deep or beautiful than that yet shared by two aging people after many long years, or than among those who saw with their hands and minds and hearts in a way far more profound than with their eyes? As to the last point, she agreed with the chaplain. Lust was not love.

"But even if love can exist between a husband and wife, it has naught to do with the contracting of a marriage," Lady Arietta observed. "Naturally, one hopes affection will grow in time. True love does in rare cases—very rare."

An impulse suddenly possessed Ana to give her head a sound shake and clear it of these women's misbegotten notions. 'Twould do little good, she knew. Ana decided to attempt a different approach.

"But what of marrying for love's sake?"

"For love's sake?" Lady Mertise appeared genuinely shocked by the suggestion. "Oh, no, no, dispel the thought, Lady Juliana. 'Twould be risky and naive to make a choice based upon feelings alone."

"True," Lady Arietta interjected. "Love would not survive, if the choice was poorly made, particularly if done so in the heat of fickle passion."

"Better that cooler heads prevail, for there is far more to consider," Lady Blythe added. "Marriage is an alliance, a joining of houses, the future of one's blood line and its security."

Ana started to take exception to the women's words, then realized, to her dismay, how she'd used a similar measure in choosing a husband. Though she'd initially felt an attraction for Gervase, and a deep fondness for him, she'd accepted his proposal in greater part for the security he could provide her. Her affection for Gervase had increased since then, and she felt confident 'twould continue to do so. She was committed to being a good wife to Gervase, though in all honesty, a part of her heart would always belong to another.

The cheerful banter of male voices filled the garden as the king and his escort entered the gate. At once, the queen rose and went to greet him, leaving behind her ladies, who quickly moved off their benches and dropped to deep curtsies.

Ana stole a glance at the royal couple, marveling again at their difference in age and at the extreme youth of the queen. It struck her then how Queen Isabella had remained silent throughout the ladies' discussion of marriage.

Ana could only wonder what the child queen thought on the subject. Isabella was still a new bride, her marriage a hasty arrangement. Rumor had it that King John had been struck with Love's arrow at the first sight of the heiress of Angoulême. But what of Isabella? Did she embrace the match? Or was it the crown she espoused more?

As the couple continued to speak, the king motioned for the ladies to rise. Ana resettled herself on the bench, at the same time catching sight of several young men peering over the hedge, one with a patch over his eye.

"I see Walter Forshay pursues you still, Lady Arietta," Lady Blanche said teasingly as she drew her thread through the tapestry.

"He's not the only admirer in the garden, I see," Lady Mertise remarked, glancing toward the fruit trees. "I believe Lady Juliana has a suitor as well."

Ana started to look past her shoulder but Lady Arietta shook her head in warning then speared her needle through the canvas. "Ignore them. They need no encouragement from us."

Ana turned forward again, found her companions busily working the tapestry, and gave her attention to the figure of the bird, looking much the worse for her stitches.

"Did you hear who is to arrive today?" Lady Blythe broke the silence a moment later. "Lady Sibylla, the Countess Linford."

"'Tis no secret why *she's* hurried apace to Wallingford," Lady Arietta said provocatively, drawing a titter of laughter from the others.

"Word must have reached her that Sir Royce has returned," Lady Mertise joined in. "She's been staying at Castle Rotherford, nearby. 'Tis one of her own, of course, but 'tis obvious she's been laying in wait for his return to

Court."

Again, knowing smiles were exchanged around the tapestry.

Ana canted her head. "The countess seeks Sir Royce?"

"Seeks?" Lady Blythe huffed a laugh. *"Pursues* is more like it."

Lady Arietta caught Ana's gaze. "None of us here were present at Westminster Palace when Sir Royce first arrived and was then sent to find you. However, Lady Sibylla was. She's since made it well known to those ladies seeking a husband that her mind is set on the hero of Acre and Ascalon."

"'Twas no less than a warning, everyone else should keep their distance of the knight," Lady Blythe added, round eyed.

"Can she do that?" Ana puzzled their words. "Does not the countess have her own husband?"

"She is a widow."

"Again."

"But she is very powerful."

"With each new husband, she's improved her station, acquiring more titles, more land, more wealth," Lady Arietta apprised. "She's exceedingly influential with the court officials as well."

"No surprise there." Lady Mertise sniffed.

"How many husbands has she had?" Ana drew her gaze over the others.

"Three, all buried."

"But why set her eyes on Sir Royce? Forgive me for saying so, but his own rank is inferior to her own."

"Marriage to Lady Sibylla would raise him to a station equal to hers. But, as to the countess's reasons, 'tis a bit of a mystery."

"What mystery?" Lady Mertise sniped, interrupting Lady

187

Blythe. "The countess is hot-blooded and her last husband was ancient and crusty. Sir Royce has proven his prowess on the battlefield and is exceedingly handsome. I suspect she wants a champion who can defend her lands as well as be a strong, lunging ram in her bed!"

Ana drove her needle into her finger at Lady Mertise's words. Thrusting her finger into her mouth, she sucked on it as the embarrassing image continued to play in her mind.

Seeing the queen was withdrawing from the garden with the king, Ana decided to depart as well. She wished to hear no more of the women's gossip.

"I best see to this. The needle went deep," she muttered, using her finger as a pretext to excuse herself.

As Ana stood to her feet, the cluster of pink campion spilled from her lap and rolled onto the ground. Seemingly from nowhere, one of the young men haunting the garden rushed forward and snatched up the bouquet.

"Ah sweet flowers that have graced my lady's lap, guarding Love's Gate!" he proclaimed loudly, slipping the bunch beneath his tunic and against his heart. With that, he hastened away.

"'Love's Gate?' Ana looked to the others. "Nay, do not tell me. I fear I can guess his meaning."

Retiring from the garden, Ana left the other ladies to their stitching and headed back to her chamber in the keep.

Ana's eyes widened. "You are Luvena?"

"Luvena Little," the miniature woman stated proudly in her high-pitched voice, drawing herself up to the full of her height.

Ana could not help but stare. Luvena stood no more than four feet high, perfectly proportioned and neatly clothed in a fawn-colored kirtle and white headdress. Regaining herself, Ana sank onto a chair to be more at eye level with the maid.

Luvena crossed her little hands, waiting patiently for her new mistress's directions, but Ana had none.

"Does my height concern you, Lady Juliana?" Luvena asked pointedly, her gaze steady upon Ana. "You will find I am as skilled and experienced a lady's maid as any who are taller, and am a devoted one as well."

"I'm sure you are, Luvena. You are recommended most highly. However, I have never had anyone attend me before." Ana's heart sank a little. "I do not know what message you might have received from Lord Gilbert concerning me, but I know nothing of being a noble lady."

Luvena tipped her head, her small lips turning up in a compassionate smile. "That is why I am here, Lady Juliana. You may trust me to see to your needs and to guide you as very best I can."

Ana gazed in wonder at the little maid, a warm joy spreading through her. She sensed she'd just found more than a maid or mentor, but a true friend at Court.

"Thank you, Luvena. I am most grateful, truly."

Three raps sounded at the door, attracting their attention. Luvena bustled to open it, then returned with her arms filled with rose-colored cloth.

"'Tis your gown, my lady, and such a pretty one."

"It has been cleaned already? The castle laundresses are quite efficient are they not? I sent it to them only last night."

"I've never known them to be that efficient," Luvena commented, unfolding the gown.

Ana was unsure she could bear to look upon it. Surely, 'twas hopelessly stained. But, as Luvena opened the gown to its full length, Ana gazed in astonishment. It bore not a single blemish, the cloth as good as new.

12

When Ana arrived in the forechamber of the great hall, she found Lord Gilbert already present. He sat apart from the other nobles on a portable chair, leaning heavily upon two canes. Godric attended him as did a second man. Ana guessed the two to be of some relation, owing to the identical coloring of their hair and similarity of features.

As she headed toward Lord Gilbert, Ana realized he appeared exceedingly fatigued. Plainly, he'd overexerted himself in coming to the hall. Anxious, she hastened to his side.

"My lord, you look pale. Perhaps you should return to your bed."

"Nay, child. A little tired is all. 'Tis to be expected. Perhaps, I should have sent Renfeld away this afternoon."

"Renfeld? The little man with the purple nose?"

"Aye, the same. He is an assistant to the queen's physick."

"He didn't bleed you, did he? Tell me he did not."

"He believed 'twould renew me for the evening if he rid me of some of the bad humors that plague me."

Ana quickly felt Lord Gilbert's head and hands and found them to be unnaturally cool. "I fear the man has caused you more ill than good. You mustn't let him bleed you again. He drains your very life away."

"Dear Juliana, you worry for naught. 'Tis the most modern curative medicine offers. 'Tis perfectly safe."

"I am not so trusting as you. Pray, do not let the man Renfeld near you again with his knives."

Lord Gilbert smiled. "How you remind me of your mother, Alyce. She, too, was strong minded. As you wish, I will not be bled unless 'tis absolutely necessary."

Ana straightened and looked to the lord's two manservants. "Godric, you and—" She paused, not knowing the other man's name.

"Brodric, m'lady. He is my cousin," the servant informed.

Ana hesitated at the name, then acknowledged Brodric with a nod. "Promise me, you'll not allow the royal physicians to perform any procedure on his lordship that he does not desire." Her gaze moved between the two men.

"We never would, m'lady." Godric looked wounded that she considered they might.

"Just like Alyce," Lord Gilbert chuckled. "Ah, look there. I see Sir Royce has taken my advice. He speaks with the Earl of Pembroke, William Marshal."

Ana spied Sir Royce on the other side of the chamber conversing with a distinguished looking man with a full head of white hair and a flowing mustache. She shifted her gaze back to the knight then allowed it to travel slowly down his length. He wore the same rich crimson tunic and black chasusses he'd worn at Dover when he stole her breath away. Even now, she felt a strange stirring inside her and a warm tingling in her breasts.

A fluttery movement drew Ana's eye and she next discovered Lady Blythe waving a square of red silk, trying to capture her attention. As Ana looked to her, Lady Blythe twitched her head to the right, as though alerting her to something there.

Curious, Ana glanced to find what might be of interest. Instantly, she discovered the assembly of nobles parting and the most elegant court lady she'd ever seen stepping into view.

"Ah, the Countess Linford," Lord Gilbert observed beside her. "I see Lady Sibylla has cast her spell over the chamber, as ever she does when she makes an appearance. Of course, 'tis likely the ladies do not welcome her presence so eagerly as do their lords." He chuckled.

Ana found, just as the others, she could scarce pull her gaze from the countess. Lady Sibylla commanded every eye in the room. Her hair was black as a raven's wing, woven with strands of pearls into a single thick braid that draped over one shoulder and down to her hips. Her gown was of a lustrous sapphire brocade, tightly laced and form revealing. While the sleeves of her undertunic fit her arms snugly to the wrists, those of her outer kirtle were cut wider, the fabric dropping in long points from beneath the elbow to the hem of her gown. A wide collar of gold set with fine gems gleamed at the countess's throat, as did the many rings upon her fingers. Added to this, an airy veil drifted in layers from atop her head, secured in place by a gold coronet.

As Lady Sibylla continued to claim the attention of all present, her great dark eyes roamed the gathering. Within seconds her gaze came to settle on Sir Royce and the Earl of Pembroke. Their interest, too, fixed upon her person. Lady Sibylla's lips lifted in a smile as she nodded in greeting to Sir Royce. Ana thought the woman looked much like a predator marking its prey.

The familiar flourish of horns announced the approach of the king and queen. As the nobles bowed and scraped, Ana observed how the countess sank into a deep curtsy with enviable grace. She held the position, eyes cast down, until the royals passed. Then, rising in one fluid motion, she turned and moved purposefully toward Sir Royce.

To Ana's surprise, the knight appeared oblivious to the countess's approach. He'd spied Lord Gilbert and now his eyes shifted to Ana's, fastening his gaze on hers. Sir Royce smiled warmly, as if pleased to find her and Lord Gilbert present. With that, he began to make his way across the chamber, directly toward them. Halfway across, Lady Sibylla stepped in his path, intercepting him.

Ana returned her attention to Lord Gilbert as Godric braced him upward, helping him to gain his feet. Brodric moved swiftly to collapse the portable chair and take it up, then offered his support to the old lord as well.

Ana slowed her pace to that of Lord Gilbert's as he shuffled forward on his canes, assisted by the two servants. She worried at the great effort he spent with each step, that the strain would weaken him further. But as they moved toward the doors, she saw him nodding right and left to this lord and that.

"Good evening to you Lord Shelton, Lady Bertrade," he said in greeting. "Have you met my granddaughter, Juliana? Ah, Sir Humphrey, do you see who I have here? My daughter, Alyce's child, is she not a beauty?" Lord Gilbert beamed with pride and joy.

Seeing his unbounded happiness, Ana dismissed all thought of urging him to return to his chamber. How could she deny him this moment?

"Lord Gilbert, you are looking much renewed and possibly two decades younger," a rich and familiar voice sounded to her right.

Ana turned to discover Sir Royce joining them, the countess at his side.

"'Tis my Juliana who has swept away the cobwebs of the years." Lord Gilbert settled a glowing smile on her. "She has the most astounding effect on a man."

Royce's gaze turned to Ana. "Indeed she does," he said congenially, his hand moving to rub at the scab over his brow.

Ana dropped her gaze away and studied her toes, trying

to ignore the guilt that pricked at her conscience.

"So, Sir Royce, this is the child you were sent to find." Lady Sibylla stepped forward, the scent of roses drifting about her. "Did you truly give her over to . . ? Oh, but the king forbids we speak of Lady Juliana's lamentable past, I am told."

Perplexed by her words, Ana met the countess's assessing gaze. Why did she feel as though those dark eyes were avidly dismantling her piece by piece?

"Lord Gilbert, your granddaughter's return must fill you with immense pleasure." The countess turned her thin smile on him. "Allow me to celebrate your good fortune with you. You both must join us at table in the upper hall where the maid can be seen by all."

Us? Ana wondered. Hadn't Lady Sibylla arrived unescorted? Glancing to the countess, she saw her extend her hand to Sir Royce, waiting expectantly for him to proffer his arm. He stole a sideways glance to Ana and Lord Gilbert, then gallantly complied.

Ana held the couple in sight, as she and Lord Gilbert followed them into the feasting hall. Tonight all eyes seemingly fixed on the two—the knight, tall and insufferably handsome, and the countess beside him, regal in bearing and bewitchingly beautiful. Ana's gaze strayed to Lady Sibylla's long fingers, laying atop Sir Royce's arm, and thought of talons poised to sink into his flesh.

At last they arrived at one of the tables at the fore of the hall, near to the dais and the king and queen. With the help of his two servants, Lord Gilbert settled himself toward the table's end. Ana took her place beside him, while opposite them, Lady Sibylla assumed a seat, claiming Sir Royce as her dinner partner.

With the trumpeting of horns, the customary washing of hands began, followed by grace, led by the almoner. Course upon course began to flow into the hall, accompanied by much bustling back and forth of servants and officials. Wine flowed, meats were broken and sauced, bread bowls filled with stews, and a new and marvelous subtlety displayed, this one in the shape of a horse.

Dinner passed pleasantly enough, for which Ana was grateful. It did not slip her attention, however, that the countess skillfully controlled the conversation and monopolized Sir Royce's attention. Yet, despite her manipulations, the knight proved himself adept at including everyone at the table in the flow of discussion.

During supper, Sir Royce saw to the countess's needs, much as he had to Ana's last night when they'd shared a trencher. Ana, in turn, attended Lord Gilbert as he required both canes to lean upon and prop himself up. Attentively, Ana selected items from the many courses and held the goblet for Lord Gilbert whenever he wished to drink. She quickly found he preferred soups and dishes with soft meats, especially *blankmanger*—a sweetened dish of chicken paste and rice, cooked in almond milk. Of this, they happily consumed two helpings together, and it pleased Ana to see the dear man so enjoy himself.

As the meal progressed, Ana felt Sir Royce's gaze straying to her time and again. He watched her, and Lady Sibylla watched him. Lord Gilbert watched them all.

As the last course was cleared away, someone called for a round dance. Many a lord and lady rose from their seats and hastened to take their places in the center of the hall. "Juliana, you should join in the merriment," Lord Gilbert prodded. "Sir Royce, you will accompany her, will you not?"

Before the knight could reply, Ana politely declined, unsure of the steps and too embarrassed to dance before the nobles. "I would much prefer to watch for now." She gave both men a small smile, knowing she must appear a timid mouse.

Lady Sibylla rose grandly from her place and cast an inviting look toward the knight. "You will not deny me the pleasure will you?"

Ana watched as Sir Royce followed the countess to join the ring of people that was forming. The music of flute, viol, and lute quickly filled the air, accompanied by a woman's high, clear voice. As the circle began to move to the right, the dancers stepped and turned in rhythm, sometimes stamping, sometimes leaping, everyone laughing and smiling. The dance no sooner ended than the music began anew, the next dance as vigorous as the one before. It reminded Ana of those enjoyed in Chinon at feast day celebrations, the steps not so very different.

Ana tried to follow the movements of Sir Royce and Lady Sibylla, but lost sight of them time and again. 'Twas only when the music stopped and they returned for a quick sip of wine that she saw them once more.

As the countess turned to join the next dance, an important-looking man with an irregular nose appeared before her, staying her steps. Ana recognized him to be one of the high-ranking lords. A duke of something, she could not recall the name. Lady Sibylla darted a regretful look to Sir Royce, then, unable or unwilling to deny the duke, she allowed him to lead her back to the center of the hall.

Royce gazed after the couple a moment, then visibly released a breath. He turned to Ana and smiled. She watched as the warmth of that smile spread upward, traveling from his lips to touch his eyes.

"My Lady Juliana, the dance is about to begin. Will you do me the honor and join me?"

"But the steps, I'm not sure—"

"'Tis a slow dance, and one I am sure you can easily conquer. Come, I shall show you." He held out his hand, his smile shining on her. "Trust me, Juliana."

As Ana laid her hand in the warmth of the knight's, he drew her to her feet and led her to where the couples formed a long line, stretching down the center of the hall.

Ana felt trembly inside, wholly unsure of herself. But as the music began, Sir Royce guided her through the paces, advising her in advance each time the moves required they briefly part. Ana's nervousness quickly gave way to a warm glow, rising inside her and radiating throughout her limbs. 'Twas more than the physical efforts of the dance that heated her, 'twas the spell of its movements and the way Sir Royce's eyes drank of her just now.

Royce found himself burgeoning with pride for Juliana as they moved over the floor. She was a vision of unaffected grace and beauty.

But 'twas not her comeliness that so affected him, though, undeniably, she gladdened his eyes and senses. Rather, 'twas Juliana's compassion, before all else, that struck his heart and impressed him deeply. Regardless of her resistance to him on their journey here, and all the frustrations she'd caused him, the maid had proven herself to be selfless and wholly sympathetic to Lord Gilbert.

Royce was unsure what transpired in Juliana's heart. He knew only that she'd yet to accept her identity or remember the past. Still, she responded to the old lord with great tenderness and genuine devotion. For that, Royce could easily forgive her the dangers to which she'd exposed them both in France, and the injuries he'd sustained.

His thoughts returned to the dance as the couples wove a sinuous path down the center of the hall. Many a lady clicked castanets in keeping with the rhythm. Others tossed tambur high in the air, only to catch them on a single, outstretched finger.

The couples parted and came back again, pressing their palms together as they met and turned in a small circle. Again they parted, and again they returned. Royce caught Juliana by her waist and lifted her up, as the dance dictated. Holding her there, he paced in a small circle once again.

Their gazes caught, Juliana's silvery halo of hair spilling forward, brushing his cheek and mingling with his beard as she delighted in the dance. For the moment entranced, Royce forgot himself. As he began to lower her to the floor, he drew her unconsciously toward him so that she slid down his length, their bodies grazing one another's. Unaware his lapse was not part of the dance, Juliana glided away, executing the next series of steps, her hips swaying entrancingly to the music.

On they danced, touching and turning, approaching and retreating, ending as the couples came together for a final time, their lips nearly kissing, the men poised over their ladies, as the strains of music faded away.

Royce's heart pounded in his chest, his breaths quick and shallow, as he gazed into Juliana's prettily flushed face. Realizing the other couples were beginning to separate, he gave into rash impulse and brushed his lips softly over the maiden's.

"Thank you, my lady, for a most remarkable dance."

Something moved in her emerald eyes, some thought, some emotion perhaps, as she too fought for breath. But as the music began again, she straightened and looked across the room to Lord Gilbert.

"Oh no, look at him. He is utterly exhausted, yet stays in the hall on my account. Excuse me, Sir Royce, I must convince him to retire now."

The maid left his side and hastened toward Lord Gilbert, where he sagged over his canes, valiantly propping himself up as he watched his granddaughter. Royce started to follow, thinking to lend his assistance and accompany them to the tower. Partway across the room, however, Lady Sibylla materialized in front of him.

The heavy scent of roses engulfed him as the countess drew close. "Come soon," she whispered at his ear. Pressing a small folded note into his hand, she then swept from the hall.

Royce paused only long enough to scan the paper. Refolding it, he slipped it into his sleeve and headed toward the table he'd shared with Juliana and Lord Gilbert. Glancing there, he saw that the lord's two servants had already assisted him to his feet and that the foursome was making their way toward the lower end of the chamber. He quickly joined them and offered his aid.

"'Tis most gallant of you, Sir Royce, but I can manage with Godric and Brodric here," Lord Gilbert replied, his voice roughened with fatigue.

"At least permit me to see you out of the keep and to the courtyard. There are a great number of steps to manage."

His eyes drew to Juliana as she uttered a small gasp.

"I'd forgotten about the steps. Do you think we'll need carry my lord?"

She raised wide eyes to Royce, and he saw in them a certain edginess that had more to do with his nearness than how to convey Lord Gilbert down the long flights of stairs.

"Carried? Have I a say in this?" Lord Gilbert spoke up.

Juliana smiled as she broke her gaze with Royce and leaned toward the old lord. "Not if the rest of us agree 'tis best for you."

Lord Gilbert lifted faded but merry eyes to Royce. "Just like her mother." He chuckled as they passed through the portal and departed the hall.

Ana helped Lord Gilbert as he leaned back against the bank of pillows, then pulled the blankets and fur throw around him.

"Good night, Juliana. Tomorrow, we'll take up our game of chess again, eh?"

"I look forward to it, my lord, though as a chess partner you'll not find me much of a challenge, I fear."

"You do not need to be, child. Your presence alone brings me such joy."

Moved, Ana dropped a kiss to his wrinkled cheek. "Till tomorrow then."

She started to take her leave, then reconsidering, turned back. The question she'd long been carrying remained, heavy upon her heart. Despite the headiness and excitements of this night, she longed to have an answer.

"My lord, I know you are tired, but there is something I have been wishing to ask since I arrived. Would you have strength for it now? A single question, only."

"For you my Juliana, anything."

The dear man uttered the words with such kindness, tears sprang to the back of Ana's eyes. Retracing her steps, she returned to the bed and lowered herself onto its edge.

"My question concerns the night of the attack on Vaux. I never knew the name of the squire who found me beneath the boat. He took gentle care of me and carried me with him on his horse to the next village. 'Tis my memory he served as squire to a certain knight, a Sir Hugh Fitz something. Would you know the knight's full name, or anything of the squire? I so wish to find him. If he still lives, that is."

Surprise washed over Lord Gilbert's features. "Then you do not know—?" He halted his words as if reconsidering what he should say. "The knight who led his troops to Vaux that night was Sir Hugh FitzAlan."

"*FitzAlan*, yes, that was the name Sir Royce spoke."

"Spoke? When?"

"On the steps of St. Maurice, when he put an end to my wedding to Gervase. He is the cooper I told you of this morning."

"Yes, I remember, go on."

"On the church steps, Sir Royce recounted how the squire gave me to the care of Georges and Marie in Vincelles. 'Twas in part how he identified me."

"In part?"

"That, by my coloring and features, and by this."

Ana drew the silver cross from the top of her gown, holding it out for Lord Gilbert to see.

"My squire gave me the cross just as he was leaving Vincelles." She smiled at the memory and caressed the cross with her fingers lovingly. "I cried frightfully when he began to leave, screamed really. He gave me his cross and told me God would keep me safe and to remember him in my prayers."

Ana lifted her eyes from the cross to Lord Gilbert and found his own intent upon her.

"Marie, my foster mother, told me that the squire was God's instrument of mercy that sorrowful night. Not only did he pluck me from the destruction and comfort me, but he brought me to them. They had no children, you see, and believed God led the squire to them, that they might safeguard me and raise me as their own."

Ana gazed across the room unseeing as she remembered that night.

"The squire also gave Georges and Marie his own coin, a generous amount. His kindness provided for more than our simpler needs though. With France's King Phillip leaving the country on Crusade, Georges feared Vincelles would fall prey to the ravaging barons as had Vaux. He moved the three of us into Angevin held territory, knowing King Richard had provided for its defense. Then too, Georges was able to expand his trade with the coin, enabling him to serve much of Chinon and provide well for us."

Ana feared these things might be difficult for Lord Gilbert to hear as he'd been searching for his granddaughter for years, and thought she was that lost child. But, returning her gaze to him, she discovered he appeared enthralled with her story, and so pressed on.

"As to the cross the squire gave me, 'twas our practice, at the rise and setting of each day, for the three of us to pray for the good squire. I would hold the cross in my hands, like so, as we prayed. I continue to do so still, each morning and night."

Lord Gilbert appeared wholly amazed at her tale and speechless as well. 'Twas not the reaction she'd expected.

"Forgive me, my lord. You are tired, and I have babbled on. I hope, if I am able to locate Sir Hugh, I might also find his squire, or at least learn of him."

Ana dearly hoped her squire yet lived and that he could aid her in her present need. She'd been unable to broach the subject of her identity with Lord Gilbert yet, but should his health suddenly fail, she'd no wish to be trapped in England or given over to the guardianship of some faceless stranger. Certainly, she could not turn to Sir Royce for help. He believed her to be the lost heiress and would do naught to help her return to Chinon.

Ana looked to the old lord, her hope rising. "In these last years, is it possible you have heard aught of Sir Hugh? Did he return from the Crusades with King Richard?"

"No, child. Regretfully, Sir Hugh FitzAlan died whilst warring in *Outremer*. He was a fine knight."

Ana wavered at his words. "And his squire? Do you think Sir Hugh's squire returned?"

A clouded look came into Lord Gilbert's eyes, and he

paused a long moment as if considering something.

"'Tis honest to say, the boy who left England as Sir Hugh FitzAlan's squire did not return. Like so many others, he lost his youth upon the battlefield," the lord said carefully, cryptically.

Ana's heart shattered. She reached out a hand and placed it upon the mattress, steadying herself.

"He is dead?" Hot tears rushed to her eyes. How would she ever bear it?

Lord Gilbert continued to gaze at her with a penetrating look. "I did not say he is dead, Juliana. But if you would know of his fate, I suggest you speak to Sir Royce."

"Sir Royce?" What could he possibly know, Ana wondered. In the next breath, a thought struck her. "Did Sir Royce fight alongside Sir Hugh'?"

"Yes, as I understand it, he did."

"Then 'tis likely he would have encountered Sir Hugh's squire."

"More than likely. 'Tis the knight who holds your answer, though I cannot fathom why he's not discussed the matter of the squire with you before now. Presumably, he has his reasons, but 'tis best to leave such explanations to him."

Lord Gilbert smiled, then the lines of his mouth eased. "Juliana, humor me, for I too have a question that seeks an answer."

Ana swiped at the tears wetting her cheeks and straightened. "Yes, my lord?"

"Sir Royce bears a notable injury on his arm. Godric could see it from the window here while Sir Royce was on the lists. What do you know of that, and of his other bruises and cuts?"

Ana moistened her lips, guilt rising in her breast. How could she divulge all that had befallen the knight without revealing her own role and how she'd fought coming here—lying, stealing, and deceiving others as she sought time and again to escape? Such a revelation certainly could not be good for Lord Gilbert's frail condition.

"Sir Royce saved me from a wild boar," she began carefully. "I'd gone into the edge of the forest with the other women to . . . well, you know. I became disoriented and wandered deeper into the wood. When Sir Royce heard my screams, he raced to my aid and killed the boar with a single stroke of his sword. He was quite heroic, I can tell you. However, the beast's tusk laid open his arm."

"Indeed?" Lord Gilbert pondered that a moment. "And what of the bruises?"

Ana took a small swallow. "Hannibal, his stallion, became unruly."

"The knight did not control his horse while you were on it?" A note of anger sharpened his voice.

"Not exactly. 'Twas my own fault for trying to mount the animal without Sir Royce present. He came to my aid, again, only in doing so, we collided, sort of. The back of my head struck his cheekbone rather hard. The bruise is looking much better though," she added quickly, cheerfully. "In another day, 'twill be gone completely."

"And the cut on his brow?"

Ana bit her lower lip. "There were two Scotsmen traveling in our company. They, er, took an interest in me. Sir Royce protected me at his own expense. They both sprang upon him, but Sir Royce prevailed."

Ana hoped Heaven wouldn't punish her for twisting the details, but she'd no wish to distress Lord Gilbert, especially as he prepared to settle down to sleep.

Seeing he remained deep in thought, Ana rose. "I should return to my chamber now," she said softly.

Lord Gilbert looked up. "Yes, my dear, of course. Brodric, see Lady Juliana safely across the ward and to her chamber."

Ana bid him good night at that and withdrew. As she passed through the portal, she heard Lord Gilbert call to Godric, bidding him bring more candles, along with parchment, pen, and ink.

Royce entered the darkened garden, the discordant creaking of the gate scraping on his ears, on his nerves, as he swung it open. Fortunately, the moon overhead shed sufficient light to brighten his way.

Following the tree-lined path, he noted two men lurking in the shadows. He'd observed them earlier in the hall, ever near the countess. By their livery, he'd realized then, they served as her personal guards. Still, out of habit, Royce's hand moved to rest on his sword hilt.

Passing through an opening in the hedge, Royce came to the heart of the garden, at its center a large fountain. Lady Sibylla waited there, bathed softly in the moon's glow.

As he proceeded toward her, she rose from the stone bench on which she sat, her gaze meeting his. Royce slowed his step, then halted before her, feeling the pull of her wide, captivating eyes. Slipping the note from his sleeve, he held it forth.

"I have come, my lady, as you requested."

"But, hopefully, you come of your own desire,"

Royce paused at her choice of words, the way she drew out the last.

"Of course, my lady."

Remembering himself, Royce bowed to the countess, as was due her station, one much higher than his own. Before he could rise, however, Lady Sibylla closed the space between them. She lay her hand along his bearded jaw and tilted is head upward.

"I would not have you bow to me, Sir Royce," she said in a husky voice.

"What would you have then?" he asked, uncertain of the direction of her thoughts, of her mood.

"I would have you to my bed."

Royce straightened at that, his heart nearly leaping from his chest. "My lady is very direct."

She gave a small shrug, her lips curving into a smile. "Is the thought of bedding me so loathsome a thought?" She moved closer, her perfectly modeled features turned up to him, her entrancing eyes gazing deeply into his own.

"Nay, lady. Far from it. I'd be the envy of every man in Christendom."

Royce's mind raced. What game did the countess play? Or did she set some trap, her guards ready to spring upon him at her signal? But, what possible enemies could he have at Court? He'd not been in England long enough to make any.

"And would that please you, Sir Royce—being the envy of every man in Christendom?"

"'Tis but a compliment I pay my lady. To be the envy of others holds no import for me."

Lady Sibylla lay her hand upon his chest, at the place over his heart. Idly, she smoothed her palm upward and fingered the laces securing the neck of his tunic.

"And what *is* of import to the great hero of Acre and Ascalon? Honor, justice, nobility? Or perhaps, something more worldly holds value for you as well—lands, titles, power?"

"My lady speaks in riddles."

She smiled. "I saw you speaking with the Earl of Pembroke in the forechamber of the hall. Tell me, is he a man you admire? One you would wish to emulate?"

"Aye, my lady. William Marshal is the greatest of knights

to live."

"And to achieve such greatness, I can well imagine the earl's advice to those who would follow his path. Regardless of a knight's prowess and success on the battlefield, or the close company he might keep with kings, 'tis only through marriage that a man may cross from the rank of poor bachelor to that of lord."

Deftly, she slid the tie free at the top of his tunic and began to spread the laces. "Were the great Marshal to advise you, he would urge you to do as he did—hold yourself in reserve for the best match, then marry high and well, gaining the most princely estates you could and all their resources. The earl, himself, waited until nearly age fifty before marrying the heiress of Striguil and gaining an earldom. You need not wait so long."

Royce caught the countess's hand as she began to slip her fingers inside his tunic. Uncannily, the earl had given him just such advice earlier this day, his words similar.

"And what has my lady's bed to do with that?"

"I need a husband."

"A husband?" He dropped her hand, his eyes narrowing with suspicion. What did the woman really seek? Certainly, a countess would not choose a knight of low rank who had yet to come into lands of his own.

"Surely there are many men—powerful barons of title and substance—who would seek that privilege."

"There are—brutal, avaricious men, who prowl at my door like wolves, ravenous for all I can bring to them and myself as well, a trophy for their beds."

She turned and began to pace before the fountain, visibly agitated. "Certain ones have even begun to harass my lands, trying to force me into marriage in order to protect my holdings. They did not know I've discovered their ruse and know their names."

"Lady Sibylla, it seems you have more need of a champion than a husband," Royce observed, taking a step toward her.

"I have need of both—a husband and a champion. If I do not act soon, the king will choose for me and award me to someone for his own political gain."

"And you do not trust John," Royce said, more statement than question.

"'Tis more than that. Thrice have I married, each husband carefully and royally selected for me, Linford's heiress. I suffered a fool for my first husband. The two after were cruel and abusive, the last being forty years older than I, his pleasures perverse. Why shouldn't I seek a match of my own choosing? I've no need for greater rank or wealth. What I require most is a protector—a proven warrior of renown—one who can defend Linford lands. You are such a man. 'Twould not matter if you held not a single knight's fief. In marrying me you will gain thirty-seven, and in addition, three castles and five manors."

Royce stood looking at the countess for a long moment, trying to find his voice, that she would willingly take him to husband and make him Earl of Linford.

"My lady's proposal is quite extraordinary. Even should I agree, the king must approve."

Lady Sibylla moved toward him, her eyes brightening.

"Align yourself with William Marshal, and the king will consent to our marriage. 'Tis the earl who is most responsible for the crown sitting upon John's brow. He also remains the king's chief counselor. None is more loyal. John knows this, though oftentimes he is unsure of the loyalties of others. But those who align with Marshal, he considers aligned with him. The king needs skilled men such as you to secure his throne. Trust me. He will not deny us in this."

Royce continued to ponder her words, seeking some

hook, some hidden snare concealed in them. And yet he could find none. Was he delusional, did he mishear? Or did this beautiful woman truly wish to marry him purely for the reasons she named? Before he gave her an answer, however, he deemed it best to learn more of the countess and the three husbands she'd buried.

"Consider my offer carefully," she whispered, closing the space between them. "Marry me and you will gain an earldom. Together we will beget a dynasty."

She grazed Royce's chest with her breasts. Then, sliding her hands over his shoulders to the back of his neck, she pressed her body against his.

"You will find my appetites can be quite insatiable. With the right man, that is. And you, Royce de Warrene, are most definitely the right man."

Drawing his head down to hers, she captured his lower lip with her teeth. She rasped the flesh lightly before releasing him. Moving against him, her mouth sought his in a hungry kiss.

Ana found the bedchamber swamped in shadows when she entered, illuminated solely by the light of the fireplace. Luvena bustled forth to meet her, bringing a candle to help guide her way.

As Ana stepped deeper into the room, she heard whisperings and soft, feminine laughter from the other side. Peering through the dimness, she spied the ladies with whom she shared the chamber, gathered at the window and gazing out.

"Luvena, put out that candle. They will see us," one hissed over her shoulder.

"Ladies of good breeding shouldn't be spying on others," the diminutive maid admonished. "And I'll not have Lady Juliana risk breaking her leg, stepping around your pallets in the dark."

"Shh, Luvena! You'll ruin everything," the youngest in the group snapped. She looked to be scarcely older than the queen.

Lady Pamela, the only one Ana knew by name, turned from the window. "Sir Royce and Lady Sibylla are in the garden below. Alone. They are standing very close, and have been talking ever so long."

"Oh! Look there! Did you see how she brushed up against him? And with her breasts, no less. How bold," another exclaimed.

"Brazen is more the word," Lady Pamela declared. "Lady Juliana, come quick. I think they're about to . . Oh yes, look there. . . ."

Unable to restrain her curiosity, Ana quickened to the window, earning a decided frown from Luvena. Shouldering her way through the others, she peered out, catching sight of two figures softly illuminated by moonlight, their forms melting to one. Ana watched, stunned, as Lady Sibylla's arms slid around Sir Royce's neck and drew his head down to her, their lips coming together in a deep, devouring kiss.

Ana fell back from the window, jolted by the sight, her heart racing in her chest.

"You're quite right, Luvena, ladies shouldn't be spying on others, and I am the sorrier for it."

"Come away, my lady. Time to bed. A sound night's sleep is what you need." Luvena took her by the arm and led her to her pallet.

Much later, having made her ablutions and undressed, Ana lay abed, her emotions roiling. She felt thoroughly miserable—angry and downcast, awash with tears that would not come. Surely, her anxiety rose from the knowledge that her dear squire had not returned from the Holy Lands. Certainly, it had naught to do with Sir Royce. Why should she care if the knight had succumbed to the countess's charms? She didn't, she assured herself. 'Twas her fears for her squire that afflicted her, that and no more.

Ana brushed her fingers over her lips, remembering the touch of Sir Royce's mouth. The image of Lady Sibylla crowded in, claiming the knight, her lips locking with his.

"Insufferable man," Ana fumed and turned onto her other side.

Catching up the silver cross, she closed her fingers around it, banishing the knight and the woman he held in his arms from her thoughts. Instead, she gave the whole of her attention to the one who mattered most to her, the one who secretly held her heart of hearts.

"Wherever you may be, most beloved squire, may God safeguard you and keep you well. And may He keep all manner of evil from your path in whatever form it may seek to afflict you. Amen."

13

Ana tossed on her pallet as a jumble of vibrant images swirled through her dreams. She caught glimpses of faces, vaguely familiar, and breath-stealing mountains and green valleys. There was also a looming structure—a dwelling— she could not quite make out, but she sensed 'twas impressive and built of stone.

A young girl suddenly appeared, perhaps seven or eight years of age. 'Twas the same girl who'd run through the corridors of Dover Castle. Her silvery hair spilled freely down her back as she stood at a table in a hall. She was not alone, but played at some game with a boy. He looked to be slightly older, perhaps ten. Each clutched a small, jointed knight, knocking and slamming the figures together as they fought a mock battle. The boy became thoroughly engrossed in their efforts, smashing his little warrior into the girl's with increasing vigor, eager to win.

"Cur! Taste my steel. Take that, and that, and that!" He pounded on her knight with abandon. His fist, a blur of motion, accidentally jabbed his piece into the back of the girl's hand, cutting her midway between the thumb and forefinger.

Screaming, the girl dropped the toy and gazed in horror at the blood dripping from her hand.

"My lady? My lady, are you all right? You cried out."

Ana frowned. Luvena? What was she doing in her dream, in this place, wherever *this* was? Ana turned onto her other side, sinking deeper into another layer of sleep.

212

"There, that is better.""Twas the blond-haired woman again, the one with wide arching brows.

Ana couldn't see her features clearly, but knew that the lady smiled as she finished wrapping the girl's small hand and placed a light kiss to it. She then took up a beautiful comb—an ivory comb with intricate carvings on its spine. She began to sing comfortingly as she drew the comb through the young girl's hair. Her voice was the sweetest Ana had ever heard, beautiful and crystal clear.

Again the images altered, but Ana continued to hear the woman singing sweetly. A lute now accompanied her fine voice and there seemed a familiarity about it all. To Ana's dismay, she could no longer see the golden lady nor the instrument. Ana seemed to be at a short distance, perhaps in an adjoining room somewhere. Confusingly, she—or was it the child?—was sitting in water, naked and wet. Several people moved about her, servants she thought. They, too, listened to the delightful song.

Abruptly, the singing stopped. 'Twas odd, Ana thought, for she felt certain the lady had not ended her song. Those around her went strangely still and silent, gaping toward the other room. Shouts sundered that brief quiet, then screams filled the air.

Ana gasped for breath, darkness enveloping her. Impossibly, she was now outside, beneath the stars, running, running, someone gripping her hand and dragging her along as they fled into the night.

Ana jerked awake and found Luvena leaning over her, patting her hand and cheek.

"My lady, you've had a bad dream. My lady, wake up."

Her heart battering against her chest, Ana pushed herself up to a sitting position. With shaky fingers, she shoved back her hair.

"Yes Luvena, just a bad dream. That is all."

Glancing about her, she saw the other ladies in the chamber beginning to wake. Servants bustled about, unshuttering the windows and allowing in the early morning light.

As her breaths evened, Ana again brushed wayward strands of hair back from her face. She halted her hand in mid-motion, stilling as she recalled the first part of her dream.

Drawing her hand slowly down, she held it before her. She need not look at it, of course, for she already knew what she would find—a small jagged scar on the back of her right hand, midway between the thumb and forefinger. It had been there for as long as she could remember.

After morning chapel, Ana headed for the northwest tower to break her fast with Lord Gilbert. On arriving, Godric informed her the lord still slept and deeply so. In accordance with his master's instructions, he directed her to the tutor Lord Gilbert had retained—Peter Coffey, by name, and highly recommended. Today, she would begin her lessons in reading and ciphering.

For the next several hours, Ana bent over a tablet of wax, stylus in hand, struggling to copy letters of the alphabet onto its surface. She wielded the stylus awkwardly, following the tutor's explicit directions. Being better coordinated with her left hand—and out of sheer frustration—she switched the instrument over to it.

"Lady Juliana! Must I tell you again? The devil rules your left hand," Peter Coffey snapped impatiently. "Use your right hand, *only* the right!"

Ana grit her teeth as she transferred the stylus back and began again. Clumsily, she dropped the instrument onto the floor. Next, she dug the point too deeply into the wax, somehow dislodging a large chunk of the material and causing it to pop free of its wood backing.

"Look what you have done to the tablet!" Master Coffey howled. "Has life among commoners allowed you no refinements? Young woman, you must have more care, more respect when handling such items. They do not come cheaply after all."

Ana glared at the man, stunned by his outburst and slighting remarks.

Oblivious to her rising anger, he continued. "The tablet can be repaired of course, but the wax will need be heated and reapplied to the board again. For now, you will have to use that portion of the tablet you have not ruined, but mind what you do."

Boiling inside, Ana took up the stylus, not realizing until a moment later she'd done so with her left hand. Before she could shift it to her opposite hand, the tutor brought down his rod with a loud *thwack,* hitting the surface of the table where Ana sat.

"Not the left!" he shouted. "You will never be an accomplished lady if you cannot follow the least of my instructions!"

"Perhaps I was never meant to be a lady." Ana shot to her feet, her temper exploding, and flung the tablet onto the floor.

"Now see what you've done. Lord Gilbert shall hear of this!"

"He most certainly will!" Ana stormed toward the door. Then, unable to resist, she halted and spun around, thrusting up her chin into the air. "You, sir, may consider yourself dismissed!" she declared boldly, then swept out of the room and fled down the stairs into the courtyard.

What had she done? Ana reproached herself as she crossed the ward, her emotions snarled into knots. She'd far overstepped her bounds. Where did she get such audacity? Yet, she knew in her heart Lord Gilbert wouldn't abide the man belittling her so. Not for one minute. He must be informed of the tutor's outrageous behavior. Her own too, before Peter Coffey could supply his own version.

Ana flexed her right hand, stretching the muscles, cramped from gripping the stylus. Absently, she dropped her gaze to the scar she bore. Indeed she must talk with Lord Gilbert, but not only of the wretched tutor.

Ana entered the tower and mounted the stairs, her emotions continuing to churn and collide within her. 'Twas not just the rudeness she'd suffered just now that stirred her feelings and agitated her so. A host of other concerns gnawed at her as well.

In part, 'twas the knowledge that Sir Royce knew something of her squire. What would he tell her, when she asked of her dear squire's fate? Would it be favorable, or would the knight's words cleave her heart in two?

Then, there was the heady dance she'd shared last night with Sir Royce—he touching his lips briefly to hers, almost kissing her. Almost. She still could feel the warmth of his breath, the tickle of his mustache, the smooth firmness of his lips. What was that about? A mere flirtation on his part? And why had he made the advance, given that within the hour he was indulging himself with the countess, savoring her kisses? Not that it mattered. It didn't, Ana assured herself. Vexingly, she couldn't seem to shut it out of her mind.

And then there were the images in her dreams, images she wasn't wholly sure she was prepared to explore, not if it meant reliving that horrible night in Vaux.

Arriving at Lord Gilbert's chamber, Ana found herself face to face with the queen's physick and barred from entering.

"Come later, child. We do but examine his lordship. He taxed himself greatly last evening, as you know. We only wish to assure he's brought no harm to himself."

"We?" Ana raised a brow, then, through the cracked door, spied the man, Renfeld, standing within. She could not see Lord Gilbert, however.

When the queen's physick again insisted she return later, Ana withdrew, but not before extracting fresh promises from Godric and Brodric that Lord Gilbert's wishes would prevail in all matters.

Reluctant to leave, but satisfied by the servants' assurances, she descended the tower stairs and headed back toward the keep. Partway there, the young page who'd sought her out yesterday appeared, burning a path straight toward her, then skidding to a halt.

"My lady, the queen wishes you to join her and her ladies in her solar," he huffed out, then gulped the air.

Ana groaned inwardly, thinking of the tapestry and how badly she'd botched the little bird with her stitches. Hopefully, the women engaged in something other than sewing this day.

"Very well." She forced a smile. "I will rely on you, good page, to lead the way."

"Come back on the morrow, Sir Royce. With luck, Lord Craven can see you then."

Royce slammed both his hands down flat on the table and leaned menacingly forward, causing the little toad of a man sitting on the other side to jump.

"I have been here seven times already," Royce ground out. "The king personally assured me I could recover my papers and the needed license today, and be on my way to Birkwell."

"*Beckwell,*" the toad corrected. "And 'tis his majesty who is responsible for the delay. He wished to examine his late brother's grant one more time. One does not rush kings."

"Of course not, especially not this one!"

Royce turned on his heel and stalked out of the building and into the courtyard. Halting a moment, he debated what he might do next to best fill time—fill time until Lord Craven returned and he could demand an audience with King John.

Royce tossed a glance about the ward, then stilled as he spotted Juliana following one of the pages to the keep. He watched the swing of her hips and swish of her skirt as she climbed the flight of stairs. Watched and remembered how those hips had swayed to the steps of the dance and rhythm of the music last night. Remembered the petal softness of her lips.

Royce shook himself from his reverie, then saw Juliana enter the keep, disappearing from sight. Suddenly self-conscious, he darted a glance around the ward to see if anyone had observed him eyeing the maid as though he was the greenest of lads. None appeared to have noticed.

Thankful to have been spared that embarrassment, he turned his thoughts toward the northwest tower. Lord Gilbert seemed a man of sound advice. Royce decided to seek his counsel on the matter of Countess Linford. Hopefully, he knew something of her past husbands and what adversaries she might own. Before heading for the tower, however, Royce thought to first divert his steps to the stables and check on Hannibal.

Half an hour later, Royce stood in Lord Gilbert's chamber, gazing on his quiet form, resting in the curtained bed.

"The physick bled him again?" Royce turned his frown on Godric. "His lordship looked perfectly sound last night."

Godric twisted his hands together, visibly distressed. "'Twas leeches they used this time. I tried to discourage Lord Gilbert from taking the treatment. But something he'd eaten—or perhaps, something he'd drunk—did not settle well with him. He convinced himself he'd feel better if the physick drained off the poisons. There was naught I could do. Lady Juliana will be angry with me."

"How so?" Royce canted his head, his brows rising.

"Brodric and I promised to not let his lordship be bled or do anything he didn't wish. Of course, his mind was made."

Royce lay a calming hand to Godric's shoulder. "Easy man. I know you cannot challenge your lord's commands. Like Lady Juliana, I am not so trusting of the royal physicks. Should they wish to practice their arts on Lord Gilbert again, send for me. Perhaps, I can dissuade him from any imprudent course the physicks press him to take."

Royce withdrew, beset with concerns for the old lord's health, but also impressed by Juliana's instincts and her pluck to assert them. Departing the tower, his thoughts remained on Juliana. He need find her and speak with her on the matter of Lord Gilbert. However, he must first see if Lord Craven had returned.

As Royce started across the ward, a feminine voice called out. Turning, he discovered Lady Sibylla approaching him.

As she joined him, she slid her arm through his. "You almost slipped away," she teased, her eyes sparkling. "Come. We must walk. I've just come from the great earl himself, William Marshal. You'll wish to know all he said."

Royce accompanied the countess toward the garden, intrigued as he gazed into her dark flashing eyes. What truly was the price of her Linford titles, he wondered, fascinated by the woman yet mindful of her proneness to brief marriages.

Ana entered the queen's solar and found the ladies working, regrettably, on the tapestry once again. Taking her place beside Lady Blythe, she took up needle and thread, her finger sorely reminding of how she'd pricked it yesterday. Ana's gaze dropped to the little bird. He really was a pathetic creature, thanks to her handiwork.

Queen Isabella smiled kindly, looking as radiant and as composed as ever. "I am glad you could join us, Lady Juliana. We were just in the midst of discussing another of Chaplain Andre's tenets of love. It states: 'The easy attainment of love makes it of little value; difficulty of attainment makes it prized.'"

Difficulty of attainment? What of the impossibility of attainment? Ana wondered dismally, thinking of her squire. She straightened at that, chiding herself. She'd thought much of her squire these last days and little of Gervase. Poor Gervase. He waited faithfully for her still, no doubt heartsick.

"Lady Juliana, what are your reflections on Chaplain Andre's tenet? Lady Juliana?" the queen prompted.

Ana wrenched herself back to the present. "Forgive me, my mind drifted a moment. Chaplain Andre—the attainment of love—well, I think . . . well . . ."

A rap at the door saved Ana from answering. She sent her thanks Heavenward for she'd not the vaguest notion of what to say.

The ladies continued to embroider as one of the pages rushed to place a sealed missive in the queen's hands. Breaking the bead of wax, she opened the letter and scanned its contents. Flushing, she smiled, then rose to her feet.

"Please continue, ladies. I shall return anon." Catching up her skirt, Isabella hastened from the chamber.

Lady Mertise's lips tilted in a thin smile. "The king must have returned from the hunt. His blood is always high when he does, as are his appetites."

A titter of laughter followed her observation.

Lady Arietta leaned forward, smiling mischievously. "I'd

much rather know of Sir Royce's appetites. Has anyone seen him or Lady Sibylla yet today?"

Ana stabbed her needle into the canvas, wide of her mark. 'Twas impossible to concentrate.

"No, but the countess was spinning her web about the knight well enough last night," Lady Mertise noted, bringing more titters of laughter.

Ana glanced up at the woman, thinking her wit and her tongue to be particularly acerbic today.

"'Twould be a high step for Sir Royce into the countess's bed," Lady Arietta mused.

Lady Blythe's eyes rounded. "Do you think that is his intent?"

"'Tis hers no doubt. And when has the countess not gotten her way?" Lady Mertise sniped. "'Tis well known, Lady Sibylla abhors cold sheets."

She shifted her eyes to Ana. Cat's eyes, Ana thought.

"And what is your opinion of the two as a couple, Lady Juliana?" Lady Mertise arched a brow, waiting expectantly.

"I don't really have one." Ana bent her attention to the tapestry, keeping it there as she stitched. 'Twas truth. She'd no opinion because she shut the topic from her mind, not wanting to court any images of Sir Royce and Lady Sibylla wrapped around one another like clutching vines.

"No opinion at all? Even if he marries her?"

"Marries her?" Ana plunged the needle into her sore finger. Bolting upright from the pain, she brushed her hand inadvertently against the tapestry, smearing her blood across the canvas and threads.

"Clumsy little fool!" Lady Mertise shrilled. "Look what you've done!"

"Mertise, 'twas an accident," Lady Blythe intervened, her gaze darting between the two.

"Humph." Lady Mertise snorted indelicately. "If her

blood hasn't ruined the piece, her stitches already have. See you there? The bird will need to be picked out." She glared at Ana. "Did no one ever teach you how to make a proper stitch?"

"Mertise, what has gotten into you?" Lady Arietta gasped. "Juliana simply did not have our advantage. She was raised among the peasants."

"Shush, both of you," Lady Blythe warned. "You know the king and queen forbid mention of Juliana's past."

Ana rose, spearing her needle into the tapestry, her heart beating madly. "You will forgive me if I leave your fine company, but you're quite right. I really don't belong here." As fast as she could manage, Ana quickened across the chamber.

"Now see what you've caused, Mertise," Lady Arietta hissed. "Someone should put a lock on your tongue."

"Why? We only tolerate her presence because the queen favors her. Good riddance, I say."

"Mertise, that is cruel!"

"And not true," Lady Blythe insisted.

"Are you so sure?" Lady Mertise challenged.

Ana could bear no more and rushed through the door, through the corridors, hurrying to her bedchamber. Entering, she was relieved to find it empty and herself alone.

A great despondency came over her, pressed down on her, like a weight of iron upon her heart. Slowly, Ana crossed to the window and gazed out. lingering there and savoring the peace.

A movement in the garden drew her eye—Sir Royce and Lady Sibylla strolling along the path, arm in arm, deep in discussion. Ana's heart sank at the sight. While she'd told the other women she'd no opinion of the two together, as she gazed on them now, she knew, deep down, she detested the thought wholly.

A sudden overpowering urge swarmed through Ana, entreating her. She wished to run and run and run, just as in her dream. But even if she should, Ana questioned what would she be running from, and what would she be running to? Did she really know?

Ana arrived late for the midday meal, finding it nearly impossible to force herself from the confines of her bedchamber to face, let alone mingle with, the court nobles. 'Twas Luvena who heartened her spirits and prodded her to go down.

"Brace yourself up with a bit of color," the little maid said, laying out Ana's rose gown. "A spot of color does wonders and will carry you through the hours. You'll look bright on the outside, even if you feel bleak on the inside. None will know, mark my words."

Luvena's guidance was the best she'd received all day, Ana decided as she entered the hall. She felt pretty and acceptable in her rose-colored gown, leastwise on the outside. Nonetheless, she hoped to take her meal unnoticed. To that end, Ana chose a place at the hall's lower end, near the entrance. She would have much preferred to sup with Lord Gilbert in his chamber, but word had come that he continued to rest.

Seeing that the king and queen were absent, Ana asked her table companions of them. One of the men, clearly annoyed to be disturbed in the midst of devouring a joint of mutton, informed her that the royals took dinner in their private chambers. Ana could well imagine what the three clacking hens—Mertise, Arietta, and Blythe—would have to say of that.

Glancing about the great hall, she tried to locate the trio. As she continued to search for them, Ana noticed how a great many of the ladies' gowns bore telltale stains—

bloodstains, obviously gained during the falcon attack on the birds in the hall. Ana puzzled that. How odd that the other ladies' gowns could not be restored while hers had been, and perfectly so.

Unexpectedly, she discovered Guy of Lisors strolling along the tables toward her. Seeing her, he smiled and stopped for a moment.

"I am almost finished with the first of my new song, Lady Juliana. 'Tis of your adventures traveling with Sir Royce. If you would indulge me, I still have questions about the boar incident."

Ana's brows rose a fraction. "If you would know what passed on the ground with the beast, I suggest you ask Sir Royce. I was in a tree."

Guy laughed. "I'll be certain to add that morsel to the verses. I only wish I could have seen his feat myself. Ah, speaking of the noble knight, there he is now with Countess Linford."

Ana cast a glance to the entrance, then just as quickly turned away. The minstrel spoke truly. Sir Royce and Lady Sibylla stood just inside the portal, pausing as a knot of people joined them there.

As Guy continued to ramble along the tables, Ana realized she'd yet to obtain a trencher or wine. For several minutes, Ana sought to catch the attention of one of the servants, but to no avail. Again she lifted her hand to signal one approaching, but irritatingly a figure stepped in front of her, blocking her view of the man.

"May I join you?" a rich masculine voice asked.

Ana instantly recognized the voice as Sir Royce's and did not bother to look up. "Are you not with Countess Linford? She'll not wish to sit so low as this."

"Lady Sibylla has been called away." He sat down next to her.

Ana glanced over her shoulder, then around the hall. Indeed, the countess was nowhere to be seen. She leveled her gaze unblinkingly at the knight.

"I am surprised you did not accompany her. 'Twould be the gallant thing to do, I am sure." Ana mentally winced, hearing the tartness in her voice. She reminded herself of Lady Mertise.

The corner of Sir Royce's lips twitched upward. "I'm not sure the countess's sister would appreciate my being present for her child's birthing."

"Oh. No, I suppose not." Ana fell silent, feeling at a sudden loss for words in the knight's presence.

"You are looking particularly lovely tonight, Lady Juliana. Your rose gown is most becoming." Sir Royce waited a moment. When she did not reply, he spoke again. "Despite your concerns over the stains, the gown appears as new, do you not agree?"

Ana raised her eyes to find him smiling. He looked as though he expected her to make some comment. But what was it she was supposed to say? As she searched her mind for possibilities, the two swains who'd pursued her yesterday passed by their table. Both wore blackened eyes and contusions on their faces. Simultaneously, the two sent glaring looks at Ana.

"What is that about?" Sir Royce's gaze fixed on the two young men, suspicion in his eyes.

"I'm not sure." Ana gazed after them as well, perplexed. "One gifted me with a bouquet of flowers, the other later snatched it away when it tumbled from my lap. 'Twas all quite ridiculous really."

"Then you are the cause of their injuries," he stated flatly.

"Me? That's absurd."

Sir Royce continued to frown at her.

"You might blame me for your own injuries, Sir Knight, and rightly so. But you cannot lay blame to me for theirs."

"Can't I? By accepting the flowers from your first admirer, you gave him to believe that you accepted his suit, that you were committing your affection to him alone."

"That's preposterous!"

"And when he later encountered your other admirer, and found him in possession of the flowers, he likely believed you to be fickle and demanded their return."

"*I* was fickle?"

"My guess is the second suitor refused to relinquish the flowers, unwilling to part with them. Obviously a fight ensued."

Ana's gaze drew back to the two swains. "The young man who snatched the flowers did seem uncommonly happy to have them," she said thoughtfully. "He uttered something about their being on my lap 'guarding Love's Gate.'"

Royce rolled his eyes. "God in His mercy," he grumbled. "Juliana, someone must lesson you about the rules of courtly love before we have half the young swains battling one another on your behalf."

Ana's eyes widened. "Why would they do that?"

"Because they are infatuated with you, and because you lead them on when you should be spurning their advances."

"You are faulting *me* for their misbegotten behavior?" Ana's voice rose as she stared at him, incredulous.

"And, you believe you own no fault?" his voice rose too, matching hers.

Ana narrowed her eyes. "Sir Knight, be warned. I have been criticized all day. I'm in no mood to endure your criticisms too."

"Juliana, 'twas not my intent to criticize you." He released a heavy sigh. "The day has held frustrations for myself as well. Here, let us eat rather than argue, shall we?"

He signaled to one of the servants, who instantly brought a trencher and goblet of wine for them to share. Ana glowered at the servant's retreating back. He was one of the servers who'd purposely ignored her.

"Would you care for some suckling pig?"

"No," Ana said stubbornly, still furious that Sir Royce blamed her for her suitors' injuries.

"Trout? Venison pasty? Mortrews?"

"No and no and no." She crossed her arms over her chest in a very unladylike manner.

The knight swiveled in place and scowled at her. "Is there anything that *would* please you?" he ground out. "What exactly do you want, Juliana?"

"Shush, the minstrel is about to sing," scolded one of their table companions, a reed-thin woman with knifelike features.

Ana groaned audibly. "I hope he's not going to try out his boar song."

The woman shushed her again. "'Tis of Sir Gawain and the Loathly Lady he's been requested to sing."

A hush fell over the hall as Guy of Lisors stepped to the center of the chamber and picked a simple tune on his lute. In introducing the tale, he explained 'twas in part that of the knight's trials—trials that tested his courage, discernment, and his truest heart. It also held the answer to an age-old question, he baited his audience, and sang on.

In order to save King Arthur from a spell of enchantment, Sir Gawain agreed to marry Ragnell, the most hideous of crones. She alone held the answer to the question that would break the spell entrapping the king. The question was this. What does a woman most want?

Ana's interest pricked at that. Had not Sir Royce just now posed the very same question to her? She slid a meaningful glance his way, assuring he was listening, then returned her attention to the minstrel. What answer would Ragnell offer? And would she herself agree?

Guy sang on. In accordance with the crone's demands, Gawain married her, to the court's horror. He would allow nothing ill to be said toward her and treated her with the greatest courtesy.

Ana flicked a glance to Sir Royce, remembering his great courtesy toward her own self at court, especially on the day of their arrival when he presented her in the hall and saw to her every need. How she wished he could have been with her today to shield her from the unkind remarks hurled at her.

Ana returned her attention to Guy's tale.

As Sir Gawain faced the wedding night with the Loathly Lady, his courage wavered. He brooded awhile, but at last rose from his place by the fire to embrace his duty and bed his bride. Turning around, Gawain discovered Ragnell had shed her ugly exterior and now was a beautiful woman, the most beautiful he'd ever seen. She explained that she too was held by an enchantment and must pass half the day in the guise of the hideous crone. She gave him the choice of having her ugly by day and beautiful by night, or the opposite—beautiful by day and ugly by night.

Noble Gawain found the choice impossible. For if he chose for his bride to be hideous by day, she would be subject to the disdain and public ridicule of others. But if he chose the latter, he must share intimacies with her as the hideous crone, grossly deformed and unbearably repulsive.

Unable to choose, Gawain gave the choice to his bride, agreeing to abide with her decision. Instantly, the spell was broken, but not only the one that entrapped Ragnell, but also the one that bound the king as well. Gawain had answered the riddle! What a woman wants most, Ragnell revealed, is to have her own way.

The story held Ana enrapt. She identified, in part, with the crone figure, seeing them both as misfits at Court—people staring, disapproving, despising their presence. Ana thought of the tutor, Peter Coffey, and Lady Mertise.

As Guy of Lisors sang the last word and plucked the final note, Ana smiled and turned to Sir Royce.

"You asked me what I want exactly, I will tell you, Sir Knight. I want the same as Ragnell—to have my own way—to be allowed to return to where I truly belong, Chinon."

The knight shuttered his look, the blue draining from his eyes, turning them steel-gray. "That I cannot give you."

"No, of course you can't. Or won't? There is no difference," Ana retorted bitterly and turned her face from his.

"'Tis not my place to grant you anything, Juliana. Lord Gilbert is your guardian."

"Perhaps, and perhaps not." She rubbed the scar on her hand, then expelled a long breath.

Where was all this to end? Ana wondered dispiritedly. How she longed to be curled up in her tiny room in Chinon, smelling the wonderful aromas of her foster mother's bread and stew, knowing Marie and Georges were near, their love ever blanketing her.

"Sir Royce! Lady Juliana!" Brodric appeared at the portal, then spying them ran apace, directly toward them, greatly agitated.

"What is it, man?" Sir Royce rose at his place.

"You must both come at once. 'Tis Lord Gilbert. He's taken a turn for the worst."

14

Ana and Sir Royce ran the full distance from the hall to the tower chamber, Brodric close behind them.

Entering the room, she discovered it to be crowded with men in flowing black robes gathered about Lord Gilbert's bed. 'Twas the queen's physick and his assistants, she realized at once. Godric stood to one side, a stricken expression on his face. Ana's heart leapt at that look, dread seizing her. Frantic, she began to shove and push her way through the wall of black-garbed men.

"What have you done to him? Get away, leave him alone!" she screamed, fighting to reach the lord's bed.

Catching sight of Lord Gilbert's face, she froze in her steps, shocked by his pallor, by his deadly paleness. Ana's hands flew to her mouth, her breath trapped in her lungs.

A hand suddenly snaked out and gripped her by the arm, preventing her from taking another step. Seeking the owner of that hand, she found herself face to face with the odious little man with the purple-veined nose, Renfeld.

"Lady, you will restrain yourself and allow us to finish attending his lordship. We've only just now completed our examination."

"Take your hand from the lady, at once," Sir Royce growled as he materialized beside Ana. Looming over Renfeld, he clamped down on the man's wrist, breaking his hold on her. "Tell the queen's physick I wish to speak with him *now*. Lady Juliana and I will wait by the fireplace. And take special care in your ministrations to Lord Gilbert. You'll answer to me should harm come to him."

Sir Royce circled his arm about Ana and guided her across the room. Almost immediately, the physick joined them. Looking up at the knight, Ana vowed she could see fire in his eyes.

"I left this chamber not two hours ago, and his lordship was resting peacefully. What happened?" Sir Royce demanded.

Ana widened her eyes over the knight, unaware of his visit to Lord Gilbert. At the same time, the physick cleared his throat, interrupting her thoughts and drawing her gaze.

"Sir Royce, Lady Juliana. In truth, Lord Gilbert has been failing for many days now. 'Tis his heart itself that is dying, ceasing to work, one portion at a time. There are signs that tell us this, and his heart's beat grows very faint."

"Nay, I do not believe you!" Ana refused to accept his words. "What signs do you speak of?"

The physick's gaze moved between Sir Royce and Ana. "His lordship has been suffering a deep fatigue, even before your arrival. Next came a swelling of his limbs, followed by a shortness of breath, and the liquids he passes are cloudy, full of poisons. These are all signs of his heart failing to do its work, the flow of blood disrupted, backing up, and of his organs failing as well. 'Tis only a matter of time."

"But he seemed so well last night," Ana protested, still unable to accept what she was being told.

"He *was* better last night, my lady." The physick turned to her, his look unexpectedly one of sympathy, understanding. "Another portion of Lord Gilbert's heart must have failed during the night. This morning there was a great amount of swelling about his back and in the veins of his neck. That I have relieved somewhat. But he's also taken with much coughing now—blood coming up. 'Tis in his lungs. There is little we can do for him, except to make him comfortable. The lord's time is short."

Ana's knees started to give way, but Sir Royce caught her about the waist and held her against him. Ana swiped at the moisture rimming her eyes and, drawing herself up, looked to the physick.

"Please, I must speak to Lord Gilbert. Do not keep me from him a moment longer."

"As you wish, my lady. I see my assistants are finished."

Her legs still quivery and her step unsteady, Ana accepted Sir Royce's arm as he accompanied her to the bed. He remained by her side as she lowered herself onto the mattress edge.

Ana's heart ached to see the dear lord lay so utterly still, ashen against the sheets. 'Twas as though he'd already departed this life. Only the shallow rise and fall of his chest bespoke that he yet lived.

Gently, so very gently, Ana lifted Lord Gilbert's hand in hers and pressed a kiss to its back. His skin was chill, as though his blood had already ceased to flow. She fought back tears, still they whelmed, spilling hotly over her cheeks, onto the back of his hand.

"Dearest lord, do not leave me," her voice broke. Shuddering with emotion, she bowed her head, then felt Sir Royce's hand settle upon her shoulder, a comforting gesture.

"Juliana?" Lord Gilbert rasped in a weakened voice. "I must have dozed off again. Juliana?" He struggled to open sleep-heavy lids.

"Yes, I am here beside you." She tightened her grip on his hand.

The old lord dragged his eyes open and gazed on her. A smile feathered over his lips. "Sweetest Juliana. You are my soul's delight. I am so overjoyed to have found you."

Ana choked back tears. "And I you, Grandfather."

"Grandfather?" His expression brightened. "You remember? Dear girl, you remember?" Tears collected in the corner of his eyes, trickling a path over his pale skin.

Ana brushed the tears away with her fingertips and smiled on him warmly. "You were right about the comb," she said evasively, for her past remained shrouded in shadows. "It has brought me dreams of many things—of scenes come to life, and of people and places."

Pleased by her words, Lord Gilbert's smile spread, but within seconds it disappeared as a spasm overtook him. Doubling forward, he clutched at his chest, coughing violently.

"Grandfather! What is it?" she cried, desperate to help him.

Instantly, Sir Royce stepped forward, bracing Lord Gilbert up, assisting Ana. Godric rushed forward with a bowl, thrusting it beneath the lord's chin as he spewed a pinkish discharge into it. 'Twas blood, Ana knew, just as the physick warned—a most unfavorable sign.

Seeing how Lord Gilbert had broken into a heavy sweat, she called for Brodric to bring a damp cloth. As Lord Gilbert's coughing subsided, Sir Royce eased him back onto the bank of pillows, and Juliana set to work, wiping his face and neck and hands.

Recovering from the bout, a smile returned to Lord Gilbert's lips, though his eyes were touched with sadness. "There is naught you can do, child. But I am content. I'd only hoped we would have more time together. I'd hoped to see you dance at your wedding."

"And you will, Grandfather, you will," Ana assured, a genuine love for the man swelling her heart. Her eyes began to blear again with tears. If only her love could heal him, if only her heart could beat for them both.

She slipped her hand into his. "Here, hold onto me. I'll

not let you go. I'll stay with you every moment, I promise. But you must promise to get well." She smiled through hot tears. "You mustn't leave me, you know. 'Tis you who makes my life bearable here on these English shores."

"And Sir Royce, too?"

Ana's brow twinged together. She cast a glance to the knight, finding him as surprised as she by the odd question.

"Yes, Sir Royce, too," she allowed, turning back to Lord Gilbert. "He's been ever chivalrous on my behalf."

Lord Gilbert rested against the pillows, seemingly satisfied by her answer. Ana set aside the damp cloth and smoothed back his snowy hair.

"You must rest now, dear lord. And when you are better, we will leave for Penhurst as you've wished to do."

He gave a small shake to his head. "I'll not be seeing Penhurst again, child."

His words clutched at her heart. "You mustn't say such things. Of course you will."

"Do not be distressed, Juliana. I am going to join my dear Thérèse, your grandmother, and your parents, too, Alyce and Robert. We shall be smiling down on you and proud, so very proud."

Tears vaulted to Ana's eyes anew. She could barely breathe. "Nay, you mustn't die." Her voice cracked. "Do not leave me here alone, Grandfather."

"You will not be alone, Juliana. I am leaving you in Sir Royce's keeping. 'Tis he whom I have appointed as your guardian."

"My lord?" Both Ana and the knight blurted together in surprise, then exchanged glances.

Lord Gilbert lifted a shaky hand and gestured to his servant. "Godric, bring the document."

Godric moved to a side table, where he fit a key to an iron-bound coffer and opened its lid. Withdrawing a folded parchment secured with cords and a seal of wax, he then started toward the bed.

Lord Gilbert fought back a cough, motioning for Godric to give the parchment to the knight. The congestion finally cleared from his throat, and he bid Sir Royce to come near.

"'Tis all there, in my own hand, witnessed and bearing my seal." He pointed a shaky finger to the document. "I have awarded guardianship of Juliana and her inheritance of Penhurst, and all it entails, to you."

Ana stared at Lord Gilbert, stunned by his words, unsure of what such a guardianship entailed or the authority Sir Royce would hold over her. Transferring her gaze to the knight, she watched as he gazed on the document, motionless as though he, too, was stunned. Slowly, he lifted his eyes to the old lord.

"You place great faith and trust in me Lord Gilbert, and for that I am honored. But I do not understand why your choice has fallen on me."

A smile played over the lord's lips. "You have proven yourself to be a man of noble character, Sir Royce—one who is steadfast, trustworthy, and more than capable of protecting my Juliana in any occasion that might arise."

The knight turned steel-blue eyes to Ana, his look perplexed. Avoiding his gaze, she glanced aside, realizing why Lord Gilbert had plied her with questions about her and the knight's journey here. 'Twas her own glowing praise of Sir Royce that had destined this moment—his being named her guardian.

"I know of none better . . . whom I might choose . . . for Juliana." Lord Gilbert choked through the words, resisting another spasm. Reaching out, he clutched for the knight's arm, a feeble grasp. "Watch over her, Sir Royce. And one thing more."

"My lord?"

"Choose for her a husband."

Sir Royce's brows shot high, as did Ana's.

"I leave the decision to you. Consider Juliana's feelings in the matter, but choose well and soon." He spoke between wheezing breaths. "Be certain the man is . . . is of sterling character . . . able to protect her . . . provide for her . . . One who will love her well."

Lord Gilbert's grip tightened on the knight's sleeve. "Promise me, Sir Royce. Choose for Juliana such a man and no less. And should you find difficulty in that decision, if your mind is filled with doubts, then look to your heart. The heart speaks truest when reason fails. 'Tis there you shall find your answer."

With shaky fingers, Lord Gilbert took Ana's hand and placed it in Sir Royce's, leaving his own atop theirs. "Take care of my Juliana, Sir Royce. Promise me."

Ana could scarcely draw a breath. She almost feared to look at Sir Royce, to see his reaction. Swallowing her dread, she forced her eyes to his and found him studying her intently. To her profound amazement, as the knight broke away his gaze, he covered Lord Gilbert's hand with his own, so all their hands were locked together.

"I give you my promise, upon my knightly oath," Sir Royce vowed solemnly.

Lord Gilbert fought down another cough threatening to scale his throat. He looked to the knight, a new urgency in his manner. "Sir Royce . . . about the past . . ." He struggled to speak, choking intermittently. "'Twas no mistake you made . . 'twas fate that led you . . ."

A ferocious onslaught of coughing erupted from deep within Lord Gilbert's throat and chest, a thick, congested sound, terrifying Ana.

"Grandfather!" Ana caught him in her arms as he

crumpled forward. Immediately, Sir Royce helped her brace him up and together they strove to relieve his attack.

Ana glanced about the chamber, desperate. Appallingly, the physick and his assistants were not to be found, having silently withdrawn.

"Godric! Come quick—the bowl, the cloth, the . . ."

She felt Lord Gilbert grow heavy in her arms, the fit beginning to pass. To Ana's relief, the frightening moment ceased, his lordship's breaths short and wheezing now.

With the greatest of care, Ana and Sir Royce lay Lord Gilbert back against the pillows. He quieted, his gaze drawing to her. As Lord Gilbert held Ana in his sight, his eyes dimmed, a long breath escaping his lips, a stillness stealing over him.

Ana's heart cracked, a strangled cry wrenching from her throat, echoing in her ears. Throwing herself across Lord Gilbert's lifeless body, she sobbed uncontrollably. She continued to pour out her anguish, only vaguely aware when Sir Royce drew her back and turned her into his arms.

Desolate, Ana wrapped her arms about Sir Royce's torso, clinging tightly, sobbing against his chest. His arms enveloped her, strong and consoling, shielding her from all the world it seemed.

Ana cried long and hard. She felt like a child again, her heart and emotions ripped apart as bitterly as they'd been long ago—long ago on the night she'd found solace in her squire's embrace . . . so like this moment in the knight's arms.

Royce oversaw the activity in the castle ward as he prepared to depart and escort Juliana and their small retinue to Penhurst.

From time to time, he glanced to the south tower, restless for one of the king's counselors to appear with the documents concerning his land. Hopefully they'd located the illusive Lord Craven who yet retained them. Royce was loathe to leave Wallingford with the matter unfinished.

Pacing along the line of packhorses and carts, he began to inspect each, confirming they were loaded and ready. As he did, he acknowledged Lord Gilbert's men-at-arms one by one, the frosty morn clouding his breath.

It came as a surprise to learn the lord maintained eight soldiers at Wallingford. 'Twas understandable, for they comprised Lord Gilbert's personal guards and ever accompanied him in his travels. Most recently, they'd seen him here, to Wallingford, where they remained awaiting his next command. Now, lamentably, they would companion his lordship back to his estate in Hampshire a final time.

According to the document Lord Gilbert had conferred on Royce, over a dozen more men-at-arms secured Penhurst, the full compliment being twenty-five. By accepting guardianship of the estate and its heiress, Royce assumed authority over them as well.

Moving on, he came to Godric and Brodric, who insisted on taking the reins of the wagon that bore the lord's banner-draped coffin. Guy of Lisors took charge of one of the luggage carts, having asked that he might travel with them to Penhurst as well. The king and queen would be departing Wallingford on the morrow, Guy explained, and he held no wish to take up the sort of scrambling life of which royals seemed so fond. For a pallet by the fire, and a bit of meat and bread, he promised to complete his song for Sir Royce.

Though Royce knew little of Guy's song, he agreed. Much might be gleaned from the minstrel, whose wandering profession took him regularly from castle to castle.

Completing his inspection, Royce made a final check on Hannibal and Nutmeg, the smooth-gaited palfrey he'd acquired for Juliana. He gave a tug to their saddle straps, and to those of the sturdy little pony that would serve Luvena.

Finished, he looked to the keep and discovered Juliana emerging, accompanied by the king and queen, Luvena bustling behind as they descended the steps. The queen's ladies-in-waiting and several Court officials followed as well. Royce quickly spied Lady Sibylla among the company.

He returned his gaze to Juliana. She moved woodenly, swathed in her fur-lined cape, the hood pulled up, her face pale and unsmiling deep within. Halfway down the stairs, she lifted her gaze to meet his. The pain he read in her eyes lanced him straight through, surely as though he'd taken a spear in his chest. Outwardly, the maid appeared carved from marble, emotionless. But within, Royce held certain, a fire burned at her core.

Leading the mounts forward, he joined the group at the bottom of the steps and bowed deeply to the royals.

"I shall miss your presence, Sir Royce." The king spoke first, motioning him to rise. "I'd hoped you would accompany me on my tour through the North Midlands—to Nottingham, Lincoln, Stamford, and such. Another time, perchance. God see you and Lady Juliana safe to Penhurst."

The king started to turn away, then stayed his step. "'Tis my understanding, according to the document awarding you guardianship, Lord Gilbert asks that you choose a husband for his granddaughter and soon."

"Aye, Majesty. 'Tis true." Suspicion spiraled through Royce at the king's interest.

King John held out a hand to the official standing nearest him. Instantly, the man produced a small scroll and placed it in the sovereign's palm.

"No doubt you will be approached by many would-be suitors. I've drawn up my own list of suggestions, which you might consider. These men, you can be assured, are all looked upon favorably by the Crown."

Royce accepted the scroll, keen to the king's plain intent to control, if not actually make, the selection of a husband for Juliana. A loyal knight would be expected to yield to the king's wishes, whatever they might be.

When King John remained silent, Isabella touched her fingers to his forearm.

"Ah, yes. I forgot to add. The queen and I desire for you and Lady Juliana to join us at the Christmas Court. 'Twill be held at . . ." John frowned and looked to his officials.

"Guildford," the queen supplied softly.

"Aye, Guildford. 'Tis my hunting lodge, south of the Thames, if you're not familiar with it. Join us there, and we will gladden the festivities by announcing Lady Juliana's betrothal and the name of the fortunate man who will take her to wife."

Royce glanced to Juliana, and though she did not so much as blink a lash, he saw the look of shock pass through her eyes. They mirrored his own surprise. The king moved quickly to award the estate and form a new alliance. His haste gave Royce pause to wonder of Penhurst's true value. It also gave rise to a new concern. If he didn't choose a husband for Juliana soon, would the king force the matter, even usurp his own authority as the maid's guardian?

As Royce started to reply to the king, Lady Sibylla left the steps, moving to his side. She lay her hand on his chest, a possessive gesture for all to see, though she directed her words expressly to him.

"Let us make the Court celebrations doubly festive with two announcements." She smiled meaningfully as she drew a scarf of red silk from the sleeve of her gown and draped it around his neck. Kissing his cheek, she further placed her mark upon him, drawing ripples of approval from those upon the steps—though not from all.

"By your leave, Majesties, Countess." Royce took a step apart of Sibylla. "'Tis best Lady Juliana and I depart and see Lord Gilbert to his rest."

He meant the words as a reminder, finding his mood increasingly irritable. The funeral rites had not even been spoken. Yet, 'twas as though everyone gathered around a living chess board, their hands clutching at the playing pieces, moving them about to their own advantage—he and Juliana suddenly naught but pawns in their games.

The maiden, who'd remained unmoving and silent for so long, started down the steps to join him, but found her way blocked when the queen unintentionally moved in front of her to whisper something to the king.

King John straightened, a slight flush coloring his cheeks as he gestured to another of the officials. The man gave over a packet of folded parchments, bound with a leather cord.

"This, Sir Royce, contains your grant from my brother, Richard, plus a license to crenellate. Though the property needs some attention, 'tis well situated, as I've said before. Improve on its fortifications, and Beckwell will stand alongside other strongholds as a powerful link in England's defenses, one of great consequence, mark my words."

Royce received the packet and slipped it inside his leather jerkin, beneath his mail and surcoat. "My gratitude, Majesty," he said, relieved to obtain the papers at last. "Until Christmas at Guildford then."

Royce bowed, bid farewell to the Countess, then, stepping forward, held out a hand to Juliana. The maid paused long enough to receive a parting kiss from the queen on her cheek, then hastened to join him. Royce led her directly to the palfrey and was pleased that Juliana seemed as anxious as he to be away. But in the next moment, she shied from the horse, hesitating to mount. Having no wish to be further delayed, Royce scooped Juliana up in his arms and lifted her onto the sidesaddle.

"This is Nutmeg," he introduced the palfrey. "She possesses a sweet disposition and her gait is smooth and steady. You'll have no trouble staying atop her. The saddle even has a back like a little chair."

Royce assured she was properly positioned, then handed her the reins. Juliana gazed down at the traces, looking perfectly daunted.

"On second thought, I'll hold the reins and lead Nutmeg," Royce offered. "You concentrate on staying in the saddle."

Seeing Luvena needed help to mount her pony, he excused himself long enough to aid her up. He'd no sooner placed her in the saddle, but a servant woman rushed forth, calling to the little maid, a bundle in her hands.

"'Tis Lady Juliana's gown." The woman handed the bundle up to her.

"Are you certain?" Luvena knitted her brows. "I am sure I packed them all."

"Yes, the laundress has had the dress for several days," the woman panted out. "There were so many gowns needing special treatment, she only now saw to Lady Juliana's."

"Hers was left till last?" Luvena's voice rose several notes. "Hopefully, 'twas not because she is the newest lady at Court."

"Oh, nay, I'm sure not." The woman shook her head.

Royce reached up and relieved Luvena of the bundle, fearing they'd be here the rest of the morning discussing the gown. "Here, I'll see it added to one of the packhorses," he promised.

After seeing this done. Royce pulled up his coif of mail, covering his hair, and mounted Hannibal. He then caught up Nutmeg's reins and with a parting nod to the royal couple and Lady Sibylla, he turned the stallion and led Juliana and their retinue through the gates of Wallingford.

Emerging from the great fortress, he directed them south toward Hampshire and Penhurst.

PART IV

A Storm in the Heart

"Love's a stern and valiant knight,
strong astride a steed;
Love's a thing that pleasures every
longing woman's need;
Love persists and keeps its heat
like any glowing gleed:
Love puts girls in floods of tears,
they rage and cry indeed."
—Anonymous

15

Penhurst Castle, Hampshire

Ana braced herself against the wind's frigid bite as she stood atop the parapet of Penhurst Castle, gazing over the curtain wall. Below, Sir Royce emerged from the gate astride Hannibal, three men-at-arms riding behind, as they set out for East Anglia.

Ana drew deeper into her mantle and hood, watching the figures move into the distance. She prayed they would reach their destination safely, before the next snowfall. The sky did not look promising. Its leaden cast was the same as it had been just before blanketing the road to Penhurst and slowing the progress of their little retinue from Wallingford. Fortunately, by then they'd drawn within five miles of the castle.

Thinking back to their arrival, Ana recalled the dubious looks that had greeted them, looks that had quickly turned to ones of grief on seeing his lordship's banner-draped coffin.

But as jolting for the castlefolk as news of their master's death was the appearance of Penhurst's lost heiress. In truth, Lord Gilbert had begun a letter to his seneschal, Edmond Kovey, apprising him of Ana's arrival in England with Sir Royce. But Lord Gilbert had continued to add to the missive and delayed sending it, until 'twas too late. Thus, when Sir Royce made their introduction, he presented both Lord Gilbert's letter announcing his granddaughter's return,

plus the document appointing him as guardian to Juliana
Mandeville and all that was Penhurst's.

Suspicions lingered on the faces of the castlefolk until
Godric and Brodric stepped forward and verified all that
had passed at Wallingford. Penhurst's soldiery were the first
to embrace Sir Royce and place themselves under his command. Many were already familiar with his name and tales
of his feats beside the Lionheart in the East. What they'd
not heard of the knight, Guy of Lisors was quick to supply
in verse. Still, it wasn't until after Lord Gilbert had been en-
tombed in the castle's chapel, beside his wife, Thérèse, that
the others began to accept Sir Royce's authority and
acknowledge Ana as Penhurst's new mistress.

Ana, on the other hand, felt grossly out of place. She also found herself the object of intense curiosity. Few would
approach her, though everyone watched her. Or so it
seemed. Ana felt miserably alone, isolated.

To make matters worse, Sir Royce arranged to depart
Penhurst this day—one day following the funeral—eager to
claim his land in East Anglia before winter descended full
force. To her disappointment, the knight refused to take her
with him. Instead, he left her in the seneschal's charge with
instructions to begin her lessons and training in the basics
of reading, ciphering, and the running of a castle household.

Ana suspected Sir Royce also left warnings with the
seneschal, lest she attempt to slip away. 'Twas her fault she
knew, for during their journey here, she'd asked again of
returning to Chinon. Where Sir Royce had assumed she'd
accepted her identity and noble station, she'd doltishly revealed she'd not. To her dismay, Ana discovered she'd trad-
ed one prison for another, Wallingford for Penhurst.

"My lady, come away before you catch your death!"
Luvena's voice sounded on the parapet's walk.

Ana turned to see the maid hastening toward her with

rapid little steps. Dear Luvena, Ana thought, she was the one true friend she had in this place, in this land. Ana sighed inwardly. How she missed Georges, Marie, Gervase, all her friends back home. Did they think as much of her, as she did of them?

"My lady, come now," Luvena urged as she joined her. "There's hot stew waiting in the hall. 'Twill put some warmth back in your bones. Mine as well," she added with a decided shiver.

Ana cast a quick glance toward the horizon. The landscape appeared empty, the men gone.

"Very well, Luvena." She smiled at the petite maid. "Perhaps after our meal we can explore more of Penhurst. There's much I've yet to see."

"Perhaps, if the seneschal doesn't have you working at your numbers." Luvena turned and led the way back to the narrow parapet steps.

Ana followed the maid down and across the courtyard to the Great Hall. Compared to Wallingford, Penhurst was a modest fortification. Its stout curtain wall was of rugged limestone, but all the buildings within were of timber, excepting the chapel and Great Hall. No mammoth keep loomed in the ward, though the defense walls bore a series of towers around its perimeter.

Penhurst had appealed to Ana from the first, as did its setting in the Meon Valley with its surrounding yew and beech forests. Though secluded, the castle was in no way cut off from the rest of the land for they'd encountered numerous little villages along the river leading here. Then, too, an old Roman road stretched from the Meon Valley to Winchester.

Ana slowed her steps, unsure how she knew of the Roman road. Yet, she felt certain of its existence.

Entering the hall, she looked neither right nor left, but

continued to follow Luvena as she directed her the length of the chamber to the lord's dais.

"Must I sit here?" Ana whispered, bending toward the maid. "I'll be alone. Perhaps you should sit with me."

"That wouldn't be proper, Lady Juliana. You are the mistress of Penhurst."

Ana straightened, clasping her hands before her. "I've no wish to sit by myself upon the dais, to be gawked at by those in the hall."

"But you cannot leave, my lady. You are expected to sup with those who serve the castle."

"Then at least allow me someone to talk to. What of the seneschal? Would he be acceptable?"

"I believe so, my lady. I'll ask that he join you at once."

As Luvena hastened away, Ana took her place on the dais, sitting in Lord Gilbert's high-backed chair. Several servants hastened forward with a bowl of stew, rolls, and a goblet of wine. She thanked them—graciously, she thought—then wondered if 'twas proper for the lady of the castle to do so. Self-conscious, she fingered the base of her goblet, aware that many an eye had begun to drift in her direction, snatching glimpses of her. What did these people think of her? Ana wondered. Did they believe her to be an impostor, a fraud, even as she felt herself to be? Blast Sir Royce for abandoning her like this.

Ana snatched up the goblet then paused as she gazed into its contents. There, she saw her reflection wavering over the wine's surface, gazing back. What was to become of her? As she'd feared, the English nobles—believing her to be an heiress—wished to quickly marry her off, Lord Gilbert had wished it himself, though out of sincere motives. The king, however, pressured Sir Royce to choose her a husband, one to the Crown's political advantage.

Ana clenched her hand beneath the table. If only she

could convince Sir Royce to not betroth her to another at all. If she understood rightly, as her guardian, he was entitled to collect the rents from Penhurst and its fiefs, and keep them for himself. Surely, that must appeal to him.

The folly of her plan lay in that 'twas almost certain Sir Royce and Lady Sibylla would marry. If Ana remained his ward and unmarried, then she would be forced to live under the countess's domination, perhaps even under the same roof. 'Twould be intolerable, Ana deemed, shifting on her chair. She had no wish to spend the nights lodged in a chamber nearby the couple, knowing they took their pleasures of one another, or of watching Sibylla swell with Sir Royce's child. And what if he should be called away? Ana would then be left totally under his wife's authority.

Gripping the goblet, Ana downed a mouthful of wine, then grimaced. 'Twas as sour as her last thought.

"Is my lady all right?"

Ana looked up to find Edmond Kovey gazing down on her, concern creasing his eyes. She forced a smile past the offensive taste in her mouth.

"I believe we shall need to do something about the castle's drink."

"As you wish, my lady. I'll speak to the butler at once." He started to turn away.

"Please, join me. I'd hoped you might answer a few questions that I have." She eyed his thinning white hair. "Did you serve Lord Gilbert very long?"

"Seven years, my lady."

Ana's hopes deflated. "Then you wouldn't have known Lord Gilbert's daughter, Lady Alyce, or Sir Robert Mandeville."

"I know of your parents, my lady, and of you as well. Lord Gilbert spoke long and often of you all. Since your own disappearance, he became obsessed with finding you."

"So I understand." Ana studied her hands a moment, as she considered what question she might ask next.

The seneschal cleared a sudden roughness in his throat. "On behalf of the others of Penhurst, may I say that we are all quite happy you were found, Lady Juliana."

Was she glad? Ana asked herself. At the moment, she felt overwhelmed and out of place and wishing to flee before she was forced into an undesired marriage. But how could she accomplish it? Who would help her? In all the commotion following Lord Gilbert's death, their travels, his funeral, she'd not once found a moment to question Sir Royce of her squire. And yet to what purpose now? If her squire hadn't returned from the East as Lord Gilbert said— whether he be alive or dead—he couldn't help her, not from *Outremer*.

Ana returned her attention to the seneschal. "Do you know of Sir Robert Mandeville's castle? 'Twas a Marcher castle along the Welsh border, I believe. Yet, 'twas not mentioned in my inheritance."

Ana winced at her own words, as they sounded so greedy. Her question didn't seem to faze Edmond Kovey, however.

"'Tis a regrettable thing, but as Sir Robert died without issue or living relatives, his holdings reverted to the Crown and have long since been awarded to another. 'Twas assumed you, yourself, were dead, my lady. Lord Gilbert alone did not give up hope of finding you."

"I see," she said quietly, recalling the mountains she'd seen in her dreams. Were they naught but fabrications?

Some part of France she'd once viewed? But when, where? Ana felt certain she'd seen nothing to compare to the mountains of her dreaming.

"If it pleases you, my lady, Lord Gilbert kept a trunk containing items belonging to his daughter and son-in-law.

Would you care to inspect it?"

"Very much so. Now, if you please." Ana set her goblet down and rose. Motioning to Luvena to join them, she followed the seneschal from the hall.

In short time, they entered Lord Gilbert's bedchamber. Ana hesitated on the threshold, feeling as though she was about to intrude upon the dead. The room was spacious, having a large canopied bed hung with silks and an immense fireplace faced with elaborate carvings. Tapestries brightened the walls, while small tables and chairs and a number of oaken trunks lined the walls' perimeter.

The seneschal led Ana to the largest of the trunks. Drawing out a ring of iron keys, he fished through them and seized on the one marked with blue yarn. Setting it to the lock, he then opened the trunk's top and stepped back.

Ana sank to her knees before the trunk, brimming with carefully preserved clothing and varied possessions of the deceased couple. Spying a small book set with jewels upon its cover, Ana lifted it out. Carefully, she opened the volume and became instantly enthralled by the glorious illuminations she found there—miniature paintings gilded with gold.

"'Tis a lady's *Book of Hours,*" Luvena offered. "It must have been your mother's."

Ana looked up at Luvena, the strangest of sensations rippling through her. "Would she have used it for her prayers?" Ana guessed.

"Exactly so, my lady. Have you seen such a book before?"

"Nay, Luvena. Never." Ana gave her attention to the pages, studying them slowly, one by one, stopping when she came upon an exquisite painting of the Virgin. She was beautiful, her blonde hair flowing to her fingertips, her small face reminding Ana of the woman in her dreams.

Ana closed the book and set it aside, her breaths suddenly shallow.

"Look here," Luvena said with a note of awe, as she removed a man's surcoat from the trunk for Ana to see. 'Twas made of fine wool—a rich blue, accented with silver.

"The garment's not quite finished," Luvena noted. "Lady Alyce must have been sewing it for your father. And see there, the red fabric . . ." She pointed into the trunk. "'Tis cut into the shape of a cross—the badge of the Crusaders. No doubt, Lady Alyce intended to sew it onto the tunic's shoulder."

Ana's gaze leapt to Luvena. The image of the man in Dover Castle flashed through her mind, and of the girl he held, reaching for something of interest on his shoulder—a red cross, perchance?

Ana shut her mind to the images, not wishing to face them at the moment. Giving her interest back to the trunk, she browsed through its costly contents—clothing fashioned in brocades, silks, velvets, and furs. Then, too, there were embroidered leather gloves, shoes of different colors, and an assortment of jewelery for both a man and a woman.

Near the bottom of the trunk, Ana felt something hard beneath the last layer of fabric. Pulling the cloth back, she discovered a small jointed knight, exactly as the one in her dreams. The scar on Ana's hand began to itch as she took up the wooden figure. Her fingers trembled.

"Edmond, did Lady Alyce and Sir Robert have a son?"

"Nay, my lady. No sons."

Ana rubbed her brow. She didn't understand this. Perhaps there was naught to her dreams and imaginings after all, only coincidence. She wanted it to be that, desperately so. Even now she could feel unnamed emotions rise in her breast and clash within her. 'Twas coincidence, she told herself, that and nothing more.

The seneschal came to stand beside her, his brows

drawn together in thought. "Lady Alyce and Sir Robert did have a nephew, however—your cousin, on your father's side. I understand the families gathered at Penhurst often. Alas, the lad's entire family died tragically of the pox when he was but ten. Do you think the toy might be his?"

Ana stared at the little figure in her hand. She didn't want to hear these words, didn't want to believe there to be anything of substance to her dreams or imaginings. For if she did, she must face the shadows that lay within her—the darkness that held her past.

Beckwell, East Anglia, near Godmanchester

Royce reined Hannibal to a halt as he scanned the horizon, vast and empty beneath enormous skies. Yet, 'twas not wholly vacant, he realized, spotting a man-built structure in the distance. He could make out battlements and a square keep jutting upward, pricking at the clouds.

As his companions drew their mounts beside his, Royce pointed a gloved hand toward the castle. "'Tis Beckwell. It appears sound enough does it not?"

"Sir?" The knight named Stephen raised a questioning brow at his statement.

"Beckwell was one of the adulterine castles that old Henry slighted when he gained his crown—so King John tells me," Royce explained. "It looks whole from this vantage, though we'll know soon enough what damage it sustained. And we'll know more when we speak with Beckwell's seneschal."

Royce bid the men forward across the open landscape, approaching the castle from its west side. As he urged Hannibal onward, it struck him that he knew not the name of the current seneschal. The position had changed hands several times to his knowledge. While at Wallingford, the royal counselors made no mention of the present official's name. No matter. He'd learn that soon enough, too.

Royce pressed on across the frozen ground. As the little band drew closer to their goal, he noticed the small village that lay beyond the castle, sprawling toward the River Ouse. The village fell short of the descriptions he'd been given. Still, any village would be an important asset to a castle, a support to its daily operations.

Royce and his men skirted the west side of the curtain wall, a handsome piece of defense work, tall and solidly built. Arriving on the south entrance side, they headed toward the gatehouse, another impressive construction. As Royce guided Hannibal onto the bridge, he saw that the gate stood open, unmanned. He knew Beckwell did not maintain a garrison, nonetheless, an unsettling feeling crept over him.

Crossing over the bridge and beneath the gatehouse archways, the four entered the castle's lower ward. 'Twas of substantial size, but where the curtain wall rose high on the south, west, and north sides, the entire length of the eastern wall was all but gone, reduced to rubble.

Royce drew his gaze slowly about the ward. The buildings stood in total disrepair—the stables, barracks, smithy, granary, and other dependencies—relics from years past, their thatched roofs rotted and caved in, their doors and shutters gone. Nothing moved within the walls of Beckwell, neither man nor beast, save for Royce's own small company from Penhurst.

Steeling his emotions, Royce guided Hannibal toward the Great Hall where it rose against the west wall. 'Twas a stone structure, considerable in size and holding some promise. It looked to have once served its lord proudly.

Royce rode the stallion directly through the wide door-less portal fronting the hall, and passed inside. Crossing over age-old rushes that still scattered the earthen floor, he brought Hannibal to a halt in the center of the great chamber. Royce lifted his gaze only to find the sky stretched overhead, the roof totally gone.

Again Royce bridled his emotions. Disappointment mingled with frustration and gnawed at his soul. He need rely on reason and sound logic, he knew, refusing to acknowledge the dull anger gathering within him, or to allow his feelings to rule him. Royce emerged from the hall and headed for the upper bailey, motioning the others to follow. As he passed through the inner defense wall—this only partially standing—he eyed the tall tower keep. He took heart, for it appeared untouched. Perhaps he'd find Beckwell's seneschal lodged there.

As his companions joined him, Royce dismounted and began the climb the timber stairs leading to the keep's entry on the second level. Gaining this, he entered in and called out several times. No answer came. Alert for any sound, Royce and his men mounted the inner stairs, ascending four stories before finally emerging atop the keep.

Stepping to the parapet wall, Royce gazed out over his newly gained land, the ruins of Beckwell at his feet. He'd been duped. But by Richard or by John?

John spoke truly when he'd said his brother Richard would not easily give up anything of value he could sell. The Lionheart had constantly exhausted his coffers for his endless campaigns. Had Richard unloaded this pile on him, expecting him to restore it at his own cost? On the other hand, John was known to be greedy and close-fisted, holding back anything of worth. Had John switched the property? Did Birkwell exist in Kent, a different estate altogether from this one before him? Did it make a difference which king had deceived him?

Disheartened, Royce braced his hands against the stone and considered his options. He'd acquired a modest fortune while in the East. Beckwell would take that and more to put it to rights. 'Twas not the castle alone that required funds. He would need to hire men-at-arms to defend it, as well as maintain the attendants and servants needed to see to the castle's smooth functioning.

A thought slipped into the back of Royce's mind. If he married Countess Linford, 'twould not matter so much whether Beckwell was ever restored. He'd instantly gain position, power, and wealth, giving him the ability to wield his knightly skills for right, to influence affairs in direct and positive ways. And if he did choose to restore Beckwell, he would have ample funds at his command to do so.

The king had been correct in one other thing—Beckwell was well situated. It lay near two important crossroads, connecting it with London and York, on the one hand, and Colchester and Chester, on the other. Market towns, such as Huntingdon, St. Ives, and St. Neots, dotted the River Ouse. Beckwell could prove an important and thriving addition, offering more than commerce but security to the region, shoring up the defense link it originally held.

Royce considered the countess. Would she accept him, despite the ruinous condition of his estate? She vowed it mattered not to her if he were landless. Beckwell should pose no obstacle to their marriage. Still . . .

Royce remained steeped in his ponderings, when one of his men pointed abruptly down at the eastern wall.

"Sir Royce, see there! The peasants are stealing from Beckwell even as we watch."

Royce gazed down into the lower ward, near the front gate. There a small army of peasants worked at lifting a block of dressed stone.

"They must not have seen us arrive. Our horses are hidden from their sight in the upper ward."

Royce watched as the peasants slid the stone into their

wagon. This accomplished, they headed out of the castle gate and back toward the village.

"No wonder Beckwell is a crumbling ruin," he vented, tasting of his anger. "What the king's father began when he slighted the castle, the peasants finish by thieving it."

"'Twould appear they steal for Mother Church." Stephen pointed to where the cart trundled directly toward the church on the village green.

"We'll see about that," Royce growled. "Mother Church is about to be visited by her unwitting benefactor!"

Forsaking the keep, he hastened down the steps to the ward, his companions close behind him. Casting himself into his saddle, Royce set his heels to Hannibal's flanks and urged him across the upper and lower wards and through the castle gate. In short minutes, he galloped furiously along the village's main road, startling the inhabitants, who darted like mice into their houses.

Pressing on to the village green, Royce hard-reined Hannibal to a halt as he came upon the church, the cart visible at the side where the peasants were beginning to unload the stone. Glancing about, Royce realized there were actually two churches here—one small and narrow, overshadowed by a newer, much grander one, not yet complete.

"Very good men. Easy now. This way." A monkish/robed figure appeared, directing the peasants in a voice as gritty as sand. The churchman proved short and round, his head tonsured, leaving a fringe of peppery hair that perfectly matched his wiry brows.

"What goes here?" Royce bellowed, causing the churchman to jump in his cowl and his scrubby brows to fly high. The workmen abandoned the block of stone and shrank back from the wagon.

"W-Why the Lord's work goes here, good knight," the churchman avowed, pulling himself up importantly, setting his jowls atremble as he did so.

"With *my* stone?" Royce growled.

"*Your* stone?"

"Aye, and you are thieving it. I am Sir Royce de War-rene, Lord of Beckwell by grant of the king."

"King John grants you Beckwell?"

"King Richard."

"But Richard is dead."

Royce's patience snapped. Did the man play him a fool or was he simply dense? "Certainly, the Lionheart is dead, but he granted me the lands of Birkwell *before* his untimely death."

The churchman gave a nervous, gravelly laugh and came forward several paces. "Birkwell? Why didn't you say so? Good sir, this is *Beckwell*. I fear you have come to the wrong place."

Royce clenched his jaw at the churchman's craftiness. He removed the papers from beneath his mail coat and held them out.

"King John assures me Birkwell and Beckwell are one in the same. Regardless, this packet contains a license to crenellate, signed and sealed by His Majesty. It specifies Beckwell by name."

"Saints in Heaven," the churchman muttered, his fingers flying to his mouth. He turned to his peasant helpers and waved them away. "Children, go along to your homes. I'll see to this matter." He gave his attention back to Royce. "Perhaps you and your men should come inside."

"No need, Father . . ."

"Friar, Friar Tupper. My assistant and I belong to a mendicant order," he added when Royce sent him a questioning look. "Just a small one—the Canons Regular of St. Augustine."

Royce caught sight of a second, much younger churchman, identically robed in a black cowl, peering from the door of the church. Royce eased back in his saddle. He was aware of the mendicants—religious who belonged to monastic communities but who carried their calling outside the monastery walls. Royce shoved the papers back beneath his jerkin and mail coat.

"Can you tell me what has become of the seneschal who was assigned to oversee Beckwell?"

"I've not the remotest idea, my son. God's truth."

"I was assured a seneschal resided at the castle and that my estate was being administered by the nearby bishopric. I even received reports from the king's accountants whilst I was in *Outremer.*"

"*Outremer?*" Friar Tupper's eyes rounded. "You fought in the Crusades? With the Lionheart?"

"That I did. But let us keep to the subject of Beckwell. What know you of the estate or the bishopric that administers it?"

The friar tugged thoughtfully on his heavy chin, his brows pulling together in a bushy line. "Beckwell belongs to the See of Ely. Benedictines there, you know. They've a community at Huntingdon also. Perhaps 'tis they who manage Beckwell directly."

Royce considered this. If they did, there was no evidence that they'd applied any of the land's income to its upkeep or improvement. The castle was a ruinous pile.

"The Crown and See remember us when they require rents and taxes, but we here at Beckwell are otherwise forgotten," the friar continued as though reading his thoughts. "No one has inhabited the castle since before I arrived. 'Tis why men such as I, and Friar Woodruff, must tend to the flock of Beckwell—laboring in God's vineyard where kings do not."

Royce afforded the man a tolerant look then guided

Hannibal around the church construction, studying its progress. 'Twas complete for the most part, excepting one wing. It even boasted a fine slate roof to shelter the worshipers. He looked back at the churchman.

"Would those be the slates from Beckwell's Great Hall?"

The Friar flushed a deep shade of red. "Sir Royce, I know nothing of your grant, or the reports you received. The castle has been moldering, unattended, for at least a decade, mayhap more. 'Tis as forgotten as are Beckwell's people. The village once served the castle, long before its slighting. Should not the castle now serve the people since the Crown will not?"

"Serve the people? How so? You build yourself a new and larger church is all, yet I see you already have one."

"An ancient Saxon structure, tiny and crumbling."

"Thus, you thieve from my castle to build a new place in which to offer your prayers?"

"To offer prayers, aye. But a church of staunch stone serves as more than a place of worship. It provides shelter in the event of an attack."

"There is the castle keep. 'Tis in good repair. I've just come from it myself," Royce countered.

"True, but it lies at a distance. Should an attack come suddenly and the villagers be unable to reach the keep, what are they to do? Think of the women and children, Sir Royce, and how defenseless they would be. As I said, the old church is crumbling. It cannot withstand a single assault. Thus we build a new, more solid, structure—one to serve God's children in *all* their needs."

Unexpectedly, the friar's arguments cast Royce's thoughts back in time, back to the night he followed Sir Hugh into the burning village of Vaux. He recalled their arrival on the green, the sight of the dead—the people cut down as they'd sought to gain the church—and the sight of those who'd survived, crouching in the church's doorway.

How did anyone survive that night? Royce wondered anew, feeling a sudden pang deep in his chest in the vicinity of his heart. Royce's thoughts strayed to Ana—his little Ana. What would have become of her had Sir Hugh's retinue not happened on Vaux that night? Or had he not lost his grip on himself and sought the river's edge? What if he'd not found her beneath the boat?

Refocusing his attention on the churchman, Royce found Friar Tupper staring at him with his hands folded over his portly belly, giving him a most solemn look.

"As the new Lord of Beckwell, 'tis my fervent hope you will support our efforts and prove a generous sponsor of our village church."

Royce grunted, still clearing the memories from his head. Obviously, the friar wished for him to approve the construction and allow the villagers to keep the stone. Royce was not prepared to give him an answer. He shifted his thoughts in a different direction.

"How long have you ministered to Beckwell, friar?"

"Half a decade." The churchman gave a small shrug.

"Long enough."

"Sir?"

"Is that your assistant lurking at the door?"

"Aye, 'tis Friar Woodruff."

"Good. Inform him he will be tending Beckwell's flock in your absence."

"My absence?"

"Aye, friar, you are coming with me. I've many questions and you, I believe, hold a good number of the answers."

"Coming? Where, sir? To the castle?" Friar Tupper blustered, his bushy brows parting wide.

"Nay, 'tis unlivable and other matters press me sorely. We ride for Hampshire and Penhurst Castle. There I expect a full reckoning of Beckwell's past."

16

Penhurst Castle, Hampshire

Activity filled the ward as Royce and his companions rode through the gates of Penhurst. At once, he spotted the differing liveries among the men there, most in the process of grooming their steeds. The visitors looked to comprise small parties of personal guards such as those traveling with him.

Had their lords come to offer their condolences on Lord Gilbert's death? Or to tell Royce of some alliance they'd shared with Penhurst's late master? As he brought Hannibal to a halt before the stables, the truth of the matter struck him in a blinding flash. The men came to offer their suits for Juliana's hand in marriage.

Royce dismounted and gave over Hannibal's reins to a groom, then strode directly toward the Great Hall. Irritation multiplied along his spine. The petitioners had descended quickly enough on Penhurst. He'd been gone less than two weeks. Likely they'd used his absence to inspect the property fully, as well as the prospective bride. His mood blackened at that thought. Setting his jaw, he entered the hall.

Few noticed his presence at first, excepting the hounds that stirred from the rushes, their tails switching in greeting. A festive air filled the hall, the minstrel's bright music a backdrop to the rumble of male voices. Servants scurried from table to table with platters of food and pitchers of drink, seeing to the needs of various lords and lesser knights. Royce counted thirty in all.

His gaze drew to Juliana where she sat upon the dais, entertaining her guests with merry conversation and winsome smiles. The most important-looking of the lords held seats beside her. They appeared utterly beguiled with the maid, outwardly at least. Royce shoved back his coif of mail, at the same time discovering Edmond at his elbow.

"My lord, welcome back," the seneschal said with a nervous smile. "We've gained a number of guests whilst you were away. They insisted on waiting for your return. Each claims to have a pressing need to speak with you. 'Tis my impression their business concerns Penhurst's lady, though none have declared it so."

"I thought as much." Royce stripped off his gloves and jammed them into his belt. "How long have they been here?"

"Three days, only, but they and their escorts have been quick to devour our stores."

Like a plague of locusts, Royce thought grimly. "And Lady Juliana, has she been amusing them ever since?"

He glanced again to the maid, missing the seneschal's response as he caught her gaze. Juliana rose instantly from her chair and took up her goblet, abandoning the dais. Royce watched as she crossed down the center of the hall, bearing the vessel toward him. At the same time, he did not miss the hot, wolfish looks that followed her.

"Welcome, Sir Knight." Juliana smiled, coming to stand before him, offering up the goblet. "Ale to ease the discomforts of your journey. 'Tis fresh."

Royce gazed at the maid, surprised that she appeared genuinely pleased to see him. "Thank you, Juliana, but a little later. For now, I've a matter to attend to with our guests, and I would prefer for you to withdraw to your chamber."

She lowered her arms, her smile fading. "Guy is not yet

finished his song."

"He is now." Royce signaled for the minstrel to cease. As the music subsided, those in the hall turned to seek the cause. "Go now, Juliana," he urged, seeing their guests rising from their places, preparing to deluge him with their suits.

"But I wish to remain," she balked. "I'm very much enjoying the company. These gentlemen have journeyed long distances to offer their sympathy for Lord Gilbert's death."

"Sympathy?" Royce spouted. "Is that the reason you believe them to be here?"

"Why, yes, of course. That and to meet the new guardian of Penhurst," she replied, full of innocence, her smile returning. "Surely, they wish to inform you of whatever bonds they shared with Lord Gilbert. They must have been fast friends of his, or supporters at least." She glanced back to the men. "They've been most kind, too. As they accept me as his granddaughter, they have sought to lighten my spirits and distract me from my grief."

Royce stared at Juliana, incredulous at her guileless assumptions. "Lady, has it escaped your consideration that these men come for more than to offer condolences or to acquaint themselves with my person?" Her brows twinged together at that. "'Tis your hand in marriage they seek. Now, I must speak with them and much prefer you keep from sight until I can be done with the matter."

Juliana paled, her eyes grown huge. "You need not speak with them at all. Just send them away, Sir Knight. I wish to marry none of them."

"'Tis my duty. I vowed to Lord Gilbert to find you a husband, and the king insists the choice be made by Christmas."

"Lord Gilbert also bound you to take my feelings into consideration."

"And I will, Juliana. Still, in fairness, I must allow each man who has traveled here the courtesy of listening to what he has to say."

"Fairness?" she cried. "Fairness to them, but what of to me?" Incensed, she hurled the goblet into the rushes, sending the contents splashing wide.

Juliana gave Royce her back and crossed to the back of the hall, exiting to where her chamber lay. As she disappeared from sight, the visiting lords and knights converged upon Royce, each trying to make himself heard.

Royce grabbed for the seneschal. He caught him by the sleeve and hauled him close. "Edmond, see these men's cups are kept full of ale and order me a hot bath. I'll meet with them once I've rid myself of my armor and the layers of dirt I've garnered in my travels."

Royce started to release the seneschal then drew him back. "I nearly forgot. I've brought with me a certain Friar Tupper from Beckwell. You'll find him in the ward somewhere. He'll be needing quarters."

Edmond bobbed his head in understanding, then raising his arms over his head, clamored for the men's attention, allowing Royce a chance to slip from the hall.

Once bathed and dressed, Royce returned and settled himself upon the dais, assuming the traditional high-backed chair of the Lords of Penhurst. Calling for a goblet and pitcher of ale, he braced himself for the coming hours. 'Twould likely require the remainder of the day and possibly the night to meet individually with Juliana's suitors.

As Royce filled his goblet, he bid the first man forward, his mood darkening. He'd returned to Penhurst chilled to the bone and chafing over his lands of Beckwell. He wasn't of a mind to confront the issue of a husband for Juliana. Not yet. But he must if he was to give the king an answer by

Christmas.

As the first suitor climbed onto the dais, Royce downed a mouthful of ale. His gaze leapt to the vessel. If there would be one compensation this day for his efforts, 'twould be the drink. 'Twas uncommonly good. Excellent, in fact. He could not remember when he'd had better.

As Royce looked to the man lowering himself onto the chair beside him, he found a battle-scarred warrior of no less than sixty years. He wore a patch over one eye, presumably missing, his other whitish and cloudy. His hair hung in stringy wisps from a balding pate and half his teeth were gone. The man identified himself as John De Grenfell, Penhurst's neighboring lord. He spoke candidly and to the point. He wanted to join the two properties and add the extra knights' fiefs to his own.

"And what of the bride, Lady Juliana?" Royce pressed.

Grenfell shrugged. "Her needs will be met, and I expect she'll breed. I've some fire left in the hearth for the task. Though, it matters not if she drops any brats. I've sons, four full grown. Henry here is the oldest and will one day inherit." He pointed to a bearish-looking man waiting by the dais. "Should I fail soon, fear not. He'll take guardianship of the lady and see to her interests."

Or his own, Royce thought, drawing on his drink. He recognized Henry as being among those who nearly salivated when Juliana swept past him in the hall. Where the elder Grenfell appeared literally blind to the maid's attributes, naught escaped the son, his appetites sharp and ravenous.

"Thank you for coming, Lord Grenfell, I will consider your suit." Royce helped him from the dais, then refilled his goblet and bid the next man approach.

The following ten suitors proved of middling years with some property already to their names. All sought to enlarge their holdings and exhibited a keen interest in warming the sheets with the maid. Predictably, their main interest lay with the land. A wife they viewed as a domestic helpmate necessary to provide an important service—the begetting of an heir. They all appeared eager to undertake that effort.

Royce called for a new pitcher of ale, as the youngest among the suitors took the seat opposite him. He was a scribe with no holdings and so timid Royce was uncertain he knew how to find his way out of his chausses. Royce recognized him to be one of the swains from Wallingford who'd trailed Juliana about everywhere she went.

As the day progressed to night and everyone in the hall continued to imbibe of their cups, the suitors became more bold, their tongues loosened, their pretenses gone.

"Have no fear, I'll treat her like the queen herself, and keep her belly filled with babes," claimed one.

"If she be shy, she won't be for long. I'll give her something warm to enjoy between her legs," boasted another.

When Royce asked what provisions would be made for Juliana should she be widowed, most named relatives to become her guardian. A few suggested she retire to the nunnery. Royce grew warm, fueled by the ale and his burgeoning temper.

Sir Ulric Bonsall was next to join Royce on the dais. The knight was thirtyish, claiming to have gained his wealth at tournaments but now seeking an heiress with land. Royce found the man coarse in his manners, but owed it in part to the drink. Bonsall claimed he was capable of protecting Penhurst and its lady and keeping her satisfied.

"Let's be honest," he said thickly, leaning forward.

"Lady Juliana is a beauty—rarest of the rare—a choice piece to gratify any husband, but a temptation to all others. I know you will agree, 'tis best to keep such a temptation out of sight."

"Out of sight? Locked up, you mean?"

"Aye."

"You'll find Juliana is a strong-willed maid."

"She'll pose no trouble, or bear the consequence," Bonsall bragged, focusing blearily on his hand as he formed it to a fist. "'Tis a *cunte's* place to obey."

Royce's knuckles exploded across the man's jaw, knocking him off his chair and into the rushes.

"Guards, remove this refuse," he bellowed, standing over the cur who did not deserve the name of knight. "See that he and his men depart at once."

Royce dropped back into his chair and stared into the bottom of his goblet. 'Twas empty again. Sighing heavily, he raised his hand, bidding the next man forward.

Edmond appeared before the dais. "My lord, that was the last one."

"Good." Royce pushed to his feet. "I can stomach no more."

"My lord?" Edmond's voice penetrated the thick wadding of wool that crowded Royce's skull. "My lord, wake up."

"Lord who?" Royce muttered, tasting of the wool in his mouth. 'Twas like an old sock—a *very* old sock. He turned to his other side.

"You, my lord," Edmond persisted. "You are Lord of Beckwell and thus, 'my lord.'"

Royce grunted at that logic and burrowed deeper into his fine feather pillow, a most welcome rest for the block of iron weighting the space where his brain should be. Everything around it seemed stuffed with wool—or perhaps old socks. He couldn't tell.

"My lord, Lady Juliana did not appear for her lessons and is yet to be found. Her maid, Luvena, is most agitated. We've looked all about, but we fear something might have befallen her ladyship."

Royce hauled open his lids and strove to focus on the man. 'Twas no easy task. "Befallen her? How so?"

"Luvena fears one of her suitors may have carried her off."

"Kidnapped Juliana?" Royce dragged himself upright. "'Tis unlikely. None seemed so desperate to do so. Besides, I doubt any could have easily managed it, given the maid's capabilities."

Swinging his feet over the side of the bed, he scrubbed his face with his hands and strove to clear his head. Royce stilled, his eyes popping open as a thought hit his sluggish brain like a bath of icy water. He'd not underestimate the maid to find some clever way to slip from Penhurst unnoticed during their visitors' many departures.

Royce cast back the bed covers, bolting to his feet, his head throbbing as he reached for his braies. "Sound a bell, or horn, or whatever you have. Call everyone out to search for Lady Juliana and have Hannibal readied."

Royce donned his garments and armor as quickly as he could manage then made his way to the ward. His thoughts ran ahead to the Meon River and what transport Juliana might have succeeded in catching there. God's teeth, he'd not anticipated this, but he should have. He never should have relaxed his vigil of the maid. Now that Lord Gilbert had gone to his rest, she'd returned to her troublesome ways.

Royce found Hannibal saddled and waiting and started to mount. Just as he lifted his foot to the stirrup, someone gave a shout, drawing his attention toward the kitchens. Juliana appeared in view as she emerged from the back of the buildings. Her sleeves were pushed to her elbows and an apron, begrimed with dirt, covered her dress. She slowed her step as she took in the commotion in the ward, blinking and obviously uncomprehending of the cause of the uproar.

Crossing the distance with long strides, Royce came to stand before her, struggling to hold rein on his temper.

"Is something amiss, Sir Knight?" She looked up at him wide-eyed.

"Where have you been?" he growled. "Everyone is searching for you."

"For me? Why? And why are you angry?"

"Because you were missing," he said between his teeth. "'Twas feared you'd been kidnapped or that you might have . . ." He halted his words, not wishing to reveal his own speculations on the matter.

"Might have what?" she persisted, giving him a long look. "Escaped? Would that I could," she said with a note of bitterness. "If you must know, I was sanding out kettles, there, behind the kitchens."

"Scrubbing pots? 'Tis servant's work," he snapped.

The maid lifted her chin, defensive. "'Tis merely work, is all, and most welcome to relieve my distress."

"And what distress might that be?" He scowled.

"The distress of knowing I am to be given to a stranger like a piece of furniture, along with the castle, to do with as he will."

Royce hardened his jaw, feeling as though steam were building behind his eyes and venting through his ears.

"You should be at your studies with Edmond, learning to conduct yourself as a lady and to run Penhurst's household."

"Does not running a household include seeing to its kitchens, Sir Knight?" she challenged.

"Overseeing it, aye, but not engaging in the labors there."

"But I am capable enough and find solace in work."

"'Tis not the issue and well you know it. You are the lady of Penhurst. 'Tis important you hold the respect of eve-ryone connected with the castle if you are to direct its affairs and be obeyed."

Juliana gave a short laugh. "And why should I wish oth-ers to obey me?"

"For their own well-being," Royce grit out. How could he make her understand? "A castle may seem naught but so much stone and timber and tillage of land. But I assure you, everyone, at every level, is dependent upon one another in some measure—none more so than upon its lord and lady. In times of the lord's absence, 'tis the lady who oversees the estate's many functionings, and if required, holds the castle when under siege. Even the knights must obey her."

Juliana absorbed his words, but then visibly shuttered her emotions. "That may be so, Sir Knight, but I own no wish to preside over a castle as its lady."

Royce arched a brow. He'd no energy to argue words with her this day. Besides, he possessed a raging headache from the quantity of ale he'd consumed, coupled with this latest excitement. Juliana was the heiress of Penhurst, and that would not change.

"Exactly what is it you wish, my lady?"

"To return to Chinon," she replied firmly, simply.

"Are we to that again? I thought you accepted you are Lord Gilbert's granddaughter."

"The truth of my identity matters not, Sir Knight. I do not belong here at Penhurst any more than I do at Court, or any other place in England. That was made most clear to me at Wallingford."

"You are of noble birth, Juliana. The king and queen themselves acknowledge that, and thus must their subjects. 'Tis more your manners and lack of learning that separates you from the others of high station, and all the more reason for you to attend to your lessons."

The maid compressed her lips, giving a stubborn set to her jaw. "You still do not understand the whole of it, Sir Knight, and I've no care to explain any further. *Please,* allow me to return to Chinon."

"Nay, Juliana, I will not. We shall speak of it no more."

"Oh, but we shall, Sir Knight," she retorted, her eyes flashing. "I can be quite mulish."

"Of that, I'm well aware," Royce muttered to himself as he bid Luvena come forward.

Royce eyed Juliana's smudged features and soiled garb then looked to the little maid. "See Lady Juliana is bathed, dressed, and at her lessons within the hour," he instructed. "And try not to lose her again this day."

His head throbbing, Royce gave orders for Hannibal to be attended, then started back toward the hall. The day had to improve, he assured himself. With Juliana found and under supervision, he could look forward to some hours of quiet and peace.

Installed in the south tower, in a chamber with a sizable window and ample light, Royce studied Penhurst's many and varied accounts. They enumerated everything from the revenues of its lands and fiefs to the garrison personnel, castle staff, household staples, on down to the stable supplies and Penhurst's offerings to the poor.

Taking up his cup, Royce glanced idly out the window, past the curtain wall, toward the barns and a drum-shaped dovecote. Contemplating the placid scene, he sipped the ale, a superior drink. He must remember to commend the alewife. Knowing he still needed to meet with Friar Tupper, he deemed now as good a time as any.

Hardly had he finished the thought, when a flock of doves burst from the far side of the dovecote and flapped furiously away in a dark cloud. Instantly, shouting tore at the silence.

"God give me strength!" Royce put down his cup and hurried from the tower. Moments later he discovered the heart of the problem—Juliana.

"Why are you here and not at your lessons?"

"I finished them." Guilt stamped her face. "You wish me to be busy, so I brought the doves some carded wool for their nests. 'Tis how to coax them to lay their eggs."

"Eggs? They'd no time for eggs!" Tomas the cook cried in complaint. "My lord, the doves were being fattened for today's dinner, and she set them free. Now we have none."

Royce rounded on the cook, taking a narrow view of the servant's uppitiness. 'Twas not his place to fault Penhurst's lady on any matter. 'Twas also a reminder that not all in the castle yet accepted the change of authority.

"If there are no birds, then I suggest we eat fish." Royce glared at the man. "Is the pond stocked?"

"Aye, m'lord," the man swallowed, his face fallen.

"Fish it is then. See to it!"

"Aye, m'lord." The man hurried off, his head bowed. Royce bent his gaze to Juliana. "There must be other things you might apply yourself to. Embroidery, mayhap?"

"Riding lessons would be more useful."

"Why? To attempt escape?" She looked away, refusing to meet his eyes or to answer. "Juliana, you are the heiress of Penhurst and your place is here."

'Tis you who wish for it so, not I."

"'Twas your grandfather's wish, and well you know it. Lord Gilbert desired only the best for you and bequeathed to you all he possessed. Do you dismiss that so lightly?"

Juliana's mouth opened and closed several times, though no sound came out. She appeared ready to burst, or to pummel his chest again. Instead, she kicked at a clump of dirt, then stalked off toward the hall, her skirt twitching.

Dinner offered no respite. As Royce shared a trencher with Juliana, she ignored him as best she could, looking exquisitely remote. Her features remained like marble, except when she ate of the fish, grimacing after each bite.

At length, she bid Guy to play Ragnell's story, then turned to Royce. "I hope you enjoy the entertainment, Sir Knight, and gain something of value from it as well."

"And what would that be?"

"Insight, the same as Sir Gawain, and the wisdom of allowing a woman to choose her own way."

"You are mistaken if you think I will allow you to choose in the matter of Chinon."

"Forgive me, Sir Knight. I forgot you spent many years in the desert, apart from the refinements of the kingdom. 'Tis likely you need to hear the story more than once," she goaded. "I can arrange for the minstrel to sing it each night till you grasp its import."

Royce shoved to his feet, growling, and quit the hall. Mayhap her one suitor had the right of it after all. A nunnery might be the perfect place to deposit the maiden and her barbed tongue—a convent whose order strictly enforced the rule of silence!

17

"What do you mean she didn't come for her lessons this morn?" Royce threw down his quill and rose from the table.

Edmond wrung his hands and started to speak. Just then Luvena appeared at the door of the tower chamber.

"What do you know of Lady Juliana?" Royce swung his temper over the maid. "Where has she gotten to now?"

Luvena's gaze skipped from Royce to Edmond and back again. "She wished to learn more of the castle and its workings, my lord, and has gone to do so."

"Without supervision?" he burst with annoyance. "She's well supervised. Several of the staff aid her."

"*Aid her?* At what precisely?" Suspicion shot through his veins.

"The fish pond, my lord."

Royce thrust his hand through his hair, then looked to Friar Tupper, who had been helping him itemize Beckwell's assets. "We'll speak anon, friar," he offered in parting, then went in search of Juliana.

Locating the pond on the east side of the curtain wall, Royce quickly spied the maid and made a straight path toward her, approaching from behind. Juliana stood at the water's edge, her hair covered with a large kerchief. The temperature having warmed, she'd set aside her mantle and wore only her kirtle, the sleeves pushed up.

As Royce closed the distance, she bent from the waist, stretching forward as she extended a pole and net to skim the debris from the water's surface. He started to call out to her, but just then she shifted quickly giving a wiggle to her shapely posterior and causing his words to wedge in his throat.

He continued to watch, his mouth gone dry, while she finished her task, then straightened and turned.

"Sir Knight!" she exclaimed.

Startled by his presence, Juliana took a swift step back. Trammeling her heel in her gown, she pulled herself off balance, and plunged backward into the pond with a large splash. The servants who'd been assisting her rushed to help, but Royce leapt into the water and reached her first. He caught her by both arms and drew her out.

Juliana spluttered, coughing on pond water, as Royce helped her regain her feet. Clearing her throat, she raised green eyes to his, peering through spiked lashes, her kerchief tangled in soppy strands of silver hair. In short, she appeared a sodden, shivering, bedraggled mess.

As Royce dropped his gaze lower, his breath caught at the sight of her kirtle plastered to her body, leaving little to be imagined. The fabric conformed to her lush breasts, the nipples pebble-hard, the circles clearly visible. She might as well wear naught. Despite himself, he felt his loins stir, an unexpected jolt of desire passing through him.

Realizing the others gaped dumbfounded at Juliana as well, Royce snatched the mantle from his shoulders and wrapped it about her. For a moment he couldn't find his voice, distracted by his swelling response, distracted too by an unreasonable anger that others had seen Juliana thusly, as good as naked, though by no fault of their own.

Deciding he'd deal with his conscience later, Royce applied himself to dealing with the maid. He caught her up as though a sack of wheat, tossed her over his shoulder, and headed for the hall. Not surprisingly, she struggled and kicked against his hold.

"What are you doing? Put me down this instance!"

"I'm seeing you back to where you belong, and I'll put you down when we are there," he asserted in a voice edged with steel. He carried her the full distance to the Great Hall and once inside, he set her on her feet again.

"Why are you angry with me? You told me to oversee the castle's affairs and I did!" she stormed in her own fit of temper. "The fish was barely tolerable last night. I found the pond befouled so the servants and I set to cleaning it."

Royce grappled with the emotions raging through him. 'Twas more the sight of her feminine attributes, displayed so revealingly before all, that had aroused his fury and admittedly more. He could not confess that to her, however.

"Overseeing means just that—*overseeing* the servants' work, not doing it for them."

"Then I've failed again, haven't I? I'll never be the lady you wish to make me. Why not just send me back to Chinon? There's no reason for me to stay here."

"Penhurst is your reason."

"'Tis a place, not a reason. People are a reason. Let me return to those who care for me, who love me."

"To your cooper?" he bit out. "Nay, Juliana, I've no intention of letting you go anywhere, especially not back to him."

"Haven't you interfered enough in my life?" Her anger flared. "Why are you doing this?"

"I've given my sacred oath to see you take your place as Penhurst's lady and see you married."

"Ohhh!" She launched herself at his chest but he caught her wrists and pulled her against him before she could attempt any damage.

"I know—I've ruined your life and you hate me. But I do hold legal authority over you and you will do as I say."

"Which is?" She tossed her head defiantly, flinging

droplets of the fetid pond water across his nose and cheek.

"For now, take another bath," he said between clenched teeth. "Here is Luvena now. Go with her, keep to your chamber, and strive to stay out of trouble. Is that clear?"

"Perfectly," she hissed, then turned on her heel and marched from the hall.

As Royce brought his gaze from the maid, he discovered he held the attention of everyone in the hall.

"Well? Have you something to say?" he bellowed.

One of the men-at-arms ventured forward. "Don't be too hard on Lady Juliana, my lord. We all understand she's had an irregular past. However, she does make the finest ale and beer ever to be swilled at Penhurst."

"Anywhere on these shores!" avowed another standing nearby, lifting his cup in her honor.

Royce felt his temper climb higher still. "Lady Juliana made the ale? *Herself?*"

"And the beer."

"She's the mistress of Penhurst, not its alewife, or its brewer," he blared.

Friar Tupper worked his way through the small knot of soldiers and servants and came to stand before Royce.

"If I may be allowed an observation, my son, I've been conversing with those of Penhurst—the garrison in particular—and, well, they all seem very happy with the improvements, quite pleased that their new mistress possesses the skills she does."

Royce's nostrils flared in anger. "I repeat, she is the lady of the castle, not . . ."

"Yes, yes, my son. But there is no reason she cannot instruct others to do the work in her stead. 'Twill improve her confidence, while adding to the smooth running of the castle. I've no doubt of it."

"If you are so enamored of her skills, good friar, then

you may supervise her efforts. See that she trains others in the craft and not merely assumes their place."

At that Royce quit the hall and sought his bedchamber. His clothes reeked of the fish pond and his boots were ruined. He couldn't help but wonder if a pitcher of ale might await him there. God's truth, 'twould be welcome.

At supper, Luvena sent word that Lady Juliana had taken the sniffles and chose to stay abed. Royce spent the time reviewing matters concerning Beckwell with the friar.

Hours later, as the castle bedded down for the night, Royce made his final rounds, checking the ward, stopping by the gatehouse, and speaking with the watchmen. As he started back, looking forward to a sound night's sleep, he spied a cloaked figure slipping along the inner wall, keeping to the shadows. 'Twas a woman's figure, of Juliana's height, heading for the stable.

Royce swore beneath his breath and followed her, keeping just beyond her sight. Did she think to steal a horse again? How did she plan to get past the watchmen and out of the gate? And what then?

As he stepped through the doors of the stable, layers of pungent odors assailed him, bespeaking of horse, leather, hay, and earth. Juliana stood several stalls down, offering the groom a costly ring, urging him to saddle Nutmeg.

Royce crossed the space in long strides, snatched the ring from Juliana's fingers, then sent the groom scrambling away. He turned on Juliana and held up the ring before her.

"I assume this came from Lord Gilbert's coffers—your mother's or grandmother's ring?" he blazed. "You have the gall to bribe the stablehand with it, that you might escape?"

"I—I was going to send Nutmeg back," she stammered, avoiding the full of his question. "I intended to ride her only as far as the river and then hire a boat."

"Hire?" He snorted. "With what? And were you going to bribe your way through the gatehouse too? Again, using what? Have you thieved more belonging to the lords and ladies of Penhurst?"

Juliana's hand went to the pouch at her waist. Seeing this, Royce seized upon it, only to find it weighted with several jeweled brooches and rings.

"You steal from Penhurst?" he snarled.

"No, not steal. If I am its heiress, then I am entitled to them. Besides, I took only what I would need."

"Now you are the heiress, are you? Either you are or you are not, Juliana. Which is it?"

She clenched her mouth tight, refusing to answer. Breaking away her gaze, she started past him. "I am going to my chamber," she stated flatly.

Royce's hand shot out, snaring her and hauling her back. "Answer me. Do you accept you are Juliana Mandeville or not?"

"Let me go," she struggled against his grip.

He tightened his hold. "Why won't you answer me? Do you claim to be the lost heiress, yea or nay?"

She continued to resist him, impatient to be free. "I don't know. I don't want to know!"

"But you already do. You called Lord Gilbert 'grandfather.' You spoke of dreams. You remembered things from you past, didn't you Juliana? Or was all that a lie, a pretense, to make an old man happy on his deathbed?"

"Nay, 'twas no pretense."

"Then you *are* Juliana."

"I don't know." She trembled beneath his hands. "Please, just let me go."

Royce pulled her against his chest, sinking his hand into her silvery hair and forcing her to look at him. "Why won't you say it? What are you concealing? Why won't you admit you are the lost maid of Penhurst?"

Tears welled in her eyes. "What does it matter who I claim to be? 'Tis Chinon, not Penhurst, that has been my home for these ten years past. That is what I remember, all I remember. That is where I belong."

She hid something. Royce sensed it, as much by her desperation to avoid the matter as by the shaking that had overtaken her body.

"You do remember something," he charged. "Something that ties you here, that tells you who you are."

"Only dreams, images." She avoided his gaze but he gave her a shake, forcing her eyes back to his.

"I ask you again. Why did you call Lord Gilbert 'grandfather'? Was it a lie?"

"Nay, I spoke truthfully," she choked out with a sudden sob. "But that doesn't mean I am certain of my identity."

Royce vented a breath of frustration. "Juliana, you speak in riddles."

"Riddles, dreams—none of it matters." Tears began to stream over her cheeks. "Lord Gilbert is dead and I wish to go back from whence I came, to the life I had before you took me from the church steps on my wedding day and turned my world upside down."

Royce tensed at her reproach, then saw through it.

"'Tis the cooper, isn't it? He's the reason you're so impatient to return to Chinon. You're intent on marrying him, aren't you?"

"If you would know, yes, I am."

"Do you love him?"

"I—I . . ."

"Or is it that you wish to marry him out of some misplaced loyalty?"

"I—I don't understand."

"After your betrothal, did he bed you?"

"Bed me?" Her lashes and brows flew upward.

"Is that why you are so intent on marrying him, because he's enjoyed your body already and you feel you must solemnize the act?"

"How dare you!" She wrenched free of his hold, her eyes fierce with anger. "You insufferable boor! Gervase did not bed me. I've never been intimate with a man."

"You claim to be a virgin?" His words stabbed the air.

"I *am* a virgin, not that 'tis your concern."

"'Tis very much my concern since, as your guardian, I am charged with negotiating your marriage."

"Ah, yes, and I am more a prize as a virgin bride to the husband you would inflict on me."

Royce opened his mouth to retort, but found himself speechless, owing to the hard truth of her words.

Suddenly she softened, her eyes becoming open wounds. "Please, Sir Knight, if a heart beats in your chest, then do not condemn me to this fate, to some nameless man to use me. Let me return to Chinon, to Georges and Marie. Gervase, too."

Royce steeled himself against her plea, against the torment he read in her face. "That I cannot do. I've given my sacred oath to your grandfather, and I believe beyond doubt you *are* Juliana Mandeville, the heiress of Penhurst."

"Stop! I do not wish to hear it!" she flared, throwing her hands over her ears.

His temper spiking anew, Royce took hold of her wrists and pulled her hands away. "God's teeth, I do not understand your stubbornness. Why do you resist the truth? Why do you resist reclaiming your past?"

"Because I do not wish to reclaim it, or remember it, any of it!" she shouted, frantic now, struggling against his hold.

Royce stared at her, stunned. "You've no wish to remember your true parents, or your life before Vaux?"

"Do not ask it of me. Leave it be, leave it be."

"Why?" he demanded, jerking her against him, bewildered by her obstinacy. "Tell me why Juliana. Why?"

She tried to draw back from him, but when he held her fast, tears flooded her eyes and tumbled over her cheeks. "Because I cannot face it. Oh, don't you understand? If I strive to remember the past, I am doomed to relive it."

"Relive it?" Royce furrowed his brows, still not comprehending.

Her eyes fastened on his, her tears falling unabated. "Whether I am Ana the miller's daughter, or Juliana the heiress of Penhurst, I can't remember anything without reliving that horrible night of the attack on Vaux." She swallowed deeply, quivering against him. "I know, deep inside, I saw my mother slain before my eyes. Others too, so many others, so much blood . . ."

She pressed her lashes shut against some image. Opening them again, she gazed past his shoulder.

"You ask if I want to remember. I thought I did once. But I cannot face it, cannot endure it again—the awful slaughter, my mother's death, the sheer horror of it all. At times, I catch glimpses of that night. And each time, I taste again of the terror I have known, a terror no one should suffer. 'Tis best to leave the past buried, as it was before you took me from Chinon."

The maid brought her gaze back to look directly into Royce's eyes, her face wet with tears. "I found happiness there, but you stripped it all away. You took me from the very people who gave me joy and love and security through the years. You brought me here to an alien land where I no longer belong, and where I am so utterly, so desperately alone."

Royce gazed on Juliana, thunderstruck by her outpouring, his heart feeling as though it had just been slammed with a battering ram.

"Alone?" He choked back his own emotion, drawing her into his embrace. "Nay, sweet Juliana, you were never alone. Nor are you now."

He felt her shudder against him, sobs wracking her slender body. Unable to bear her sorrow, Royce brushed his lips against her hair, her temples and cheek, then sought the soft warmth of her mouth, closing his over hers, comforting her with his kiss.

Honey. Her lips were sweetest honey, soft and pliant beneath his. Her sobs quieted as he prolonged the kiss, and her shaking became faint tremors in his arms. Heartened, Royce yielded to impulse, deepening his kiss, wishing to draw all the pain from her and let it become his own.

"Juliana, my precious Juliana," he murmured against her lips, as he continued to console her, owning no wish to cease, nor the will to do so. He felt her hand lift uncertainly to his bearded jaw, then slip to the back of his neck and head, her body pressing against him.

"Royce." She voiced his name in a breathy whisper.

Her unexpected utterance fed the fires already burning within him. 'Twas the first time she'd ever spoken his name, and the sweet sound of it roused a desire he'd long suppressed. Desire and a towering need.

Swiftly, Royce lifted Juliana in his arms and carried her to where a pile of fresh hay filled one of the stable's corners. Kneeling down with her, he lay her back, covering her with his body, his mouth never leaving hers. He coaxed her to open to him, felt her yield. Plunging in, his tongue sought hers. She met him tentatively at first, then grew more bold as she learned his play. Giving in to their passion, their mouths possessed one another's, their tongues coupling in a quickening dance. Juliana wrapped herself around him, making a pleasurable sound deep in her throat.

At her encouragement, Royce left her mouth to lavish kisses over her face and along her neck, seeking the hollow at the base to press more kisses there. Feeling her arch against him, he pushed back her mantle and cupped her breast, nearly rejoicing to find she wore only her kirtle.

Lord's mercy but she filled his palm fully, as he knew she would. He reveled in its warm pliant shape, in its weight. He drew his thumb across her nipple, drawing a gasp from her lips, a gasp that soon turned to a moan as he continued to caress her and felt her hardened beneath his touch. Juliana's senses were awake to him. The very thought caused a fine madness to take hold of him, to bare her flesh and savor her fruits.

Royce covered her mouth once more, seducing her with his tongue as he slid his hands to the back of her gown and fumbled with the laces there. She must have dressed herself, and hurriedly, he guessed, for the laces were loose and untied.

Loosening them further, he parted the cloth and opened the neckline. Drawing the gown from her shoulders, he pulled it downward, exposing the creamy swell of her breasts, kissing a path over them as he did, advancing steadily toward the prize. Seized with impatience, he swept the fabric away, laying her breasts naked as he bent to press a kiss between them. Instantly, his lips met with cold metal.

Startled, Royce braced himself up, then spied the silver cross guarding the treasure he ached to possess. The cross rose and fell with her breasts, as Juliana panted for air. Her eyes, darkened with desire, fixed on his, questioning why he'd stopped.

Royce wished to groan aloud as he gazed on her perfect breasts awaiting him, ready for his ravishment. But the cross might as well have been a sword to forestall his plunderings.

'Twas his gift to her long ago, and now a reminder of his knightly duty. Juliana was his ward. Would he deflower her as though some willing chambermaid, despoil the heiress of Penhurst for her bridal bed?

"What am I doing?" Royce pulled painfully away, mastering himself with the greatest of difficulty. "Juliana forgive me."

The questioning look in her eyes turned to one of confusion, then hurt. She reached for the front of her gown, covering her nakedness as she scrambled to her feet and fumbled back into her clothes.

"You need not worry, Sir Knight," she said briskly. "I'll not tell Lady Sibylla or ruin your plans."

"Lady Sibylla?" His muddled brain could make little sense of her words. He started to reach toward her. "Juliana —"

"Please, there is nothing more to say." Clutching her mantle tight about her, she fled the stable.

Royce rose unsteadily and moved to the door. Bracing his hand on the wood frame, he watched the maid flee across the ward, astounded by his own actions, as much as by all else that had just passed between them. If she'd despised him before, she must more so now.

Slowly Royce straightened, considering what he should do. Deciding his course, he left the stable. He would depart Penhurst on the morrow.

Friar Tupper leaned out from the last stall and watched as Sir Royce strode from the stable. Assured that he and his drinking companion were alone once more, the friar struggled clumsily to his feet, sloshing the ale from his cup as he did.

"Good friend, would you know who this Lady Sibylla is?" He shifted his stance to better observe the knight where he retreated across the ward. "Is the lady Sir Royce's wife?"

Guy of Lisors rose slowly, steadying his cup as he brushed the straw from his garments. "Nay, leastwise, not yet. But if the countess has her way, I suspect the two will announce their betrothal at Christmas. 'Tis then, by the express wish of the king, that Sir Royce must announce his choice of a husband for Lady Juliana."

"Indeed?" The friar pondered that, rubbing his finger across his bottom lip. "And what do you know of the two?"

"Sir Royce and Lady Sibylla?"

"Nay, the knight and Lady Juliana."

The side of Guy's mouth dragged upward in a crooked smile. "Here, you'll need a bit more ale for that."

He nabbed the pitcher from where it sat on the floor of the stall and replenished their cups.

"I first encountered the couple at Le Mans when I joined a group of travelers heading north to Rouen. The entire group was abuzz with news of the knight."

"He's a Crusader, is he not?"

"Aye, and a hero of some renown. But the reason for the excitement was due to the knight's feat of the night before. The others claimed he slew a boar single-handedly."

"Single-handedly?" Friar Tupper choked on his swallow of ale. "Can it be done?"

"By few and at great risk. I am told Sir Royce slew the beast most courageously to save Lady Juliana."

"God's truth," the friar mumbled in awe, then tossed back another mouthful of ale.

"But there's more." Guy topped off their cups and launched into a most remarkable tale of the couple, ever at odds, the maid defying the knight at every turn, attempting to escape, even filching his horse and setting Scotsmen on him.

Guy chuckled. "I'd originally intended to stop for a time

at Rouen then head on to Paris. But I became so fascinated by the two, I decided to follow them to England and watch the progress of their story."

"There is still more?"

"Much more, and I am setting it all to verse, preserving it for time to come."

"And are you nearly finished, my son?"

Guy shook his head then sighed. "'Tis my sense the *lai* doesn't take up the story of the knight and the maid at quite the right place. Nor does it yet possess an ending."

"Perhaps, you will have one come Christmastide and can entertain the Court."

"Mayhap, but I've found where Sir Royce and Lady Juliana are concerned, naught is predictable."

"Such is life, my friend." Tupper clunked his cup against the minstrel's, as if toasting that thought, then returned his gaze to the now empty ward. "On the other hand, God doth work in mysterious ways."

18

Ana counted herself among the lowest of the low, her guilt unbearable as she gazed out her bedchamber window.

For so many years, she'd saved herself for her beloved squire. When 'twas clear he would not return and she agreed to marry Gervase, she'd kept herself chaste for their wedding bed. Now, deplorably, she'd betrayed them both with the knight. She would have given herself willingly to Sir Royce, like the most shameless of wantons, had the squire's cross not stopped them both, jarring them back to their senses.

She'd not seen Sir Royce since that night, nearly three weeks past. He'd departed Penhurst before dawn, leaving word only that he did so on a matter of import and for Edmond to oversee her lessons. Sir Royce had been quick enough to leave, Ana reflected. Was he as regretful as she of their tryst in the stable?

How had it happened? she asked herself an endless time. They'd both been swept up in the emotion of the moment. He'd sought only to comfort her at first, of that she was sure. But quite astoundingly, his efforts ignited a fiery desire in them both.

Heaven forgive her, she'd welcomed his kisses and caresses and craved much more. Even now she could still feel the knight's mouth upon hers, his hand fondling her breast, his beard prickling her flesh as he kissed a path down her neck and lower still as he undressed her. Ana felt her breasts tighten at the memory, a fire beneath her skin spreading through her.

Moving from the window, she wiped a hand across her brow. Though she'd set her mind and heart firmly aright, her body continued to betray her. She should seek the confessional, yet to whom would she confess? Penhurst's resident priest had left the estate to meet with the bishop in Winchester. Ana felt too embarrassed to confess to Friar Tupper and then be forced to face him from day to day.

Perhaps she was overly sensitive, but it seemed as though everyone watched her, in particular the monk and the minstrel. Was it possible, by something in her manner, they could tell she'd frolicked in the hay with Penhurst's guardian, allowing him liberties with her person?

A horn sounded long and loud from the gatehouse, announcing the approach of visitors. Shouts quickly rang out and were repeated throughout the ward. Sir Royce had returned.

Heat stung Ana's cheeks. How could she face him? The knight had seen her half naked and knew well her responsiveness to his advances. Knew she had been willing and ready to surrender herself to him completely.

Ana drew the silver cross from her gown and let it hang suspended over her breasts, a reminder to them both. With that, she hastened to the hall.

Ana called for ale as she entered the back of the Great Hall. After receiving the goblet from the maidservant, she headed toward the entrance to meet Sir Royce.

Regardless of her embarrassment, she need confront him on matters that remained unspoken between them. Above all, she wished to learn of her squire and what the knight knew of his fate. Since Sir Royce's return from Beckwell, there'd been scant opportunity to do so. First, there'd been the suitors who'd immediately descended upon him. Then there were the continuous clashes and heated words between her and the knight. Time and again Ana had found herself too furious to speak with him, let alone broach the subject of her squire. But she would not allow the stable incident to delay her further. She would have her answers.

Despite her resolve, Ana felt her knees wobble as she continued across the chamber. Before she could reach the lower end of the hall, the door opened and Sir Royce entered, his figure tall and impressive as ever it was. Pushing back his coif of mail, his eyes sought hers. Ana felt acutely self-conscious as he held her gaze, then skimmed a swift glance over her, pausing briefly at the cross. His eyes returned to hers, his mouth pulling into a smile.

"Lady Juliana, I am glad to find you well. I've brought someone to see you. No longer need you feel alone upon these shores."

Ana knitted her brows at his words. But as her eyes drew to the portal, she discovered Georges and Marie entering. The goblet slipped from her fingers at the sight of them. Rushing forward, she flung her arms about her foster parents, her heart bursting with joy.

The three clung to one another fiercely, weeping, kissing, hugging, overcome with happiness to be reunited. An eternity passed before Ana could compose herself enough to speak again. She looked to the knight and thought to see moistness glossing his eyes. He was responsible for this. Though she was unsure exactly of his motives, she knew he did it for her.

"Thank you, Sir Knight, I am quite overwhelmed by your kindness and generosity. You have my endless gratitude."

"Then I would ask a favor."

Ana's heart skipped a beat. What he might require of

her for so magnanimous a gesture?

"I would much prefer you call me by my given name, rather than by 'Sir Knight.'"

She breathed again, relieved, then silently chastised herself. Did she really think he would ask her to complete what they'd begun in the stable?

"Of course, Sir Royce," she managed, his name still strange upon her lips.

Ana felt herself color, remembering all too well the first time she'd spoken it and the intimacy they'd shared. Uncomfortable under the knight's gaze, she turned back to her foster parents.

"What news from Chinon?" She looked from one to the other.

It did not escape her that Gervase had not traveled with them. She could only assume the knight remained intent on her marrying a noble of his own choosing. 'Twas a disappointment, still she would know of her cooper and argue the matter with Sir Royce later.

"What of Gervase? How fares he?" She could see Sir Royce removing his gloves in the edge of her vision but avoided his gaze. "Is Gervase well?"

Georges and Marie exchanged uneasy glances. Her foster mother then took Ana's hands gently in her own.

"Child, I know how you must miss him, but 'twas not possible for him to come. He remains in Chinon, celebrating his marriage to Gytha, the vintner's daughter."

"Marriage?" Ana gaped, shocked by Marie's words, then began to shake her head in denial. "Nay, Gervase would not wed another. He promised to wait for me. Say it isn't so.

"'Tis true, child," Georges confirmed as he moved to her side. "Gervase was not the man we'd thought him to be. After you left, he used the knight's coin to expand his cooping business and align himself with Jacques the vintner who supplies the royal fortress."

"Jacques? But he gave a cask of wine to *our* wedding," she protested.

"He's now given Gervase his daughter."

Ana's heart plummeted. Gervase? Married to the vintner's daughter? Shock quickly gave way to anger.

"How convenient that he may now fill his casks with wine, rather than ale, and fill his coffers with silver servicing the nobles of Chinon," she vented, infuriated.

But anger next turned to anguish, the strain of the past weeks and months overtaking her, and that of all the years before engulfing her. Ana hugged herself against the pain as tears surged to her eyes, a blackness sweeping through her. She melted to her knees as the wreckage of her life tumbled about her. Did Heaven itself conspire against her?

"Dearest Ana, I am so sorry to tell you like this," Marie joined her in the rushes, surrounding her with loving arms. "Cry, my dear. Cry all you want. You waited so long to marry—to find just the right man—and now he's gone off with another. 'Tis hard when one loves a man and is so callously betrayed."

"W-What?" Ana gulped back hot tears. "Nay, *mere* Marie, you do not understand."

"Understand what, child?"

"I didn't wait to marry because I was seeking to find the 'right' man. My heart already belonged to another. I waited in hopes my squire would return for me. But he never came." Tears dropped like rainfall over her cheeks.

"The squire?" Marie's brows bunched together. "The one who brought you to Vincelles?"

Ana nodded, wholly miserable, aware she held the attention of all in the hall, and that Sir Royce had stepped closer. She didn't care. Not anymore, not when she felt so desolate.

"I know it sounds foolish but 'tis true. I prayed that my

gallant squire would return unscathed from the East and seek to find me. Here, I wear his cross always. Do you remember the night he gave it to me?"

Marie smiled. "You screamed out for him when he started to leave. 'Twas all I could do to hold you."

Ana closed her hand around the metal. "I prayed for him from that moment on, year after year, asking God to watch over him and keep him safe. But I also prayed that my squire would return for me. He never did."

Ana stroked the cross's texture with her thumb, a heavy sadness in her heart. "How foolish I was to expect he'd remember a skinny little peasant girl, or that he might hold feelings for me. Finally, I faced the truth, that in all probability, I would never see him again."

Her head sank forward. "'Twas then I accepted Gervase's suit. I believed him to be a good, reliable man, one whom I could stand proudly beside in life. Obviously, I was wrong. Given a bit of coin, he was quick enough to improve his lot and replace me with another. And so I am forgot again."

Ana gripped the cross tight, the metal biting into her palm. "All my prayers and faithfulness were in vain. God hasn't been listening. He's forgotten me too."

Stinging with feelings of abandonment, by God and by man, an unreasoning fury took hold of Ana. She dragged the cross and chain over her head and cast it into the rushes, then fell into Marie's arms and dissolved to tears. Vaguely, she realized Sir Royce moved to retrieve the cross from where it lay. She wished he would just leave it there, forgotten as was she. But he would not and in the next instance came to stand before her, the cross in his hand.

"Juliana, about your squire—"

Despair seized Ana, momentarily displacing her anger as she glanced up at the knight. "Will you break my heart further still and tell me something grievous of my squire I'll not wish to hear?"

Surprise, mingled with confusion, touched the knight's eyes.

"Lord Gilbert said my squire did not . . . did not return from the East." Ana swiped at her tears. "He said you might know of him . . . that you fought alongside the knight he served, Sir Hugh FitzAlan."

Sir Royce hesitated at her words, his look unreadable. "Aye, Juliana," he voiced softly at last. "I fought alongside Sir Hugh in many a battle." Slowly he lowered himself to a squatting position beside her in the rushes. "But that was only after he'd dubbed me a knight on the field of Acre."

Reaching out, he took her hand, enclosing it in his own, drawing her gaze to his. "Before that time, I served Sir Hugh in another capacity. In truth, I accompanied him from England to meet the Lionheart at Vézelay and proceed on to the Holy Lands . . . attending him as his squire."

Ana stilled, the air trapped in her lungs. As she regained herself, she snatched back her hand, incredulous. "What are you saying? That *you* are the one who found me, in Vaux?"

She scrabbled to her feet, disbelieving his claim, unable to make sense of it or compass it fully. How could this man, who'd disrupted her entire world and set it on end, possibly be her most noble squire? How dare he suggest it. Did he do so merely to appease her?

"Why are you saying these things? Do you mock me?"

"Nay, Juliana—"

"Then do not claim to be my squire," she blazed, indignant. "Do you think I would not recognize him? You are *nothing* like my squire. Y-You look nothing like him. Do you play me for a fool like Gervase?"

Her heart and nerves raw, unable to bear more, Ana raced from the hall, feeling Sir Royce's eyes boring into her back.

Royce turned the cross in his hand, contemplating the piece as he soaked in his bath, the water having long gone cold.

Was it possible? Juliana loved him?

Nay, not him, he amended. 'Twas the squire who held her heart. Calf love, he assured himself in the next instant. Surely her feelings were that and no more. Yet, she'd waited faithfully through the years for his return, keeping herself chaste from all other men, refusing to marry until convinced she'd never see him again.

Royce continued to contemplate the cross as he mulled Juliana's startling revelation. He found himself flattered, humbled, touched to the core. Still, 'twas the squire who possessed the maiden's heart—the youth she remembered, rather than the battle-worn knight he now was. The time they'd spent together since his arrival in Chinon couldn't have endeared her to him one jot. No wonder she spurned the very thought of his being the one for whom she'd waited so long.

He should have revealed his identity to Juliana sooner, Royce chided to himself. He should have made her listen to him. Yet, even if he had, would she have believed him then? He released an exasperated sigh.

Royce took up the steel mirror from beside the tub and studied his reflection. He'd changed greatly from the scrawny lad of ten years past. Had he not grown into his looks, he doubted he would recognize himself either. Still, there must be something that remained familiar about him.

He considered his bearded face in the mirror, rubbing at the whiskers that covered his upper lip and jaw. Just then, the servant attending his bath reappeared.

"Is there anything more you require, my lord?"

"Aye, there is."

Ana lay across her bed, her face pressed against the pillows, her emotions spent. When a knock sounded at the door, she pressed her lashes shut. She'd asked to be left undisturbed. Did no one understand how desperately she needed to be alone for now?

"Luvena, I know you mean well, but I told you, I do not wish to take any food or drink," she called when she heard the door open.

"Nor does she bring any." Sir Royce's rich voice sounded from the portal.

"Please, leave me be." Ana turned her face into the pillows, her stomach clenching.

"That I cannot do, Juliana. Not until you hear me out. God did not abandon you. Nor did He me."

Ana's temper flared. Did the man still insist he was her squire? "I asked you to leave!"

She turned to rise and push the knight back out the door if necessary. As she stood to her feet, she froze in her footsteps. Sir Royce filled the portal, the cross suspended about his neck over fresh clothes, his face clean shaven.

Ana stared, astounded by the transformation. Slowly, he crossed the chamber to stand before her. She remained voiceless as the light from the window bathed his features—features familiar to her. Ana lifted a hand to his face in wonderment, beholding her squire gazing back at her, years older and splendidly handsome.

"'Tis you," she voiced softly, tears filling her eyes. "My gallant squire. But Lord Gilbert said you had not returned from the East."

He smiled on her, a most wonderful smile, so different without his mustache and beard. "Lord Gilbert said Sir Hugh's *squire* had not returned. 'Twas because that lad was a squire no more, but a knight who'd won his spurs." He reached out a hand and brushed the tangled strands of hair from her face and thumbed away her tears. "I suspect your grandfather wished for me to be the one to tell you of my identity."

Ana nodded mutely as she continued to drink in the sight of him, still awed by his transformation. His eyes appeared much bluer in this moment, she noted—a most marvelous shade.

"You once asked how I knew of the cross you wore and of its engraving," Sir Royce reminded, his hand moving to the piece. "I spoke truly when I said 'twas once my father's. The knight's ancient oath has been inscribed there for as long as I've known—from the time I inherited it, and wore it, before giving it to you."

"'Twas a great sacrifice for you to do so. It must be very precious to you."

Ana lifted her hand to touch the cross where it lay upon his chest. Before she could withdraw her fingers, he caught them in his.

"Juliana, I cannot fault you for not recognizing me. I have changed much with the years, not only in appearance, but I've become a different person as well—no longer the green squire, but the knight I'd sought to be. 'Twas an angelic little sprite who inspired me through the years, a silver-haired waif I discovered beneath a boat, so lost and alone, so terrified and in need of saving."

He drew her to him and gazed deep into her eyes, causing warm shivers to ripple through her and her knees to soften.

"Upon my oath, I never forgot you, fair maiden." His rich voice grazed her senses. "'Twould be an impossibility, I assure you."

Raising her hand to his mouth, Sir Royce pressed a kiss

to its back. As his lips lingered warmly there, a horn sounded from the gatehouse. Within moments, the seneschal appeared at the door.

"My lord, Penhurst has more visitors!"

Sir Royce continued to gaze into Ana's eyes. "I'm not of a mind to speak with more suitors today. Tell them to return another time."

"'Tis no suitor, my lord. 'Tis the Countess Linford who arrives with her escort. She's entering the ward as we speak."

19

My dear, Royce." Lady Sibylla extended her gloved hand, glinting with jewels, from where she sat upon her palfrey. Though wrapped from head to toe in sable, her eyes and cheeks glowed bright, livened by the cold that sharpened the day.

Ana watched from the door of the Great Hall as Sir Royce lifted the countess from the horse. Lady Sibylla slipped her hand through the knight's arm and drew close to his side, remarking on his smooth-shaven face as they started toward the hall.

Ana retreated, heading for the exit at the far end of the chamber, thinking to seek her private quarters. She'd no wish to face the countess with her eyes puffy and red from crying. Besides, her emotions remained in a broil, the day's joyous surprise and jolting revelations keeping them off balance.

As Ana passed through the back portal, she impulsively restrained her step. Keeping from sight, she observed Sir Royce and Lady Sibylla enter the hall and cross to the fireplace. The countess accepted a goblet, at the same time lowering her fur hood. Many in the hall stilled in their steps, clearly struck by Sibylla's elegant beauty.

"Why this is excellent!" the countess praised, having sipped of the goblet. "Penhurst must have a very fine ale maker. You must give your servant my compliments."

Ana squeezed her hands at her sides. She was the one responsible for the drink, much more a commoner than a lady. As she continued to gaze on the countess, she felt keenly aware of the gulf that separated them.

Ana shook herself. She could no longer deny she was, in fact, the heiress of Penhurst—unpolished, perhaps, but still of noble blood. Even so, Ana knew she could not begin to compare to Countess Linford.

"You must be surprised to see me, Sir Royce." Lady Sibylla purred throatily. "I am on my way to Wiltshire but diverted my route here to bring you letters from the earl of Pembroke."

"William Marshal? Is it urgent?" Sir Royce's voice carried his surprise.

"Urgent insofar as he is anxious to have you join him in the affairs of the realm." Lady Sibylla touched her gloved fingers to his chest, directly over his heart. "You have impressed him. After you departed Wallingford, I tarried and took the opportunity to indulge in several lengthy conversations with him." Her fingers moved upward to stroke the base of his throat. "Once you are Earl of Linford, he holds specific plans for you, ones that will place you in the crown's inner circles."

"You were able to learn all that from Marshal? You are quite remarkable, my lady."

Lady Sibylla smiled at the compliment. "More so than you guess. Leastwise, I hope you will find that to be true. But we can discuss these things further, after I've freshened and changed."

As Sir Royce called for a servant to see the countess to her lodgings, Ana withdrew and returned to her chamber. Lady Sibylla spun a web of enticements about Sir Royce, offering what few women could—wealth, power, position, and beauty to be freely claimed. What man could resist such an offering? Ana wondered, feeling a throb in her heart.

Two hours later, unable to avoid making an appearance any longer, Ana arrived in the hall and moved to assume her chair on the dais.

Sir Royce rose at once from his place. At the same time, Ana's gaze drew past him to the countess, nodding in greeting when their eyes met. As Ana allowed the knight to seat her, she noticed he already shared a trencher with Lady Sibylla. She could blame no one but herself, she knew. She was inexcusably late to supper.

"I invited your foster parents to join us at table but they declined, saying they would feel more comfortable in the hall," Sir Royce confided to her quietly as he gave a nod to where they supped and conversed with Guy of Lisors.

"How gallant of you to have asked them." Ana exchanged smiles with Georges and Marie across the distance then brought her gaze back to Sir Royce, sending him an appreciative look.

"Perhaps you would find an agreeable table companion in Friar Tupper this eve."

"Yes, I would like that." She smiled, finding herself edgy at the knight's closeness, the sight of her beloved squire, reflected in his face, still fresh and unsettling.

At Sir Royce's signal, the servants brought forth a trencher, goblet, two bowls, and two spoons. The good friar joined her and applied himself to ensuring they'd an ample amount to eat and drink.

Ana glanced down the table to Lady Sibylla, who was currently laughing at some jest she'd just shared with Sir Royce. Ana felt pale in comparison to this vibrant woman with dark, dancing eyes. The countess wore a gown of scarlet silk, the rich color setting off her flawless features and swanlike neck. She used her hands gracefully, expressively, gems sparkling on each of her long, slender fingers. Again, Ana felt ordinary, unexceptional, in contrast to Lady Sibylla's sophistication.

"Hell holes," the monk whispered beside her, catching Ana's attention and sending a meaningful look toward the countess.

As he clicked his tongue beside her, Ana saw how the lacings on the side of of the countess's over- and under-gowns had been positioned, one atop the other, and loosened to expose her bare flesh beneath. Ana widened her eyes at the immodest display and reached for the goblet.

"My dear, Juliana. Whatever has happened to your hands?" Lady Sibylla leaned forward. "They are red and rough like a laborer's. You really must take care of them. However will Sir Royce find you a husband? Fortunately, I have just the remedy—extract of roses and linseed oil. I'll give the receipt to your maid."

The countess returned her attention to Sir Royce. "Have you made progress in finding Juliana a husband? There must be someone suitable on the king's list."

The knight's eyes briefly met Ana's before he dropped away his gaze to study his wine. "I am considering it, and we've had a fair number of suitors arrive at Penhurst," he allowed stiffly.

"Good. Then you'll be able to announce your choice at Christmastide." Lady Sibylla rose from her chair. "We really should speak of the Earl of Pembroke's missives in private. Why don't we take a turn about the ward?"

"As you wish, my lady."

As Sir Royce and the countess excused themselves from the table, Ana found her appetite had deserted her. Leaving Friar Tupper to the bounty piled upon their trencher, she sought her foster parents, bid them good night, then quit the hall for her bedchamber.

Ana slipped into bed, grateful Luvena had warmed the

sheets well with a pan of hot cinders. While the maid finished the last of her chores, Ana stared at the canopy overhead.

What were the countess and Sir Royce doing now? Was Lady Sibylla in the knight's arms once more, savoring his kisses? Ana tried to blot out images of the two in the royal garden at Wallingford but failed miserably. Worse, she felt the sharp horn of jealousy.

She'd no right to feel thusly, Ana chastened herself. Had she not treated Sir Royce abominably from their first encounter on the church steps in Chinon? Had she not done all in her power to turn him from her and to oppose him in every way?

Yet, despite their constant contest of wills, they'd been drawn to one another like lodestones. 'Twas the night in the stable, in an explosion of emotions, that the barriers had crumbled between them. Ana had welcomed the warmth of Sir Royce's lips upon her flesh, the strength of his arms surrounding her, his hands exploring, possessing her.

She'd berated herself for betraying her beloved squire in the embrace of the knight, unaware the two were the same. Yet, since that night, she'd also been keenly aware of the feelings she harbored for Sir Royce—feelings she'd ignored and suppressed. Feelings that, nonetheless, ran deep through her heart.

Now, knowing the truth of his identity—despite their special bond of long past and the intimate moments they'd so recently shared—she'd no right to expect him to set aside Lady Sibylla in favor of her—to reject a countess who offered him an earldom, for an heiress of only modest means.

Royce de Warrene was no more the squire she'd loved through all these years. He'd become a knight of distinction, one with a glorious future awaiting him as the Earl of Linford. Come Christmas he would announce his engagement to Lady Sibylla and that of herself to another.

Ana bit her lip, fighting back a rush of emotion. How would she endure it?

"I'll lay out your gown for the morrow," Luvena called from where she opened the clothes chest. "Which would you prefer, my lady?"

"The rose-colored one," Ana replied, wholly dispirited. "'Tis my favorite and Sir Royce's too, I think."

Luvena reached into the trunk. "Oh, see here! I never opened this bundle—the one the laundress gave me when we left Wallingford. I suspect 'tis someone else's gown. You are missing none."

The maid brought the bundle to the bed and freed its wrappings, revealing a rose-colored gown, the exact shade as the other Ana possessed.

"By the saints!" Luvena exclaimed softly as she unfolded it. "'Tis a twin. But look here, the laundress did not get out the stains. They look to be streaks of some kind. Streaks of—"

"Of blood," Ana uttered in amazement, recalling the debacle with the falcons and the birds in the royal feasting hall. "Sir Royce must have ordered a second gown to be made for me."

"Ah, Sir Royce is the very finest of men." Luvena sighed.

Guilt flooded Ana anew. How horribly she'd dealt with him—lying, stealing, telling him time and again that he'd ruined her life. And through it all, how kindly he'd dealt with her, even bringing her foster parents to Penhurst this day. The knowledge sat as burning coals upon her heart.

"Think of it Royce, the great Marshal offers you a place beside him. Once you are the Earl of Linford, he desires to mentor you, groom you in matters of the crown."

Sibylla toyed with the brooch securing Royce's mantle, then lifted her dark, seductive eyes once more to his. "Consider, William Marshal grows old. When he passes, you will be in a position of high authority, next to the throne."

Royce caught her fingers. "I did not realize you were so ambitious, Sibylla."

"My ambitions are for you, darling." She freed her hand and brushed her fingers along his throat. Again he trapped them in his.

"I would remind you, Countess, I am a warrior, seasoned in battle, not politics. My own aspirations spring solely from the knightly code—to defend the church, the land, and its people, to champion what is right and good against injustice. It does not include self-aggrandizement or the coddling of kings."

Especially one who would cheat his own knights of what was rightfully theirs, Royce added mentally, then amended the thought. Likely, he would never be sure which of the sovereigns had played him false—Richard or John.

"But 'tis through the king you can realize your goals—all of them, my darling. From a station of import, you can accomplish more than you've ever conceived."

She drew her fingers from his and fumbled with his brooch once more. "Then too, King John will surely beget an heir on his queen and soon, as much as he beds her. What if something should befall him?" She gave a light shrug. "Kings are mortal after all. What then of the child king? Instead of affecting the lives of a few, you could affect the lives of an entire kingdom by safeguarding and guiding its heir. If you position yourself well now, that is, and take advantage of Marshal's offer."

Royce stared at the countess through the dimming light, startled by the height of her ambitions. Sibylla took hold of his hands and, drawing them beneath her mantle, placed them on her sides, over the open lacings on her gown. Instantly, Royce felt her bare flesh warming his palms, as she intended.

"Your future stands before you, destined to shine as bright as William Marshal's. I promise, you shall find in me a most capable consort."

Royce could not deny that her vision stirred his blood, or that her words held appeal. Sibylla offered him an earl-dom and opportunities beyond his dreams. How much more he could achieve as an earl of the kingdom, than one of its small barons? He held the promise of that luminous future in his hands, in the person of Lady Sibylla. He'd be a fool not to seize the gift she offered and marry her. Yet something dragged at his soul, and the words he need speak, committing himself to the countess, failed to climb to his tongue.

"Did I tell you how handsome I find you without your beard?" Sibylla stroked her fingers over his cheek and jaw. "I look forward to helping you fulfill your appetites as well as your ambitions."

Sibylla pressed her lips to Royce's, her distinctive scent of roses wreathing him, weaving a fragrant web.

Ana held to a small distance as Sir Royce lifted the countess onto her palfrey and guided her foot to the stirrup. Smiling out from her swath of furs, Lady Sibylla placed a kiss to her gloved fingertips then touched his cheek.

"Until Guildford," she said, her features glowing with anticipation of that event. At her signal, Linford's select guard surrounded her. Then, with a parting glance to Sir Royce, she allowed them to escort her from Penhurst, passing from the inner ward and out the main gate.

Sir Royce watched the countess's departure, remaining motionless for several long moments after she disappeared from sight. Turning at last, he met Ana's eyes, his look pensive.

She took a small swallow, unable to guess the path of his thoughts, unsure she'd wish to even if she could. By his countenance, something must have passed between him and the countess last night. She dreaded to know. Would he announce their engagement at the Christmas Court after all? Was there yet a breath of hope he would not?

As Sir Royce came to stand before Ana, his lips parted as if to speak. But, seeming to change his mind, he glanced to the ground and toed at something there.

"There are matters—accounts—to which I must attend this morn, Juliana." He raised his eyes once more, looking deeply into her own. "I trust you will apply yourself to your studies until I join you again at dinner."

'Twas a statement, not a question. Ana made no effort to reply, a heaviness settling into her heart. The countess possessed Sir Royce's thoughts, as soon she would his person by benefit of marriage. In time to come, Ana knew she would occupy naught but the shadows of the knight's memories as she had for so many years past.

Dispirited, Ana gazed after Sir Royce as he took his leave of her and headed across the ward for the south tower. Taking hold of herself, she glanced to the hall where Edmond waited to begin her day's studies.

Unable to bear giving herself to hours of instructions, her emotions welling afresh, Ana turned on her heel and headed away from the hall.

20

Grandfather, what shall I do?"

Ana sat on the floor of Penhurst's chapel, leaning against Lord Gilbert's marble tomb, wholly miserable. "Truly, Heaven must have been listening to my pleas for, at last, I've gained my heart's desire. I've found my squire, only I am destined to lose him once more."

She lifted her hand to the side of the tomb and touched it lovingly, then released a long sigh. Her thoughts strayed momentarily, following a different path.

"I hope you are smiling down on me, Grandfather, and that you know I do accept who I am—Juliana Mandeville, daughter of the Marcher lord, Sir Robert Mandeville, and his wife, Alyce, and your only grandchild. I've known that truth deep in my heart for a time, but resisted it."

She swiped at the moisture rimming her eyes. "I am so grateful for the time we shared together. If only it could have been more, much more. If only I could have your guidance now. I admit, there is still little I can recall of the years before Vaux. At times, I catch glimpses—of my parents, I'm sure, and of my nursemaid. In truth, I'm still afraid to open a door on the past."

She shifted where she sat and dropped her hand back to her lap. "You knew much of my past, didn't you? Even of that horrid night, though not in its fullness as surely I must, somewhere deep inside me. You also knew of Sir Royce, that he was the one who found me, my valorous squire. How shamelessly I've treated him. Surely, I've sinned against Mother Church and am in sore need of confession."

"Confession, my child?"

Ana bolted upright, nearly leaping from her skin. Glancing in the direction of the voice, she discovered Friar Tupper at the back of the chapel.

"Good Friar, you gave me such a scare! I thought I was alone, among the dead."

"Forgive me, my lady. 'Twas not my intent. But if you are in need of confession I should be happy to hear it."

Ana detected something in his tone, in his eyes. Could he possibly know of her tryst with Sir Royce?

"'Tis best to unburden your soul of any misdeeds you might carry and receive God's grace," he advised in his gravelly voice.

"I—I would like that. Should we move to the confessional?"

"Nay, child, the pews here will do. Come." He motioned her to the first of the benches, joining her there. "You may begin when you are ready."

"Y-Yes, of course," she faltered, self-conscious. "Bless me father, it has been . . . Well, I haven't been to confession since I left Chinon, and I've sinned quite regularly since."

The friar's wiry brows rose several inches. "Go on my child, what is your—are your—sins?"

Ana launched into a hurried account of how she'd defied Sir Royce from the day he carried her from the steps of St. Maurice and how her actions had placed him in mortal danger from the wild boar, then led to a host of injuries during her subsequent attempts to escape.

"I've continued to disobey Sir Royce at every turn," she admitted. "Several weeks past, I took some of the Penhurst jewels and tried to bribe the stable groom to help me escape back to Chinon. When Sir Royce discovered me, I lied and took out my anger on him and, and . . . oh dear . . ."

Hot tears blurred Ana's vision. "I didn't know it was him." Her voice came out in a squeak.

"You didn't know he was Sir Royce?"

"Nay, that Sir Royce was my squire—the one who'd found me and protected me that horrible night in Vaux."

Friar Tupper scratched at his fringe of hair. "And you are telling me you wouldn't have lied, or stolen, or done any of these other things had you known he was your squire?"

"But of course I wouldn't have!" Ana blurted, aghast that he would even think it of her.

The friar gave her a fuddled look. "And why would that be?"

"Because I didn't know the knight was the squire, or the squire the knight and, and . . . because I care for him so very deeply! In truth, I love him."

"Which 'him' would that be?"

"Both! I love them both. Only, they are one and the same."

"Are they? 'Twas the squire for whom you waited. You held no warmth for the knight, certainly no love. And need I remind you, the lad of ten years past is not the man of today?"

Ana looked through her tears at the churchman. "But they are, good friar," she said full of conviction. "Sir Royce may have done and seen much in the years between, but his heart has not changed. He has proven himself, again and again, to be the most estimable and chivalrous of men. Only yesterday, he restored to me my foster parents, seeking to ease my sorrow. But I've . . . I've made him so very miserable."

Fresh tears escaped her eyes. "He will marry Lady Sibylla and think no more of me. I will lose him forever, which is what I deserve, though he was never truly mine. The countess offers him great station and power, I know. But her husbands have a way of dying. Luvena told me so. Perhaps I've condemned him to a terrible fate and 'tis all my fault."

"Your fault? I cannot see that 'tis y—"

"If he'd not been obliged to take me to Wallingford, perhaps he'd never have met her—or leastwise, met her after she'd married another. Or if I'd treated him with love and kindness as he deserves, perhaps he would not have been so quick to consider wedding the countess."

Ridden with guilt, Ana grasped the monk by both sleeves. "Please, Friar Tupper, grant me penance, hours of penance, as I most certainly deserve."

"I think you've been living your penance, child," he muttered, half to himself. "But perhaps some is in order. Make amends by doing what Sir Royce has asked of you. See to your lessons and learn all you can about the estate and its running. Your little maid can help you with personal refinements—how to walk, hold genteel conversations, all that."

Ana squinched her brows together. "I don't understand."

The friar patted her hand. "In matters of the heart, I cannot advise you, but of this I am certain. 'Tis time to take your place as the Lady of Penhurst."

"You mean, I should smooth out my rough edges, learn to oversee the servants?"

"Much more than that. If you will indulge me a little scripture, St. Paul writes: 'When I was a child, I spoke as a child, I felt as a child, I thought as a child. Now that I have become a man, I have put away the things of a child.' As I entered the chapel just now, you were speaking to your grandfather, saying you accepted who you are."

"I do." She palmed away her tears.

"Yet, I suspect, you still think of yourself as Ana, the brewer's daughter. 'Tis time to put away the things of that past, and of the child Ana. 'Tis time to embrace yourself as Juliana, and to become all you can possibly be—a noble lady of whom your forebearers could be proud. One that will gladden Sir Royce's heart and earn his respect"

"Gladden his heart? And make them all proud? Yes, I would like that." She felt something warm and akin to a smile spreading through her. "Are you sure 'tis penance you give me?"

"You will find it so, once you apply yourself to the task in earnest."

She leaned forward and kissed Friar Tupper on the cheek. "Then bear witness. I leave Ana, the brewer's daughter, here in this place, and go forth as Juliana Mandeville, Lady of Penhurst."

"Too young, too old, possesses a fell temper . . ."

Royce worked his way down the list of suitors, crossing off names. He abhorred being pressed to make a decision in the matter of choosing a husband for Juliana. Yet, the king charged him to name her future spouse in just a few short weeks when the Court gathered at Guildford. Thankfully, Lady Sibylla had departed Penhurst soon after her arrival. Despite her good intentions, her presence drained

his energy, clouded his thinking and judgment, and aggravated his moods.

He put pen and ink to parchment once more. "Squanders his money, a poor administrator, lecherous, a drunkard, given to eccentric excesses . . ."

Royce skipped over several names with whom he could find no obvious fault. He'd return to them later, he decided. Perhaps he could find some shortcoming that would allow him to strike them from the list.

Royce tossed down his quill and shoved his hands through his hair. What was he doing? He wasn't trying to find Juliana a husband. He was trying to find reasons to reject every suitor named on these lists.

He leaned back, tilting his chair on two legs, his thoughts on Lord Gilbert's will and the final words Penhurst's lord had spoken to him. He'd urged Royce to watch over Juliana, to choose her a husband of "sterling character," one who would love her. He'd further said Royce should look to his heart if his mind was filled with doubts.

The heart speaks truest when reason fails. 'Tis there you shall find your answer.

As Lord Gilbert's words echoed in his mind, Royce was unsure what his heart spoke, if it spoke at all. Lord Gilbert had placed his faith in the wrong man, Royce feared. He had no wish to choose any man to take Juliana to wife. Still, he'd given his oath to her grandfather to see her wed. Strange, only a short time past he couldn't wait to be rid of the maid. Now, he despised the thought of her not being near.

Unable to tolerate another minute in the confines of the tower chamber, Royce rose and headed for the stable. Saddling Hannibal, he rode out toward the Meon River. Giving the stallion his lead, Royce spent the morning savoring the calm and quiet of the winter landscape, sorting through his thoughts. Rather than finding peace, however, as he returned to the castle he felt even more conflicted.

Approaching Penhurst, Royce spied Friar Tupper pacing slowly through the barren orchard, meditating with a small breviary open in his hands. Royce reined in Hannibal, dismounted, and sought out the churchman.

"Good friar, might I have a word with you? I find myself in dire need of confession."

"You also?" The monk's bushy brows rose. "I mean, how so, my son? You wish to confess here? Now?"

"Aye, if 'tis possible." Full of high energy, Royce fell in pace beside him. Confession was ever good for the soul and would help clear his mind. "My duties as Penhurst's guardian plague me night and day," he conceded. "My temper is short, I find fault in everything, I've been unreasonable with the servants, and even yelled at my men when 'twas undeserved. Worse, I cannot seem to restrain myself from these—these fits!"

The monk pondered his words. "Does something provoke these outbursts, my son? Something you've not told me?"

Royce felt his stomach tighten in a hard knot. He was loath to divulge what truly lay at the root of his dour moods. "Aye, I am in the midst of choosing a husband for Lady Juliana," he allowed at last. "I'm chagrined to say I've dealt with her suitors unfairly, striking nearly all their names from the lists, sometimes for the shallowest of reasons."

"Curious. Very curious."

"Tell me friar, how can one judge their desires objectively—whether what they want is selfish ambition or selfless sacrifice?" Royce asked, changing the direction of his thoughts. "From what place is it best to benefit others—from position, power?"

"From the heart, my son." Friar Tupper held him with his steady gaze.

Royce considered that. "Lord Gilbert said to look to my heart."

"In the matter of Lady Juliana?"

"Aye . . ." Royce's voice trailed off as he turned his thoughts then broke them off. "What penance, good friar? Surely I must have penance?"

"Penance? I'm not certain you've confessed a sin."

"For my anger and unfairness, then. I'd feel better to do penance."

"Everyone is a self-flagellant. We could begin my own order," Friar Tupper muttered. "Very well, pray one Our Father, three Hail Marys and look, henceforth, through the prism of your heart in those things that most matter."

"That is all?"

"All? 'Twill be enough when times of testing come, when your heart wars with your head, and clear answers are not apparent."

Feeling no less conflicted than before, but more at peace for having spoken with the friar, Royce headed back to the tower and the repugnant task that awaited him.

Juliana applied herself eagerly to learning all there was to know of the estate she'd inherited and its orderly functioning. She quickly discovered a system more complex than she'd initially grasped, one dependent on an extensive household, both domestic and military in character.

Penhurst's most valued member was its faithful seneschal, Edmond. 'Twas he who administered the estate, oversaw the castle personnel including its garrison, maintained the lord's financial accounts, and carried out legal responsibilities to the community as need required.

As part of her efforts to educate herself in all matters concerning Penhurst, Juliana accompanied Edmond on his rounds, having him explain, from the broader points to specific details, the various duties he was executing. In this way, she quickly learned of the lands and fiefs Penhurst held, its acreage, produce, and revenues, as well as the courts it periodically held.

'Twas Juliana's delight that Georges and Marie agreed to remain permanently in England. She was determined that they would hold an honored place with her at Penhurst. Thus she included them in all she did, even having them accompany her to meet those who served the castle, from the men-at-arms who guarded it down to the kitchen knaves. Together the three examined the storerooms and their stock, inspected the kitchens, spoke with the laundresses, and visited the stables, Juliana taking apples for Hannibal and Nutmeg.

To her surprise, she found that managing others and seeing their duties were properly carried out proved as demanding as doing the work itself. She understood now what Sir Royce had tried to impress on her and decided her days of cleaning fish ponds were at an end.

Juliana grew comfortable in directing the servants, finding some had slackened in their chores during Lord Gilbert's long absences. She ordered the rushes changed throughout the castle and strewn with costmary and pennyroyal, required the kitchens to be scrubbed down, and assured ample meat was salted and smoked for winter. Depending upon her foster parents' mastery of brewing, she asked them to oversee the staff normally responsible for the production of the castle's beverages and to instruct them in their own techniques.

In the hours left to her in the day, Juliana applied herself to her lessons in reading and ciphering. She also improved her skills at chess, thanks to Guy of Lisors. And when she discovered a lute once belonging to her mother, she asked him to teach her to play it, along with a few songs. At other times, in the privacy of her chamber, Juliana practiced walking with a smooth fluid gait and softened her hands with lavender oil—Luvena's receipt—and improved her talents with a needle.

"Do you think he will like it?" she asked Luvena as she broidered an eagle on the tunic she'd made for Sir Royce, her Christmas gift to him. She worked the emblem in gold on black, the colors of the Lords of Penhurst, the eagle rising with wings spread.

"He cannot help but like it, my lady." Luvena smiled. "I'm sure he will wear it with great pride."

Juliana sighed and glanced to the window. She'd found happiness in her new life at Penhurst. Yet, for all her efforts, she doubted Sir Royce took notice of the progress she'd made. More and more he avoided her, keeping to himself in the tower. The days closed fast now on the time they would depart for the king's hunting lodge on the Thames. She knew she must trust Sir Royce in the decisions he would make concerning her. Still, she could not dispel the gloom that hung over her, knowing he would not only announce the man she would marry, but his own intentions to take Lady Sibylla to wife.

"I have brought you a small repast. You did not appear for dinner and I thought you might be hungry." Juliana entered Sir Royce's cramped tower chamber, a cloth-covered tray in her hands.

"You worry for me, Juliana?" He smiled as he glanced up from the table where he sat, parchments stacked in neat piles on its surface.

She returned his smile, her pulse quickening as his eyes continued to hold her, their steely cast warming to blue. Setting the tray before him, she withdrew the linen cloth to reveal a plate of cold meat, cheese, bread, fruit, a wooden cup, and a pitcher of ale.

As she took a step back, to her pleasure, Sir Royce's gaze continued to linger over her. She'd taken pains with her appearance, hoping to appear a lady of refinement, however modest her accomplishment in that regard might be.

"I never thanked you for my new rose gown." She smoothed her hand over the beautiful fabric. "In truth, I'd not realized there were two identical gowns until Luvena opened the laundress's bundle and found the stained one."

"I could not bear your unhappiness when the first was ruined," Sir Royce offered. "'Twas your favorite and you prized it so. Besides, the color suits you well, Juliana, and is most flattering. If you would know, it pleases me greatly to see you wear it."

Juliana fumbled for words in the face of his compliment, his gaze still warm upon her. "However did you manage to match the fabric and color?" she finally managed. "The gowns are perfect twins."

"I'd bought an excess of the fabric at Dover when I'd arranged for the original gown made. I suppose, even then, I knew how becoming the color would look on you." His smile drew upward. "I brought the extra material with me to Wallingford. Before I could gift it to you, your gown was ruined, and hence, I engaged a court seamstress to make a second."

Amazement filled Juliana along with a familiar twinge of guilt. When they'd landed at Dover, she'd already caused Sir Royce an excess of trouble and continued to remain headstrong and difficult all the way to Wallingford and after. She'd not deserved such goodness.

"'Twas indeed most kind and generous of you, Sir Royce," she said softly, pulling her gaze away.

Her eyes strayed to the stacks of parchments, pausing over one that appeared to be a list of names, many with lines drawn through them, though not all. A sudden chill stole through her, chasing away the warm feelings she'd enjoyed these last moments with the knight.

"Juliana, I—"

"Will you join us at supper this eve?" She cut his words short, not wishing to know what he might say concerning the matter of her suitors or of either of their impending nuptials. "*Mere* Marie has overseen a fine stew made for this evening's meal. I'd hate to think of you languishing over matters that would keep you here and undermine your health. Besides, I dare say you'll need your strength for when next you meet the countess."

Unable to hide her bitterness, Juliana turned and hurried from the room.

As dawn broke, Royce sat with his lists and accounts, staring out the tower window. He'd sat long into the night with Friar Tupper, arguing the matter of Beckwell's church and the stone used to build it, filched from the castle wall. The friar urged that the church be allowed to keep the stone. Royce contended he could not secure his castle without it. His personal wealth would only stretch so far, and he need install a garrison at Beckwell and hire a simple staff.

To that end, he'd spoken with Georges and Marie about coming to Beckwell and supervising the brewing and cider-making, at least initially, as he strove to bring the castle back to life. They agreed most graciously, to his relief. Though he'd never ask them to leave Juliana, once she married, her husband would make the decisions concerning Penhurst and its residents. Royce told the couple they were always welcome at Beckwell and would ever have a place in his hall.

Royce's thoughts drifted to Juliana. She'd worn her hair differently at supper last night, more elaborate and wound with colorful ribbons. 'Twas Luvena's handiwork, he was sure. He hadn't meant to disappoint Juliana when he said he much preferred her hair loose and flowing. Yet he could see the ache in her eyes.

What a clumsy ox he'd become. Juliana had worked hard to improve herself and assume her place as Penhurst's lady. And what did he do but offer criticism when he should have given praise. Repentant, he made a mental note to have a new gown made for her, one for the Christmas Court. She would need a new mantle and slippers, as well, to compliment the gown. He liked to see Juliana dressed attractively, as much as he liked to see her shining hair unbound.

Royce glanced down at the remaining names on the list of suitors, those he'd not scratched through. Seized with frustration, he crumpled the list in his hands and threw it across the room. Juliana and he were to leave on the morrow for Guildford, where he would seal both their fates. Royce sank his head into both hands, his heart warring with his mind, waging a fierce battle there. How was he to choose?

PART V

Christmas Revels

"Love without anxiety and without fear
Is fear without flames and without warmth.
Day without sunlight, hive without honey,
Summer without flower, winter without frost."

— Cretien de Troyes

21

Guildford, Surrey

The hunting lodge at Guildford proved to be a massive square keep, rising from a great mound of earth that overlooked the River Wye. Sir Royce informed Juliana 'twas one of King John's favorite residences, built by his father, Henry II. Adjacent to the palace stretched a vast amount of forested land, a private park, stocked with game for the pleasures of the hunt.

As their retinue pressed toward the castle, Juliana drew her gaze over the stark woodland, its leafless branches lifted like a thorny headpiece, nicking at the dreary gray sky. The bleakness of the day only added to the bleakness she felt in her heart. Shortly, Sir Royce would announce his decision, but what would that decision be?

Many at Penhurst worried with her, and for her as well. She'd seen it in their faces when she departed, especially *pere* Georges and *mere* Marie. She'd seen it many times since in the eyes of her traveling companions—dear Luvena, Guy of Lisors, even the men-at-arms.

It warmed Juliana to know she'd found a place in the heart of the castlefolk at Penhurst, as did Sir Royce. But this journey to Guildford would change all. Subject to the pronouncements made here, Sir Royce would soon take up residency at Linford Castle as its new earl, while at Penhurst, another would take his place.

Passing through the gatehouse, they came upon a thick

324

congestion in the castle ward. There the entourages of many a lord and lady attending the Christmas revels unloaded their baggage wains. Leaving instructions with his men, Sir Royce aided Juliana and Luvena from their mounts and, together with Guy of Lisors, led them to the keep.

As Juliana faced the flight of steps looming before her, she braced herself against the hours and days to come. A small voice within urged she trust Sir Royce. Had he not proven himself a man upon whom she could rely? Still a heavy foreboding weighed Juliana's heart as she set her foot upon the first of the risers.

Colorful liveried guards greeted their party as they gained the top of the steps and crossed through the threshold of the keep. Holly and ivy bedecked the entry while minstrels filled the air with festive tunes welcoming all to Guildford. Juliana held close to Sir Royce as they moved slowly forward in a misshapen line, the guests identifying themselves to a steward to check against his list. When at last Sir Royce gave their names, an official standing to one side and robed in dark clothes stepped instantly forward.

"Sir Royce, Lady Juliana, His Majesty is in anticipation of your arrival. I am to take you to his presence at once. This way, if you will."

Sir Royce tensed visibly at the man's words while Juliana fought back a sudden light-headedness. She'd not expected this moment to come so swiftly. Indeed, she'd hoped the king would not require the knight's decision before tomorrow, Christmas Eve, or possibly later still.

Leaving Luvena and Guy to see to their lodgings and trunks, Juliana and Sir Royce followed the official up several winding flights of stairs to the king's private chambers. Juliana's heart pounded as much from the climb as from the impending audience. There was no escaping her fate now, or delaying it. Best to face it straight on and know what the future held.

The official led them to a handsomely appointed room where tapestries, interspersed with antlers, covered the walls. Approaching a second door, flanked by armed guards, the official rapped several times then spoke with someone unseen on the other side. Motioning Sir Royce and Juliana to follow, he ushered them into the adjoining chamber.

Across the room, King John paced before a table strewn with documents, drawing on the contents of his goblet. Pausing long enough to replenish the drink from a pitcher, he renewed his pacing, jutting his fiery head forward as he wrestled some thought. As he caught sight of his visitors he turned and cast a hard gaze over them. Instantly, Sir Royce bowed low and Juliana dropped into a deep curtsy.

"Good! You are here. Rise, rise," the king commanded, his tone brusque, agitated.

Gesturing for those who attended him in the chamber to leave, he seated himself on a chair before the fireplace. He continued to study Sir Royce and Juliana closely, his eyes shifting from one to the other. Apprehension slid along Juliana's spine. Was the sovereign always in such a cramped mood when he was about to discuss the impending betrothals of his nobles?

"Is the name Rennart de Friston familiar to either of you?" he asked abruptly.

Royce exchanged glances with Juliana. "Nay, Majesty. I've never heard the name."

"Nor, I, Majesty," Juliana added softly, deeming the question odd.

The king dragged on his beard. "A knight, calling himself by that name, arrived here at Guildford yesterday. He holds a position of some import at the French Court as one of King Philip's ministers." John pronounced his adversary's name with obvious distaste, then cleansed it from his tongue with a swallow of wine.

"The documents Friston carries bear this out," the king continued. "But he makes another claim, one that is most disturbing. He contends he is Lady Juliana's cousin on her mother's side, through an aunt—Madeleine Soutere of Senlis."

"That is not poss—" Juliana started to object but the king raised his hand, staying her words.

"Friston brings a letter from the church of Senlis, confirming the record of his baptism there as the son of Madeleine and Geoffrey Soutere. The document appears authentic, though the church's seal is poorly made, its stamp somewhat difficult to discern."

King John rose and moved to stand before Juliana, searching her eyes. "In short, Rennart de Friston claims the right of guardianship to Penhurst's lady and her estates, and contests the awarding of that position to any other man." John's gaze swung to the knight. "To point, you, Sir Royce. He argues the English branch of the family did not approve of his parents' marriage and that Lord Gilbert had refused to recognize the couple's offspring, though they were legitimately conceived—two daughters and a son. Friston demands his rights as Lady Juliana's blood relation and vows to take the matter before the courts and the Pope if he must."

Juliana looked to Royce, alarm surging through her.

"But that cannot be." She returned her gaze to the sovereign. "Lord Gilbert said my mother regularly visited her aunts in Senlis and Chalon—one widowed, her children having died in infancy, the other cloistered. 'Twas why she and I traveled to France with my father ten years past. While he set out on Crusade, we repaired first to Senlis and were on our way to Chalon when we stopped at Vaux. The family was not estranged from its French relatives."

John took up his pacing again. "The thought of giving this man, Friston, guardianship of you, Lady Juliana, is particularly loathsome to me. And though 'twould please me to intervene on your behalf, unless the baptismal documents can be successfully challenged, there is little I can do."

He stopped his pacing and faced them both. "Mayhap, 'tis best you meet the man."

Juliana turned to Sir Royce, her heart beating high in her throat, as the king spoke to the guards outside the door. What cruel trick of fate was this, that this man should materialize from seemingly nowhere and be allowed to take possession of her and all that was Penhurst's?

Her temples began to throb while a sickening despair spread through her limbs. Juliana felt herself waver, but Sir Royce caught her at once, steadying her as he held her near. She lifted her eyes to his, finding concern sharpening their steel-blue depths. Her lips parted at that look. Just as she started to speak, a knock sounded at the door and one of the guards appeared.

"Majesty, by your leave—Rennart de Friston."

As the guard stepped aside, a bullish man of medium height and pitch-black hair entered in. His garments bespoke of his high station—fur-lined velvets and a heavy gold chain and medallion about his neck. Juliana's gaze drew to the puckered scar running along the left side of his face. It reached from hairline to jaw, dividing his beard with an obvious part where the hair no longer grew.

An icy cold swept through Juliana. As she continued to look upon the ugly mar, her temples began to throb, a knifelike pain stabbing her there. Unbidden, an image arose before her mind's eye—fire, dancing along the edge of a sword blade and staining it red.

Friston bowed before the king, then rising, he sought Juliana with his watery-blue eyes, so pale they appeared nearly colorless. Her breath solidified in her chest as he held her gaze, a smile unfurling across his lips, long and thin and chill.

"*Demoiselle,* at last we meet. I confess, you are just as *maman* described. Somewhat older, of course, no more the little stick she said you were. I am your cousin, Rennart."

Again he bowed, but as he straightened, he cut his eyes up at Juliana in an eerily familiar way, jarring loose some memory within her, some dark fragment from the past.

Juliana pressed against Sir Royce, trampling upon his boots, an unholy fear seizing her. She sensed she knew the Frenchman. Exactly how or why or when she encountered him she could not say. But of one thing she held certain, they shared no common blood between them.

"I realize my sudden appearance, even my existence, must come as a shock to you, *demoiselle.*" A glitter appeared in his eyes as he took a step toward her. "But then, I, too, was shocked to learn you had returned from the dead. The news was slow in reaching my ears at the French Court. I'd long thought you had perished at Vaux."

Sir Royce transferred Juliana from his booted feet to a place directly behind him, then shielded her with his body as he confronted the man. "I find it strange, Friston, that you never assisted Lord Gilbert in all the years he searched for his granddaughter."

Again a shimmer appeared in the man's pale eyes. "He could have had my aid, had he wished it. On the other hand, he was the only one who seriously believed the child yet lived." His watery-blue gaze fixed on Juliana. "I admit, I am most grateful to learn I was mistaken."

Pivoting, he turned to the king."Majesty, I have presented you my documents attesting I am Lady Juliana's sole living male relative, and thus her rightful guardian. By law on both sides of La Manche, I believe my rights of kinship supplant those of anyone named as guardian in Lord Gilbert's will." His gaze veered to Sir Royce. "If the document states the heiress possesses no male relations such as myself, as I suspect it does, then it invalidates itself by its own falsehoods."

The king's gaze drew to Sir Royce as well. "Does the will assert there are no male relatives?"

"It does." The knight nodded gravely, causing Juliana's heart to sink further.

Friston smiled his serpent's smile. "*Eh bien*. Unless any objection can be made, and if I have your consent to assume guardianship of my cousin, Majesty, I confess 'tis urgent that I return to the French Court. Lady Juliana and I need depart for Paris at once."

Sir Royce and King John each started to protest, but Juliana's voice rang out first.

"Nay, I'll not go with you!"

"You have no say in this, cousin." Friston speared her with a wintry glare, turning her blood to ice.

"I may not, but my husband does," she countered boldly, notching up her chin, her pulse pounding.

"Husband?" King John and the Frenchman blurted in unison.

Juliana quickly stepped before Sir Royce, seizing both his arms. "Tell them, my love. Tell them how we were secretly married at Penhurst. Tell them how you alone hold governance over me, as my husband and Lord of Penhurst." She pleaded silently with her eyes, her fingers digging into the solid muscles beneath his sleeves.

Royce gazed at Juliana, astounded by her claim. Yet, as he looked into her eyes, he found naked fear choking their green depths.

"Is this true, Sir Royce?" the king demanded, surprise

rather than anger filling his voice. "Did you and Lady Juliana marry? And without my knowledge?"

Royce continued to lock gazes with Juliana, at a loss to respond. If he said yes, he would cast aside an earldom plus a wealth of opportunity to benefit others, opportunities that would place him in the highest circles of power that revolved around the king. But if he denied Juliana's words, she would be given over to Rennart de Friston, a man who clearly terrified her.

Again, he felt himself torn, cold reasoning warring against fiery instincts over the landscape of his heart. 'Twas the same battle he'd fought these many long weeks and without resolution, the opposing voices clashing within him, clamoring to have their own way.

Look henceforth through the prism of your heart . . . Friar Tupper's words echoed through the din.

The heart speaks truest when reason fails. He heard Lord Gilbert bid him, as if from the grave. *'Tis there you shall find your answer.*

Royce closed his lids, aware of Juliana's fingers still digging into his arms. Shutting out the chatter of his mind, he reached within. Suddenly, in that welcomed silence, the turmoil he felt began to dissipate. All became so simple, so clear as he gazed into his heart. At its center, he found Juliana.

Certain truths became clear as well. While there was much to be accomplished and many to succor, there were also many paths he might take in order to achieve his goals. But what manner of knight would he be this day without Juliana? None at all, he knew, remembering back to that gruesome night in Vaux and to the transformation that took place within the heart of a weak-kneed squire, all owing to a little waif of a girl.

As he ended that thought, an overpowering conviction

gripped Royce. Destiny bound Juliana and he together, as much in this moment as it had that dark night long ago, even as it had when Lord Gilbert sought him out at Westminster Palace and he'd been given the quest to find her. Since the lord's death, Royce knew he'd been unable to decide on a husband for Juliana for the simplest of reasons. The name of the man he would choose did not appear on any of his lists—that of his own.

Opening his eyes, he sought Juliana's and smiled, an effusive joy welling up within him, a sense of rightness that he should claim her as his own. But as he transferred his glance to Friston, a fierce protectiveness took hold of him, his mood darkening, his warrior instincts sharpening.

"Lady Juliana speaks truly. We are indeed wed." *In heart if not in fact,* Royce added mentally, knowing he'd need seek the confessional before all this was done.

Juliana eased her hold, a relieved breath escaping her as she looked up to him with eyes full of gratitude. Royce slipped his arm around her, drawing her against him as he addressed the king.

"Forgive us for not consulting you, Majesty. 'Twas an impulsive decision on our parts. After we'd been reunited in Chinon, we formed, shall we say, a special attachment during our journey to England."

At least that was truth, Royce thought to himself. He had the scars to prove it.

"We became quite inseparable, actually," he continued, thinking of how he'd tethered Juliana to him on occasion, as warranted. "Our relationship continued to deepen once at Wallingford." He recalled the heated dance they'd shared, his lips brushing hers. "As you know, I vowed to Lord Gilbert on his deathbed to watch over Lady Juliana and to find her a suitable husband. I believe my service in *Outremer* speaks of my abilities and skills. I am able to defend the lady and her lands. Given our feelings for one another, I felt myself to be the most suitable choice."

"Majesty, do you accept this, this contrivance?" Friston burst out.

Royce ignored him and looked again to the king. "Lady Juliana and I would have waited to announce our intentions at the Christmas Court, but in truth, we found our longing for one another increasingly ungovernable." Their passionate encounter in the stable leapt to mind. "Thus, rather than sin, we married in haste."

Juliana's brows rose high over wide, rounded eyes, as though she, too, thought of the stable and feared he would say more.

"And yet your bride wears no ring," Friston challenged, blackest anger lashing his features. "Neither of you do."

Juliana thrust her hands into the folds of her gown. "I— I have a ring. We both do. We didn't wear them because, well—"

"Because we didn't wish the fact to be known until we'd spoken first with His Majesty and sought his, er, blessing," Royce quickly added.

"How comforting to know." King John appeared to be taking some amusement in his struggles.

Friston continued to scowl. "I do not believe you. There are no pale marks upon her finger, or yours, where a band might have been worn. And to be blunt, Lady Juliana possesses a virginal quality about her, an innocence that betrays that she's never known a man."

Furious at the man's gall, Royce swept Juliana behind him once more. "Take care in what you say of my lady, Friston, or we will yet cross blades."

"Then let us do so," the Frenchman sneered. "But first, produce the priest who married you. Let him be called to court." Friston turned his burning gaze to the king. "Majesty, I have supplied documents giving proof to support every word I've claimed. Sir Royce must be required to do no less. If he is to be allowed to assert his rights as Lady Juliana's husband and claim the lordship of Penhurst, then he should provide proof of his marriage to her."

King John lifted a brow at that, then glanced to Sir Royce. "'Tis reasonable enough. Can you produce the churchman, Sir Royce?"

Curse the meddling Frenchman, Royce fumed. He was like a badger who'd bitten into his prey and wouldn't let go.

"Aye, Majesty. 'Twas Friar Tupper who performed the ceremony. He is presently visiting Penhurst from Beckwell."

Friston's eyes narrowed. "Majesty, while this friar is being summoned, I insist Lady Juliana be lodged apart of Sir Royce, until their marriage can be confirmed or denied. 'Tis my understanding the papal legate is due to arrive here tomorrow. I hope to have no cause to seek him out with any complaints."

"Do not dare to threaten me, unless you wish to discover what lies in the bowels of Guildford's keep!" the king barked, standing eye to eye with the Frenchman. "I will send my own men to fetch Friar Tupper, lest you next claim his cooperation was influenced. Gratefully, Penhurst is not far, and we'll soon have an answer. Meantime, Lady Juliana will stay with my queen and other arrangements will be found for you, Sir Royce. I assume, Friston, that you have your own hole to climb into somewhere?" The king glared at the man.

"Comfortable enough quarters, Majesty. I shall withdraw to there now." He sketched a bow and started for the door. Pausing, he shot a glance back at Royce. "Until the matter is resolved, be assured, *chevalier*, Lady Juliana, I will be watching."

The "other arrangements" found for Royce were in an isolated corner, high in the keep, a tiny chamber on the topmost floor. 'Twas a snug, out-of-the-way room that the king suggested, claiming to have used it on occasion himself—before his recent marriage, of course.

No sooner had Royce moved in his small trunk than a priest arrived at his door, bearing a message from John.

"I am to await your instruction, Sir Royce," the priest said as he removed a small scroll from his sleeve and handed it to Royce.

His interest piqued, Royce unrolled the parchment. The message it bore was brief, but the meaning clear.

> The cunning fox spreads word of his presence and purpose at Court, as well as your claims concerning Lady Juliana. Acting the aggrieved relative, he now openly demands Lady Juliana submit herself to an examination by the royal physicians. If she proves yet chaste, he will appeal to the papal legate and have the marriage nullified, assuming your friar confirms one exists.
>
> The examination I will allow but have delayed till the morrow. To do otherwise invites suspicion and further interference. Meanwhile, I send you my priest, Father Andrew Des Roches, to aid you in whatever way he might. He may be trusted.
>
> John Rex

Seeing Royce re-roll the parchment, Father Andrew stepped forward and cleared his throat.

"I am to advise you, what with the continuing arrivals at Guildford and the Court diversions planned for this evening, that your presence will not be missed. Nor will that of Lady Juliana. His Majesty said you would understand."

Royce tapped the scroll thoughtfully against his palm. "That I do, Father. That I do."

Juliana sat woodenly in naught but her linen chemise while Luvena combed out her hair. The other ladies in the bedchamber were busily applying the final touches to their appearance and departing for the Great Hall below. Juliana, however, had no wish to leave the confines of the room. She feared encountering Friston and was far too embarrassed to face Sir Royce.

Dear Lord, what had she done? She may well have ruined Sir Royce's opportunity to marry the countess and become the next Earl of Linford. She'd acted solely on impulse, the sight of the Frenchman panicking her to the bone. If only she could attach his face to some place or time, but her mind would not give up the memory.

On the other hand, she'd thrust Sir Royce into a most difficult situation. She must right things for him—seek out Lady Sibylla and explain what had happened. Despite Sir Royce's gallantry, Juliana could not allow him to sacrifice his own future for her sake.

It still amazed her that he'd supported her wild tale that they were wed. Had he done so because of the special bond they shared? Because he felt some obligation to continue saving the "little sprite" who'd "inspired him through the years," as he'd said of her? No matter, he'd proved himself a most chivalrous knight, jeopardizing much for her this day—a bride and an earl's coronet. She must amend things for him, even though doing so would break her heart.

"Are you sure you do not wish to go down, my lady?" Luvena asked as she finished working her hair into a thick braid. "There will be the most splendid amusements this eve—mummers, tumblers, little dogs leaping through hoops."

Before Juliana could answer, a knock came at the door. Luvena bustled across the room to open it, and Juliana next heard a male voice, speaking low and rapid.

"I seek Lady Juliana. Is she here?"

"Aye, Father. That she is,"

"Then inform her she is to come with me at once."

"She will first need dress—"

"At once!" he insisted. "There is no time."

Juliana caught up her fur-lined mantle from where it lay over her trunk and quickly wrapped it about her. "Luvena, who comes?"

"A priest, my lady, and two of the king's guard." Juliana joined the maid at the door and confronted the churchman, her stomach knotting. "Where is it you wish to take me? If to Rennart de Friston, I warn you I'll not go."

"My lady, I am Father Andrew, His Majesty's spiritual advisor. I am to bring you to the owner of this."

Opening his palm, he held out a silver cross, the same cross she'd worn these ten years past. Taking it from him, Juliana forgot all else and nodded.

"Of course. Please lead the way, Father."

No sooner did Juliana emerge from the chamber than new fears seized her. Sir Royce must be hugely angry with her for all the trouble she'd caused him this day. On the other hand, it struck her as extraordinary that the king's own priest should be sent to find her and escort her to the knight. What was this truly about?

Juliana braced herself and continued to follow the priest along the corridors, hazy with torchfire, the guards tracking behind. They climbed high in the keep, arriving at last before a door in the southwest corner. Father Andrew rapped thrice then pushed the door open and stepped aside. Motioning her through, he then closed the door behind her.

Juliana drew a breath as she took another step into the chamber. There, waiting before the fireplace, stood Sir Royce, as strikingly handsome as ever. She hesitated as his eyes pulled to her, expecting to find them fired with anger. Instead, they were weighted with thought, his look sober, unreadable, causing her to tense all the more.

Uncertain of his mood, Juliana clutched her mantle close and moved cautiously into the room. "Sir Royce, I—I am so sorry . . . for the trouble I have caused you . . . but thankful too. Once more you have saved me, it seems."

She tried to form a smile but found her lips suddenly dry. As she moistened them, the motion drew Sir Royce's eyes, his gaze lingering upon her mouth.

"When Friston tried to claim me, I could scarce think," she continued, self-conscious, her words jumbling together. "I knew only to seek your protection, which I did, by saying you were my husband. The man is evil, I'm sure of it. How, I don't know, but he's no cousin of mine. Heaven knows what he wants with me—"

In a single step, Sir Royce closed the space between them, drawing her to him and dropping a kiss to the top of her head. "Shhh, Juliana. 'Tis all right."

Surprised to find herself solaced in his arms, rather than tasting of his anger, Juliana glanced slowly upward. "I promise to explain everything to Lady Sibylla—"

"Do not worry about Lady Sibylla."

Juliana sought his gaze at that, sensing something amiss. "What is it, Sir Royce? Why have you sent for me?"

His eyes quested hers a long moment, then he eased his hold of her. "Perhaps you should sit down, Juliana."

She pulled away, stiffening. Something indeed was wrong. "What has happened? Tell me. I'll not break or throw myself into a fit."

"Nor would I expect you to, my brave Juliana, though you may still decide it best to sit." He brushed the back of his fingers over her cheek, then coupled his gaze with hers. "These past weeks, you've asked me to allow you your own choice. That I will do this night, though the choice I must offer you is far from any you might have expected."

"Go on," Juliana prompted when he paused overlong, steeling herself for his next words.

"At the insistence of Friston and by the command of the king you are to undergo an examination on the morrow by the royal physicians. They will verify whether you yet be a virgin or not. If so, our ruse will be exposed and the Frenchman will reassert his claim over you."

Juliana wavered at his revelation. "But still, we can maintain we have spoken our marriage vows—"

"An unconsummated union can be dissolved and Friston stands ready to appeal the matter to the papal legate."

"I see." Juliana's heart sank to the vicinity of her toes. "You said there is a choice?"

"I see but two alternatives, Juliana. Either we allow the truth to be revealed, in which case you will be given over to the guardianship of your 'cousin'— "

"Oh, nay, we cannot do that! There must be another way. Anything. Tell me what I must do and I shall. What is the other choice?"

Sir Royce cupped her face in his strong hands. "We must lie together this night, as though truly man and wife, so that on the morrow you will in truth no longer be a virgin."

Juliana's pulse pounded in her ears as she stared up at him. She couldn't seem to get any sound past her lips.

"I am sorry, Juliana, there is no delicate way to put this. To keep you from Friston, you must give me your maidenhead."

She felt herself color hotly.

"There are, shall we say, less *natural* ways to—" He shook his head against the notion, then sighed. "Friston will not abandon his claim easily. He may insist you face the prelate and even take an oath. You must be able to claim with all honesty that we have been intimate. To lie to the papal prelate would be as if to lie before God, a sin. 'Tis best we—"

"I understand." She must have swayed for Sir Royce's hands moved to steady her, capturing her about her waist and by her arm.

"Juliana, I've no wish to dishonor you, and certainly would not take your gift without benefit of vows, but I cannot marry you. I've already spoken with the priest, but as 'tis Advent, no marriages may be performed either now or before Twelfth Night. He can make no exceptions."

Confusion crowded her brain. "You asked him to marry us? But, of course, you did. You are ever a man of honor. I wouldn't have agreed, of course. I won't marry you."

Her words brought a startled look to Sir Royce's eyes, but she'd not deny him the brilliant future he deserved. She loved him too much to stand in his way.

"I will truly speak with Lady Sibylla," she assured, her heart tearing.

"Juliana, listen to me—"

She pressed her fingers to his lips—warm, wonderful lips—and stopped his words.

"Your countess need know nothing of what passes here. 'Tis no secret I was betrothed before coming to England. Let her believe I arrived on these shores already deflowered."

He caught her fingers in his. "Juliana, I appreciate what you seek to do. Let us speak of it another time. Still, I've no intention of bedding you without some benefit of vows.

This much I can offer you—our own betrothal, blessed by the Church."

Juliana blinked at Sir Royce's insistence. The vows of betrothal were as solemn as those of marriage, though not as binding. "Very well. Once Friston leaves Court, we can have them quietly dissolved. Meanwhile, we must reveal them to no one, especially to Lady Sibylla. Agreed?"

"I will promise you this, Juliana, I will keep our secret for now and will leave the choice with you as to what shall be done about our vows in time to come."

"Then, I can ask no more. Best call in Father Andrew and proceed, lest any new twist of fate befall us today."

Sir Royce pressed a kiss to her forehead, then moved to the door and ushered in the priest. Father Andrew addressed Juliana and Sir Royce briefly on the weightiness of their vows, then instructed them to repeat the words of betrothal, requiring they pledge to take each other to husband and to wife in the future, "if the Holy Church consents."

As Juliana and Sir Royce affirmed they would, the priest next called for the rings of betrothal. To her surprise, Sir Royce produced a gold band with flowers carved round it and slipped it onto her finger. Satisfied, Father Andrew blessed their espousal and withdrew from the chamber.

Juliana found herself alone once more with Sir Royce, their hands still joined as they stood in the center of the tiny chamber, its prominent piece of furniture a bed for two. She grew heated in the heavy mantle she wore, her gaze fixed on the floor, knowing what they now must do.

Juliana grew charmingly shy before Royce's eyes, cocooning herself in her mantle. As he drank in her exquisite beauty, he reminded himself 'twas to be her first joining, the moment thrust upon her, the circumstance far from what any maiden might desire.

He vowed in that moment to make the experience as agreeable for her as possible. How fragile she seemed, as she stood before him, her lashes lowered, her shoulders trembling. Royce tipped up her chin with his fingertip, coaxing her to look at him.

"Juliana, how much do you know of what passes between a man and a woman?"

Skittish as a doe, her eyes met his briefly then darted away. "Only what *mère* Marie told me, a few days before I was to wed."

He frowned at that, finding little encouragement there. 'Twas likely Juliana was as chaste in mind as she was in body. Bedding her without frightening her was going to be a challenge.

"Perhaps you would care for something to relax you. I've brought ale from Penhurst, if you prefer it."

Juliana shook her head. Shutting her eyes, she stood rigid as a marble column and just as straight. "Nay, no ale. I'll be fine. Let's see this done with."

Royce smiled inwardly, touched by her innocence as well as by her courage. At the same time he felt his own tensions ease. There was but one solution for this night—to lead with his heart.

"Juliana, look at me." He took her face gently in his hands. "I am not going to attack you like some animal. I'm going to make love to you. *We* are going to make love."

"We?" Her eyes flew open to his.

"Aye, we. 'Tis the only true way for a man and a woman to join together as one and to seek their pleasure."

"Pleasure?" A look of disbelief appeared in her eyes, then she flushed prettily. "I suppose there is that for the man. Are you sure you wish to do this? Make love to me, that is?"

"More than sure, my Juliana." *More than you could possibly imagine, my heart.*

He smiled, then skimmed his hand over her lustrous hair and the thick braid draped over her shoulder. His attention drew to the ribbons securing the braid. He tugged on the satiny strips and freed them one by one.

"You revealed to me, not long ago, how you'd prayed for me through these years. How you longed for my return."

"'Tis true," she said in a small voice, her gaze returning to his.

"I am here, Juliana, and you are my betrothed. Do you trust me?"

She nodded, her green eyes darkening as he began slowly loosening her braid, freeing her tresses from their confinement.

"Will you trust me—now, in this moment, and for the hours to come?"

She went perfectly still. So still, Royce thought she'd stopped breathing. But then she lifted her hands to her throat and opened her mantle. Slipping it from her shoulders, she let it drop to the floor.

Juliana trembled as she stood before him in her thin chemise, the fabric transparent before the fire's light. Royce's blood fired in his veins as he gazed upon her—her breasts visible through the light veil of linen, as was the outline of her legs. His cross hung suspended about her neck. This time, rather than curbing his ardor, it called to mind the many ties that bound them—important as any, the vows they'd just spoken.

"I trust you." Juliana's soft voice drew his gaze back to hers. "Above all others, I trust you, Royce."

Her words filled him, warmed him. "Then do not fear me, my heart." He drew the lustrous fall of hair from her shoulder, then traced his fingertips over her slender neck. "I only wish to love you, Juliana."

Her lips tilted in a smile at that. She took his hand and drew it to her breast, offering him her silent answer, offering him herself.

His heart brimmed with love for this woman. Gathering Juliana to him, Royce's mouth descended over hers, claiming her with his kiss. He explored her lips, savored their softness, forcing himself to proceed slowly, though in truth, he yearned to devour her whole.

Relishing the weight of her breast in his hand, he began to caress her, grazing her nipple with his thumb, then stroking circles around its tight, tender bud. She gasped at his touch, her lips parting. Royce waited no invitation, but plundered the recesses of her mouth, tasting, probing, mating her tongue with his.

Juliana met him haltingly at first, then more daringly, as she joined him in a sensuous dance of tongues. He felt her body lean into his, her womanly softness yielding against his solid frame.

As Royce continued his seduction, his hand left her breast to slide down her spine. Cupping her sweet backside, he pressed her hips against him, bringing her into contact with his burgeoning desire. She started at first, but he held her firm, deeming it important she know something of what was to come, of what to expect. Soon, her resistance dissolved, her body softening against him once more. Juliana's arms twined about him as she gave herself to the pleasure of their kisses.

Aching to hold her warm flesh, Royce eased up her chemise, then slipped his hand beneath. Sweeping his palm upward over her bare hip and waist, he sought her breast once again. Briefly, he teased the taut globe of her nipple, then abandoning her lips, he lifted the fabric, uncovering her lush treasure, and took her in his mouth.

"R-Royce," Juliana moaned as a liquid heat passed through her, pooling between her legs. She gripped hold of Royce, certain her bones would melt as he cherished one, then the other, of her breasts. Her skin tingled, vibrantly alive and sensitive to his touch. Hazily, she realized he was drawing off her gown and next found herself naked in his arms. Embarrassed, Juliana started to cover herself with her hands but he pulled them away.

"Do not hide, Juliana. You are beautiful. Let me see you—all of you."

Her heart beat wildly as Royce drank in the sight of her, nothing withheld from him, her every pore exposed. Desire burned in his eyes, near scorching her with its intensity. In the next breath, he recaptured her mouth with his. Slipping his arms behind her knees, he swept her off the floor, into his arms, and carried her to the bed.

Juliana felt the mattress give beneath her as Royce lay her upon it then covered her with his body. He ravished her with kisses, loving her with his mouth and tongue. Leaving her lips, he began a downward journey, trailing a fiery path to the hollow of her throat and over her shoulders. He paused to feast on her breasts before shifting lower to lave his attentions on her stomach and abdomen.

Juliana squirmed when he continued lower still, tracing his tongue over her thighs, behind her knees, down to her ankles. Pressing kisses upward again, he moved slowly, tormentingly, toward her most secret place. She ceased to breathe as she thought he would touch her there. Instead, he rose momentarily, ridding himself of his clothes, leaving her aching and on fire for him.

She dropped her gaze away as Royce undressed, but then curiosity overcame modesty and her eyes drew to him. He stood with his back to her as he divested himself of the last of his garments—his chausses and braies. As her gaze traveled over his hard length, she thought him magnificently sculpted, leastwise from behind. He turned toward her then, their eyes meeting. Juliana glimpsed only the muscled planes of his chest and shoulders as he moved quickly to rejoin her, flesh searing flesh as he did.

Royce drew her into a deep kiss, their naked lengths pressed together. Juliana fought her shyness. Had she not longed for this moment, when Royce would return from the East and claim her as his own? She'd not deny her love for this man, or her desire for him, nor allow timidity to get in the way. Suddenly impatient to touch him, Juliana spread her hands over his chest, then along his rib cage. Exploring his back, she roamed downward toward his buttocks, but her fingertips reached only midway.

How wondrously he was made, she thought, then realized Royce smiled at her. As she returned his smile, he kissed her deeply, then initiated another downward journey. Currents of fire traveled through her as he possessed her breasts. At the same time his fingers caressed the sensitive flesh of her inner thighs, teasing her legs apart. As she allowed him the access he sought, he covered her feminine mound with his palm and began to massage her there.

"Do you trust me, Juliana?" He spread kisses over her stomach.

"Yes," she whispered, her pulse skittering.

As he continued to massage her, she felt a throbbing response between her legs and pressed against Royce's hand. Instantly, shockingly, he slipped his fingers inside her. Juliana bolted against him, but he persisted in his invasion, stroking her intimately, unrelentingly, awakening an array of new senses within her and commanding each one. Some part of her brain told her she should protest, but as pleasure spread through her feminine core, her body wantonly craved more. She opened to Royce fully, like the petals of a blossom, welcoming his possession.

Royce caressed Juliana's swollen desire, his own need near to bursting, his hold on himself tenuous. As he brought her to the brink of fulfillment, she writhed beneath him, her breaths coming short and quick.

"Juliana, do you give yourself to me?" he rasped, continuing to love her with his fingers, at the same time settling himself between her legs.

"Yes, please . . . Royce . . ." Her nails dug into his back and she moaned against him.

Royce set his jaw. Drawing her legs around him, he pressed into her, met the dread barrier, then drove forward with one swift thrust and sheathed himself in her. Juliana cried out, her hips arching against him, forcing him deeper inside. Royce stilled, struggling to master himself as they both lay panting, Juliana's femininity clamped tight around him, searing hot. He began quieting her with his kisses.

"There will be no more pain, my darling. We are one."

"I am no longer a virgin?" she asked breathlessly. "We are done?" Disappointment traced her features, bringing a smile to Royce's lips.

"Nay, Juliana, we've only just begun."

His blood flowing hot and thick, Royce loved her anew, savoring her breasts and bringing gasps to her lips as he began to move inside her. Guiding her hips with his hands, he rocked her against him, setting the pace. Their breaths quickened as on and on they strove together in an age-old rhythm, faster and faster. Suddenly, Juliana's eyes flew wide.

"Royce!" She convulsed against him, gripping him covetously as spasms overtook her, catapulting her to another realm.

Juliana's contractions carried Royce with her, triggering his own climax. Surging against her, he joined her in that fiery ecstasy, roaring as the twin sensations of pain and pleasure ripped through him, and he began emptying himself into his beloved.

Together they rode their passions to rapturous heights, their hearts afire, as their bodies and souls melded to one.

22

"Sir Royce, you pace like a man whose wife is ready to give birth. The physicks do but examine your bride. Here, have a goblet of wine. They'll not disturb your sporting ground, you have my word."

Royce turned on his heel, his gaze meeting the king's grinning face. The sly fox well knew the source of his unrest. 'Twas King John, himself, who'd manipulated last night's events like a master puppeteer.

Not that Royce was complaining of the passion he'd shared with Juliana. Their union had been astounding, unimaginably satisfying, in spirit as well as body. But 'twas Juliana's first sexual experience. He despised that she must now undergo this crude, personal inspection—that she must disrobe, even if partially, for these men's prying eyes. Royce didn't care if they were royal physicians, the entire affair made his blood boil. Juliana must be mortified, and there was naught he could do about it.

If his concerns for her were not enough, Royce knew 'twould be obvious Juliana had forfeited her maidenhead to him brief hours ago. She'd still be healing, likely inflamed, from the act. Then, too, she carried his seed. Should the physicks openly announce as much, Royce might next find himself crossing swords with Rennart de Friston, posturing as the outraged kinsman and demanding recompense.

Was Friston Juliana's kinsman? Royce held his suspicions. At the moment, the Frenchman stood near the fireplace, waiting for the outcome of the examination. Though he did not pace, he fidgeted constantly—flicking his thumb against his forefinger, pulling on his earlobe, crossing and re-crossing his arms. 'Twas clear he was impatient to gain charge of Juliana and depart England. He'd voiced that desire with irritating frequency.

It struck Royce as odd that Friston's interest lay solely with the heiress and not with her land or the wealth it might bring him. Not once had Friston asked of Penhurst or of its dependencies. Royce narrowed his eyes over the man. What were his true intentions toward Juliana?

The creaking of the door on the opposite wall drew Royce's attention. There, three physicians, garbed in flowing black robes and little square hats, filed out of the queen's chambers—these reserved for her ladies-in-waiting and where, this morning, Juliana's examination took place. Coming before the king, they bowed with a flourish and rose.

"Majesty," the senior physick among them began importantly. "We've completed our directives and have determined the following concerning the lady's—"

The king's hand shot up. "A simple yea or nay will suffice. I've no need of an analysis of the lady's intimate parts. Is Lady Juliana a virgin or not?"

"We only thought you would wish to know—"

"Yea or nay?" the king barked, quelling the man's tongue with his glare.

"Nay, Majesty. Lady Juliana is not a virgin. And recently bedded too," the physick added quickly.

"Of course *recently*. She's only just married," the king spewed as though the man was dense.

Allowing the physicians no quarter to divulge more, he signaled for them to withdraw. Royce expelled a breath of relief as the king's gaze traveled between himself and Friston.

"We must now wait on Friar Tupper's arrival to confirm

or disclaim any marriage. Until such time, Lady Juliana will continue to remain under my protection. One exception I will make, however." The king's gaze fixed on Royce.

"Since 'twas Lord Gilbert's own wish that you hold guardianship of his granddaughter, and since your claims to being her husband are thus far borne out, you may publicly escort Lady Juliana to all services and holiday festivities at Guildford. In private, however, she will remain in my queen's chambers and under guard. I trust you both find that agreeable." The king's eyes shifted to the Frenchman.

Friston bowed stiffly to King John, his features hard, tense. "As you will, Majesty." He started to leave then turned to Royce. "Be assured, *chevalier*, unless a valid marriage can be proven, I will claim my rights to my cousin by all means necessary. Meanwhile, as I said before, I'll be near and watching."

As the Frenchman quit the chamber, the king moved to Royce's side. "When first I sent you on your quest to find Lady Juliana, I said I'd no intention of losing any of the realm's fair maidens. I meant that. I'll especially not lose any to the French Court or to its king—the wolf who nips at my heels and hungers after my lands." He cocked a brow at Royce, a twinkle in his eyes. "Of course, Lady Juliana is no longer a maiden, is she?"

John grinned wide and clapped Royce on the back as if to congratulate him. He then looked to the queen's chambers where the door stood closed once more.

"Your lady will need time to dress and compose herself. No doubt, Isabella will wish to keep company with her for a time. My young queen is none too happy about all this, be assured," John confided. "Come. Let us see if Marshal has arrived. He promised to bring wine from Pembroke."

Royce glanced to the door, chafing to be with Juliana and assure she was well. Having no recourse, however, he followed the king from the chamber.

Two hours later, Juliana emerged from seclusion in the queen's chambers to accompany Royce to the feast, about to commence in the hall below. She kept her lashes lowered as she joined him, too embarrassed to meet his eyes after their passionate lovemaking last night, followed by the morning's events. Royce would have none of it, however. Gently, he framed her face in his hands and urged her to look at him.

"Are you all right, Juliana?"

Heat flooded her at his touch, her senses stirring as she remembered how his hands had moved over her, how she'd surrendered to him totally.

"Juliana?" he asked again, concern filling his voice.

"I-I'm all right." She nodded. Still she could not bring herself to meet his gaze.

"What is it? I caused you pain last night, perhaps more than I realized." His concern turned to worry. "Or is it the physicians? Did they harm you in any way?"

"Nay, Royce. I am fine, truly."

"What then?" His hands slid to her shoulders.

"It's just that . . . what we did together . . . in the dark . . . I even scratched your back."

"Ah, sweet Juliana, do not be embarrassed by what we shared. I am not. I shall treasure those moments always, as I hope you will."

Royce enfolded her in his arms, kissing her tenderly, giving her no chance to reply. Juliana's heart raced as she melted into him, his clean, manly scent surrounding her. Sweet Jesus, how she wished to remain in his embrace always. If only that could be.

"Come now, my lady. 'Tis Christmas Eve, and you'll not want to miss the spectacles planned for today's feast."

Juliana smiled up at Royce, meeting his eyes finally, her heart full of love for her gallant knight. Placing her hand atop his forearm, she accompanied him downstairs, assured no one else would know of what had transpired between them. But as they joined the bright assemblage of lords and ladies in the fore chamber of the great Hall, many knowing glances turned their way.

"Congratulations to you both!" one man called out while another gave a friendly clout to Royce's back, echoing the greeting. More crowded round them.

"Secret nuptials? Shame on you, sir, for depriving us the merry ceremonials of a wedding and a bedding!"

"Can't say I blame you," interjected a long-bearded knight. "Your bride is a delectable creature. If you find you need help fulfilling your duties, I am near."

Many good-natured jests and winks were tossed Royce's way, while the ladies fluttered about Juliana giving her hugs and kisses on her cheeks, the entire Court seemingly abuzz with news of their supposed marriage. A few men sent disgruntled looks Royce's way. Juliana recognized them to be suitors who'd offered unsuccessfully for her hand.

As the flow of wishes continued, Juliana tugged on Royce's sleeve. "Royce, everyone knows about last night!"

"About last night? Nay, my heart," he replied for her hearing alone. "But, they do assume we've lain together. 'Tis what newly wedded couples do, after all—make love, every day, many times over."

"What?" she squeaked. "You mean, they think . . ?"

"Aye, many times over." He beamed, unabashed, as he accepted another couple's well-wishes.

"Royce de Warrene, you are not the least embarrassed. You even look pleased by their assumptions."

"Enormously, I'll not deny it. I'm proud for others to know I've claimed you as my own." He dropped a kiss below her ear. "My only regret is that I've not enjoyed your sweet favors as ofttimes as everyone seems to think I have. Mayhap we should seek to remedy that."

"Royce!" Her gaze flew to his, his admittance sending a secret thrill spiraling through her.

"Ohhhh, Lady Juliana, I am so happy for you!" gushed Lady Blythe, appearing beside her and clasping her hands.

For a moment, Juliana caught sight of Friston's black-clad figure across the room. She quickly turned back to Lady Blythe. At the same time, Royce slipped his hand to the small of Juliana's back, a possessive but reassuring gesture. Had he spied the Frenchman as well?

Juliana began to relax and enjoy the attentions showered on her and Royce. Just as she warmed to her role as a new bride, Lady Sibylla swept grandly into view. Without hesitation, the countess walked straight up to Royce and slapped him hard across the face. Her nostrils flared as she flayed him with dark, furious eyes, her features brittle with anger. She cast a withering gaze over Juliana, then hoisted her chin high and, giving them both her back, stalked away.

Royce rubbed his jaw. "'Twould seem our happy news did not set well with Countess Linford."

"Indeed." Juliana glanced after Sibylla, the magic of the moment gone, reality crashing down on her like a wave of frigid water. Juliana knew she must speak with the countess, explain what had happened, and set things aright between her and Royce. Juliana had promised she would. 'Twas one promise she loathed to keep.

Trumpets blared as the king and queen appeared and led the noble crowd into the hall, calling for the celebrations to begin. Noon stretched toward eve amid extravagant feasting on peacock and swan. Marvels of entertainment punctuated the courses—presentations of wind and stringed instruments, and singing ensembles that danced the carols.

Mummers in fanciful costumes flooded into the hall, reciting verse and tossing dice with guests, rewarding the winners with rings of gold.

While the festivities swirled around them, Juliana was ever aware of Friston. His eyes seldom left her and he appeared seemingly at every turn. On the other hand, she remained painfully conscious of the countess, who held a place befitting her station, far above that of the minor barons where she and Royce sat. The distinction served only to fortify Juliana's resolve for what she must do.

When the day's dinner and entertainments concluded, the nobles retired to their chambers to refresh themselves and prepare for the evening supper and diversions yet to come. Juliana took the opportunity to send Luvena to Lady Sibylla, requesting an audience. Luvena soon returned, however, having been recognized as Juliana's maid and rebuffed.

Juliana next sent for Guy of Lisors, knowing him to be trained in letters. When he arrived, she asked him to record and deliver a missive to Countess Linford as a personal favor. Tears rimmed Juliana's eyes as she dictated the words, her sorrow not lost on the minstrel.

"Write that Royce de Warrene is the most chivalrous of men—the most brave and wonderful and most self-sacrificing of all. He seeks only to protect me from the Frenchman, Rennart de Friston, whose intentions toward me are questionable at best."

She swiped at the tears that had begun to fall. "Write that naught is as it seems, and that I urge her patience. When the matter with Friston is resolved, all will be explained. She will find Royce's honor untarnished. She will also find him free and able to marry her." Juliana bowed her head, tears spilling hotly over her cheeks.

"My lady are you certain you wish me to deliver this? Perhaps Sir Royce should see it."

"Nay, he'll seek to change my mind. He is too noble for his own good. He is a great man, with a great destiny to fulfill. I know it in my heart. I also know I am a stone about his neck, an anchor that will weigh him down. I can bring him only a baronial lordship, while Sibylla can bring him an earldom and the power such destiny requires."

"But my lady, you love him. Is this not so?"

Juliana nodded sadly. "With all my heart, which is why you must deliver the letter, that he may become the man he must, for the good of all, not just one—not just me."

"But what of you, Lady Juliana? Will you seek another match? Another man to become Lord of Penhurst?"

"Nay." She shook her head firmly. "Royce alone holds my heart. There is no other, nor shall there ever be. I shall seek cloister. Go now, friend." Her voice broke as tears blurred her vision. "Deliver the missive. Help me give my love the future he deserves."

"As you will, my lady." The minstrel withdrew on silent feet, leaving her to her private misery.

Guy of Lisors closed the door quietly behind him and started down the corridor, his mood heavy. He'd almost completed his *lai* of the couple, with all its surprising twists and turns. Their story needed only a proper resolution—or rather, a satisfying one.

He considered the missive in his hand, thought of Lady Juliana's heart-wringing words, of the sacrifice she was prepared to make. Again he considered the message and the outcome it would likely bring. He didn't care for that particular ending to the couple's story. Not at all.

Folding the parchment in fours, he slipped it into his tunic. Guy's thoughts ran ahead of him as he changed his direction and took another passageway. There was one thing he could do. One thing that might make a difference.

The revels and feasting lasted deep into the night, many of the nobles disguising themselves in elaborate costumes to perform stories in dance and song. They posed as dragons and wildmen, elephants and angels. Juliana might have been able to set aside her unhappiness for a time and enjoy the fun had it not been for Lady Sibylla's vivid presence and Rennart de Friston, ever shadowing her about the hall.

Royce occupied her every moment, however, engaging her as they dined and leading her into dance after dance, keeping her wholly to himself. He grew pensive at times, his gaze settling intensely upon her. Juliana wondered if he brooded over what Friar Tupper would say once he arrived at Guildford, and what would come of their dilemma. Royce confided that he'd sent ahead two of Penhurst's men-at-arms to apprise the friar of what had taken place. Hopefully, they'd reach the monk before the king's men.

Juliana smiled at Royce as they came together in dance. Executing the steps, they turned and touched palms with the person at their left. Juliana froze, discovering Friston there, and snatched back her hand. The man was everywhere.

"Keep your distance, Friston," Royce snarled, stepping between them. Taking Juliana by the arm, he guided her from the floor.

Unnerved by the Frenchman and exhausted from all that had occurred since her arrival at Guildford, Juliana asked Royce to escort her back to the queen's chambers. There, he kissed her long and deep, ignoring the presence of the guards, leaving her breathless and craving more.

"Do not worry on the morrow, my heart, or the morrow after." He pressed his lips to her temple. "I've asked you to trust me, I ask you to still. All will work itself out."

For hours after, Juliana lay awake on her pallet, consumed with thoughts of Royce, questioning the course she'd taken regarding the countess. Life would be unbearable without him. She hadn't loved another since first she met him, nor would she ever, for all the days that she lived.

Christmas Day dawned crisp and clear, a dusting of snow having fallen overnight. The lords, ladies, and their royal hosts crowded into Guildford's chapel to attend High Mass and parade their holiday finery.

To Juliana's secret delight, she and Royce arrived looking every inch the Lord and Lady of Penhurst—he wearing the tunic she'd made for him, bearing the golden eagle, and she wearing his gift to her, a beautiful new gown of rich brocade, fashioned in Penhurst's colors and all lavishly embroidered. As she and Royce presented themselves as a glowing, newly wedded couple, she could almost believe the deception.

Standing beside Royce, Juliana shifted from one foot to the other as the Mass drew out, everything sung, chanted, and sanctified with incense. Distracted, she allowed her gaze to roam the chapel, an impressive chamber rising several stories high and having a gallery that ran along the upper level. There, the windows in the outer walls were positioned directly across from the gallery's archways, forming a clerestory of sorts where one could walk, but at the same time allowing in daylight to illuminate the space below.

As the choir began to sing the *Gloria* in parts, Juliana glanced toward the voices, but a movement in the upper gallery pulled her gaze back. She started as she discovered the Frenchman framed in one of the archways above, staring down at her.

Juliana's temper snapped, the frustrations and uncertainties of the past days colliding within her. Everywhere she turned, Friston was there. Why would the man not leave her alone? What did he want with her?

Shaking with anger, she shot him a hostile look, wishing it could lance him straight through. He continued to stare at her, showing no emotion but altering his stance. Juliana tensed, recognizing something in his eyes, something in his expression that unnerved her, something cold as death.

Her pulse drubbed solidly in her veins as she transferred her gaze to the Frenchman's gruesome scar. The image of blood, bright and red, flashed before her mind's eye. For a fleeting moment 'twas as though she gazed upon his open wound, freshly wrought and bleeding.

Juliana's knees buckled and she fell against Royce. Instantly, his arms went around her.

"Juliana, what is it?"

"I—I'm not sure." She gripped his arms, depending on his strength to hold her up.

Her heart pounding, Juliana lifted her gaze to the gallery once more, but Friston was gone.

Friar Tupper shivered within the folds of his mantle, gladdened by the sight of Guildford Castle as it came into view. He looked forward to thawing his bones before a fire and learning why he'd been brought here under royal guard.

All had happened in a blur. Barely had the king's soldiers arrived at Penhurst, when two of the men-at-arms from Lord Royce and Lady Juliana's escort returned. If they bore him some message, he'd not received it. The royal guards allowed no one to speak with him before they hastened him away.

The friar pondered that. Some trouble must have befallen the couple. What, precisely, was beyond his imagining. Lord Royce was to announce his choice of husband for Lady Juliana, as well as his own intentions to marry Countess Linford. Tupper found both thoughts as depressing as the winter's barren landscape. He'd hoped the knight would take his advice and look to his heart. Lord Royce and Lady Juliana loved one another deeply, 'twas obvious. If they would only admit as much to each other, they could get happily on with life, and the countess could see her way back to Linford.

Something must have happened at the Christmas Court. Had Lady Juliana fled once again, distressed by Lord Royce's choice of husband? Even so, what would that have to do with himself, and why would royal guards be sent to veritably abduct him and deliver him to Guildford?

The friar continued to puzzle the matter as the guards conducted him inside the castle compound, up a long flight of stairs, and into the great square keep. All was a marvel to his eyes and ears at first, but he quickly found himself isolated in a stark little room with a single bench and only a small brazier by which to warm himself.

Tupper rubbed heat into his arms, feeling much like a prisoner. *Prisoner.* His heart jumped at the word. What if Lord Royce had reported his activities at Beckwell—those of dismantling the walls of its tumble-down castle to build the village a new church? Mayhap the king took offense and decided that he, the one responsible for the pilferage, required lessoning in Guildford's dungeon!

He rose with a need to pace, but just as he did the door opened and a man appeared—a Court official by the quality of his garments and the ornate staff he carried.

"You are Friar Tupper of Penhurst?" the man asked.

"Friar Eugenius Tupper of Beckwell, actually," he admitted nervously. "I've only recently begun tending the flock at Penhurst. Their resident priest, uh, broke his leg while in Winchester. Perhaps, he is the one you seek."

"You *are* the same Friar Tupper who serves the Lord and Lady of Penhurst?"

Tupper bunched his brows at that. The knight held Lordship of Beckwell, not Penhurst.

"Lord Royce and Lady Juliana, they are known to you?" the official pressed, his tone edged with impatience.

"Aye, that they are." Tupper drew up his girth with an air of importance, not caring for the clerk's abrupt manner.

"Follow me," the man ordered flatly and whisked from the room, thumping his staff with each stride he took.

Friar Tupper trailed behind, nettled with concerns and cold to the bone. Mounting stairs to the castle's main floor, they proceeded to a set of double doors, flanked by more guards.

The official rounded on him. "You will bow low to His Majesty and remain so till bidden to rise. You will then speak only when spoken to, is that clear?"

"M-majesty?" Tupper gulped. He was doomed. The king knew.

"Come!" the man ordered as the guards opened the doors. "Remember what I said."

Tupper shuffled in after the man, dreading his fate, sending up hasty prayers. The official halted, thumped his staff thrice, and announced him by name in a booming voice. Tupper blanched as the man stepped aside and he found himself standing before the king.

John was more impressive than he'd supposed, fiery in coloring like his brother and father, fiery in temperament, too, he'd heard. He occupied a small throne with casual grace, regal in his silks and gems, his gold crown slightly crooked upon his head. To the king's right stood Sir Royce, and to his left a man who looked to be of knightly class, his hair and beard black as a crow's wing, his eyes obsidian.

A dozen other nobles occupied the chamber as well, sitting on high-backed chairs in a row. The scene resembled a legal court. *God have mercy,* Tupper pleaded for deliverance as he bent in as deep a bow as he could manage.

"Rise, Friar Tupper," the king commanded.

Blessedly, there was no hint of anger in the royal voice, or in his eyes. The king beckoned to someone unseen, standing just beyond a door at the back of the chamber. In the next moment, Lady Juliana entered, looking ghostly pale as she came before the throne and dropped into a curtsy. The king bid her to rise and stand before him, roughly in the center of the room for all to see.

"You are acquainted with Lord Royce and Lady Juliana of Penhurst?" The king's eyes shifted back to Friar Tupper.

There it was again—the knight being named as Lord of Penhurst rather than Beckwell.

"You are acquainted with the couple?" the king repeated.

"Aye, Majesty." *Couple?* Why did he sense he was being fed clues in some matter?

"Might you also be acquainted with Sir Rennart de Friston, who comes to us from King Philip's Court?"

Tupper glanced to the French knight. He had a hardness to him, especially about the eyes. The word "sinister" came to mind. "Nay, Majesty. I have not had the, uh, pleasure."

The king opened his mouth to say something more, but again the official returned, thumping his staff, this time announcing Aberto Ruggerio, papal legate from Rome. Friar Tupper scuttled aside as the worldly looking Italian moved past him.

"Majesty." Ruggerio sketched a bow in deference to England's king. "I come at the request of Sir Rennart, who has brought his claims, and those of the lord and lady, to my attention. I submit that, as His Holiness's emissary, I should lead the questioning in this matter."

King John exchanged a swift glance with Lord Royce.

Lady Juliana, looked to both as well, clearly anxious by this development.

"The claims concern the Crown, not the Church." John's eyes flashed, reminding of a lion roused.

The legate stood his ground. "The claims as to guardianship lay with the Crown, I agree. But those concerning the sacrament of matrimony lay with the Church. 'Tis the Church that ultimately judges the legitimacy of marriage vows, or permits the dissolution of them."

Tupper's brows rose at that. Clearly, the last a pointed reminder to King John of the Church's role in granting his annulment to his first wife, whom he'd hastily discarded upon attaining his crown. That and a reminder of the Church's blessing upon his recent marriage to Isabella of Angoulême. But did the legate also refer to other nuptials?

"Very well," the king growled, then looked to the friar. "You have been summoned here to settle certain claims that have been asserted by Lord Royce and Sir Rennart concerning Lady Juliana. Consider well your answers. The lady's future is dependent upon them."

The king's look bore into him. What was he expected to draw from it? Tupper wondered, at a loss.

The legate, Ruggerio, turned to him, gauging him with his sharp, beaded eyes. "By your cowl I see you are of the Black Canons."

"Aye, a mendicant brother and priest, attached to St. Botolph's Priory at Colchester."

"A notably less disciplined group than those who follow the strict Rule of Benedict," the legate commented dryly. "No matter. The question I must put to you is simple and direct. Both Sir Rennart and Lord Royce claim authority over Lady Juliana and her lands—Sir Rennart as her blood kinsman, Sir Royce as her husband."

Tupper struggled to keep his astonishment from his face. A blood kinsman and a husband? Lady Juliana had possessed neither when she left Penhurst.

"My question is this. Did you marry Lord Royce and Lady Juliana as they claim?"

Stunned, the friar's gaze leapt to the two, seeking some sign as to what he should say. He delighted in the idea of the two as married, flinched at the possibility of the lady being given over to the Frenchman. Still, being a man of God, he could not lie.

For a moment he floundered for an answer, then spied the band of gold on Lady Juliana's finger. Lacing his fingers together over the curve of his generous stomach, he smiled at the legate.

"Good brother, as you know, in our calling as priests— of any order—'tis not we who actually 'marry' the couple. We but serve as witnesses as the bride and groom exchange their vows before God."

"Of course, I know that," the legate retorted as though the friar were thick-skulled. "Specifically—did you or did you not witness the couple exchanging vows?"

Tupper smiled hugely inside. "Exchange vows? Oh, aye, indeed I did." *Many vows, usually very testy ones, exchanged often and with great passion.* "Truly, before God and before man, Lord Royce and Lady Juliana are eternally bound."

"As man and wife?" the legate snapped.

"As much or more than any two could be."

Ruggerio shot a look to the Frenchman, both men's aspects growing so dark the friar wondered if they'd made some prior agreement between them—one that had just failed.

King John rose to his feet. "The matter is settled then. The marriage is confirmed. I award Lady Juliana to her husband's keeping, and recognize Royce de Warrene as Lord of

Penhurst as well as that of Beckwell. As Penhurst is a barony of import, bringing with it rank and title greater than that of Beckwell, I further acknowledge Royce de Warenne's right to be addressed as 'Lord Royce,' as benefits his station—now doubly so."

The King eyed the French knight. "Sir Rennart, give my tidings to Philip when you return to his Court. Meanwhile, if you are the lady's kinsman as you claim, I encourage you to make peace with her husband. 'Tis the Christmas season after all."

Nearly purple with rage, Friston gave a curt bow and quit the chamber, casting a venomous look over the lord and lady as he did. The legate followed him out, his face set in grim lines.

"'Tis time for more celebrating, do you all not think?" The king's beard parted with a wide grin. "Lady Juliana you'll wish to prepare." He motioned for one of the attendants to lead her away, a curious gleam in his eye. "You also," he tossed to "Lord" Royce who stared after the lady as she disappeared through the chamber's rear door.

Tupper bowed low, as did the rest, when King John abandoned his throne and quit the room, saying something of finding his queen.

As the friar rose, Lord Royce joined him, clamping a hand to his shoulder. "Thank you, Friar. You have my endless gratitude. You have saved Lady Juliana from a direful fate this day."

"Truly, my lord? I'm happy to be of help." Tupper chuckled. "And here I feared being cast in the dungeon."

Lord Royce's brows shot up. "Why so? Is there something you have done?"

Tupper gave a small shrug. "Filched a bit of stone from my lord's castle wall to build Beckwell a new church."

"Friend, you may keep the stone. You have well earned

it this day." Lord Royce smiled in earnest.

"Thank you, my lord. You'll not regret it." Friar Tupper paused and rubbed his jaw. "About your vows with Lady Juliana, I sense there are more that yet need be spoken between the two of you—after Twelfth Night, mayhap?"

"Hopefully so, good friar. 'Twill all depend on the lady."

23

Royce headed for his chamber, the enormous relief he felt lightening his steps, his desire to rejoin Juliana hastening them.

After leaving Friar Tupper, he'd dispatched two of his men to watch Friston's movements and assure he left Guildford. With the Frenchman's plans foiled, his claims denied, there was naught for him to do but depart for France. Yet Royce did not trust Friston and would not rest easily until certain the man was gone from this place.

Royce's thoughts circled back to Juliana. He would change for the evening's revelries and then seek her out. He intended they should celebrate the night through. With matters decided in their favor and Friston no longer an impediment, naught stood between them. Except convincing Juliana to marry him.

Arriving at his chamber door, he shoved it open and crossed the threshold. He came up short as he discovered Juliana within, wrapped in a silken robe and sitting on a stool. Luvena tended her hair, combing through its length so that it fell like a silvery waterfall over Juliana's shoulders and past her waist.

On seeing him, Juliana rose at once, their gazes meeting, coupling, across the silence. Royce's heart swelled with love and pride for his lady. So many trials had brought them here.

"Congratulations, my lord!" Luvena bubbled, bustling forward and patting his arm. "I told Lady Juliana the same.

Such secrets to be keeping! Wonderful ones, though. Surely God smiles on Penhurst that you should be its lord and she its lady." Her smile filled her round little face. "My lady's trunk is moved in beside your own," she chattered on. "His Majesty's command. You are to share the chamber together now."

"Thank you, Luvena." Royce's gaze dropped to the maid then returned to Juliana. "Could you give us a moment?"

"Of course, my lord. Call should you need me." Luvena glanced between the two. "But of course, you won't." She tittered then slipped out the door, closing it behind her.

Consuming Juliana with his eyes, Royce started toward her, but she quickly joined him halfway, her arms slipping around him. As she lifted her face to his, a tide of emotion broke through Royce. He sought her lips and possessed them, so great was his relief, so intense was his love. To Royce's joy, Juliana met his kisses with equal ardor, their mouths suddenly afire with want of one another. When their lips parted at last, and he drew back to gaze on Juliana, he found tears wetting her cheeks.

"What's this, my heart? 'Tis no time for tears, lest they be ones of joy." He brushed them away, smiling.

Her hold on him only tightened. "Royce, I was so frightened. I feared I'd be taken from you. Friar Tupper was clearly at a loss, unsuspecting of our plight when he arrived. Then the legate appeared—"

"Shhh, my darling. 'Tis over." Royce kissed her cheek, her brow. "Friston departs even as we speak, and the legate is satisfied, thanks to Friar Tupper's quick thinking. You are safe, my darling."

"Safe in your arms as ever I've been." She lifted her hand to his cheek. Her emerald eyes darkened with a look of longing, but also of worry.

"What is it, Juliana? Does something trouble you?"

Her gaze dropped to his lips, and she traced them lightly with her fingertips. When she raised her eyes again, they were filled with a piercing sadness.

"If only we could leash time itself and remain in this moment forever. But 'twill not last."

"Why do you say that, my heart? Time is no hindrance. Our future lies clear before us."

An even deeper sadness pervaded her eyes. "Indeed, the future waiting before us is clear, as is all required of us." Her look of sadness turned to one of urgency. "Love me, Royce. Before this moment is lost to us forever, love me once more."

Slipping her arms about his neck, she drew him to her, pressing her lips to his. Royce felt her tremble as she gripped him close. 'Twas as though she feared he would vanish. Giving himself to her kiss, he deepened it. Whatever her concerns, he'd not deny her this moment, nor any other. God willing, they'd enjoy a lifetime of loving.

Juliana opened her mouth beneath Royce's, urging his invasion, her tongue boldly seeking his. If she must tend her days in a nunnery then she wanted to make love with him one more time—wanted to touch Heaven with him just once again.

As their kisses caught fire, Royce gathered her up into his arms and carried her to the bed. She pulled impatiently at his clothes, trying to free him of them. He obliged, shedding them hastily before returning to her. Equally impatient, he pushed aside her robe, found her already naked and ready for him. Juliana smiled as she heard him groan and felt him harden against her. She gloried then in the feel of his lips moving over her, his tongue tasting her and trailing patterns over her flesh, gloried in the heat of his mouth upon her breast.

Juliana explored him eagerly as well, daringly so, wishing to know and memorize every detail about him, wishing to hold them forever in her heart.

Anxious that they should be joined, she wrapped her legs about his. Indulging them both, Royce pressed forward, penetrating her depths, uniting them as one. Slowly, rhythmically, he began to move against her.

Juliana arched against Royce as he rode her steadily. Once more, he captured her lips, seducing her thoroughly before turning to ravish her breasts. His tongue wrought delicious sensations—sensations that turned to ones of molten heat, spreading from the tips of her breasts downward to center between her legs.

Tension coiled inside her as she rocked against Royce, the feeling building, expanding, into a thousand tiny points of desire, aching for release. Suddenly, raw need overtook her and she surged against Royce, rushing toward an unseen precipice. He guided her hips with his hands, matching her pace and taking them both over the edge.

Juliana shattered against Royce, and he against her, as their passions exploded, hurtling them out of time and place. On and on, together they strove, their love blazing so bright as to rival the stars.

Spent at last, they drifted slowly back to earth. Feeling a deep peace and happiness, Juliana molded herself to Royce, wondering how she would ever exist a single day without him.

Juliana and Royce paused at the portal of the Great Hall, arriving belatedly, having made love yet again.

She'd brought on the moment, Juliana realized, still glowing with satisfaction and the lingering pleasure of it all. They'd been both nearly dressed, Royce sitting upon the stool drawing on his boots, when she asked him to lace her gown. Instead, he grinned wolfishly and drew her down atop his lap, prompting her to straddle his legs. She felt him fumble with his chausses, then him filling her. Drawing her gown off her shoulders to her waist, he laid siege to her in earnest. Juliana sank her hands in his hair as he took her—a quick, primal, breathtaking possession that left her shuddering against him.

"You are beautiful flushed with love," Royce whispered, dropping a kiss to the curve of her neck.

Juliana smiled up at him, her skin prickling, still highly sensitive to his touch. As she and Royce entered the hall and found a place at a table, she suspected she was pink from head to toe, their recent exertions apparent to all.

Servants quickly provided them with a trencher and wine, the second course about to begin. Throughout the hall, musicians entertained on harps, viols, tabors, and drums, while one juggler balanced his sword by its point on his chin, and another twirled plates on long sticks.

If only this happiness could last, Juliana thought to herself. If only she could offer Royce all he required to ensure his bright future, that he might remain with her always. She'd not think on it now, she told herself, stealing a glance at his fine features. She would savor every moment granted them, knowing soon she must relinquish him to the countess.

As Juliana glanced about the chamber, she felt comforted to not find Friston lurking anywhere. He was truly gone from her life. Leastwise, she hoped so. Still, the question remained, why had he sought to claim her?

When the horns sounded, the parade of dishes recommenced. Juliana saw a great pie carried on planks into the hall, braced on the shoulders of six squires. She recoiled at the thought it might contain birds. Happily, tiny tumblers emerged from the pie, to everyone's surprise. As everyone dined and supped their way through the evening, enjoying the endless Court spectacles, Juliana reflected that she was far from the life she once knew in Chinon. As for the time before that, she still had no clear memory of it, but certainly she'd never experienced anything like this in her parents' castle.

As the latest course was cleared away, a procession of mummers whirled into the hall, carrying torches and dancing to the minstrels' tune. Tonight their costumes were even more elaborate and fanciful than before—monkeys and peacocks, goats, swans, lions, and unicorns.

Juliana laughed and clapped at their performance along with Royce, and when they invited her to partake in their dance, Royce encouraged her to join in the play. The lords and ladies formed a line on one side of the floor with the mummers opposite, leading them in a series of steps. Enjoying herself, Juliana turned round and round, laughing heartily. But her smile died when she glanced toward Royce and discovered Lady Sibylla engaging his interest.

She forced her feet to keep pace with the others, her partner a seven-foot vulture, his disguise complete with feathered wings and a mask having a large hooked beak. As the dance ended, the mummers escorted the lords and ladies to the fringes of the dance floor, then began leaping and twirling as they headed toward the lower hall.

Juliana sought Royce, but found Lady Sibylla had drawn him off to the side wall. Just as Juliana's gaze alighted on them, she saw the countess smooth her hand over Royce's chest, then raise on tiptoe and kiss him full on the lips.

Juliana turned away, the sharp horns of jealousy goring her heart. Sibylla had obviously received her letter and accepted its contents. Now Juliana must honor her own words and see through her promise. But how could she bear to give Royce up? How could she bear the thought of him making love to the countess as he had to her?

Composing herself as best she could, Juliana spied Friar Tupper at the lower end of the hall enjoying a tankard of ale, steeped in conversation with his tablemate. Unable to face Royce at the moment, she began to move toward the monk, wishing to thank him for today. She would need speak to him of her betrothal to Royce, and of dissolving it. Tomorrow, perhaps. Tonight was hers and Royce's to enjoy, thanks to the good friar. At least, it had been, she thought, glancing to where Sibylla occupied Royce.

As Juliana stepped onto the edge of the dance floor, the mummers swirled about her, playfully dancing circles around her and carrying her along with them as they made their way toward the hall's portal at the lower end. She gave herself to the diversion, allowing them to include her in their fun, since they moved in the direction where the friar sat. As they neared his table, however, she found herself swept on with the merry group, past the archways and screens passages and out the door. The colorful troop continued to frolic along the corridor, leading her further and further from the hall.

"Please, I wish to go back." Juliana tried to elbow past a large frog and a camel.

As she pushed her way through the crush of revelers, she came up against a wall of black feathers. Glancing up, she discovered the vulture with whom she'd previously danced. He towered over her, or rather, the mummer's headpiece did. It peered down at her with black pebbly eyes, tipping its head this way and that, so that the raptor looked to be scrutinizing her as if for its next meal.

A shiver passed through Juliana. "Please, let me through."

She started to shove past the huge bird but its wing shot up. 'Twas no wing at all, but a feathered cloak, she realized, as it enshrouded her totally, a hidden hand closing over her mouth.

Juliana struggled against the mummer's hold as he dragged her into a separate corridor, then thrust her hard against the wall. Pain exploded through the back of her head as it contacted the stone. Dazedly, she felt the hand leave her mouth, replaced by cold steel pressing into her throat.

"Not a word," the man hissed in her ear.

Juliana ceased to breathe as she recognized the voice of Rennart de Friston.

"I am sorry, Lord Royce." Lady Margaret smiled politely. "I don't know where your lady is. She didn't return to our table after the mummers left."

Royce uttered his thanks then drew his gaze over the chamber once again. Where had Juliana disappeared to? Noting Guy of Lisors speaking with Friar Tupper at the lower end of the hall, Royce started their way. Mayhap one of them had caught sight of her.

"Lady Juliana was dancing with the mummers, last I saw her," Guy supplied, moments later.

"I as well," Friar Tupper added.

Royce expelled a breath. He disliked not knowing where she was, especially since she'd left without a word.

"I'm beginning to regret encouraging her to join the others. I'd expected her to return to our table once the dance was finished."

"But, I saw her after that, my son, amidst the mummers as they capered out of the hall."

Royce's gaze vaulted to the monk. Most of the players were nobles in disguise. Likely, they'd returned to their quarters to change from their costumes. Had Juliana returned to their own chamber as well? But why? Could his speaking with the countess have provoked her to leave?

"I must find her," Royce mumbled, heading for the door.

Friar Tupper and Guy followed directly behind, offering their help. On questioning the castle guards posted outside the door, the soldiers pointed them in the direction the mummers took. Asked further if they'd seen a lady with the performers, one with silvery bright hair, one man nodded.

"Aye, a beauty. She favored the queen."

Royce hastened on, following the corridor, the minstrel and monk behind him. As they approached the passage's end, a young man with a cap of blond curls stumbled out of a side room, holding his head, blood streaming through his fingers. Royce caught him as the fellow's knees folded and eased him to the floor.

"'Tis Lord Edward Haverlock's son," Guy voiced with some surprise, recognizing the noble.

Royce looked to the young man's wound, a nasty gash on the side of his head. "Who did this to you?" he pressed.

"Don't know . . . a man. . .black hair . . . scar on the side of his face . . . stole my costume . . .

"Friston," Royce spat the name. "What was the costume? What does it look like?"

"V-Vulture . . . tall, very tall."

"God's wounds, Juliana was dancing with Friston all along! He must have her now."

The young man sagged heavily against Royce, losing consciousness. "See to him, Friar," Royce charged, giving Haverlock's son over to the monk's care.

Rising to his feet, Royce debated what to do next. Friston's unwavering determination to gain control of Juliana boded ill. Very ill.

"Guy, call out Penhurst's men-at-arms. Have them check all of Guildford's gates. See if anyone departed. I'll have others search the castle, room by room, though 'tis more likely he'll try to reach the river with my lady. He seemed intent on leaving English soil as swift as he could."

Royce started back down the corridor, then pivoted, calling back to Guy.

"Tell my men I'll join them as soon as I am armed. Should Friston harm Lady Juliana, he's a dead man!"

"Smile, my lady." Friston pressed the tip of his knife into Juliana's side as they exited the keep, past a pair of guards, and started down the long flight of steps.

"Is this how you treat your cousin?" She taunted as he continued to clutch her against him, the blade hidden beneath the folds of her mantle.

He made no reply, but on reaching the bottom of the stairs, forced her across the castle's inner ward. He afforded a few friendly nods to those they encountered, presumably wishing others to think them late-night revelers who sought some private spot.

Juliana shuddered, part from fear, part from the bitter cold. At least the Frenchman had allowed her the feather cloak to wear. Her silken gown and mantle were little protection against the frigid air, a fresh layer of snow having fallen earlier and the breeze now moving off it, whipping particles of ice into her cheeks. Friston fared better. He'd retrieved his own heavy mantle along with his sword, hidden in a storage room. At the same time, he discarded the vulture mask.

Friston propelled her toward the stables, but when two soldiers appeared, making their rounds, he shoved her against the wall of the nearest building, trapping her there with his bulk while he buried his face in her hair. To any who looked their way they would appear lovers. In truth, his knife was set firmly between her breasts.

The back of Juliana's head continued to ache where she'd hit it, but now her temples began to throb also. She winced at the pain, a fragment of memory flickering before her mind's eye—Friston again, the side of his face bleeding. What did it mean? She couldn't quite grasp it.

The soldiers strode on, coarsely cheering the Frenchman to "snatch a bit" for them. Friston darted a glance about the ward and assured they were alone. Once more, he began dragging Juliana along with him.

"You'll never get through the main gate. 'Twill be barred for the night and heavily guarded." Juliana hoped what she said was true. Cities locked their gates at dark, why not the king his castle?

"We won't be using the main gate."

Friston gave her a hard smile, one that raised the hair on the nape of Juliana's neck. Holding her arm in a bruising grip, he drew her past the outbuildings, toward the west gate in Guildford's curtain wall. She recoiled, realizing it to be the entrance to the royal game park.

"Why are you taking me here? I thought you were eager to sail for France."

"I am, and I shall."

"Through the park?" she pressed, skepticism in her voice.

"The river runs below the castle and I've hired a packet there. We'll reach it through the woods."

"But how? The park is enclosed." Juliana resisted him, not trusting the Frenchman, not liking the idea of venturing into the darkened forest, stocked with all manner of beasts for the hunt. Friston drew her on, his knife a sharp reminder to do as he said.

"Naught but a deep ravine compasses the park," he finally replied. "'Twill be manageable enough."

"For you, mayhap," Juliana shot back. When the

Frenchman said nothing, a black fear seized her. Possibly he'd no intention that she should leave the park at all. "There is still the gate into the park. 'Twill be locked and guarded too," she argued, her heart racing.

Friston eyed her, his look impenetrable. "Like the boat, that too has been taken care of."

As they approached the looming gate, oaken and iron studded, Juliana saw that a single guard kept watch of it. She started to cry out and appeal for help, but Friston jerked her toward him and seized her lips brutally with his own. Silencing her, he continued to pull her forward. To Juliana's alarm, the guard only laughed and drew out his keys. Unlocking the small wicket door set within the larger gate, he opened it and allowed them through.

When they continued on without stopping, the guard followed behind. "Aren't you forgetting something, friend? The rest of the coin you promised?"

Friston halted, pulling his lips from Juliana. "Sorry, the woman has me so hot, I forgot. Here you are."

As the guard moved behind them, Friston reached toward his waist, momentarily releasing his hold on Juliana. She stumbled back, then saw her chance to run. But before she managed another step, Friston wheeled round, plunging his knife into the man's stomach. Slipping a second knife from his belt, he slit the man's throat in one quick movement.

Filled with horror, Juliana watched as the guard sank to the snow, choking on his blood. A wave of dizziness assaulted her, pain piercing her temples, all about her pressing in.

Juliana broke into a run, panicked. Suddenly, the edges of her vision dimmed, and she found herself hurled back in time. She was a child of eight again, fleeing the manor house, heading for the nearby stand of trees. Aldis, her nurse, hurried her on, while behind them the village burned and the people screamed their terror.

Juliana stumbled onto her knees and hands, jarring her back to the present as her fingers turned to ice in the snow. Picking herself up again, she forced herself on, her feet numbed with cold in her thin slippers.

Gratefully, the full moon reflected off the snow, brightening the landscape to near day, making its features distinct—patterns of black and white. The forest's edge lay near. If only she could reach it, perhaps she could find cover and hide.

Royce, where was he? Had he missed her yet? Could he find her? She saw how the snow appeared churned, then remembered the king had hunted with his barons this morn. Her heart sank, realizing she was leaving no clear path for anyone to follow. Remembering the mummer's cloak she wore, she began to yank feathers off the fabric, dropping them as she rushed on.

Juliana took no more than five steps when a weight slammed down on her shoulders—two hands, Friston's, dragging her back down to the snowy ground. She clawed forward, but he rolled her onto her back then lay atop her, jamming the bloody knife blade beneath her chin.

"Will you kill me next? Like the guard?" she challenged, her heart beating wildly. "Why? Is this how you claim your rights to your kinswoman? Penhurst is not so grand a property to do murder for it."

"Come now, Lady Juliana. Do not play me for a fool. We both know, I am not your cousin."

"We do?" She feigned innocence, the pain in her temples spreading.

"Aye, 'tis easily read in your eyes. I knew, once you returned to your homeland—to places familiar to you, 'twas only a matter of time before you regained your memory."

He slackened his pressure on the knife, hauled her to her feet, and lowered the blade to her ribs. Then, catching her by the arm, he forced her on toward the forest's edge.

"Why should my memory matter to you? Who are you?" Juliana managed to drop another feather unnoticed.

Friston gave her a sidelong glance but did not answer directly. "Pity that the people of Chinon are such braggarts. News travels swiftly, especially when 'tis so remarkable a tale as your own—a peasant maid, revealed to be a lost heiress of noble blood, carried off from the church steps on her wedding day by a knight of the English realm. Had the townsfolk not been so avid to boast their news, word still might not have reached me of the maid who'd survived the bloodletting at that cursed patch of earth named Vaux."

"Vaux?" Juliana went to stone in his grip, causing the Frenchman to lurch to a halt. She flinched again as fresh pain shot through her temples, some image trying to emerge. "What do you know of Vaux?"

"Enough."

"I'm not the only survivor," she felt suddenly compelled to say. "There were others."

"Villagers only. None from the manor house save you. I confess, on learning of your existence, 'twas a relief to discover you'd no memory of the event. Again the townsfolk of Chinon were most helpful, especially a certain cooper who'd lost his bride."

"Gervase?" she uttered his name, aghast. How many times had he betrayed her, knowingly or not?

The Frenchman dragged her on with him. "Better for you to never regain your memory, Lady Juliana. But how can I trust you won't?"

"Why does it matter?" she countered. "'Twas ten years ago. What is Vaux to you?"

He halted, rounding on her. "Nothing, and everything.

Vaux's lord was responsible for the death of my only son and heir, and that of my wife, who could not bear the loss."

Juliana's breath left her at the revelation, but he'd already transferred his attention elsewhere. Seeing they stood at the rim of the forest, Friston stared into it as if to consider what might lurk there. Releasing Juliana, he drew his sword from its scabbard and raised it before him. Moonlight danced along the steel's honed edge, riveting Juliana's gaze. The sight touched some memory deep inside her, something dark, long buried.

The throbbing in her temples multiplied, a searing pain arcing over the top of her head. As Friston turned his scarred face toward her, his sword glinting in his hand, an explosion of images burst forth in Juliana's head. Screaming, she clutched her head in her hands and crumpled to her knees, her past flooding back in vivid detail.

Royce bolted to his feet at the sound of a woman's scream. "Juliana!"

Judging the direction of her cry, he quickly turned back to his companions at the wicket door where they crouched over the slain guard.

"Guy, remain here. Tell the others where we've gone. Kenric, Harbin, let's get this gate open and the horses through."

Again came the scream, tortured, haunted, curdling Royce's blood.

"Catch up with me!" he called, not wasting a moment further as he headed across the open field toward the woodland.

Scanning the long stretch of trees where the forest began, he knew Juliana and Friston could have entered them at any point. Equally frustrating, the snow lay turned all about, offering no help, no clear tracks to follow.

His eyes drew to a dark, regular shape outlined against the moon-brightened snow. A feather. Another lay just ahead, and shortly beyond, still another. All were of similar size—chicken feathers, dyed black, like those on the mummer's costume. Royce smiled. Juliana had left him a trail to guide his steps.

"I shall not fail you, love," he swore, lengthening his stride, following the path she'd marked.

Gaining the woodland's edge, his thoughts shifted to Friston. Royce unsheathed his sword and cast himself onward into the forest, an unholy fury raging through his heart.

Juliana panted for breath, her lungs stinging with cold as Friston dragged her with him through the brush and trees. Still the flood of images came, her past alive within her once again.

She saw herself bathing in a small chamber, just off the main hall in Vaux's manor house. Her mother's beautiful voice floated through the partially open door as she sang a familiar tune and plucked the strings of her lute.

Abruptly, the music stopped. Shouts sounded, then screams and the clanging of metal. The servants in the back chamber rushed to peer through the door, as did her nurse Aldis. Alarmed for her mother, Juliana climbed from the tub, catching up a towel and hurrying to join the others.

Chaos reigned in the hall, soldiers in black garb pouring through the front entrance, their swords drawn and slashing, most within unarmed. The Mandeville men-at-arms ringed her mother, defending her furiously though sorely outnumbered. One by one they fell, the rest ever tightening the circle around Lady Alyce and fighting on.

Another man in black garb moved into view. He appeared the leader of the rest for he bellowed out orders. Juliana saw his face only fleetingly as he crossed swords with Eadric Montfort, captain of the Mandeville guard, the last left standing now, protecting her mother. Eadric fought skillfully and with a swipe of his blade sliced open the side of the man's face. Just when Eadric would have finished him, another of the attackers came at him from the side, running him through.

Juliana's scream mingled with that of her mother. She watched terrified as Lady Alyce launched herself at the man with the slashed face. He brought his sword hilt down against the side of her mother's head, battering her again and again before drawing his blade across her throat. Beautiful Alyce fell, tangled in her veil, her life's blood soaking the rushes. As the carnage continued, the man turned in Juliana's direction, his face bleeding, firelight glancing off his sword. 'Twas Rennart de Friston.

"Come away, come away!" her nurse hissed, yanking Juliana along by the hand and fleeing out a back door.

Juliana felt another yank to her hand then realized 'twas Friston forcing her steps forward through the snowy forest. Ahead, still at some distance, she saw the flicker of torchlights through the trees. Her heart lurched as she recognized their source to be the boats on the river. The Wye lay far nearer to the game park than she'd thought. Distressingly near.

Her thoughts reached back to Vaux, to when she and Aldis escaped the manor house and fled for the river that lay behind it. They first gained cover in a stand of woods midway between the manor and river. From there, they witnessed further bloodshed as soldiers spilled out of the manor and began slaughtering the sheep in their folds and anything else that moved. Beyond the manor's enclosure walls, fire engulfed the village and screams rang out. Juliana could not see what horrors passed there.

"We must reach the water," Aldis told her. "I see two row boats by the mill house. We'll take one and use the river to get away. Now, run child, as fast as your feet can carry you, and pray we'll not be seen."

With that, they dashed hand in hand toward the mill. Reaching the river safely, Aldis worked frantically to right one of the overturned boats, Juliana helping her. But as they did, the miller and his family emerged from their house, hearing the clamor from the village and seeking its cause. Unwittingly, they drew the soldiers' attention.

"Quick, under the boat before they see you!" Aldis ordered Juliana.

Slipping beneath, Juliana clutched the toweling about her and peered out again. Her eyes met with the sight of the soldiers converging on the miller, his wife, and daughters and mercilessly cutting them down. The soldiers then directed their gazes toward the boats.

Juliana scooted back, shaking violently. She suddenly realized Aldis was not with her. Hearing the thud of footsteps passing, she dared to look out again. Dread filled her soul as she saw Aldis running along the river bank, drawing the soldiers after her, away from the boat. Within scant minutes, the men descended on her, their blades slashing, stabbing.

She must have fainted, Juliana realized, for her next memory was that of Royce, lifting the boat off her. She was terrified at first. But when he took her up into his arms, she spied the red Crusader cross upon his shoulder, the same as her father wore, and knew the young man would not hurt her. God had sent him expressly to save her.

As she pulled her thoughts from the past and focused on Friston, anguish fused with anger in Juliana's heart.

"You were there! You led the others and ordered them to kill everyone at Vaux." She tried to pull free of his grasp but failed. "You killed my mother and our Mandeville guards. Why?" she screamed, balling her free hand and striking at his back, his shoulder, then at his chest as he turned toward her.

He snared her wrist easily and dragged her over to a tree, thrusting her against it. "'Twas their misfortune and yours to be guests of the Lord of Vaux. I did but repay the misery wrought on my own lands, my own family."

"And so you sought revenge?"

"Nay, *justice*. Who could have known that, once Philip returned from Crusade, I would climb so high in rank, to serve as minister to his right hand? Or that 'twould be revealed the wife of Vaux's lord had shared blood ties with the king—the king whose favor I now held?"

Friston's gloved hand slid up and around Juliana's neck, gripping her with a light, deliberate pressure.

"So you see, my sweet, your existence is a complication. One I cannot abide. You can identify me, place me at Vaux on that fateful night."

Juliana grabbed for his hand as he increased the pressure on her neck. At the same time, she thought to hear a sound off to her left, a rustling in the bushes. As her attention returned to Friston, she found him brushing his lips against her hair.

"'Tis a shame I cannot let you live. You've grown to be quite a beauty."

Juliana shrank at his look, but he took no notice as he trapped her with his body against the tree.

"I wouldn't mind having a piece of what you gave de Warrene," he breathed at her ear. When she averted her face, he caught her jaw in his hand and forced her to look at him. "Come now. Again, the truth is carried in your eyes. You're no virgin. Not anymore. You know the game. And the park is for sporting after all."

Juliana struggled as he pressed his lips against her throat, but found she could not win free. Her mind reeled as he pushed her cloak aside, the sharp air instantly chilling her through the thinness of her gown. What had he done with his sword? Juliana wondered wildly. Propped it against the tree, she thought. But the knives he'd returned to his belt.

Again came the distinct rustling of brush nearby.

"Something is there. An animal," she gasped out, trying to distract him.

"Only a night scavenger. Nothing to interfere with us."

Friston started to force his kiss on her, but the sharp snapping of twigs and low, snorting sounds drew up his head. As he focused his attention toward the noise, Juliana seized the moment and grabbed for the knife in his belt, pulling it out. The Frenchman's hand shot to hers, deflecting the blade, but not before it caught him in the side. Recoiling at the pain, his grip slackened, providing Juliana the opportunity to shove from beneath him and break free.

Juliana ran blindly through the forest, swatting away the tangles of growth and low branches. She could hear Friston hot behind her, cursing as he gave pursuit. Despite the aid of the bright moonlight, vision remained poor in the woods with no clear path to see. Juliana followed her instincts as she hastened on, but moments later her foot caught on something unseen, sending her sprawling, then tumbling downward.

Juliana screamed as she plunged down an incline. Instantly she realized 'twas the ravine that enclosed the park. Brambles, stones, and woody debris slowed her fall, a thicket of shrubbery finally stopping her. She raised onto her elbows and saw Friston standing at the top of the embankment, his blade glinting. He appeared to search for her, the dim light and brush concealing her position.

Glancing into the inky depths of the ravine, Juliana wondered how far it stretched to the bottom and what form of wildlife might move there. She discarded any idea of scaling down it in order to reach the other side and climb out. Instead, she returned her attention to the rim of woods overhead. Cautiously, she began climbing upward, at a wide angle, moving away from Friston and back in the direction of the wall that surrounded the keep.

Just as she gained the top, successfully eluding the Frenchman, she heard a thrashing in the bushes, then saw something large and dark trot through the brush. 'Twas the size of a sheep. Only sheep were not so massive or with humped backs. Nor did they grunt or snort like this animal.

"Oh God, no, not again!" she muttered beneath her breath, catching a glimpse of the animal's hideous mouth, its teeth bristling. 'Twas a boar. Was there something about her that drew these creatures? she wondered, frantic. But as she mentally took hold of herself, she perceived a way to use the creature to her advantage.

Quickly, Juliana felt for rocks and sticks—anything she could throw and that would carry a distance. She then looked about for a sturdy tree—the nearest one she could climb that would give her refuge. Deciding on one at the edge of the ravine, she began to move toward it.

She still had a short distance to reach the tree when Friston came into view. If only she could draw the boar's attention to the Frenchman—throw the rocks and sticks close to where he stood, create enough noise to seize the animal's interest. With luck, the boar would attack, possibly disable him or worse. Would that make her a murderess if the pig should kill him? Yet, if she did nothing, Friston would certainly kill her.

Before Juliana could think further on it, Friston shouted out, seeing her, and started toward her. He made sufficient noise to attract the pig, still it made no attempt to charge. Worse, the Frenchman was closing on her own position.

She'd no wish to find herself at the end of its tusks. Frustrated at the beast's passivity, she hurled several stones into the bushes at it, hoping to rile its temper. A high, discordant squeal told her she had.

Juliana's heart quickened with excitement and dread, seeing Friston turn toward the creature as it emerged from the bushes, obviously maddened. Quickly, she ran for the tree, scrambling up and onto its lowermost branch. She began to climb higher, then halted at the bellow of a man's voice. 'Twas not the Frenchman she heard, but Royce!

"Friston!" Royce roared as he appeared in the clearing, his sword braced before him as he faced the Frenchman, unaware of the danger nearby. "Where is my lady? What have you done with her, cur?"

Desperately, Juliana sought the wild pig but could not immediately spot it. Still, the danger was no less. She'd stirred the beast, and once it set its narrow mind to attack, it would do so, undeterred. But instead of having one target, it now had two. The boar could kill either man, or both, with a swipe of its tusks.

"Royce!" she cried out. "There's a boar in the brush!"

At the sound of her voice, Royce glanced in her direction, distracted. Instantly, Friston sprang forward, his sword slashing. Royce met Friston's steel with his own, their blades clanging as he warded off the blow then rained down one of his own. Together the two knights battled, their swords ringing as they hammered and hewed at one another.

Juliana watched, her heart frozen in her throat as the men warred on, a deadly match that could have but one end. A shrill squeal jarred her from the scene. 'Twas then she spied the boar to the right of the men, at a short distance, pawing the ground and clashing its tusks over its teeth.

Realizing it was poised to attack, Juliana started to climb from the tree, yelling and tossing sticks as she did, trying to divert the beast's attention to herself. But it ignored her fully. Single-minded, the boar drove toward the two men, its ears pricked and eyes rolled back as it entered the fray. For a moment the forms melted together in the dim light, men and beast scuffling, then a horrid scream rent the air—a human scream. One of the men suddenly rose up, his form separating from the others as he gripped his sword by the pommel and plunged it downward. A hideous squealing followed, then silence.

Juliana began to shake violently, not knowing who'd survived. But as the man straightened to his full height and turned round, she recognized him to be Royce.

Dropping the final distance out of the tree, she flew to him, wrapping her arms about his middle and squeezing him tight. She started to look toward Friston and the animal, but Royce quickly turned her away.

"Nay, love. Do not look there. The boar laid him open with his tusks. Friston is dead."

Juliana buried her face against his chest. When she pulled away a moment later, she saw that he was wounded. "Royce, your wrist, it's bleeding!"

"Saving fair ladies in distress has its dangers." He smiled, still regaining his breath.

Juliana drew the handkerchief from her sleeve and tied it about his wrist, stanching the flow of blood.

"Friston was the one, Royce—the one who led the attack on Vaux and killed my mother and our guards."

"You remember this? You've regained your memory?"

"Everything," She nodded soberly, shaking with cold and emotion, the strain of the night overcoming her.

A look of concern crossed Royce's face and he drew her to him, wrapping his cloak around her. "Come away. We'll send others to see to matters here. Let us return to the keep and seek a warm fire. You can tell me all then. You are safe now, my heart."

"I am, as long as you are near." Juliana smiled up at him.

He smiled too, then kissed her gently, lovingly. Lifting her from her feet, Royce carried Juliana back to the keep, secure in the protection of his arms.

PART VI

The Lady's Choice

"All other love's worth naught,
And every joy meaningless to me
but yours, which gladdens and restores me."

—Castelloza, born c. A.D. 1200
woman troubadour

24

The royal physician finished dressing the wound on Royce's wrist, then collected his bandages and implements and started toward the chamber door.

"You'll have a scar, of course. 'Twill match the other." He gestured to the long, puckered line on Royce's forearm. "Both are from a boar, you say?"

Royce nodded where he sat on a stool, bare chested, inspecting the generous wrappings that swathed his hand and wrist.

As the physician departed, Juliana left the fireplace where she stood and joined Royce. "I caused you this," she said, laying her hand lightly upon his shoulder as she gazed at his wounded arm. "You've been in danger ever since finding me in Chinon."

Royce remained silent a long moment as he gazed up at her, searching her eyes. He covered her hand with his own, rose, and drew her to him.

"I will wear my scars proudly. Let them stand as proof of my love for you, and as a warning to any who would try to bring you harm or seek to take you from me."

"Royce . . ." Juliana's voice caught, emotion crowding her throat. "You love me, truly?"

"Aye, lady. You slipped into my heart long ago and have possessed it ever since." He gave her a smile, then his look turned serious again.

"Marry me, sweet Juliana," he said softly. "Stay with me always. Let my name and my strength protect you. Let me love you all the days that are ours." He pressed a kiss beneath her jaw, then to the curve of her neck.

Juliana leaned into him, relishing his seduction as his lips moved down her throat. But thoughts crowded in, nagging thoughts of futures and destinies yet to be fulfilled.

"Royce, you promised me a choice, concerning our betrothal vows. Remember? You said the decision rested with me, whether we would keep them, or break them."

"That I did, and I'm a man of my word." He found her collarbone, traced it with the tip of his tongue. "Choose to stay with me, love. Pray, do so now, lest I go mad with want of you."

"But what of the countess?"

"What of her?" He continued his attentions, pressing a kiss to her shoulder, his hands moving to her back.

"I saw you together . . . in the hall." She found it difficult to hold a thought as Royce fumbled with her laces.

"Lady Sibylla was only wishing us both well."

Juliana pulled back, eyeing him. "Royce, she was kissing you! She expects to have you for herself. I sent her a letter so she wouldn't be angry with you, explaining all was not as it seemed—that when you said you'd married me, all you were doing was protecting me."

"'Twasn't all that I—we—were doing." He smiled impossibly, loosening her laces with his uninjured hand.

"She needn't know that. She *mustn't* know that."

"Why not?" He parted the back of her gown.

"Because you must marry her."

He paused, frowning. "Do you no longer love me, sweet Juliana?" He gave her a wounded look. "You told me you'd waited for me through all those years."

Juliana choked back a sudden anguish, pain fissuring through her heart.

"Of course I love you, Royce. More than life, do I love

you. But you've a great future before you, and I will only keep you from it. Lady Sibylla brings you an earldom and the resources you will need. She is the one you must marry. My letter clears away any misunderstandings so she will accept you. So you see, nothing stands in your way from taking her to wife."

"There might yet be," Royce replied solemnly. "If this is the letter you sent." He drew a small square of parchment from his belt and held it up.

Juliana's eyes widened. "Guy didn't deliver my letter?"

"He did, but to me." Royce's lips pulled into a smile.

"But I thought . . . Well, the countess kissed you . . ."

"As I said, she was wishing us well. Like the rest of the Court, Sibylla believes us already married. I didn't disabuse her of that notion. In truth, I told her ours is a love match. That I had decided I would have you for my bride and no other. 'Twas something I determined, myself, before you ever dispatched your missive."

Juliana gave him a skeptical look.

"Haven't you looked inside your ring, my love? I had it inscribed for our betrothal."

Juliana's gaze dropped to her finger. "I haven't taken it off my finger since you put it there."

"Then take it off now, and I'll place it on again when you marry me. See for yourself its inscription."

Slipping the ring from her finger, Juliana looked inside, finding an engraving there. She tried to sound out the letters, then looked to Royce for help.

"It reads, *'Vous et nul autre.'* You and no other."

Love welled in her heart for Royce, overflowing and leaving her speechless.

"Marry me, Juliana." He started to lower his head and kiss her, but then pulled back. "Unless you do not love me as passionately as I do you."

Juliana flung her arms around him, tears of happiness burning her eyes. "I do love you Royce, with all my heart. You know that I do. But what of your destiny?"

"My destiny, sweet Juliana, is you." Turning to the fireplace, he cast the letter into the flames. Then, looking to her once more, he smiled. "I should warn you, I intend to claim my destiny this very moment and to hold it now and forever more."

As Royce's lips descended over Juliana's, he drew her gown off her shoulders, pulling it downward and letting it drift to the floor. Juliana made no objection as he caught her up in his arms and bore her to the bed. There they gave themselves to each other and to destiny, their hearts afire as they became one in the brilliance of each other's love.

As Twelfth Night ended, passing to a new day, the small wedding party gathered in the royal chapel at Guildford. Friar Tupper presided over the candlelit ceremony, the king and queen in attendance along with a select few, including Guy of Lisors, Luvena, and Georges and Marie, who had been brought from Penhurst.

Joy sang in Juliana's heart as she and Royce spoke their vows and exchanged rings and, at last, were pronounced husband and wife. Penhurst now truly had a new lord. She was sure Lord Gilbert smiled down on them, well pleased.

Royce kissed her soundly before all, causing her to flush, then they accepted well-wishes from the others and withdrew into a room off the chapel. There a light repast awaited—spiced wine, honeyed cakes, almonds, and more, covering a table. In the center of the table, amidst the food, rested an ornate coffer encrusted with jewels.

"You must open it," the king urged Royce and Juliana, a grin splitting his beard as he and the queen joined them.

Juliana looked on as Royce lifted the coffer's lid. Within

lay two scrolls. The king continued to grin like a mischievous child, and the queen smiled wide as well.

"Go on, read them," the king prompted merrily.

Royce lifted out one of the parchments and unrolled it. A stunned look crossed his face as he read the words it contained.

"Majesty, I hardly know what to say." He glanced to Juliana then back to the scroll. "The king grants a substantial sum of money, plus provisions, and twenty knights to improve and fortify Beckwell."

"As I've said before, Beckwell's location is prime, both for trade and defense. I wish it restored." The king pulled on his beard. "You might start with the curtain wall. 'Twas in a piteous state when last I saw it."

Juliana saw Royce exchange glances with Friar Tupper.

"But Beckwell's grant is only half my bestowal—the lesser half. Look at the other parchment. Look, look!"

Juliana peered at the writing on the second scroll as Royce opened it. Though she still struggled to decipher the markings, Royce suddenly could not speak.

King John's grin stretched so wide it seemed to touch his ears. "I have granted you Chelford Castle."

"Chelford?" Shock ran through Juliana. "Is that not the Marcher castle once belonging to my father?"

"Aye, the same, and now it pleases me to return it to the Mandeville bloodline." The king's gaze shifted to Royce. "I confess, 'twas Marshal's idea, but he is right. You have proven yourself to be a knight of worth, one who can hold that which is entrusted to him. I need such men as you, especially to secure my Welsh border. 'Twill not be an easy task, but Chelford is well manned and supplied—fifty knights."

'Twas Juliana's turn to be speechless. No longer was Royce a minor baron, but one of true import.

"Ah, lest I forget, seek out the earl," the king instructed Royce. "There are matters Marshal wishes to discuss with you, and I will want a full accounting when we meet for Easter at Canterbury."

Juliana at last found her tongue. "Majesty, if I may ask, what became of the family who held Chelford after my father?"

"They were without issue and have no relations fit to command the castle when the last lord recently died. I trust you two will see your halls well populated?"

"We will certainly make every effort." Royce smiled at Juliana, a sparkle in his eyes.

As everyone's drinks were replenished, Guy offered to entertain with a special gift of his own.

"My *lai* is at last complete," he announced as he began to pick out notes on his lute. "'Tis a tale you will no doubt recognize—a most splendid tale—though not of my own creation. I have but humbly recorded it, that it might be told and retold in many a hall, for years and centuries to come. 'Tis a love story for all time.

"So listen carefully, friends, as I sing to you of a certain squire who gave away a highborn maid to the common folk, only to later return a great knight and rescue her from her fate. Theirs is a tale of dangerous trials and adventures, of a love sorely tested but at last realized."

Juliana looked to Royce, his arm going around her as they shared a smile.

"Does this tale have a name, minstrel?" the king called out in good cheer.

"Aye, Majesty, a most fitting one, which well suits the spirit of the piece. In truth, 'twas chosen by our groom, himself, in honor of his bride." Guy glanced to the couple as he began fingering a tune. "Lords and ladies, make yourselves comfortable as I sing for you the tale of `His Fair Lady."'

'His Fair Lady?"' Juliana smiled up at Royce, pleased and flattered by the title. "You chose the name for me?"

"Aye, love, for you are that—a true and fair lady and the one who holds my heart." His eyes warm upon her, he drew her into a heady kiss. As Guy's voice filled the small chamber with song, Royce's mouth slowly parted from hers.

"Come love. Let us to bed. We know how the minstrel's story ends."

"Ends? Nay, my darling." Juliana brushed her lips across his, her joy overflowing. "'Tis only the beginning."

AUTHOR BIOGRAPHY

Kathleen Kirkwood is the pseudonym for award-winning, best-selling author Anita Gordon. Having an abiding love for history, she enjoys setting her stories in distant times and places long past. To date they include Medieval adventures and Late Victorian paranormal romances. After forty years of travels and raising children in various locations, Kirkwood and her husband have returned to the Southwest, where they first met. Currently, she is dusting off and revising her backlist for release in digital and print format. She is also working on a new novel, a haunting tale set on the Chesapeake Bay and the shores of historic Southern Maryland. Look for *Pirates' Moon* *in late 2012. Visit her at:*

Web Site: *www.kathleenkirkwoodhistoricals.com*
Blog Site: *http://kathleenkirkwood.blogspot.com*

ALSO AVAILABLE
in print and e-book formats:

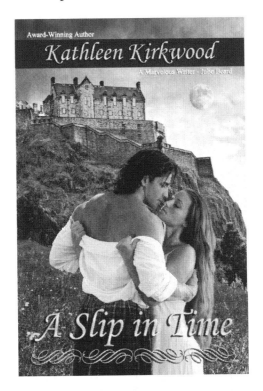

A Highland Chieftain . . .
A Victorian Lady . . .
drawn irresistibly through
the portals of time . . .

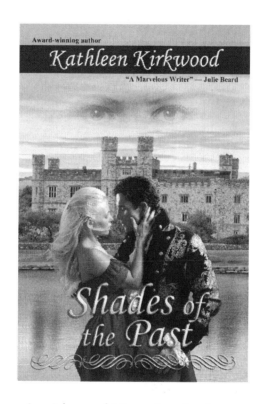

A widowed Victorian Lady . . .
A mysterious Viscount . . .
A remote and ancient castle . . .
Where ghostly residents stir anew . . .

COMING SOON

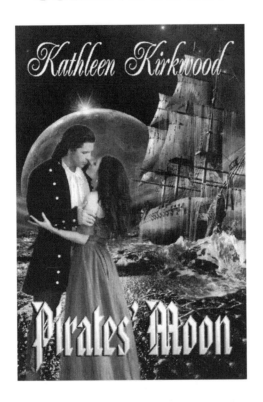

Once every quarter of a century,
On the night of the blood red moon,
A ghostly ship sails forth,
Out of the mists of time . . .